READING GLASSES

Stories Through
an Unpredictable Lens

Edited by
Amy Holiday and Jessica A. Walsh

Hypothetical Press

Reading Glasses: Stories Through an Unpredictable Lens
Edited by Amy Holiday and Jessica A. Walsh
©2014 Hypothetical Press
Cover art ©2014 by Shelley Szajner

Individual stories are copyrighted as follows:
"The Malocchio" ©2014 by Bruce Capoferri
"The Icarus Option" ©2014 by John Farquhar
"Starstruck" ©2014 by Gregg Feistman
"The Passing of Millie Hudson" ©2010 by J. Keller Ford
"The Beach House" ©2014 by Christine L. Hardy
"Fox and the Rose" ©2014 by Amy Holiday
"The Highborn" ©2014 by K.A. Magrowski
"Sifkin's Fence" ©2014 by Ray Rebmann
"Mason, On His Way Home" ©2014 by Randy Ribay
"The Hearing of Memory's Voice" ©1993 by J.J. Steinfeld
"Mrs. Rabinski" ©2014 by Richard Voza
"Unquiet Mind" ©2014 by Jessica A. Walsh
"Reading Glasses" ©2014 by Neal Wooten

Earlier versions of "The Hearing of Memory's Voice" previously appeared in *Dancing at the Club Holocaust* (Ragweed Press, 1993) and in *Jewish Dialog* with the title "Amnesia." Used by permission of the author.

"The Beach House" was the winning entry to the South Jersey Writers' Group 2013 Summer Contest, themed *Another Jersey Shore*.

ISBN: 978-0-9898189-9-5
Library of Congress Control Number: 2014916681
First Printing September 2014

Dedicated to the members of the South Jersey Writers' Group,

and to our friends, family and the Kickstarter community
for all their support.

To Sharon,
Who rocks Bat Girl!
Love,
Red Robbing Hood
11-1-14

TABLE OF CONTENTS

READING GLASSES:
STORIES THROUGH AN UNPREDICTABLE LENS

Sifkin's Fence

Ray Rebmann

Are there places within ourselves we keep locked up? Places we are afraid to go because we fear to discover their secrets, and what those secrets reveal about ourselves? I wonder about that as I walk, my son's voice egging me on. I don't know if I am walking toward something, or away from it.

My son insists there are pockets of overlooked magic carried over from other times. "If those forces are not somehow appeased or released, they can harm you," he said the last time we spoke. I'd had a particularly hard day at work and I found him standing in his mess of paints and canvas in the back bedroom, as usual, instead of contributing in some way around the house or looking for a damn job. I'd come to expect this sort of mumbo jumbo from him; home all day dabbing paint on canvas pretending to be an artist.

"In order to truly live, we must seek out those pockets, and those places within ourselves, and face them fully and learn their knowledge, working with it to allow us to grow and make changes for the better; to make our lives complete."

"My life would be a lot more complete if you would tear yourself away from that mess and get a job," I replied, standing in the doorway.

"The magic reveals itself to the artist's eye," he said, ignoring my comment. "We all have a bit of the eye, Dad. Even you, though you deny it." He leaned back, studying the blobs of color on canvas from a different angle. "But if you choose to see, and you look hard enough, it will reveal itself."

"Such nonsense doesn't pay the mortgage," I countered. "Life swallows whole and treats with utmost cruelty those who insist upon trying to keep to special paths of their own making."

1

"There is energy existing outside the province of reality. Those who are discerning enough can harness this energy to help them achieve their goals, and overcome whatever it is that is hurtful as they seek to keep to the path of their own making."

"The path of your making is more like a path of least resistance. Least activity, least productivity. You've wasted gallons of paint and bushels of brushes thinking about this gibberish while I fought traffic and slaved from dawn till dusk trying to make ends meet, yours as well as mine." He stood in that smelly room, not listening to me, squinting at his *creations*, paint smeared all over his face and clothing. Incense burned, but it didn't disguise his worst kept secret: that he's back there smoking pot all day.

Finally, he looked up at me. "Dad, you've blinded yourself to what's possible," he said. Next thing I knew, I was holding him pinned to the wall by the throat.

"Dad, why are you so cold and unfeeling?" he asked calmly. It infuriated me that he didn't fight back.

"Don't let me stand in the way of your seeking those magic pockets so long as your search carries you away from my door and gets your hands out of *my* pockets," I said through gritted teeth.

His mother exploded into my peripheral vision, screaming hysterically, cursing and wildly flailing a broom handle . . . at *me!*

"Give him a chance. You're always picking at him," she shrieked. "He's working so hard . . ."

I let him go and he slumped to the floor, rubbing his neck and coughing slightly. I turned to my wife. "If he's working so hard, then what the hell am I doing all day? I have a say in matters involving my household and my family!"

The words continued louder and harsher, cutting deeper and deeper until the police were called and I was led away. It seems my wife and son didn't want me around anymore.

Sure, I could have done what they expected of me; admit I'm a hot-headed old man, set in my ways, pig-headedly sticking with old-fashioned ideals, and consider the passionate pleadings of my son to look at matters from another angle. *His* angle. But why should I?

When my wife sided with my deadbeat son, I was forced to reconsider things. But instead of apologizing, I reconsidered my marriage, and I walked.

I didn't go quietly. Rather I slammed every door shut behind me before walking out into the night, through with my marriage and family, the hypocrisy of my actions exposed as the soft underbelly of my existence.

I instantly protected myself, covering any vulnerability with a hard veneer of cynicism and indifference. I walked away from the city of my birth and childhood; away from my friends and the home I'd created as an adult, along with the wife I had created it with.

I didn't stop walking until Philadelphia had receded into a distant haze, wandering far into the wastelands of southern New Jersey, following the shoreline of the Delaware Bay. I vaguely recall sleeping in cheap motels and eating greasy food at shabby roadside diners. Mostly I just walked.

Drawn on, perhaps by a force I did not understand and didn't care to consider, I passed through bustling suburbs then quiet, well-kept farmlands, and finally entered places long abandoned and forgotten. Where the pine forest ended, the tidal marsh began, and each step carried me deeper into an alien world. Finally, a sign caught my eye.

SHELLBANK
OYSTER CAPITAL OF –

Part of the sign was broken, so who knows what lofty rights they were claiming. I continued down the dilapidated road into town, where a small patch of tumbledown Victorians poked sagging eaves out of the high marsh grasses. A few cypress trees dotted the landscape, sun-bleached white and tortured into all sorts of grotesque poses by the wind.

Finally, as if reaching a preordained destination, I stopped walking.

Before me stood a large house with a wide, weathered porch where several people sat in rocking chairs spread out from another. They stared at me as I approached, lined up like a jury in a courtroom about to render their verdict. As I got closer, I noticed they were ancient; wizened human relics. They did not exchange any words with one another, or greet me. Each rocked creakily, isolated inside individual bubbles of existence.

A man, clean-shaven and seemingly closer to my age, emerged from the shadowy doorway.

"Hi, stranger," he said.

"Hello," I called from my place at the bottom of the sagging steps. Many pairs of eyes turned in my direction.

"You lost?" asked the man.

3

"Not really," I said. "Just . . . traveling."

"Where to?" he asked, frowning.

I hesitated, not knowing how to answer that. I still hadn't figured it out.

"Nowhere to go, huh," the man said, understanding. His eyes seemed tired. The old people on the porch just creaked their rockers back and forth slowly.

"Want a job?"

I hesitated again, and he stepped forward. "How about a cup of coffee?" he asked.

That was one question I definitely knew the answer to. I climbed the collapsing stairs carefully, and followed him into the house.

Over coffee, the man – Mister Sanders – explained that he needed someone willing to oversee the daily commonplaces of the senior citizens rest home. That explained the old folks.

"You've worked with all kinds of people?" he asked, refilling the chipped mug in front of me. "Good enough," he'd replied when I indicated that I had vast experience with the species. "What else do you need to handle this crowd, after all?"

I nodded. Senior citizens I could handle, assuming they weren't into magic places or seeking harmony with invisible forces or whatever.

You'll be on your own here," he informed me, wearily.

"No different than everywhere else," I replied. "Besides, I have nothing left to lose."

Clearly, I was his man. After an awkward silence, he offered me a relieved grin, presented me with the keys to my new kingdom, and left the premises without a backward glance.

I made my way back out to the porch and surveyed my new environment with a curious sort of ambivalence. It was readily apparent that the town was in the advanced stages of dying, not unlike many of its residents. All I saw were old folk. On the porch, and a few huddled together out in the garden, apparently farming dandelions. The rest home appeared to be the center of life in Shellbank, the only place where anyone resembling a living soul could be found.

Up the road a piece, a crew of road repairers was finishing up painting a pair of solid yellow lines down the road's center. Their work stopped at what I presume was the border of Shellbank. Two cars that had been fuming impatiently, waiting for the flag man's signal, zipped past the rest home stirring only the dust.

Headed through Shellbank toward...anywhere else.

"No stopping in Shellbank; just passing through..." a toothless rocker quipped, without missing a creaky beat.

This was my welcome into Shellbank society.

Later that afternoon, I met the entire community gathered at the home's historical club meeting. It was an odd gathering. There was no idle gossip prior to the start of the meeting and no one sat together; empty chairs and invisible lines separated and divided one from another.

The presider, an older gentleman, wordlessly shuffled to the fore and cleared his throat. The room assumed a death-like stillness. He lifted a thin booklet from amongst his stack of papers and the audience grumbled with obvious displeasure. With a look of disgust, the presider placed it at the farthest edge of the podium. He mumbled over some notes, something about the significance of the Revolutionary War on local fishing three centuries ago. The audience collectively shifted in its seats.

Finally his monotone trailed off, and his attention turned reluctantly to the booklet. He nudged it as if to check that it wouldn't bite. He appeared to be waiting for someone from the audience to rush to his rescue and bear the unholy thing away.

Finally, the presider nodded at the pamphlet and, while still not actually touching it, expressed tepid thanks to its creator, "young Will Dietz." Listening carefully to his mumbling, I figured out that Dietz had researched, written, and designed the booklet, a compilation of the families of Shellbank and their lineages.

Normally, I would have thought that such a personal family history would delight older folks. But not this group. Murderous expressions greeted the announcement. They shifted uneasily in their seats as the presider made it clear that the club had neither sought such a history, nor did it now appreciate the existence of such a document. I surmised that Dietz must have employed the darkest of arts to create his masterpiece. Ignoring the many hateful scowls directed at me, I picked up one of the pamphlets from the otherwise untouched pile on a corner table. Figured I'd better get to know my new home.

Skimming through the tedious list, I realized that at some point everyone in Shellbank stopped having children. Shellbank's current crop of humans was its last. Elderly Wilfred Dietz *was* the youngster of the community.

Well, excluding yours truly, of course.

As the presider complained about the multitude of spelling and punctuation errors in Dietz's work, the other relics suddenly came to life, their participation consisting of snickers, guffaws, and sneers. All chorused in agreement that Dietz had wasted his time and was now wasting theirs. I concluded that time here was little else but wasted. But their anger ran deeper than mere dissatisfaction with errors in grammar.

Dietz suffered alone, stoically, two rows back. I said nothing and kept my head down, lest their nasty barbs find me on their way back to smite Dietz. I studied the pamphlet, concentrating on the section in which residents provided their most significant memories from lifetimes endured in Shellbank. Time and again, there were references to a place or landmark called Sifkin's fence. The memories expressed were not very memorable, or very clear for that matter. But each offered a comment involving this Sifkin's fence.

I put aside the pamphlet and tried to focus on what was being said around me, but the level of abuse had become vitriolic, almost to the point of violence. I felt embarrassed for them. They were too old to behave so viciously.

"I don't want to get off on the wrong foot here," I began loudly, standing and interrupting the uproar. They turned evil old eyes my way. "I know how hard it is to sift through material to put together a piece like this. I think Mr. Dietz ought to be commended for his effort."

The presider shot me a sidelong glance and leaned against the podium in a pose that relayed these ancients' attitude toward anything that did not share their decrepitude. Contempt permeated the meeting chamber.

I recognized his pose. It was the same one I'd assumed during my last conversation with my son when he tried showing me his latest "work". I had refused to look and he accused me of being unreasonable. "Wanna paint? Try the walls, they could use a coat," I had responded.

The intensity of ancient eyes boring into me broke my reverie. It seemed my efforts had fallen on deaf ears. Instead of feeling badly about the way they were behaving, the ancients simply turned their anger and resentment toward me. For being young and daring to voice a differing opinion, I supposed. Even Dietz glared at me.

"Could any of *you* done better?" I sneered.

No one cared enough to rise to the challenge.

"I'm reading these little remembrances you have in here," I continued, dodging daggers from hate-filled eyes. "What about this Sifkin's fence? Nearly everyone mentioned it."

As innocuous as my comments had been, the reaction in that room when I mentioned Sifkin's fence was tumultuous.

The presider gaveled me out of order. Chairs went awry in all directions as the ancients climbed over one another in an effort to get the farthest away from me fastest.

Over the commotion, the presider brought the gathering to an abrupt close. A cacophony of cane rapping and walker squeaking followed as everyone rushed for the door.

"Wait!" I shouted, with the bullheaded witlessness of youth. "This Sifkin's fence is obviously an important symbol to this community," I offered, trying to somehow appease them.

The presider could have sided a barn with all his hammering on the podium.

"Perhaps if our young caretaker were not so presumptuous as to impose his views without knowing that which he speaks, he would be more temperate of tongue," the presider hissed.

I shut up at that point, stunned and confused. Dietz shook his head vigorously.

The members shuffled their walkers and rolled their wheel chairs and pecked their canes out of the room, without a backward glance.

"I was always the impetuous youngster upsetting everyone at these meetings until you came along," Dietz guffawed when we were alone. With his stooped shoulders and deeply wrinkled face, Dietz hardly qualified as a youngster, but I suppressed the urge to chuckle at his comment.

"What did I say?"

"Sifkin's fence."

"They mentioned it in your book. I figured it was some sort of lover's lane rendezvous or something."

"Or *something* all right," Dietz croaked. "I guess you'll be revising my history then. I can't wait to read how it turns out."

"I guess so." I couldn't help noticing how relieved Dietz looked.

"Well, don't count on getting a lot of cooperation." he said on the way out.

"Do yourself a favor, young man. Forget about Sifkin's fence and worry about getting more variety on the breakfast menu other than oatmeal and powdered eggs."

Dietz was right. No one would talk to me. About anything. At meals, before television hour; they avoided and evaded me with an agility and speed that belied their advanced years.

So once again, I walked.

I traversed every square inch of Shellbank. A faded word written on a cedar shingle nailed to a tree at the edge of town provided my first tangible clue.

Sifkin's fence, I finally learned, was a broken-down cedar pole fence surrounding a patch of overgrown weeds. Inside the broken circle of Sifkin's fence was a crumbled house with caved in cedar shake roof. The emaciated skeletons of a few shutters hung on desperately from windows that, from the looks of it, hadn't contained a pane of glass since the Great Depression. What great hold could this fence and the place it enclosed have on these relics?

I was intrigued. Not so much by the eeriness of the place, but the fact that my interest in it united the community in dislike for a new enemy. Their communication with me was limited to monosyllables, punctuated by icy silence, and that only served to raise the level of my intrigue. Besides, there was nothing else to intrigue me at this point in my life.

I suddenly found myself with a purpose. I needed to find out about this Sifkin and his fence. I needed to learn what hold it had on these people that made them so reluctant to talk about it.

Sitting in the library, I rummaged through the yellowed records of the county, dating back before the American Revolution. Through the pages of local history, I followed the adventures of the usual cast of pioneers and settlers. Farmers, fishermen, hunters, woodsmen. They hacked out a way of life in a place that was surprisingly generous with its tillable soil, seasonal climate, wood products, fish and game.

Ironic, perhaps, given what time and indifference had done to the surrounding area, but Shellbank was an idyllic place in the minds and hearts of those forbearers.

I learned that Henry Sifkin had inherited his father's oyster business on the Delaware Bay. Sifkin Senior had been an enterprising black man at the turn of the twentieth century, and he taught his teenage son, Henry, the tricks of navigating through the hard life on the water. But he also made sure that Henry learned to read and write. The elder Sifkin wanted his son to do "better" than struggle against the elements to obtain a livelihood. But after graduating at the top of his class in the county high school, and earning a scholarship to Lincoln University, Henry followed in his father's footsteps and took to the water.

Stubborn sons and disappointed fathers. How history takes us 'round and 'round.

Henry married a young woman named Sara Spaulding. He built a modest house for his new bride on the outskirts of the hamlet—the remains of that house I had visited earlier.

A few years after the Sifkins settled on the fringes of Shellbank, the railroad came through, snaking a line down along the western edge of the Sifkin property.

Sifkin was soon shipping fresh oysters wrapped in burlap and stored in great iced barrels to folk in the city. His business prospered and grew.

The county records tell of the birth of George to Sarah and Henry Sifkin, with the birth taking place at home. They give a date and a description of George as male and Negro. After those statistical entries, the record goes silent.

I used my new found information as a weapon, a battering ram that I employed to gain entry into the fortress of reticence.

I started with one of the men, Potter. During that first group meeting, he'd seemed livelier. I hoped he'd prove less hostile than the others.

Potter was a fisherman. The weathered leathery look of his sun-browned skin was my first clue.

"Used to be drum fish and black fish in these waters so thick you could walk across t' Delaware. Some of 'em big as torpedoes from a submarine," he reminisced.

He nodded at my pen; his signal for me to begin taking down his remembrances.

"Clam and oyster too. You could reach down to the bottom with the nets and they'd come up full ever' time. Any fool could make a livin' on the water in them days." I could tell by his tone of voice that the "fool" in question was not himself.

"Old man Sifkin was an oysterman and a good one," Potter said suddenly, perhaps recalling my actual reason for interviewing him. "A lot of men hereabouts worked for him one time or another. He always knew where to drop his nets, no matter what the season or the weather.

"There was a son named George. George was why that fence was built in the first place." Potter now settled back comfortably in his chair, confident that he had hooked his audience. I scribbled busily.

George Sifkin helped his father haul firewood and the burlap bags full of oysters when the boats came in, Potter told me. But George couldn't do much more than that.

"He was an idiot. A retard," Potter said.

The locals had other names for him, even less kind. Potter would not repeat them.

George wasn't capable of taking care of himself and had to be supervised constantly. So Henry built a fence around his property to confine him, and that fence marked the boundary of George's world.

"George wasn't allowed outside of the fence or to play with the rest of us kids," Potter continued. "It wasn't so much because of him being a colored. He was peculiar. We'd go down in groups to the Sifkin place just to watch him on t'other side of the fence. Sometimes, nothin' happened. Sometimes, the strangest things."

Potter admitted that the children, himself included, often teased George, but that he was so "gone in the head" he never seemed to notice or mind. One day, Potter recalled, the children had been treating him real bad when George came close to the fence and seemed to be trying to say something. The youngsters threw empty oyster shells at him.

"We didn't know any better. Or care," he acknowledged. "We didn't think he had sense enough to feel anything. Our aim was good. Near ever' one was a hit. And those shells was hard, some had pretty sharp edges too. George never thought to dodge. He just stood there and got hit. I forget who 'twas, Bobby Dietz maybe, he threw a thick oyster shell that caught George good on the right cheek." Potter shook his head slowly, his voice assuming a far-off timbre. "George didn't react. He just stood there and looked at us a long time, blood streakin' down the right side of his face. Finally, we saw a tear move real slow down the left cheek. Seemed like it took an hour to make its way down and we all just stood there stone still and watched."

It was clear to me that when Potter saw that tear, it had been a revelation.

"He knew. He understood what we was doin'. Mebbe even why we was doin' it."

But that never stopped him, or any of the others, from continuing with their abuse in the days that followed, Potter admitted regretfully.

He became more animated as he recalled George Sifkin's dog. A golden retriever, a beautiful dog none of them had ever seen before.

"I could never figger how it came to be there," he said, still puzzling it out. "Had to have come from under the house," he shrugged. "Must've been cooling itself in the shade. George, he turns away from us and starts playin' with this dog. All our shoutin' and shell tossin' had no effect. Him and that dog played fetch and tumbled about and paid us no mind. It was like there was nothin' beyond that fence; just him and the dog in the whole wide world."

Potter recalled mentioning the dog at the supper table and his father raged at him. 'The Sifkins don't have no dog', my papa shouted. 'Henry Sifkin loves that boy more than any man can love a son despite that child's . . . *condition*. He isn't a fool to trust his idiot son with any kind of animal,' he said, imitating his father.

"But we all seen that dog."

Potter and the other children had been spooked by that and other things like it that they had witnessed in their many visits to Sifkin's fence.

"George could do things like that on his side of the fence. He wanted a dog there, there was a dog there. I don't know how to explain it," Potter rasped in a voice, now fierce, defying me to disbelieve him. "He had powers. We didn't try to understand him; never tried to cross that fence. We just knew he didn't belong in this world."

Potter slumped in his chair, breathing heavily, as though the strain of telling was more than he could handle. He angrily brushed aside my attempts to question him further.

"My granddad used to tell me how whales used to come up the bay this far. And after a day's killin', the beach would be stained red with carcasses ever'place. The air was thick with flies feeding upon those bloated carcasses. Now that was a time, long before Sifkin and the fence. A time when life and death both held sway in this place and folks was sure which way the world turned and knew the seasons and the reasons why things happened as they did."

Potter pulled his fishing cap tight over his forehead to shield his eyes from the noonday sun. He slammed the screen door behind him and went off to check his crab pots, down by the bulkhead; likely to find nothing, as usual.

Sally had flirted with me one morning as I served orange juice and corn flakes so I thought I might have a chance of getting her to talk. When I suggested as much, she invited me to her room.

I found her putting on make-up and fussing with her hair. I'm not sure why she bothered. No one ever came calling and no one ever went anywhere. She took great pains to make herself look as much younger as the miracles of cosmetology and the art of grooming would allow. She did it for me, I guess.

She stared at herself in the mirror for a long time after I asked about Sifkin's fence.

"I remember one day, just like most days in Shellbank, but long ago," she whispered, her voice assuming a theatrical air. "You know them days when there's nothing to do and a pesky hot breeze gives no relief; only riles the 'skeeters. Folks just sat on their porches and stared; trying not to move too much. Just fanning themselves and waiting for sundown and, God willing, a break from the heat. The only sounds were flies buzzing and the creek, still and muddy, sizzling as it dried up."

She turned away from the mirror and faced me. "I went for a stroll and happened to find myself passing by the Sifkin's house," Sally recalled. "There was George playing alone in the yard the way he always did, no matter what the season. But on his side of the fence, there was snow."

She paused, for dramatic effect, I suppose. Satisfied that she had my full attention, she went on.

"There he was, running and laughing as the snow fell. The ground was covered and he tossed handfuls of snow into the sky. He spots me and bends down. He comes up with a snowball and throws it at me. I just stood there, surprised, waiting for it to hit me. Truth to tell, it was so frightfully hot, I was hoping it *would* hit me . . . but the snowball vanished just as it reached the fence."

Sally paused, searching my face for reaction.

"I know it sounds crazy. I never told a soul because you know how folks are 'round here with their malicious gossip. Anyhow, George went back to his play like I wasn't there. So I continued walking. "Things like that were always happening near Sifkin's fence," she continued with a faraway look. "Lookin' back, I suppose we all had seen strange things, had strange things happen to us; but no one ever talked about it. We were all of us afraid of what was on the other side of that fence. We never went over it."

She paused, looking at me intensely, before continuing.

"That's what caused the trouble."

I barely heard what she said, her voice had dropped so low. She had a frightened look on her face. She glanced around the room anxiously, like she was afraid someone was listening, ready to burst into the room to tear her apart for saying too much.

I waited patiently, something new for me; something I had never done with my son. Sally cleared her throat, which brought me back to the moment . . .

"You see, there was a little girl . . ." she began.

When I left Sally's room, I was shaken, with a ringing in my ears. The ringing continued, only it turned out to be the unfamiliar music of the home's official telephone, announcing a rarity in these parts: an incoming call.

My son had tracked me down and was calling from some place that sounded far away. Canada, maybe. Canada had become a favorite point of destination for people of my son's artistic temperament.

"Seeking your pocket of magic in some safe faraway place?" I asked scornfully.

"Surprised to hear from me, Dad?" he parried, sadness in his voice. I'd come to find that voice annoying. But now, I admitted grudgingly to myself, I wanted to hear it despite the anger rising within me.

"Delighted as always." I pushed the words out through clenched teeth. "Although, I wouldn't want to keep you from more pressing business at your easel."

"Dad, can there be peace between us?"

I pictured him lost in the world, nothing but his dreams and a fistful of paint tubes to carry him through. *Why did you reject everything I tried to teach you*? I wanted to ask. I wanted to warn him for the millionth time that life was a test, an ordeal especially hard for those distracted by the false euphoria offered by dreams.

"It doesn't have to be this way with us, Dad," he continued.

But I wasn't listening. I saw a future of destitution and street corners; him squatting in the gutter drawing caricatures of passersby in hopes of scrounging together enough loose change to underwrite his glorious delusions. I couldn't help myself; that was how I saw him. I could not understand what he was doing or thinking and it frightened me well beyond the point of mere generational revulsion.

I was never good at hiding my scorn and I needed him to hurt, to think that I had given up caring.

"Peace, eh son? Give peace a chance? Let love make the world go 'round? It doesn't. No more than that magic art you're always going on about."

"You have a lot of misdirected anger boiling away your heart and soul, Dad. I feel sorry for you. Someday, that anger will explode out once and for all and it will blow you so far away that you won't be able to crawl back. You should look for your bliss and let it release you."

"Is that some of the psychology you learned in college when I was paying a lot of money for you to take accounting courses instead?"

I sensed him withdrawing, drifting away from me, carried off on a wind that I wished would blow my way.

"You win, Dad."

He paused, long enough to give me a chance to say something to turn things around. I outwaited him, stubbornly. He finally served up his last pitch.

"I know you don't care, but a gallery on Rittenhouse Square is hosting a showing of my paintings this weekend. It could be a big break. I'd like you to come see my work."

I said nothing.

"All right, Dad. Anyway, I called because I just wanted to let you know that I love you."

"Love is all you need," I sang before returning the phone to its receiver.

I didn't know what it was about the person he'd become that angered me so.

His head was filled with silly ideas and romantic notions, typical for an inexperienced youth trying to figure things out. Typical of someone who hasn't had all the feel-good sentiments about one's

14

fellow man stamped out by long-term exposure to the short-comings of the species.

That was to be expected. Life had yet to disappoint him. Maybe I envied him for his unabashed innocence, but I didn't resent him for it.

I resented him for showing me who I am.

When confronted with such ferocious truth, I had walked until I reached this end of the world.

His voice echoing its declaration of love through the phone line directly into my head became too much to bear in the confinement of the home.

So I walked again. And once again, I didn't know if I was walking away, or toward, something.

As if on cue, moonlight appeared to guide me. A golden beam illuminated the path leading upland from the home. I understood right off where the beam wanted to lead me. I followed it to the Sifkin house.

I heard music. It was crickets. All around me, crickets. Then, the crickets went still. And so did I. I stood rigid for a long time, enveloped in the sheer silence permeating the place.

I caught a flash of shadow from the other side of the fence and, for an instant, thought I saw my son; thought that perhaps he had come to this god-forsaken place to torment me. I knew that was ridiculous, and figured it to be a shadow or a shrub distorted by moonlight and an agitated imagination. I tried to relax, and leaned on one of the sturdier fence posts. In that moment, the air changed; the darkness turned grainy, charged with static, and the marsh seemed to hold its breath.

A distraught man materializes in front of me, straight-backed, as if in a daze. He carries the lifeless body of a little girl, her smooth white arm dangling.

Through this ancient ghost, behind the safety of his fence, I see George Sifkin.

He frolics in the moonlight, tossing handfuls of light into the air. No, not light; snow. I see him laughing, but I don't hear a sound. His lips move in a wide grin.

Suddenly, shadows appear all around me; puncturing the golden glow as they emerge swiftly and silently from the darkness sur-

rounding Sifkin's fence. The townsmen of Shellbank as they had been long ago: the fathers of Potter and Sally and Dietz and all the others now haunting the rest home. They gather at the fence in communal rage. Their darkness, grainy and incomplete, contrasts with the vivid color of George Sifkin who is playing with his dog and laughing happily in the snow, mindless of the madness coming his way from the other side of the fence.

They call to George, coaxing him with sweet lies to come to the fence. When he does, they drag him over the fence, his body going limp as they haul him into the moonlight. There is no jeering, no cursing or banter of bravado. Just mute, cold concerted rage.

The boy looks around, uncomprehending, his animal innocent eyes probing until they lock onto mine. For an eternal moment, he gapes at me beseechingly, his eyes begging the question why. I avert my eyes and slip behind the cedar tree at the corner of the property.

George sobs uncontrollably, but offers no resistance. Suddenly, another flash of moonlight shoots between branches now swaying in a hot, harsh wind, and the tree limbs part revealing . . . ME!

My face; its expression is uncomprehending and resentful. In my hands, I hold the other end of a rope, providing counterbalance to the weight of George Sifkin's body as it now dangles, lifeless.

It ends quickly. The men disperse as stealthily as they had come.

I see a young Sally hiding in the reeds, frightened, yet wide-eyed curious. I see Dietz, holding his father's horse, and Potter pushing back his fishing cap to whistle in amazement like he'd finally hooked the ultimate big one. They are young and old at the same time, ageless and unable ever to be young again, there and not there. The way I had been.

Wind ruffles the tall grasses, and the scene of horror dissipates. The wind blows hot, wind that Hell released upon Shellbank the night George Sifkin left this place; wind that hasn't stopped blowing to this day.

The next morning, Wilfred Dietz found me unconscious outside Sifkin's fence. Unhappy that their breakfasts hadn't been brought out for them, the residents of the home became positively alarmed when no one showed up to dispense morning medications. It was decided to send out a search party to find me.

"I figured I might find you hereabouts," Dietz muttered. He fidgeted and wouldn't look at me.

"How is it that your little history neglected to mention what actually happened here?" I asked testily.

"Strange things happened here all the time. I was only ten years old when the 'incident' occurred. No one ever talked about it. We convinced ourselves that we could never be sure that it really happened at all. We figured that maybe it was just one of those tricks George was always playing."

Dietz took a deep breath and swallowed several times. He began to cry, sobbing silently as he forced himself to remember it all. No evasions. No tricks. *History.*

He told me about the Willard girl, who most likely had wanted to play with George's dog so she'd climbed over the fence. Instead of the dog, she encountered George, excited to finally find someone on his side of the fence.

The girl probably became frightened and tried to run. George, excited and not knowing what to do, grabbed her and most likely tried to quiet her by placing his hand over her mouth. That only frightened the girl more and she struggled, so he held on tighter and tighter.

Until he'd snapped her neck.

A worker coming back from the ice house spotted the girl's body lying in the middle of the yard and ran to tell her father . . .

. . . and then the rest of it.

I helped Dietz sit, as he choked on his sobs.

"After everyone had left the Sifkin place that night, I stayed, hidden, and watched," Dietz said. "I just knew something more was going to happen.

"Sure enough," he continued, "when all was quiet, a beam of moonlight flashed on the hanging tree. And there was George Sifkin, alive again, yanking the rope from the limb and lowering himself to the ground. After he freed himself, he whistled for the dog, which came loping out of nowhere. The two of them wandered off down the path to the bay, where Henry Sifkin's boats were anchored. Last I ever saw of either of them."

Dietz explained that the folk of Shellbank had expected Henry Sifkin to exact a terrible revenge. But he didn't. He surprised them all one night by simply leaving Shellbank; taking his family and as many of his possessions as he could carry. He boarded one of his oyster boats and sailed away into the world.

Shellbank arose the morning after to find that the boats Henry had left behind had been scuttled beyond repair. The ice house had been burned to the ground, as well. Shellbank quickly learned how economically dependent it had been upon the industry and largesse of Henry Sifkin.

Shellbank stopped living. Even the oystering dried up, leaving little more than a bleached shell. The place began the long process of withering away that produced the dried out husk I discovered.

Henry Sifkin had not sought revenge, but with his show of noble disdain, he had exacted a terrible retribution from Shellbank by revealing the simple truth about the place and its people.

I had learned at the library that Henry Sifkin's other children, grandchildren and great-grandchildren had multiplied and spread across America; becoming doctors, lawyers, and teachers, statesmen and warriors; people of property and substance; respected members of numerous communities.

While Shellbank dwindled and diminished. The men of Shellbank began to die off afterward. Some went quickly, from oddball ailments no one had ever heard of; others more slowly, from the effects of alcohol and idleness and guilt.

Some tried to leave, to make new lives for themselves. But they always came back to Shellbank. Alone. Battered bitter by failure. It was as if they *had* to come back and live out the lives they had made for themselves in this place.

It would be easy to examine what had happened with the comfortable detachment and wisdom of hindsight afforded by the 1960s, and resolve that George Sifkin had been lynched by an angry white mob because he was black and handicapped. Because he crossed a line separating him from the rest of the community, a line that was not in the least invisible back in "those days."

Dietz explained it better as we sat in the shade of a tree near the remains of Sifkin's fence. He told me that George Sifkin's differences didn't really have to do with his skin color or mental state, although both made it easier for folk to justify their actions during the long lonely conversations each had with himself.

"He lived in his own world, on the other side of that fence," Dietz said, his voice quivering.

"It was a place the rest of us couldn't go. We didn't understand it and it frightened us. It made us angry and we resented him because he was simple and happy. It made him less human and more of an abstract symbol or something, something put here to test and torment the rest of us; something forbidden and out of reach, and even though we didn't understand it, we wanted it. There was something magical about that place, about George Sifkin. When we couldn't have that power for ourselves, we destroyed it."

The residents of Shellbank gathered around us. There were many sheepish looks exchanged, some tearful. All held themselves solemn and anxious. They seemed to be expecting me to say something, to comment on their dark secret.

"Histories have beginnings and endings," I suggested. "One phase ends before the next can begin and run its course. Perhaps . . . perhaps Shellbank has not properly concluded the incident at Sifkin's fence."

The next meeting of the Shellbank Historical Society gathered at a long-forgotten church. I helped Potter and the presider tear away the planks that were put up long ago to block the entrance.

Several of the members went inside, while the others mingled uneasily at the door. The presider emerged from the church carrying a small, but heavy, wooden cross. Several people gathered to help him carry it.

They limped and shuffled slowly down the dirt path leading back to the Sifkin place. They appeared hesitant and ashamed, yet they struggled forward.

The presider took the lead as his father had done ages ago as the last minister of the church. He nodded at Wilfred Dietz who propped the cross against the fence post. One by one the others approached, bearing honey and dandelions, and wreaths of marsh grasses.

No one looked into the Sifkin yard. Dietz shuffled back to stand beside me under the cedar tree. Sally tried to arrange the flowers but her fingers trembled so much that she made a mess of it. A few others shambled forward to help.

The presider tried some words, but found no comfort in language. Memory ruled here, and memory was not showing mercy this day.

I looked beyond the fence post and spotted something moving out of the shadow of the house. I squinted in the harsh sun, and stopped when I saw a figure emerge into the light.

My son.

In that precise moment I began to understand places within myself, and I understood what the townspeople of Shellbank had to do.

"Go inside the fence!" I exclaimed.

They looked at me like I was mad.

"You have to see the world from inside the fence, the way George Sifkin saw it," I said in a pleading whisper, as the figure of my son faded.

They hesitated. I led them, one by one, to the fence urging each to enter. Dietz, Potter, Sally, the presider. Soon, they were all inside. Only I stood outside the fence.

"To bear witness," I said to them. But the truth is, I still felt unsure about my own feelings.

"We're here to finally recognize a wrong that we, as a community, committed long ago," the presider said, finding his voice.

"We can't go back. And there's not much to look forward to. Perhaps we do this now that our sin has been finally brought to light, out of fear and in the selfish hope of assuring ourselves a cleaner slate if and when we meet our maker.

"We're sorry, George. We didn't know what we were doing." The presider paused, letting the heavy air from the bay punctuate and carry his speech to his listeners. "Let's try to make some sense of this with the time we have left."

As the presider walked slowly away, he nodded toward the Sifkin house. Silently, they all slowly began making their way back toward the path. A cool breeze, coming from the Sifkin place, swept over us. It ruffled the calico of the dresses and played with the thin strands of hair cobwebbed on the heads of the men. It lifted Potter's fishing cap, sending it dancing ahead of them as they headed down the path, dust devils leading the way. I took a long inhalation of the air.

"I smell snow," I said in awe, or reverence.

"Wonderful," Sally cooed in a girlish voice. "You know, I feel like going on a picnic." Other voices murmured giddy agreement. I watched as they shuffled down the path past the rest home and headed toward the marsh, vanishing, one by one, inside the swaying wall of marsh reeds and phragmites lining the side of the road. I did not follow. I understood that another path was meant for me.

Instead, I waited by Sifkin's fence, like Wilfred Dietz had done all those years ago, expectant that something else might happen.

Did I figure to see George Sifkin, returning at last to complete the pitiful story of this forsaken place? I *did* see someone watching me from the other side of the fence. But it wasn't George Sifkin.

My son. His shoulder-length hair blowing freely in the breeze. He carried brushes in one hand and embraced a canvas under the other arm. He smiled and beckoned to me with a wave of his paint-stained hand. Then he held up the canvas to show me.

A life-sized portrait of George Sifkin smiling happily as he romped in the snow with his dog. Bringing me back to the moment, I recalled Dietz's parting words:

I know what I saw. George and the dog vanished inside a curtain of reeds at the water's edge. I figure we won't be whole until we follow a bit in his footsteps.

Now, I know how it should go at the end of a story. Resolution.

I should cross the fence and go to my son and let the mystery that still lingers in that place be the guide of my actions. But what mystery? Innocence? Anger? Remorse and reconciliation? I ponder and consider.

I'm not sure that I'm ready give in yet and throw myself upon another's strength and embrace a magic that isn't really my own, to see me through this troubled existence of mine.

Once again, I walk instead, choosing to follow the double yellow line leading away from Shellbank, back to familiar places I had fled in moments of fear and weakness.

But now, it is a world I feel more willing to properly explore.

Maybe I'll head to a certain art gallery on Rittenhouse Square.

I'm happy to walk every step of the way.

Mason, On His Way Home

Randy Ribay

They look like birds with broken wings, Mason thought, his face pressed against the cool concrete of the sidewalk, his left eye stinging. He could already feel the heat of the blood rushing, stretching the skin taut as it swelled. He watched as dozens of pages fluttered in the gusts of the passing cars until a rush of air lifted them upward in a quick arc. They floated back down, sweeping in graceful parabolas until they landed, only to be kicked up again a moment later by the next passing car. Mason found the sight hypnotizing, like watching waves break against rocks. A grating voice from above returned him to the situation at hand.

"What now, bitch? I fucking dare you to say that shit again."

When he did not respond or move to stand, a foot slammed into his side. Pain jolted through his ribs. Mason winced, watching the fliers flap, waiting for the pain to subside.

"He's not gonna do anything, man. Just leave him," said a second voice, higher than the first, cracking from puberty.

"Nah, I want him to say it again. To my face." There was a moment of silence. The boy stepped in front of Mason's nose and then crouched. The boy's black, untied skate shoe blocked Mason's view of the fluttering pages. "Think you're so fucking brave saying it to my back. Say it again, bitch. To. My. Face."

Mason briefly considered this great injustice of the world, the fact that some people so readily insulted others but were such bad sports when insulted back.

He croaked, and then cleared his throat.

"I . . . heard . . . your mom . . . gives great head, too . . . *Oof!*"

The boy kicked Mason two more times in the stomach.

"Ever talk about my mom again—" *kick*— "or my sister—" *kick*—"and I'll fucking kill you!" *Kick.* The boy spit on Mason's face and kicked him one more time. Mason allowed the momentum to roll him onto his back. He closed his eyes and listened to the papers and the passing cars.

"Alright, you happy now? Can we go?" said the second voice. "We're lucky someone hasn't already stopped."

If anyone actually cared, they would have, Mason thought.

"Yeah, I'm done with this piece of shit," said the boy.

Mason heard them climb onto their bikes and pedal away.

Pulling one sleeve over his hand, Mason wiped the boy's saliva from his face. Pain pulsated around his eye and along his side. He tried to tell himself it was all in his mind, which scientifically was true, and hoped that acknowledging the sensation as nothing but mere neurological pulses would diminish the sting. It worked for a moment, but the pain returned, like sunlight after a small cloud has passed.

He waited several minutes and then slowly opened his eyes, the right one still stinging. The sky looked like rain, an infinite sheet of grey cloud, moving imperceptibly.

Mason thought he might go home and take a nap, but a paper slapped into the side of his face. It was one of the fliers he was supposed to be passing out on Main Street, advertising the weekly specials at the sandwich shop where he worked.

Mason pushed himself up and saw the rest of the fliers scattered across the road, up and down the length of the block. One hundred and fifty fliers that should have been in the hands of hungry Saturday morning shoppers. Mr. Phareal had warned Mason that someone was going to keep an eye on him to make sure he didn't merely throw them away. Mason knew this bluff was typical of the old man's humor. Nobody was watching him.

I could just leave the fliers, return to the shop, and say I passed them all out already, he thought.

But he knew that wouldn't work. Even if there was no spy keeping tabs on him, the shop was only a couple blocks away. In all likelihood, Mr. Phareal would eventually drive by, see the fliers, and know that Mason had lied. He would be disappointed.

I should have ignored that kid, Mason thought. *It's not like he was the first to say that. Hell, he's not even the hundredth.*

But Mason was not the type to ignore an insult. He stood and brushed the dirt from his clothes, then pulled up his shirt and examined his side. There was no blood, but the reddish purple of a burgeoning bruise had begun to blossom beneath his light brown skin. He poked its epicenter and winced.

He gathered as many fliers from the road as he could without venturing into traffic. Mason smoothed the meager pile against a telephone pole and then walked downtown.

Maybe it was because they were dingy and marked with tire tracks, but after an hour on bustling Main Street not a single person had taken a flier from Mason. When he held them out, people averted their eyes and shook their heads stiffly. Mothers used a protective arm to shepherd their children away from him. The elderly crossed the street and then crossed back once they had achieved a comfortable distance. Teens pointed and laughed. One took a picture with her phone.

His limping gait, fat lip, and swollen brow probably didn't help his salesmanship. He couldn't blame people for not wanting to take a flier from someone who resembled a mad scientist's henchman.

Mason checked the time and called it a day a few hours early. He threw the fliers into a nearby garbage can, put his hands in his pockets, and headed back to the sandwich shop.

The bell jangled when he opened the door. Mr. Phareal, all alone, turned away from the mounted TV, expecting a customer. Disappointment and then concern flashed on his face.

"Jesus H. Christ, son. What happened to you?"

Mason sat down in one of the booths and craned his neck toward the TV. "*Jurassic Park*," he said. "I love this movie."

"You hear me? You got a concussion? What the hell happened?"

Mr. Phareal held a rag over his palm and pressed the lever for ice on the soda fountain. "Here." He tied the ends of the rag together and handed Mason the impromptu icepack as he sat across the table. His skin was jet-black, but his short hair was the grey of an overcast sky.

Mason pressed it against his temple, enjoying the chill but not the stench of food that permeated the cloth. "I tripped."

"Some trip."

"You can say that again."

"Some trip."

Under normal circumstances, Mason would have at least cracked a smile, but this time he didn't react. He continued to watch the movie while Mr. Phareal searched his face. "Seriously, son, what happened? Someone say something about your mom again? Look, I know she—"

"I tripped," Mason shrugged, avoiding eye contact. "I passed out the fliers. You should expect an avalanche of customers at any moment."

On the screen someone found a severed arm.

Mr. Phareal sighed. "You remember that stray you picked up when you were a little kid?"

Mason didn't respond, but his thoughts turned to his late cat, Sir Sprinkleforth III.

"When that cat died, you were devastated for weeks. Didn't want to come out of your room, didn't want to talk to no one, didn't want to do nothing. It was like your world had ended. You just cared so much for it."

Mason stared at the TV, fighting tears. Holding it in.

"But the world didn't end, and eventually, you understood that. Well, the same thing's going on now, only I'm afraid you're not gonna pull out of it. But you need to. The world is still here. You're still here. Your dad's still here. And I know I'm going to sound like a real old head when I say this, but you've got your whole life ahead of you, son. It's true, even if it sounds corny. Look, I know that when your mom—"

Mason shot the old man a look that made him stop speaking. "I don't want to talk about her."

Mr. Phareal held up his hands and then continued more carefully. "I just hate to see you like this. Always angry. Always looking for a fight you can't win. Sometimes you just got to let go and keep on going, because if you don't, you'll find out that what you've actually been holding onto is a bomb. If anyone knows that, it's me."

Mr. Phareal looked at Mason, gauging whether or not his words hit home. Sighing, he said, "Go home. Rest. Tell your old man I said hey."

"Thanks." Mason slid out of the booth. He went to the back, punched his time card, and then left through the backdoor, still holding the pungent towel of ice to his temple.

The rain fell in light but steady drops; the kind of rain that could turn the world grey for days. It pattered on the bus shelter where Mason sat, leaning against one of the scratched up Plexiglas walls. He stared at the gutter, watching a tiny stream of detritus flow along the side of the road and into a nearby sewer grate. Car tires hissed back and forth, punctuated by the slosh of a nearby puddle.

What the fuck is wrong with people? Mason thought, not for the first time. *Why do they always have to give you shit for things you have no control over? I can't wave a fucking magic wand and fix everything.*

Like a dam holding back a thousand miles of river, Mason fought to keep out any thoughts of his mother. Though a few months had passed, the pain was as fresh as his black eye. He fixed his eyes on the world outside the bus shelter.

A dark object floating its way toward the drain caught Mason's eye. It was the size of a quarter, and it seemed to be twitching—no, wriggling. Thankful for the distraction, Mason stepped out of his self-pitying reverie and into the rain. He bent down at the curb to get a closer look.

It was a turtle. A tiny turtle.

A tiny head, a tiny tail, and four tiny limbs poked out from beneath its tiny, dark shell. The legs moved in a frantic effort to swim against the current, away from the maw of the drain.

Perplexed by his find, Mason reached into the cool, debris-filled water with both hands and scooped it out of the gutter. He darted back into the bus shelter, set the turtle on the bench, and then crouched to examine it at eye level. It withdrew its limbs into its shell. Mason sat back down and waited for it to reemerge.

Mason didn't know much about turtles. Its dark shell, still shiny with moisture, was such a deep brown that it was nearly black. Flecks of orange and yellow randomly speckled what he had seen of the tiny turtle's body, and its belly was the impossibly bright orange of glowing coal.

"Where did you come from, little guy?" Mason asked the turtle, his voice high and soft as if talking to a child. He nudged it with his finger to no effect. Mason tried to estimate the distance to the nearest pond or forest or ocean or wherever a turtle might live.

He continued to observe the turtle without touching it. First, it stretched its little head out and lazily blinked its wide-set eyes. It opened and closed its small beak of a mouth a few times as if

27

tasting the air for danger. Finding none, it extended its limbs fully and began to meander across the bench, its progress slow and uneven. Whenever it wandered too close to the edge, Mason would cup his hands and hold them beneath the turtle as a safety net. But it never fell. It always turned around just in time and then headed off to explore a different direction with the sad delusion of freedom.

Suddenly, a wave of dirty water sloshed out of the gutter and onto Mason, soaking his pants and shoes. He cursed the bus under his breath. Impassive, the bus squealed to a stop in front of the shelter and the doors hissed open. Without thinking, Mason swept the turtle into his hands, and slipped it into his pocket before stepping onto the bus.

The driver took in Mason's disheveled state, and gave him a look. Mason knew that look. *Don't you try to cause any trouble.*

Mason flashed an insincere smile, swiped his pass, and then walked toward the back as far from the other few passengers as possible. Once seated, he ducked low and pulled the turtle from his pocket. He cupped his hands around it and peeked through his fingers.

Mason carried the turtle to his desk. He pushed aside a stack of half-finished homework, and rearranged his pre-calc and *U.S. History from 1865* textbooks to form a makeshift triangular pen with his laptop as the third wall. Satisfied for the moment, Mason changed into dry clothes and then surveyed his room for a more permanent habitat for his new friend.

Four months ago, this would have been a much easier task. His mom had always forced him to clean his room on Saturdays. His phone, laptop, and Xbox controllers had always been held hostage until he made his bed, put away his clothes, organized his desk, and vacuumed. Curtains drawn back, sunlight streaming into the room, she would give a thorough assessment as Mason stood in the doorway, his hands itching for electronics.

But with his mother gone like last year's dreams, his father couldn't care less about domestic order. Books and video game cases were strewn about the floor amidst clothes that leaked like vomit from his open closet and dresser drawers. His sheets were a tangled mess and revealed part of the bare mattress. It was through this mess that Mason rummaged while the turtle waited on his desk like the calm in the center of a storm.

He rejected everything he found. A cereal bowl from last week with some solidified milk in the bottom—not flat enough. A sandwich container with green fuzz in it.

"Man," Mason said over his shoulder, "somebody really needs to clean this place up." He stood and turned to the turtle. "Hang on. I'll be right back." He left the room.

Mason returned out of breath, dragging a storage bin. It was short and wide, the kind designed to slide underneath a bed. A piece of peeling masking tape clung to one side with the words "Mom's Sweaters" written in fading marker in his mother's even handwriting. It no longer held Mom's sweaters.

"Hey, little guy," he said, peering over at the turtle. Its tiny claws tapped against the cheap wooden desk as it searched for an exit. It bumped against the spine of a textbook, and then tried to scale the vertical surface.

"I found you a freakin' turtle mansion." Mason kicked some clothes out of the way and set the container onto a piece of floor he hadn't seen in months.

Mason left the room again, returning with a large McDonald's cup held carefully between both hands. He tilted the cup into the plastic container and water splashed across the bottom. It flowed across the surface and then settled in small pools. After several more trips, the homemade habitat eventually became a shallow pool of water featuring a large stick, some rocks, a few small islands and tracts of "land", a toy tree, and several plastic dinosaurs to keep the turtle company.

Stepping back, Mason surveyed his work.

"Hey, Son," came a sudden voice from behind.

Mason turned. His father stood in the doorway. His eyes were blurry and his short fro was pressed flat on one side. His face was unshaven and he was wearing a ratty, faded blue robe.

His presence surprised Mason, as usual. Though he was home whenever he wasn't teaching mathematics at Mason's high school, his father mentally resided elsewhere. Mason often thought of himself as an orphan.

"Hi," Mason said, turning back to the turtle's new home.

"What you doin'?" he asked.

"Playing video games," Mason replied over his shoulder.

"Okay. Just keep it down, alright?"

"Yeah, okay, Dad."

Mason's father nodded, scratched his beard, and then drifted away, presumably back to the couch in the living room.

Mason closed the door behind him. He scooped the turtle gently into his palm, and it retreated into its shell. Mason set the turtle down onto one of the islands he had made from a handful of dirt from the front yard. Mason observed, eager to watch the turtle frolic in the lap of luxury.

For a while, nothing happened. The shell sat on the dirt, seemingly lifeless. But after a few minutes, its small head peeked out, followed by its limbs. Finding its footing, the turtle clambered down the dirt to the edge of the water.

"Go on," Mason said, his voice a whisper.

As if understanding his words, the turtle slid into the water. Its head and shell bobbed at the surface. Its small legs kicked furiously, propelling it around the miniature pond in uncontrolled arcs. After a few seconds, it eventually made it to one of the islands and climbed ashore.

Mason smiled. "Good job, little guy. You must be hungry now."

Mason left the room and headed into the kitchen. He pulled open the fridge, surveyed the meager contents, and pulled a browning head of lettuce from the vegetable drawer. Returning to the turtle, he tore off a leaf and placed it next to the turtle.

The turtle approached the lettuce and appeared to sniff it. Mason wondered if turtles had noses and made a mental note to look it up later.

"Sorry, that's all we have right now. Dad hasn't gone food shopping in like . . . forever. I promise I'll pick up something later."

Mason was so absorbed watching the turtle explore, he didn't notice that his room had gotten so dark he could barely see. He stood and stretched his stiff limbs, then turned on the light.

"I think I'm going to call you 'Raphael'," Mason said.

The turtle looked up at Mason and shook its head almost imperceptibly.

Weird, Mason thought.

Playing along, Mason tried again. "Fine. Maybe you're more of a 'Leonardo'."

Again, Mason thought he saw the turtle move his head from side to side, more emphatically this time.

I must be tired.

"Donatello? Michelangelo? Splinter? April O'Neil?"

The turtle responded to each suggestion by shaking his head in definite rejection. Amused, Mason stopped talking. *It's probably just responding to the sound of my voice. I bet if I speak gibberish it'll shake its head again.*

So Mason mumbled random syllables, but the turtle did not shake its head. It stared at Mason with what seemed like a quizzical expression.

Mason looked around his room. Maybe there was a hidden camera somewhere and this was some sort of elaborate prank his friends were playing on him. Then again, Mason didn't really have friends anymore.

Mason turned back to the turtle. "So you know what I'm saying?"

The turtle nodded its tiny turtle head.

Christ, Mason thought. He brought his hand up and touched his swollen eye. It stung. *That punch must have jacked up my brain.*

"No," a voice said.

Mason turned, but the door was still closed. He looked back at the turtle.

"Hello, Mason." The voice was deep and laced with a sonorous English accent.

"What. The. Fuck?" Mason shook his head to clear it and then looked back down at the turtle.

"Yes, I'm the little one with the fancy shell."

"What—how—is this real? Did I get a concussion?" Mason wondered whether he was imagining all of this, while his body lay on the side of the road and his brain hemorrhaged away. He had read a short story like that in school once.

"No, no, sir, you're quite well. Although I do not understand why you insist on calling me out of name."

Mason looked around again. Spotting no hidden cameras, he turned back to the turtle. It seemed to be speaking to him, but it was not moving its mouth. Also, it was a freaking turtle.

"I was trying to give you a name," Mason said, lowering his voice in case there was a camera somewhere.

"Why, how would you like it if I tried to give you a name? I've already got one, thank you very much, and it's a fine name if I do say so myself. What is it with you humans and your need to name every single thing you come across?"

Mason shrugged, not knowing how to answer for all humanity. "So what is it? Your name?"

The turtled cleared its throat somehow. *"Ahem. Void, at your service."*

"Void?"

"Yes, Void." The turtle named Void squinted its eyes and looked at Mason askew.

"That doesn't sound very English."

"Why the bloody hell does a turtle need to have an English name?"

Mason shifted uncomfortably. "It's just . . . I don't know . . . I thought that with your accent and all . . ."

"What accent?" Void asked.

Mason leaned back. "Never mind. Sorry. I'm Mason. It's nice to meet you, Void."

If he was going off the deep, he may as well dive. Mason extended his hand.

Void merely looked at it. *"Yes, I know your name."*

Mason withdrew his hand. "Oh, yeah. That's right. How *do* you know my name?"

"I'm a turtle," the turtle said, as if that explained everything. It turned away from Mason, crawled across the dirt to the sad lettuce leaf and nibbled it slowly. Mason thought he saw the turtle make a face before it turned and slipped into the water. For several minutes, neither Mason nor the turtle said anything else. The room was quiet except for the soft splashes of the water and the muffled sound of the television floating through the walls.

Void swam around for a few minutes and then climbed onto one of the dirt islands, the one with the tree taken from an old Lego set. He remained motionless for several more minutes.

"I've gone crazy," Mason said aloud. In his head he pictured a future that involved rubber walls.

For a moment, there was no response, and then Void sighed. *"Do we really need to go through this again, chap? I assure you that you are completely sound of mind. Well, maybe not completely. Mostly."*

"If I'm not going crazy, then why am I talking to a fucking turtle?"

The turtle backed up a few steps. *"I say, no need for such profane language."*

Mason rubbed his eyes. "Sorry. Can you just please explain to me what's going on. I mean, I'm pretty sure most people don't talk to turtles named 'Void'."

"Right. I expect they don't—other turtles have other names. Yet, you have a point. Perhaps I should have explained this all first." Void

moved forward and Mason could swear the turtle sat. *"You saved me."*

"I did?" Mason remembered pulling the turtle out of the gutter before it fell into the drain. "I did."

"Yes, those sewers are absolutely vile places for turtles. You cannot even imagine. There are—oh, I cannot bring myself to describe the horrors. Suffice it to say, I would not have lasted long."

The turtle looked around.

"And I must say, while it is not my original home, you have managed to create something beautiful."

"Thanks," Mason said, glancing at a small cave he had made in the corner of the bin from pebbles and dirt. "But you'll grow. You'll become too big for this place. "

"In time, yes. But for now, it is perfect."

"Do you want me to take you home?"

The turtle craned its neck toward the large stick in the opposite corner and its face took on a wistful expression. *"Oh, I am afraid that I can't go home. It was destroyed. For a new golf course, I think? But so it is. Sometimes things change and we must simply go forth."*

Mason waited for further explanation. After a few beats of silence, Mason leaned over and straightened the tree. "So now what? I saved you. Do I get three wishes?"

Void slid back into the water, waded in a semi-circle, and looked up at Mason. *"Actually, yes. Well, kind of. It's only one wish, really. And you cannot wish for just anything."*

"Why not?"

"Why, I haven't that kind of power. What do I look like to you? A sloth? No, no. What I can offer is more of an option, I suppose."

"What's the option?"

"I can give you a shell."

Mason scrunched up his face in confusion. "What? A shell? Like your shell? Don't you need it? Besides, it's kind of small; I don't know what I'd—"

"No, not my shell. A shell. Your very own personal carapace."

"For what? Luck?"

"For using whenever you are in danger. It will protect you, as mine protects me. It really is quite wonderful."

"That's not even possible," Mason said. Then he remembered he was talking to a turtle, having the longest conversation he'd had with anyone in the past few months. He imagined himself walking around with a shell. What would the other kids say?

"What's my other option?" Mason asked.

"Oh, simply to not have a shell."

Mason eyed the turtle suspiciously. "Why wouldn't I want a shell?"

"Well, as useful as it can be, those new to the thing can come to rely upon it too heavily."

"What do you mean?"

"If you never confront danger, but simply hide from it all of the time, you will never get any stronger. Your body will weaken and wither. No, no, you must learn when to confront and when to retreat."

Mason considered the turtle's words. His mind went to the fight earlier that day, when that boy had talked shit about his mother. Certainly a shell would have been useful then. If he had a shell, he could have retreated into himself and just hunkered down until his attacker grew bored and wandered away. It wasn't the first time he had gotten into a fight, and he was sure it wouldn't be the last.

"The shell," Mason said. "I'll take the shell."

"Are you sure?" Void asked. "It will become as much a part of your body as your hands or your feet or your lungs or your brain or your heart. It will shield you from the world as much as it will separate you from it."

"Yes. I'm sure."

"Alright, then. Go to sleep. When you awake, my friend, you will be part of the carapace club. Use it wisely."

With that, Void disappeared into the small cave of pebbles in the corner of the bin.

Still confused, Mason changed into sweat pants, turned off the light, and slipped into bed. He closed his eyes, and though his mind raced with all of the possible advantages of having permanent protection, he expected to awake in a hospital room, alone, peeing into a bag as his life beeped away.

*

Mason awoke the next morning in his room. Sunlight streamed through the window, washing everything in the light of a new day, making even his piles of dirty clothes appear noble.

Yawning, Mason rubbed his eyes. His back felt stiff and he needed to stretch. With considerable effort, he rolled uncomfortably onto his side. On the floor next to his bed, he noticed the elaborate turtle habitat he had constructed the day before. The turtle was nowhere to be seen.

"Good morning," Mason said anyway, and then vaguely recalled having a strange dream in which he had a lengthy conversation with the turtle. He could not remember what they had talked about exactly, but he did remember the turtle had an unusual name.

Void. What a weird fucking turtle name. Sounds like the name of a Decepticon.

After easing back into consciousness, Mason sat up on his bed. He winced as the stiffness of his back phased into a sharp ache. *Damn—that kid really did a number on me.*

But when Mason moved his hand to rub the soreness, he did not find the soft warmth of swollen flesh. Instead, his hand hit something cold and hard, like a large, flat stone whose surface has been smoothed by decades beneath a river.

What the fuck, he thought. His eyes opened wide and he felt fully awake. He stood and craned his neck to look behind himself. Panic set in.

He felt around his back with both hands, trying to understand what was stuck to him. Everywhere he touched he felt that combination of smoothness and hardness. The hard edge extended below his butt. Arms bent behind him, he traced its arc in a complete oval. When his hands returned to the bottom, he readjusted his grip and tried to pull the disc-like surface away from his body. But when he pulled, it hurt as if he were trying to pry off a fingernail.

Moving his hands to his stomach, he found more hardened surface covering the front of his torso like a suit of armor. Nearly the same light brown as his skin, it was smoother than whatever covered his back. He knocked on it several times and a hollow feeling resounded within his chest.

Finally, it hit him. The shell. The turtle had asked him if he wanted a shell. He had said yes. Only it wasn't a dream. It was real. And now he had a shell.

"Void!" Mason called, dropping to the floor and peering into the cave. "Void! Come out here."

After a few moments, the turtle slowly crawled out of the cave. It looked at Mason.

"Take it back. I don't want it anymore."

The turtle merely looked at Mason. It did not nod. It did not shake its head. It did not look at him quizzically, and it certainly did not speak.

Mason raised his voice and said, "Take it back."

The turtle continued staring at him.

Mason struggled to stand. "If you don't take it back, I'm going to take you outside and throw you into the nearest gutter."

Silence.

"What you shoutin' about, Son?"

Mason swung around to find his father's face poking through the door.

Mason scrambled to his feet. "Um, nothing, Dad. Just my video game. Sorry."

His father eyed the small TV set atop Mason's dresser. It was off, the screen blank. His gaze shifted back to Mason and examined him for several moments. Finally, he said, "You look different. What's up?"

Keeping his back out of his father's view, he said, "Nothing. Sorry. I'll turn it down."

"You wearin' a new sweater?"

". . . Oh, this? Yeah, you like it?" Mason mimed pulling up some material over his shoulder, as if he were actually wearing a sweater instead of a giant turtle shell encasing his torso. "I bought it using money from the sandwich shop."

Mason's father rubbed his chin, then his eyes. "Hmm. You know you're supposed to be saving that for college." He took a step inside Mason's room.

"Speaking of the shop, though, Mr. Phareal called last night. Said some stuff that kept me awake all night. Made me take a real hard look at myself. How I been actin' and how I ain't been any kind of real father to you since we lost your mom . . ." His voice trailed off as he examined a mark on the doorframe. He scratched at it with a nail. "I think maybe it's 'bout time we face some of this."

Without any conscious effort, Mason's arms, legs, and head retracted into his shell and he dropped to the floor with a thud. Mason could not explain how he had done it or how it was even possible. He found himself wrapped in a warm, thick darkness and an echoing quiet. Even with his eyes open he saw nothing.

A million miles away, he heard his father calling his name over and over again. The world began to sway. His father must have been rocking the shell back and forth with a slippered foot, in a half-assed effort to rouse him. After some time, the swaying stopped and the world grew silent again. Mason counted to one hundred and then slowly peeked his head out of his shell.

He found himself alone, belly up in the middle of his room. He looked down and saw the underbelly of his shell, but not his arms or legs. The sight was surreal.

He began extending his arms and legs. The process was slow and surprisingly painful, like the pins-and-needles feeling after sitting in a strange position for too long. But once his limbs were fully extended, Mason found himself stuck on his back. He rocked back and forth several times, flailing his arms and legs, and finally righted himself. He stood.

I really hope there's no hidden camera, he thought.

He looked at the small turtle as it nibbled a piece of wilted lettuce. He listened for his father but heard nothing. Not knowing what else to do, he bolted from the house, the back of his thighs bumping against the bottom edge of the shell with each step.

He felt eyes staring at him in disbelief every time a car passed. Luckily, nobody stopped. Maybe they thought that he was simply a weirdo wearing a costume in the middle of the summer, or perhaps they were just too intent on making it to church. Mason thought about sticking to the tree cover instead of the sidewalk, but the thought of running into a raccoon or possum filled him with an inexplicable fear.

When he left the house he had decided to go to the sandwich shop. He needed to talk to someone, and the turtle was out of the question. He didn't have any close friends, and he was nowhere near ready to talk to his father, so that left only Mr. Phareal.

There's no way he'll believe me. He'll probably have me committed . . . maybe that's what I need . . . But when Mom left it was good to talk to him about it . . . even Dad wouldn't let me talk about it . . . so maybe he'll understand. Maybe he'll know what to do again . . .

The backs of his thighs were chafed and his calves were sore. He cursed himself for leaving with neither bus pass nor wallet. He started to feel hot and lightheaded from the merciless sun, and he regretted his decision to eschew the shade for the safety of open space.

"Look who it is," said a familiar grating voice behind him.

Mason had to turn his whole body to look at the kid, the one who had given him the black eye and probably a few bruised ribs. He was on a bike, and behind him pedaled two other kids who looked just as predatory as their leader.

Mason retreated into his shell as instinctively as blinking. He felt the thud of the shell settling on the ground as he welcomed the safety of his sanctuary. In a moment there was violent motion, as if he were on a boat in the middle of a storm with his eyes closed. He guessed that the three kids were trying to beat the crap out of him. But he felt no pain. It was beautiful. He heard the kids' voices rattling distantly in a muffled staccato.

"Hey, Pussy! Why don't you come out of there and face me man-to-man? Or man-to-turtle—whatever the fuck you are!"

The voice was more focused as it echoed around the walls of the shell. It sounded like shouting through a tube. Mason supposed that the kid was speaking directly into the shell's neck hole.

Maybe I should go out and just take the beating, Mason thought. *I can't hide in here forever. Or can I?*

"Your mom's a real fucking slut, dude. I heard that after she got done with the principal, she blew every other teacher on the staff. My uncle works in the E.R., and he said they pumped like five gallons of cum from her stomach the next day." The kid laughed obnoxiously.

Mason never actually heard the part about the principal from his father. As far as he knew, his parents had such a bad argument that his mother just decided to leave. Of course, when school started up a few weeks later, Mason heard all about the affair. It was all anyone talked about. And when your mom sleeps with your principal and they both leave their families and jobs to run away together, you become a popular target. Mason had wanted to transfer, but his father refused to consider it since Mason was a year away from graduation and he was only two years away from retirement.

"So you just going to hide like some fucking faggot?" said the voice.

Mason did not move. He did not respond. He was crying now. He hoped they couldn't hear his sobs.

"I hope you fucking die in there," the voice said. Then, more distantly, probably to his friends, "Let's go. He isn't worth the sweat on my taint."

Mason remained in the shell for what felt like hours. He no longer knew if his eyes were open or closed. His mouth felt parched and his limbs stiff. The sun was baking him inside his shell. But he did not care. This was the best option. Nobody would even notice that he was gone. Not his mother. Not his father. Not his classmates. Perhaps Mr. Phareal, but he'd probably move on as he'd advised Mason to do.

Mason did not have to fight anymore. He did not have to protect or defend or take any more hits. He could stay in the warm darkness and gradually slip into inky obscurity.

"Mason! There you are! Mason? You hear me?"

Mason struggled to comprehend the words. Waking would require a Herculean effort, far more strength than he had left.

"Mason! You in there, Son? I been lookin' all over for you! Mason!? C'mon!"

He now recognized his father's voice. It was clear and echo-y, like the boy's voice from earlier. Mason listened but didn't move.

"I'm sorry, Son. Please. Please." The words were choked, almost sobs. "Please. Please. Come on out. We need to talk. There's so much we need to talk about."

Mason thought about shooting out of the shell and screaming at his father that there was nothing to talk about anymore. That everything was fucked up and that's how it would always be so they just needed to accept it.

But he didn't say anything. He waited. His father waited. And Mason couldn't help remembering lying on his bed with his eyes closed, trying to will away the ongoing argument between his parents in the next room. The words were indistinguishable sound waves sieved by the walls, but their tones carried through clear as light. He listened to the voices rising and falling, rising and falling, like the sea. One would grow with intensity and speed, gathering momentum before finally smashing into an oncoming wave, and then settling, both swallowed by silence, by calm, then the soft swaying of another wave forming. This went on for hours. Mason had considered putting on his headphones, but like a passerby gawking at a car accident, he couldn't not give it his undivided attention.

Eventually, the storm subsided, giving way to sounds that made Mason think of waves lapping softly in the calm ocean. The occasional soft murmuring tones spoke of resolution, of apology, of a return to normal.

But then his mom burst into his room. Her eyes were red and her mascara smeared in streaks down her cheeks. She moved swiftly to Mason, who sat up at the unexpected intrusion. She kissed him once on the forehead, once on the cheek, once on the lips. It felt final, it felt religious. Her lips were soft and warm and waxen with the wetness of her tears.

"I'm sorry," she said. "I love you so much, Mason. You'll never know."

She turned and walked out before Mason had a chance to react.

Mason felt a sledgehammer to his heart, his brain. He stumbled, crying, to his parents' room to ask his father what the hell had just happened, like a small child waking from a nightmare. But the door was locked. Mason knocked and knocked, but his father never opened the door, never even responded.

Mason returned to the present. He replayed his father's plea in his head and considered his father's apology, his proposition for their future.

But he stayed in the darkness.

A moment later, the world lifted, rocking gently. He realized that his father was carrying him.

Time passed, but Mason couldn't say how much. Gravity pulled, and he felt stops and starts and small jostles. But the rocking always began again.

A long time later, everything stopped. The world was still, dark, and silent.

Maybe he just dropped me off on the coast and peaced out, Mason thought. *I can't blame him.*

Mason strained his ears listening for seagulls or waves or any clue that confirmed his fear. But he heard nothing. He considered emerging from the shell. But he was safe and warm. Nothing on the outside world could match it. So instead, he submitted to the darkness and fell asleep.

Mason awoke some time later, groggy and disoriented. The events of the last twenty-four hours came back to him like debris from a shipwreck washing ashore. At first, he thought it had all been a dream. But then he sensed the shell, surrounding and containing him. It no longer felt like a separate thing.

He thought about what to do next. There was still the matter of where the hell his father had taken him. After the bit of rest he had gotten, the safety of the shell no longer seemed like a viable life plan. If his father had taken him to the coast, he figured he may as well slip into the ocean and start his new life.

Mason slowly extended his legs, his arms, and then his head.

He found himself on his back staring upward into a field of improbable stars. The pinpricks of light crowded the evening sky with startling clarity. The moon hadn't risen yet, or it had already set. Mason didn't know which.

"Hey there," said Mason's father.

Mason titled his head toward his father. "Where are we? Are you setting me free?"

Mason's father laughed and shook his head. "Setting you free? What are you talking about? We're at home, son."

Mason tried to sit up, confused by his father's claim.

"Let me help you," his father said and then helped him. Mason righted himself and sat up.

He looked around. They *were* home. They were sitting on the roof. The neighborhood was spread out in the shadows below them. Orange street lamps illuminated patches of sidewalk and parked cars. He looked up again and remembered.

When he was younger, he and his father used to slip through the guest bedroom's window and onto the roof on clear summer nights. His mother had hated it, fearing they'd slip to their deaths. But that never stopped his father from waking Mason in the middle of the night and bringing him outside to look at the moon or Orion or the International Space Station floating by. When had they stopped? Why had they stopped?

"I'm sorry," his father said, gazing upward.

Mason sighed.

"I'm sorry," his father continued. "I ain't been any kind of dad since your mom left us."

"Tell me something I don't know."

His father let out a small laugh. "I deserved that. I was just . . . I don't know . . . I was in so much pain. I loved her so much." He started to cry.

His father's tears made him uncomfortable, so Mason looked at the sky and tried to find half-remembered constellations.

"When she left," his father continued, "I just . . . I just didn't have the strength to do anything, you know? I loved her so much. So goddamned much."

Mason listened.

"I didn't understand, and I didn't want to believe it was true. I kept hopin' she was comin' back . . . back to me . . . to us. I'd close my eyes and pray to God she'd come back . . . I asked myself why a million times and came up with a million questions . . . What had I done wrong? Why hadn't I been enough for her? I'd have given her anything, forgiven her anything, if she'd just come back."

"Me too," Mason said.

His father looked at him, tears in his eyes. He cuffed the back of Mason's neck, just above the rim of the shell. "I know she's not comin' back. I've accepted that. I've accepted it."

A tear slid down Mason's cheek. "She's not, is she?"

His father shook his head. "I can't lose you too, son. I just can't. I feel like I'm about to break apart, like my insides are screaming and shutting down, and I know you probably been feelin' this way too. Only I was too selfish to realize that."

Mason knew. For months they had lived parallel lives, suffering alongside each other, but separately. Only now did Mason realize their pain was actually unifying.

Mason rested his head on his dad's shoulder, and his dad put his arm around Mason. And his dad's arm no longer found the hard shell. Just the warmth of skin and muscle beneath Mason's shirt.

"Maybe we can help each other," Mason said, oblivious to his return to normal. "To hold it together. To repair each other."

"That's just what I was thinking," his father said, squeezing Mason's shoulder.

Mason considered the future. "And fuck Mom."

His dad didn't respond, and Mason feared he was in trouble. But then his dad let a single chuckle escape. More laughter followed, rising and gaining momentum until his dad's whole body shook. Mason smiled and laughed too, not at what he had said, but that they were laughing on the roof above Mr. Phareal, above Void, above the kid who punched him, above his mother.

A neighborhood dog barked somewhere a few houses away. A car pulled into a driveway the next block over. People slept. The lights of an airplane glided across the western horizon.

Mason and his father continued laughing. They laughed until they cried, until they couldn't breathe anymore, until they nearly fell off the roof.

Starstruck

Gregg Feistman

"Christ, you scared me!" I said, whirling around.

"Sorry, didn't mean to."

Casey the heartbreaker was standing behind me.

"I was just wondering if you had the final spectroanalysis results yet," she said.

"Almost, boss. They should be done by tonight."

"Well, if they're done by dinnertime, bring 'em with you, and why don't you join us for a change?"

"Okay, will do."

She flashed her million watt smile and went back down the corridor. I watched her walk away; always a pleasant sight. Casey and I were friends, but that's all it would ever be. Her husband was back on Earth and every guy on the station wanted to fill the role, at least temporarily. I gave her credit for staying faithful; it couldn't be easy.

I turned around and resumed watching my instruments. The analysis was progressing steadily, which was good. Any kind of spikes, or anomalies in engineer-speak, would mean starting the stupid thing all over again. It had already been running for two days.

I liked my little corner here. Tucked away, dark and quiet, but the window offered one hell of a view. Even though I saw them every day, Saturn's rings never ceased to amaze.

I tore myself away from daydreaming and focused back on my work. I don't know how much time had lapsed; I was concentrating so hard I never heard her.

"Boo."

"Not funny, Casey," I told her, not turning my chair around this time.

"I'm not Casey."

I looked up and saw her reflection in my monitor. I spun around.

"Where did you come from?"

She was tall, blonde, leggy, fine-featured and beautifully proportioned. She wore a bright blue jumpsuit, designating a health professional. But she was missing a name patch.

She smiled mischievously. "Out there," she said with a wave of her hand.

"Did you come with the latest transfer crew?"

She shook her head. "Sorry if I startled you."

"That's okay, I just didn't know anyone else was around. Who are you?"

"Ava Green."

"Nice to meet you. I'm Aaron."

"I know. I've wanted to meet you for a long time, Aaron. I've been very interested in you."

"Really? How do you know me? Have we met before?"

"Not formally. I read your personnel file. I sought you out specifically. You're a particularly interesting subject."

"Am I? Why is that? What do you mean you 'sought me out'?"

"Let's just say I study life. I've been doing it a while," she added.

"You don't look that old." I figured she was in her mid-thirties.

"Why, thank you," she said.

"What else do you know about me?"

"Many things. And I hope we'll get to know each other even better," she insinuated.

I was intrigued by this new blonde, but something about her was a little strange. I reached for the alarm, but she stayed my hand. Something about her touch prevented me from pushing the button. It was warm and inviting, not threatening. But I'm not naïve.

"Mother!" I suddenly called out. "Head count!"

"There are currently one hundred and forty-two members of the crew aboard the station," the female-sounding digital voice responded.

Exactly how many there should be. Not counting the woman standing in front of me.

"How many at this work station right now?" I asked.

"Scanning . . . One."

Ava laughed, the sound throaty and sexy, her jade green eyes dancing. "God, men are so predictable."

"Are we?"

"You always respond better to a female voice, even a computer-generated one. It must be hardwired into the genes."

"So," I said to her, "what are you? A 3-D hologram?"

She smiled playfully and stepped close, firmly taking my hands in hers and planting them on her hips. "Do I feel like a hologram?" she asked.

"No," I said, nearly choking.

She laughed again, let go of my hands and stepped back. "I'm a friend."

I cleared my throat. "Thanks, but I've got all the friends I need."

"I'll bet you don't have one like me," she said.

"Yeah, for one thing, the computer doesn't register you as being alive," I noted.

"I've heard the computer's personnel recognition function has been malfunctioning."

"Yeah, I'll have to check that," I said skeptically. If nothing else, she was well informed. The damn thing had been acting up for weeks and the tech crew couldn't find what was causing it. It even failed to recognize me one time.

"You don't have to worry, Aaron, I'm very real. And I'm here to work with you. Maybe offer you some choices."

"No, thanks. I'm okay where I am."

"But you haven't heard them yet."

"I don't need to. I've made all the choices I'll need."

"Maybe you'll change your mind." She was still smiling.

"I doubt it."

"Well, we'll talk later."

She turned and started walking away. I watched her go round the corner and then bolted after her. I couldn't have been more than a few seconds behind her, but when I got to the corridor, she had vanished. Back at my station, I wondered if I had hallucinated the whole thing. But she was no hallucination.

In fact, I recognized the name. Dr. Ava Green was a well-respected astro-psychologist. With the expansion of space exploration, new fields of study had cropped up, astro-psychology being one of them. Those of us who had been on board for a while were studied to see if we deviated from the baseline psychological profiles we came here with. So now it was my turn.

I had been told this was coming and wondered when my own personal shrink would show up, but I still didn't like it. The next few weeks with Dr. Ava Green would be filled with regular appointments, chatting about "how I felt being here" and "did I like my co-workers?" and "did I miss Earth?" Easy answers: "Okay", "I guess so", and "No". The last thing I wanted to do was get my head examined. But I had no choice; I had to go through with this farcical bullshit if I wanted to extend my stay here. And since I had nowhere else to go, I wanted my stay extended as long as possible; forever if someone could arrange that.

"So, you've been here for six years?"

"Yup," I said.

"What's it been like?"

I shrugged. "Mostly routine."

"Tell me about the routine."

"Routine is routine."

Ava put the electronic pad down on the low table between us and looked at me.

"You're not being very helpful, Aaron."

"I'm answering your questions, aren't I?"

"This is our third chat, and I still feel like you're keeping me at arm's length," she replied. "I know you don't want to go through this, but everyone has to, so let's just make the best of it, okay? You wouldn't want me to label my final report on you 'elusive' and 'uncooperative' would you?"

What I wanted to tell her was, I don't give a shit what you label me, this is a giant waste of my time. Instead, I answered "no."

"I'm hoping you'll trust me," she told me.

I shrugged again. "Sure."

"Why did you volunteer to come here?" she asked.

"I needed to get away. I knew they'd accept me; there just weren't many candidates left with my qualifications. The next group was being trained, but they weren't ready yet, and they needed people right away. After all that had happened . . ."

"Zaren certainly changed the world," she admitted.

"The world needed it," I said. "He wanted his cure for cancer to be made readily available. But the corporations privatized it for huge profits. He was right to incite the common man to revolt."

"And when he turned political?"

"He said what had needed to be said for far too long, in my opinion," I told her. "People had finally had it with the ever-increasing amount of corruption and greed. Zaren's arrest the night he accepted the Nobel Prize was the wake-up call the world needed."

"And when all the armies stood down?"

"It's amazing how fast things changed," I continued. "Poverty, disease and a host of other things all gone in a dozen or so years? Nobody expected things would move that quickly. Breakthroughs in medicine, design, biology, engineering, materials science, propulsion technology. Just incredible."

"A new era," Ava said. "Hence, here we sit."

"Here we sit," I repeated. "No more wars to spend on, so out into space we go. Moon bases first, then the disaster that was Mars, and now this space station.

"Jupiter's moons, next. I'll go, if they ask. And it looks like I'll have plenty of time to do it."

"Yes, of course," she smiled. "Which brings us to your current project."

"Why none of us here on the good station *Hestia* age very much? We haven't been able to find the cause. Not yet, anyway. We're not traveling at the speed of light, so Einstein's Theory of Relativity doesn't apply. All we know is living here, we age about one month for every Earth year. And when people go back to Earth, they age normally like nothing ever happened. No side effects, either."

"Why do you think that is?"

I shook my head. "No idea. We've been studying it for the last several years, but it could be anything—radiation, the gas giants' gravitational pull, dark matter, or something we don't know about yet."

"How do you feel about this?"

"Hey, a longer life just for working out here? I'll take it. Hell, I haven't even hit forty-five yet."

She paused. "Why did you come here?"

"I told you, I volunteered."

"Why? It's not the easiest life here."

"I'm sure it's in my file," I said darkly, not liking where I thought this was going.

"Most of the facts are there. But I want to hear it from you," she said. "I want to know how you felt."

"No."

She leaned forward and peered into my eyes. I could smell her fragrance and thought there was something in her look. Sadness? Maybe it was empathy.

"I know it's painful, but tell me about Gabrielle."

I didn't answer. Couldn't really.

"Please?"

"I've spent six years trying not to think about it."

Her green eyes held me steady, not blinking.

"It was an accident, Aaron," she said softly.

"Was it? Where were you in those days?"

"Here and there."

"But you weren't *there*."

"No, I wasn't," she admitted.

"Then you don't know. 'Accidents' always had a question mark attached to them back then."

"Why was that?"

"I don't know, that's just how it was."

"Go on."

"It doesn't matter. In every revolution innocents always get caught in the crossfire, right?" I paused. "Maybe it was my work back then. Or hers. But something made the authorities take the beautiful, funny, intelligent love of my life and our baby daughter from our home that morning."

"They were released the same day."

"But they never came home."

She picked up the tablet and swiped through some documents.

"You only left the house for the funeral," she said. "No one saw or heard from you for months, then one day you signed up for the *Hestia* and were here shortly thereafter. One might say as quickly as you could."

"What do you expect?" I asked angrily. "My world was gone. I didn't give a *damn* about the rest of the world. It could all go to hell."

She looked up. "I can understand how you felt," she said gently.

"No Doctor, I really don't think you can," I said bitterly.

"You could have started over eventually."

"What for? I had no reason to, not there. I just hoped 900 million miles would be far enough."

She put the pad down, leaned in and locked eyes with me.

"Was it?" she asked. "Have you ever thought that maybe while you're out here, something might come along to help turn things around again?"

I stood up. "I think we're done for today."

"Do I really believe my eyes?" Thompson said as I joined the little group. "Is Aaron actually being social for once?"

"Hey, give him a break," Casey said, scooting over. "He can be social. Here, have a seat."

I put my tray down next to hers and sat.

"Looks good," Dean said, glancing at my dinner.

"This new generation of food processors has really come a long way," I agreed.

"And the botany module grows the real thing, no more artificial tastes," Casey added. "Hey, I reviewed the results of your report," she told me.

"And they're confirmed?"

She nodded.

"Let me guess," Thompson said, "still nothing?"

She nodded again. "So we're back to square one."

A groan emanated from around the table.

"Hey sorry, guys, but we go again until we find something."

"What if there's nothing to find?" Dean asked.

"Then we try something else," she answered. "That's why we're here."

"Don't you ever stop working?" Thompson asked her. "I mean, it's okay to have some fun here too, you know." He eyed Casey, giving a self-satisfied smirk.

"We've been over this. You and I have different definitions of fun," she said, staring right back at him. "I'm very happily married."

"But your husband's pretty far away right now. Two years is a long time, right?"

I caught Dean shaking his head as Casey went in for the kill.

"For your information, he and I had lots of fun before I left, and we'll have even more fun when I get back," she told Thompson. "Your concern for my well-being is touching, but don't you worry, I send him regular reminders every week. And no, you can't see them. Besides, I *know* I have nothing to worry about, and neither does he. It's called trust. When you love someone, really truly love them, you trust them and they trust you. Why don't you ask your ex-wives about that?"

Dean sniggered as Casey took a bite of food. I had to grin too. There was a reason Casey had become team leader within the first year.

"Hey, how are your sessions with the shrink going?" Thompson asked me, clearing his throat.

"Fine," I said.

"She probing your deepest, darkest secrets?" he asked.

"She's just doing her job," I told him.

"I'll bet," he smirked. "How many more times you have to meet with her?"

"A few more, I guess."

"Well, if I were you, I'd keep it going for as long as you can," he said. "And hey, when you're done, maybe I can sign up for some time with her. One on one sounds good to me, a man can get lonely up here by himself, nothin' but work to keep him company. And she's pretty damned gorgeous, or hadn't you noticed?"

"Shut up, Thompson," Casey told him.

Dean couldn't hide a smile. "You know, bub, life here might be easier if you didn't think that all the women were placed here solely for your enjoyment." He shook his head again.

"Oh, come on," Thompson said, "a little ribbing never hurt anyone. You guys have become way too serious lately."

I finished my meal and got up. "Excuse me."

"Oh hey, stick around," Dean said. "What's your hurry?"

"I've got some work to do," I told him.

"Relax a little, Aaron," he said. "There's a card game later, why don't you join us? Low stakes, promise."

"Maybe another time."

I took my tray to the recycle station and went to the exit. Casey was waiting for me.

"Are you okay?"

"I'm fine, thanks."

"Listen, don't let Thompson get to you. He's all talk anyway. Dean threatens to throw him out of an airlock at least once a day."

"I know."

"And I'm sorry if I upset you by talking about Alex waiting for me on Earth. I know you don't . . . I mean, I hope I wasn't being insensitive. I didn't mean to make you feel . . ."

"I know. It's okay, really, I'm all right," I told her.

"You sure?" she asked with concern in her brown eyes.

"I'm fine, thanks."

"You really have work to do?"

"Yes, I really have work to do. I have an idea or two on a new direction to try and I want to jot some things down and run a few quick simulations."

"They can wait 'til morning. Why don't you come and play cards with us?"

"I will, another time. It's okay, really."

She looked at me again, a mixture of sadness and lingering concern. "Okay, I'll see you in the morning."

I left and walked down the corridor towards my living quarters, taking the long way. The constant hum of the station's environmental systems throbbed in the background. When I first came here, it bothered me, the lack of complete silence no matter where I went, even in my quarters. There was always some reminder we weren't on *terra firma*. Now, I don't even notice it.

Okay, so I lied to Casey, I wasn't okay. In truth, it really wasn't what she or Thompson *said*. It was the topic. I had gotten good, real good at pushing Gabby from my mind every time she popped into it. And then my discussion with Ava brought it all back. How I had fallen hard the very first time I saw her, how I had relentlessly pursued her, how she had knowingly, teasingly made me wait before agreeing to marry me, how happy we'd been. And then the baby came. I had gotten very good at forgetting it all. Maybe too good.

Since our last talk a few days ago, I hadn't seen Ava. I felt awkward; a little guilty for blowing up at her. Maybe she had seen it before with others. She'd probably seen all kinds of behaviors. But I didn't think I did myself any good. I hadn't exactly made a strong case to stay here.

After another long loop, I went to my door. I pressed the wall panel, the door recognized my handprint and slid open, complimented by the low hissing of compressed air.

Ava was standing there.

"How did you get in here?" I asked. The door hissed closed.

She smiled mischievously. "I slipped in under the door."

"What did you do, steal my handprint?"

"Something like that," she said, still smiling.

"I don't know if anyone's told you, but that's a serious offense around here. Listen, I'm going to have to ask you to leave."

"That's not very gallant, Aaron."

"I can be the most un-gallant man you'll ever meet," I told her. "But I guess you know that already."

She shook her head. "I very much doubt that, you're not that type." She took a step towards me. "It's been a couple of days, I thought you might be happy to see me."

"This isn't office hours, Doctor."

She laughed. "True. Listen, I'm sorry I pressed you. You have the right to keep some things private. But I hope you understand repressed feelings can come out in other ways, in behaviors possibly detrimental to you or to others on the station. It's my job to identify them, if they exist, and help you find ways to deal with them."

"Sure, I understand," I said, "you were just doing your job. I get that. And I'm sorry I blew up at you. But you don't have to worry about me, Doctor. I dealt with what happened a long time ago. I'm not a danger to anyone, not even me. So is that what you came here for?"

"Mostly."

"What else?"

"To make amends."

I shook my head. "No need."

"It was obviously a traumatic event in your life, Aaron. It was bound to affect you."

"I'll say," stating the obvious. "I came here."

"And you've never thought about returning to Earth?"

"Why?" I snorted.

"It's home," she said.

"Not my home."

"It's where you were born."

"And it's where I *died*, Doctor. That life is over. Now I have this one."

She paused, processing that. After a moment, her green eyes seemed to soften a bit.

"Tell me this, then," she asked. "Do you ever get lonely?"

"I don't think about it."

"Most people get lonely from time to time, especially those without close family ties or friends. It's normal," she said. "There are ways to combat loneliness."

"I stay busy. What about you? Do you get lonely?" I asked.

She nodded, a quick glimpse of that melancholy showing through. "Sometimes."

"Then maybe you ought to work up a profile on yourself, Doctor."

"Or maybe we should talk about something else."

"Like what?"

She took another step. We were standing pretty close. Her scent filled my quarters. "I want to get to know you better. And I want you to get to know me."

"Why?"

She stopped, surprised. "Why?"

"Yes, why? Why me?"

She stepped away and became serious.

"You're forty-four, your parents died before the revolution began," she began, speaking almost clinically. "You lost your wife and family tragically, you've got no siblings or attachments back on Earth, and it's quite clear you have no intention of ever returning. You volunteered to come to this station to get away."

"So you know my personnel file and have been working on my psychological profile," I said. "Is that my official report?"

"Except you found life here wasn't what you hoped it would be. Oh, you find the work interesting enough for the most part, and you get along with your colleagues, but the truth is, you just exist. You're lonely, lonelier than you ever want to admit. So you've shut yourself off. You said it yourself—you died that day."

Her words stung. Deeply. She was right and I hated that.

"Please leave," I said.

"Aaron," she said gently, and I saw that mournful look in her eyes again, this time more pronounced than ever. "I know what loneliness is like, better than you, better than anyone here. Let me give you a reason to open yourself up again to possibilities. I like you, and I want to be with you. I've chosen you. Can't that be enough for now?"

"Just like that?"

"Just like that."

"What am I, a sympathy case?"

"No, of course not." she said.

"And what about later?"

A small, sad smile crossed her face. "There is no future, there is no past, there is only now."

"I'm guessing this isn't part of your standard therapy. You know, you have quite the bio, Doctor. And I did some checking on you too. For instance, there's no record of when you arrived. Care to explain that?"

"I arrived when you first saw me. Are you always so suspicious?"

"Sorry, not good enough. I have some questions for the woman who obviously wants to shake up my routine."

"Well, I'm here now," she said simply.

"If you really want to be with me, I need to know more."

"You'll know more in time, a lot more, everything. I promise."

She took another step towards me and I stepped back towards the door.

"Don't be frightened," she said.

She reached up and unzipped her suit. Shrugging it off, she stood naked in front of me.

"Do you really want me to go?"

It was hard to take my eyes off her. I'm sorry to admit it, but beautiful women have never just offered themselves to me. It was then that I heard the little voice screaming loud and clear in my head to get her out. I ignored it.

"There *is* no future, there *is* no past, there is only . . . only . . . now!"

Propped up on my palms, I looked down at Ava, her face aglow with pleasure, her blonde hair matted and damp, strewn about on her shoulders. I stayed that way for another moment or two, then rolled off of her.

I laid back and turned my head to look at her. Her eyes were still closed, the sheen of her perfect skin glistening with sweat. We were both breathing heavily.

"Being profound, again?" I asked.

"Telling the truth," she answered. She opened her eyes and lazily rolled over to lay partly on top of me. "You know it's true," our chins meeting, her eyes boring into mine, the heat of her body radiating in my quarters.

"I suppose."

We laid together in silence, her head resting on my chest, me staring straight up at the stars through the window in the ceiling. Saturn's rings would be coming into view soon. The chime from the wall sounded. I sighed.

"Time for your shift," she said. Her hand slid down my stomach and kept going. "What if I don't let you report on time?"

"Then someone will wonder and they'll come looking."

"I very much doubt that," she said.

I got up, crossed over to the wall, hit the button and the sink slid out, water already filling it. I washed my face and got into my clothes, knowing full well she was watching me the entire time.

"I have to leave for a while, but I'll be here when you get back," she told me.

"I figured you would." I had hoped she would.

I touched the wall plate and the door slid back. I stepped out, the door closing behind me.

The weeks passed. Just about every morning we woke up together. I went to work; sometimes she stayed after I left. What she did while I was gone, I didn't know. I assumed she worked. I pressed her once and she got upset with me, saying she was preparing something but not revealing any details. At first I thought it was her final report on me, but after a while I thought maybe not. So I let it go, learning not to ask too many questions. I was enjoying her attention too much, I guess.

I checked the logs and there was an extensive file on her. Impressive credentials, as I had heard, lots of research and publications in top psychological journals. Quoted extensively; national and international presentations galore, too.

"What are you thinking?" she asked late one night, lying on her stomach as I idly traced my fingertips around her bare shoulder.

I hesitated, not wanting to ruin the mood.

"For the first time in a very long time I'm happy, and sometimes . . . sometimes I wish this could go on forever."

She turned her head to face me, one eye hidden behind a fall of jumbled hair.

"Do you remember a few weeks ago, when I said I had a proposal for you?"

"You called it an 'opportunity'." She had cut off the conversation, saying she wasn't ready yet, and put me off every time I mentioned it.

She sat up, naked from the waist up, and took a deep breath. "It's time I told you who I really am."

"You're really not an astro-psychologist, are you?"

She laughed. "Actually, I am, in a way. But I admit, I'm not exactly what I appear to be." She paused for a long time. I waited. "I'm star-born."

"What exactly does that mean?"

"I am made up of matter and energy."

"Everything is made up of matter and energy," I replied.

She shook her head. "No, you don't understand. What your science sees as the energy of a solar flare actually contains bits of living matter. Your technology is not developed enough to detect it. Most of this living matter dies in the void of space within nanoseconds, but some of us, a very few, have a stronger will. We coalesce and become sentient. And because we're made up of star material, we can take any form we choose."

"So you chose a human woman?" I asked, surprised.

"Now, yes, because I have a reason to. But I have been other forms, other genders. Some you are familiar with, such as a tree or a whale. But I have also been a mountainbeast, a rockcreature, an airtern, and thousands of others from planets your species have yet to discover."

"And that's what you do? Become other creatures, other species?"

"Yes."

"Why?" I asked.

"I was born in a solar flare, so my natural state is gaseous. But I've always been curious. I study life in all its forms. I've learned the best way to do that is to become other life."

"So what are you doing here?"

"I've visited Earth many times and of all Earth's species, humans have always intrigued me the most. But like all terrestrial life, humans have a beginning and an end. The lifespan is different for different creatures on many planets, but all eventually die. I however, do not."

"You're immortal?"

"Not quite," she smiled ruefully. "I'm star-born, so my ultimate fate is tied to my star's. My life will end when my star's life ends."

"And which star is that?"

"The one you call the sun."

"So you'll die in another, what, six or seven billion years?"

"Yes, as humans understand time. And when the sun becomes a red giant, it'll throw off more energy and matter and I will be re-born. It's a never-ending cycle." She paused. "Have I frightened you?"

"No."

"Good. I don't wish to frighten you, Aaron. After all, I'm here as I am because I chose you."

"For what?"

"For all the science you understand, for all the science other civilizations more advanced than yours understand, there is one constant in the universe. And it's not defined by science. It's a feeling, an emotion. Loneliness. A being like me, having lived countless lives as something else, understands loneliness better than anyone."

The look in her eyes was back and this time it was overwhelming. Her whole body seemed to slump.

"Surely you've had companions before."

"They all die," she said, barely audible. "I am tired of death. It's been my one constant companion. But now I want another companion, a different one, a *living* companion by my side, to live as I live, learn to know what I know."

"Me."

"You."

"What exactly do I get out of this?"

"I will be whatever you wish, take on any appearance you desire, fulfill any dream, any fantasy or craving you aspire to. All I ask is that you stay with me."

"For how long?" I asked.

"You will not age."

"I don't age now, at least not much," I said.

"None of you do, for a simple reason. I don't wish you to."

"What!?"

She nodded.

"So you control that too?" I asked. "How? Why?"

"The people here are some of the best of your species. I needed time to study them before I made my choice. It's why I became an astro-psychologist. I've studied you and chosen you. You very well may outlive your own kind. But you'll never be lonely again. *We'll* never be lonely again."

"So that's your proposition?" I asked.

"Yes, and your opportunity."

"How would I become like you?"

"I will change you."

"How?"

59

"It's difficult to explain. It will happen, that's all," she shrugged. "Please don't worry. You won't suffer or feel any pain, I promise."

"What would I have to do?"

"Nothing. If you agree, you will just become like me."

"And then what?"

"Anything you want. I can guide you across the galaxy; show you things you haven't even imagined yet."

I was silent for a long time. I had never expected this. And I wasn't totally sure I believed her.

"What's the catch?" I asked.

She smiled, her mood brighter. "No catch. Just you and I forever."

"There's always a catch."

"You think like a human," she teased.

"It comes with the territory."

"Only a slight change. Let's just say you'll become more aware, that's all."

"Of what?"

"Of everything. It's hard to explain, you'll have to experience it."

I was quiet for a while. "I'll have to think about it."

She shrugged and laid back down in my arms. "Of course."

The days and nights passed. The only change in our routine was Ava didn't spend every night with me. In fact, there were some days I didn't see her at all. In truth, that was okay; I needed time to think. Our formal sessions were over. She continued role playing her astro-psychologist guise, meeting with other crew members. I guess it was her way of still fitting in. Sometimes I wondered if she was sleeping with them too. Did she make any of them the same offer she made me? I can say that when we were together she was practically insatiable. Perhaps it was her way of giving me an incentive, a preview of what was in store if I said yes.

I knew I had to give her an answer. She had waited long enough. Although for a being that's pretty much immortal, the phrase "long enough" probably doesn't mean much.

A fluid pump became jammed and needed replacing. No big deal, a two-hour spacewalk was all that was needed. Just part of the regular maintenance the crew had to go through to keep the facility operating. It was my off-shift, so I volunteered.

No matter how routine the spacewalk, one step outside and you're confronted by the eternal vastness of the cosmos; how insignificant you are. It's sound psychological practice to be reminded you're not alone out there, even if it's just to replace a jammed fluid pump.

I trusted the control team with my life, which is what you always did when you took a spacewalk.

"How's it look out there?" Casey's voice rang in my ears.

"Gorgeous. I never get tired of the sight. Saturn's rings look particularly lovely today. Almost as lovely as you."

"Keep your mind on your work," Casey said. I heard the smile in her voice.

Dean's voice boomed in my ears. "Find the pump yet?"

"I should be coming up to it in a minute," I said.

I was on a long tether, attached to the hand grab at the airlock for safety. I gave a quick squeeze on the control nozzles on my suit and floated over to the panel covering the pump. Using a hand tool, I loosened the panel until one side swung free. The pump was right there. I unhooked the clamps holding it, pulled it out, and replaced it with the spare I'd brought. I hooked up the clamps again, closed the panel and began to tighten it.

"Pretty much finished," I said.

Dean's voice boomed in my helmet. "Ah, Aaron, we've got something here."

"Huh?" I said as I tightened the last fastener.

"I'm getting a reading. There's an energy wave . . . it's spiking like crazy . . . holy shit!"

"Aaron," Casey's voice broke in, "get back! Now!"

"What is it?" I asked, my hands moving to the maneuvering nozzles.

"Damn it, move!" she said. "There's a huge energy wave riding the solar wind coming right at us! Probably a solar flare, but I've never seen one like this! Get in here!"

I gave the nozzles full thrust and it shot me towards the airlock like a bullet. I got there and reached for the hand grab, but it was too late. In an instant, a blinding light enveloped me. I shut my eyes tight as I thought I heard Casey's scream. The solar wind pressed me against the outer door of the airlock. Blindly, I fumbled for the access panel. Something grabbed my left hand. There was a noise in my ears, like the sound of rushing waves getting louder. Beyond that I thought I could maybe hear the frantic cries of Dean and Casey calling me.

Everything faded.

I felt myself floating, no spacesuit, no tether. I opened my eyes. I was surrounded by stars. But I had never seen them quite this way before. They weren't just pinpoints in the night sky. They shimmered, hummed, vibrated, pulsed with energy on all different frequencies, each one a unique rhythm. The closest thing I can think of to describe it was music. But this went far beyond any music I'd ever heard. The notes, while all over the tonal range, seemed to blend together into a coherent pattern. I'm sure no one had ever heard or seen the stars or anything else like this before. It made for a symphony of sorts. A symphony of the cosmos.

But this went beyond hearing. I could actually *feel* the energy of the universe coursing through me. I felt so peaceful as I drifted, for how long I've no idea, completely empty of thought, just listening to the stars and feeling the pulse of the universe.

After a while, a voice interrupted my tranquility. It was feminine, soft and musical. I couldn't tell where it was coming from, but it was there.

"Hello, Aaron." It was Ava.

"Hello."

"How do you feel?"

"This is amazing. You were right, I hear and feel everything. So incredibly . . . idyllic."

She laughed. "I've never heard it described that way before."

"I feel very peaceful."

"I can tell. Anything else?"

I thought about it. "I'm happy, maybe for the first time in my life, really, truly happy."

"You remember what that's like? Feeling happy?"

"Yes."

"Even happier than when you were human? With Gabby?"

"Oh yes. I was happy with her, but this . . . is . . ."

"Is what?"

"I . . . don't know. I can't really describe it. Freeing, maybe? It's like . . . I'm not weary anymore." Something warm ran down my cheek. I caught it with the tip of my tongue. It was salty.

"You are free," she said, "free of everything you knew that confined you and held you back. I'm pleased you feel that way now, I really am."

"It was you on that solar flare, wasn't it? Or were you the flare?"

"Both. You remember it?"

"I remember everything," I said. "Is this it, is it over?"

"Yes."

"How come I can't see you?"

"Think of seeing me," she said, "and you will."

So I did. And she appeared, floating next to me. She looked the same, but seemed to radiate with an inner glow I hadn't seen before, burning bright.

"Is your sadness gone?" I asked.

"Yes, thanks to you," she said. "Listen."

I did. I heard a new note in the symphony of the stars.

"That's you, isn't it?"

"Yes, do you like it?"

"It's beautiful. Will I have a sound too?" I asked.

"Yes, I can hear it already. It's wonderful."

"I can't."

"You will," she reassured me.

"What about the station? Is it still there? Is everyone all right?"

"It's still there," she said. "And yes, everyone is fine."

And as I thought of the *Hestia*, it appeared in front of me. But I knew what was happening inside at that moment too. Casey and Dean were frantic, sounding the emergency siren and calling for help. They were going to launch a search and rescue, using some of the minipods attached to the station. They were trying to reach me. I could hear them, but I didn't respond. I just watched.

"You like them, don't you?" Ava asked.

"I like almost everyone on the station. Those two are some of the best."

"You can see them whenever you want," she told me. "Or you could go elsewhere."

"Such as?"

"Anywhere you'd like." I felt her hand grasping mine. "I'll take you."

But I wasn't ready for that, not yet. So we stayed at the station and she seemed okay with that. I guess I just felt most comfortable with the familiar. She told me that in time—whatever that phrase meant now—I would cast off what I had known and embrace my new abilities. Maybe she was right, but for now I still wanted to be part of my former life, even down to taking my regular shift.

"It's time to get up," she said. "You don't want to be late."

"Will you come too?"

"Of course," she said. "I promised you I'd be there."

With effort, I got out of bed. Ava was already dressed in her crew jumpsuit, straightening her hair and examining herself in the mirror. She had a subtle glow, an inner radiance making the small room dull in comparison.

"You look great," I told her.

"Thanks, so do you."

Leaving my quarters, we held hands and started walking to the other side of the station. We walked silently and if I didn't know any better, I would have said we were the only ones on board being it was so quiet. But everyone else was already at the assembly.

We stood in the back and no one seemed to notice us. The head of the station, Dr. Williams, stood in front, cleared his throat and looked around.

"Thank you all for coming, I know this is difficult. We are here to remember a valued colleague and friend. As you know, Aaron was taken from us under mysterious circumstances, which aren't yet fully explained. The investigation continues. But we're not here to dwell on that, but rather to commemorate a life lived. His scientific contributions were important, but more important were the lives he touched."

There was some muffled sobs and Ava leaned her head towards me.

"They miss you," she whispered.

"Yeah, who would have thought?"

I looked into her eyes. They were gleaming.

Williams went on to say a few more platitudes and then a couple of other people spoke. It was touching. I got along with everyone, but I can't say I was ever really close with anyone. I know that sounds strange coming from someone who worked with mostly the same people for years in a confined space, but it was true. I saw now, in my loneliness, I never really let anyone in.

I turned my head back as a female voice spoke.

"I always admired Aaron, but more than that, I liked him."

I liked you too, Casey.

"He was a good guy," Casey was saying. "Always willing to help. And he was one hell of a scientist. Dr. Williams spoke of his scientific contributions, which I know you're all aware of. But what you don't know, was the size of his heart. He probably struck most of us as a bit aloof, but this," she held up a file chip, "reveals much more about the person he really was."

As she inserted it into a console, I turned to Ava.

"Did you leave that for her to find?"

"I wanted them to have one last memory of you," she said. "I hoped you wouldn't mind."

I turned back just as the large viewscreen overhead flared and my face came into view, ten feet high.

Aaron Kramer personal journal, day twenty one ninety five. Five days ago was my six year anniversary on Hestia. I didn't tell anyone, didn't want a fuss, I guess. Still, some of my colleagues surprised me with a cake at dinner. I felt silly, but they were all so genuine about it I decided to join in the fun. And you know what? It was fun. These are the best people I've ever met. I left Earth for my own reasons, but I never expected to bond with these people. I don't think I ever want to go back. I want to stay here, with these people, doing what I do, helping them do what they do. And if nothing else ever comes of it, at least I can say I was here.

The picture winked out and all eyes returned to Casey. She was crying.

"Aaron, wherever you are, I want you to know, you'll always be remembered," she said.

There was a moment of silence as people lowered their heads, and then the assembly broke up and people started to drift away.

"That was nice, don't you think?" Ava asked.

"Yes, very nice," I replied, as I turned towards her. "Except I never said any of that. That was you up there, wasn't it? Where's my real journal?"

"Exactly where you left it," she said.

"Untouched?"

She nodded. "Are you mad at me?"

"I'm not sure. I feel like my privacy's been invaded. I guess it's silly to hold on to human emotion at this point, isn't it?"

"No," she said, "it's instinct, it's what you know. Don't be ashamed of it."

"I'm not."

I was still looking at Casey. She was at the front of the assembly, talking to people. I decided to go say hello. Or maybe goodbye. I left Ava's side, made my way to the front of the room and walked up to her. Her eyes were still wet as she thanked people for coming and they thanked her for her words. I reached for her hand but she turned away just as I was about to grasp it. I thought I brushed it, but I couldn't be sure.

"She doesn't know you're here," Ava said, standing next to me again.

"I think she does."

"It's weird," Casey was saying to a few members of the crew. "It was almost as if I could feel Aaron's presence among us."

"Not very scientific of you, Doctor," someone responded and they all laughed.

"No," Casey said smiling, "but I'd like to believe it anyway."

"I am here," I said aloud. No one reacted.

"Aaron," Ava said quietly, touching my arm.

"So this is the way it is now?" I asked.

Ava nodded. "Yes."

"I knew there had to be a price to pay."

Ava just looked at me, her face not revealing anything.

"You made it seem so easy, so natural. Like going through an airlock. I'd come out and nothing would change. Except everything has changed. I'm more aware, but they're not. I try to reach them, but they don't hear me. They don't know I'm here."

"No," Ava said. "You're beyond their understanding now."

"But I can be anything I want, that's what you said, that's what you do," I said.

"Yes, but my origins are star-born. You originated as something else. Once that form of life has been altered, it's changed forever."

"How come they saw you? Interacted with you like just another member of the crew?" I asked.

"Because I allowed them to. It was necessary to find you, study you. It took extra effort, but it was worth it."

"And I can't do that?" I asked.

"No. "

"So I can never be human again?"

"You can take human form whenever you like," Ava explained. "You can live among them, see them, hear them, do the things they do, but you can never live as human again."

I let that sink in for a moment.

"You should have told me about this," I said a bit harshly.

"Would it have made a difference?"

And that was the great question. In truth, I don't know, probably not. But I wasn't ready to share that with her. Maybe she knew it anyway. Maybe that's why she chose me to begin with.

"I don't know. But I never agreed to this." I spun around, and acting very human, quickly strode out, double-timing it back to my quarters. I didn't know if Ava was following me or not, and frankly, I didn't care. No one noticed me, of course, as I made my way through the station, and even if they had, I wouldn't have noticed them. My only goal was to reach my quarters. Arriving, I smacked the wall panel. Oddly, the computer still recognized my handprint and the door slid open. Of course, Ava was standing there.

"Aaron—"

"Stop. Don't say a word."

She stepped back and I went in, the door closing behind me. I went straight to my computer console and opened the directory.

"It's not here," I said, scanning the files. "Where is it?"

"Where's what?"

I spun around, took one stride and grabbed her by the shoulders.

"Don't play games with me! Where's my journal, the one you said was untouched?"

"Aaron, please, you're hurting me."

"Since when can a star-born creature feel pain?"

"When I take a flesh and blood form, I feel what it feels," she answered. "Pain and pleasure. You know that. Please . . ."

I released her and walked away, sitting down on the bed. "I never agreed to this. You changed me before I said yes."

"There wasn't a choice," she said.

"Of course there was. And it was mine to make," I said bitterly. "Not yours."

"No," she said. "Aaron, I sent my report on you back to Earth. They wanted you to return."

"What?"

"I had to give them my professional opinion."

"As Doctor Ava Green, astro-psychologist."

She nodded. "They read the report and determined it was time to bring you home."

"*This* is my home."

"Not to them," she said. "You were to be on the next transport. They thought you had been away long enough, they were going to try and reintegrate you. I knew you would never allow that and I couldn't bear to think of what might happen to you if they failed. I just couldn't let that happen, not after everything I went through to find you."

"You could have changed me on Earth if you were that worried about me," I said.

"It would have been much more difficult."

She came over and sat down next to me, stroking my head, massaging the back of my neck. My anger dissipated.

"I don't want you to be angry with me," she said softly.

"And I don't want to hurt you," I said, not looking at her.

"I know how happy you were with Gabby. But she's dead, Aaron, and going back to Earth would just remind you of her. This way is better. You've got a second chance. And we're going to be together. Forever," she said. "I'll give you whatever you want."

"I want . . . my personal journal."

She pressed something into my hand. "Here."

I opened my hand. It was a file chip.

"Why did you take it?"

"I didn't think you'd need it anymore," she said.

"Well, you were wrong." I let out a deep breath. "I need to be alone right now," I said, staring at it.

Without a word, she got up and left. The door closed behind her and I looked up. I walked around my room, looking at everything making up my home for the past six years, all my 'worldly' possessions. There wasn't much and it didn't take all that long. Unconsciously, my hand rested on a small box I had brought with me. Picking it up, I opened it and stared at Gabby's wedding ring, the only thing she had with her that day that I was able to recover. In my mind's eye I saw her vividly, catching her by surprise, the playful look of love emanating from her eyes burning into my consciousness. No wonder I had kept the box closed for all these years.

Looking out the small window on the far wall, Saturn still turned, her rings glistening in the distant sunlight. It seemed silly to be standing here staring at it when with just a thought, I could be there, floating among the millions of pieces of rock, ice and dust making up the rings. But I still wasn't ready.

Despite Ava's intentions, if there was one thing I was going to leave my old life with, it would have to be more than just a good memory. I had to leave the truth behind. I had to tell my story.

I sat down at the console and inserted the file chip. In the moment it took to load I thought about what I wanted to say. When I was ready, I hit 'record'.

"Hi, it's Aaron. I know you're missing me but I don't want you to worry, I'm okay. I'm going to tell you an amazing story, and I swear it's all true. It started when I met Doctor Ava Green, the astro-psychologist. Except that's not really who, or what, she is."

The rest came tumbling out; everything that had happened. How my life, my very existence, changed, and how I felt about it. I knew now I'd be leaving the station. When I finished, I replayed the recording, making sure I hadn't missed anything. As the last words faded away, I felt strangely complete; like it was the last thing crossed off a long to-do list I had hung onto for too long. I could now start fresh. I ejected the file chip with the recording and looked at it for a moment. I knew where I'd leave it so it would be found, and looked around one last time to say goodbye.

With a thought, I stood next to the bed where Casey was sleeping. She stirred and turned over on her back. I crossed to her desk and inserted the file chip. The next time she went to her console, it would play automatically. After her nice words about me at the ceremony I figured she should be the first one to know. Besides, we had been friends. I looked around one more time. Finally, I crossed over to Casey's bed and bent down to stroke her soft hair with my hand. Whether or not she felt it, I'll never know. She didn't move.

"Thanks, Casey."

I stood up, took a deep breath, closed my eyes and thought one last thought.

"Are you ready?" Ava asked, as I floated among the stars again.

"Yes."

Her hand pressed into mine and I felt her soft lips on mine.

"Then I'll take you on the journey of a lifetime."

And with that we said goodbye and left to roam among the stars.

Unquiet Mind

Jessica A. Walsh

If I tell you I can't sleep, it sounds as if I have something keeping me awake at night. If I tell you I don't sleep, you may think I suffer from insomnia. The truth is that I can't sleep. I *don't* sleep. I have never slept.

Fourteen years ago to the day was the last time I saw my mother, I wish I could turn off, as she used to put it. Not for the first time, I wish I could stop thinking, shut down, and sleep. I hate this day and I'm only three hours into it.

The man I went home with is sound asleep, face down in bed. I struggle to remember his name. It doesn't matter. Nearly two years ago, I had my first drink and enjoyed the effects very much. I decided to test the limits and see if I could pass out like I had seen so many people do. I learned only that I could black out. I'd be awake, but when I sobered up, I had no recollection whatsoever of what I had done, who I'd done it with, or how I had gotten to where I was. I found the experience exhilarating. It was the closest I could come to sleep and I welcomed it immensely. And so began a long stint of absolutely reckless behavior.

Behavior that has since only been curbed by sheer boredom and depression. Most of the time I find it more appealing to spend my long, lonely nights with a book cuddling my furry four-legged companion, Quinn.

Some nights however, like this night, my need for physical touch is unbearable. However short lived, I bask in feeling wanted, needed, having someone close to me, having their undivided attention. I soak it up like a sponge absorbing rain after being left in the sun.

After a while, I dress quietly so as not to disturb the handsome stranger I am walking out on. I close the door softly and let myself

71

out into the cold night air. The temperature feels exactly the same as it did the night I left my mother. It is impossible not to think of her. And Ray.

My mother was a recluse, paranoid and overprotective. I hated her for it. It was too late for she and I by the time I learned she was only like that because of me. She loved me. One of the memories I keep in the most protected part of my soul is from when I was very small, when she would sit me in her lap and hold me against her chest and rock slowly back and forth, humming. The hum made my cheek buzz, and it calmed me. In those moments she was perfect and strong and not afraid, and it was just the two of us and she loved me and I loved her.

But the rest of the time, she was afraid. Her fear imprisoned me, and I was too young and too curious to be held captive.

I watched her sleep, eyes closed, and counted her breaths. I experimented on what it took to "wake" her as she called it. I'd cough ever so quietly, then louder, and louder still until she jolted awake.

"Are you sick?"

"No. I just had something in my throat," I lied.

"I told you. No eating while I'm sleeping. It's not safe for a child to eat unsupervised."

"Why can't I sleep?"

"Well," she hesitated, "because you're different."

"Different how?"

"Different because you don't sleep like I do."

She taught me to read and write, but there were no books in our house. I learned only what Momma knew, and as I grew older I learned fear and mistrust and suspicion. She told me stories of her own invention, stories about children who were different. "Like you," she would say, sadly. I was never special, just different.

"Momma, what is A-S-S-A-L-T-E-D?" I asked one day, coming upon a new word in one of her stories.

"Assaulted. It means to hurt someone. It's what happens to children who are different."

For years her misspelling made me think that I was kept inside so that no one would strip me naked and rub my skin raw with salt. The image made me shiver. I was glad to be safe with her in our little apartment; I wasn't so lonely, and she wasn't scared. We had a content routine, like old friends, and we enjoyed one another. We quietly sang silly songs, Momma teasing about my off-key singing. I'd giggle and intentionally sing even worse and she'd teasingly put her hands over her ears.

But as I got older the rooms grew smaller, the air staler, Momma's presence suffocating. Her friend, Ray was the only thing that brought change and excitement. His stories were more fun than Momma's, and he told silly jokes. He brought me treats, like paper and coloring books, and always wanted to see what I drew. He also brought groceries for us; I didn't realize at the time that he was our lifeline, keeping us alive and protected.

One time while she was sleeping, I pulled a chair up to the counter to reach into the highest cabinet. The chair tipped, and the loud bang woke her up. She found me crying on the floor holding my wrist, the purple book I had retrieved lying open a few feet away. I could tell that she was scared more than angry.

She made me bend and twist my wrist. It hurt, but I could do it. "It's only a sprain," she said. "It'll be okay. Ray can look at it when he comes. And as for this," she reached for the book, "it's mine."

"What are those?"

"Photos," she answered.

"That's you," I said, pointing at one of them.

"Yes. With my older sister."

"Sister? Where is she?"

"She's gone, Reven. No more questions." And with that she collected the album that I would never find again despite my best efforts. "You'll need to rest that wrist for a few days," she said as she went back into her room.

Rest. It seemed unfair that I had the power to rest parts of my body, but not my mind.

After I fell off the chair, the rule was that I had to "rest" while she slept, which meant I had to lie still and not do or touch anything until she woke up.

Although I tried, I found resting impossible. I lay awake daydreaming about the world beyond our apartment and dared myself to sneak outside. *No. Lie still.* I concentrated on locking my limbs but sparks singed my muscles. Anger and frustration ignited a fire in my chest that raged up into my head, creating a searing heat of adrenaline that left my body through my fists and legs, kicking the couch, pounding the pillow, my body contorting out of my control as the fury escaped, guttural screaming scraping my throat, the salty taste of the damp pillow case. But my limbs eventually gave up, and I would lie with clenched muscles and fists, controlling the rage so I could be still.

My mind, though, never stopped.

I wanted to scream in her face, but I was afraid – not of her – but of the Officials. Momma told me that children weren't allowed in the building and if anyone heard a child's voice they would report us. "You don't want the Officials to take you away, do you?"

So instead of screaming, I played tricks while she slept. I blew on her, poked her, dripped droplets of water on her, just to see what it would take to wake her. But mostly to pass the time. She usually woke up angry. One time she was *really* angry.

"Damnit, Reven! Why do you do this? Can't you just let me sleep?"

"I'm bored. I wanna sleep. What is it like?"

"It's like . . ." she was thinking. I waited patiently. "Turning off for a while, I guess. But you're different, so you need to learn to lie quietly."

"Why can't I sleep?"

"Because your grandfather is a bigoted bastard, that's why!" she shouted.

I jumped. This was the first time she hadn't said, 'I don't know.'

She reached for me then, drawing me close. "I'm sorry."

I allowed her to envelop me and I melted into her chest. Despite my anger and confusion, I always felt safe and calm in her arms.

"Why can't I go outside?" I whispered into her ear as she stroked my hair.

"Because it's not safe."

"Why isn't it safe?"

Her arms tensed around my back, and she pushed me backward. Shocked, I remember staring up at her through oncoming tears. "Because people are evil and can't be trusted, damnit! Now leave me alone!" She stormed into the bathroom and slammed the door.

My four-year-old mind figured this "grandfather" person was the evil villain going around 'assalting' them, rubbing their skin raw with salt.

I was only half wrong.

Back in my apartment, I pour myself a generous helping of scotch. It's now four in the morning. I don't know if that makes it too late or too early to drink. Out on the fire escape, my breath hangs in the cool air as I look up at the stars, then down at the city streets below; the same streets I walked for the very first time fourteen years ago tonight.

I cannot prevent my eyes from searching the manicured grid of concrete, bordered by tree-lined curbs below for our old apartment building. I will myself to remember some detail – a building name, a street name, something. But there was never a reason to teach me our address. I'd never need to find my way back if I never left.

My glass empty, I climb through the window into the warmth of my apartment. I close the window, catching my reflection in the glass. For a split second, I see my younger self in the reflection behind me, running toward the window, fists raised.

I look down and form fists with my own hands, examining the raised scars.

Thankfully, only a few more hours to kill before work.

I practiced resting as best as I could and longed for the day when I would grow out of not sleeping and finally be able to go outside. When I was about eight years old, I climbed out onto the fire escape. That was the first time my mother ever slapped me.

Ray visited later that day. I overheard Momma venting to him, saying how bad I was becoming; that she didn't know what to do with me.

"Come on, Nina," he said laughing. "What do you expect?"

"This is not funny. Someone could have seen her."

"No one knows who she is."

"Fine, but look at her, Nina. She's restless." Then lowering his voice to a whisper said, "Let me take her out for an hour. For ice cream? I saw the schedule - no one's out today."

I twitched with excitement. Sitting in time-out in the kitchen, I willed her to say yes.

"No. Out of the question." My heart deflated. "You start that now and it'll never stop."

Ray sighed. He came into the kitchen and kissed my cheek, whispering, "Sorry, kiddo. I tried."

I was crushed, but I was already in trouble, so I didn't push it. After he left, I asked Momma who Ray was.

"A friend," she answered.

"Why does he come here?"

"Because he is a friend of ours and that's what friends do."

"When did you become friends?"

"That's enough now, Reven." And that was that. It didn't make sense but I knew better than to question her.

I began looking forward to Ray's visits more than anything. I kept track of his visits in my diary, the one he left under my mattress when Momma wasn't looking.

One time, fourteen days went by without a visit from Ray. He had never stayed away that long before. My heart skipped in anticipation at every footstep in the hall, followed by crushing disappointment when no knock followed. We had run out of food, but a different hunger grew in my belly as I waited. It burned as images of Ray whirled in my head, one moment lying in a street bleeding, the next him saying to a faceless stranger that we were no longer worth the trouble.

Fear ignited the fire that rose to my head. We needed Ray, he was our lifeline. I needed to find him somehow and tell him that we relied on him. I ran to the window and threw it open. I had one leg over the sill when Momma grabbed me, pulling me back inside.

"Let me go!" I screamed, flailing around in her arms, the fire of fear controlling my limbs.

She begged me to stop, to calm down. "Reven! Someone might hear you and call the Officials!" I screamed louder, drowning out her urgent pleading, and flailed my limbs harder, not caring if I was hurting her. I *wanted* to hurt her. She pushed me away, hard, and slammed the window closed.

The heat took over my whole body sucking the air out of the room; out of the whole world. I was suffocating.

My mother reached for me, blurry beyond the fire of rage, beyond my control. I slapped her, my hand acting on its own, making contact with her soft cheek, twisting her neck. The sound snuffed the flames to dull gray smoke, leaving me gasping in the aftermath of my fire's destruction.

I can still see her stunned face as she gasped and dropped to her knees, gazing as if she had never seen me before.

I can also still hear her words, permanently engraved on my memory.

"What happened to my sweet girl?" she sobbed.

I hated her. Where was Ray? I didn't care if the Officials came. I hated her so much. She had been threatening that my entire life and they had never come. The heat sparked again; I needed air. I needed to find Ray. I needed to be away from her.

I charged the window and slammed my fists into the glass, putting all my effort into destroying the very thing that confined me. Momma did not try to stop me. I pounded until the glass cracked, then rammed my fists through the cracks until I could no longer lift my arms and I collapsed.

Momma scooped me into her arms, pressing me against her and she sat back against the wall.

She held my head against her chest and gently rocked side to side. "Shhh. Shhh. Everything will be all right. Momma's here."

And everything did feel all right.

That moment, right before my life changed forever, is how I try to remember her. Her comforting touch, the smell of her hair, clean and familiar. But regret disturbs that peace, crowding out comfort and softness, jagged like broken glass. I will never be her sweet girl again.

But I would still give anything if she could just hold me and tell me everything would be all right.

Five am. "Want to go si-si?" I ask Quinn, who looks up happily and wags her tail. She raises all thirty-five pounds of her mass onto her black hind legs and plants her white front legs on my stomach. I laugh as she dances excitedly and grab my jacket. I don't have to hide from people anymore, only guilt and anger, and I'm just as restless now on my own as I was stuck in that tiny apartment.

A knock on the door interrupted our calm. Momma's face turned to panic, and cut off my breath. I clung to her. They had heard me and we were going to be separated, just as she always feared.

An urgent whisper from outside. "It's Ray. Quick, let me in."

I broke Momma's hold and threw open the door despite her urgent plea to wait, that it may be a trick. Ray stepped in, pushing me out of the way to shut and lock the door in an instant.

He reeled toward us. "What in the hell is going on in here!?" he whispered angrily. "Reven, I heard you screaming all the way in the stairwell." He saw the broken glass, the blood on my hands, my mother's shirt streaked with red. "What the hell happened?"

"This is YOUR fault, Ray!" my mother returned.

"My fault? How is this my fault?"

"You're the reason she's upset!"

No Momma, please don't say that. Don't make him go away. He's all we have. "No it's not!" I screamed and was greeted with an urgent "SSSSHHHHHHH!" from both of them.

"Calm down a minute and take a deep breath," Ray said rubbing his face and inhaled deeply, slowly releasing it. "Now. Reven. What's wrong?"

My mother began to answer for me. Ray raised a finger in her direction. "Nina, stop. Let her talk." He turned to me. "Reven?"

"I . . . I . . ." I stammered between hiccups and sniffles. "I got scared, I guess."

"Scared of what?" Ray asked.

"Scared that you weren't coming."

"See, Ray! I told you it was your fault."

"Do you have any idea how hard it is to keep coming here without letting anyone on to me?" His voice rose above a whisper. "You were granted clemency here. I'm not supposed to have anything to do with you! You can't have it both ways, Nina!"

This is the first I heard of any of this so I stayed quiet, hoping they'd continue, seemingly having forgotten I was in the room.

"Haven't I proven myself after all these years? Let me get her out of this goddamned apartment!"

"Proven yourself!? Look what happened today! We're lucky no one has busted the door down by now."

"You've established your reputation as a recluse, as you were supposed to. But don't make Reven one too! I swear on my life I won't let anything happen to her!"

Momma looked as though she'd been injured. "We have been just fine all of these years!"

"Because of me! You would have both starved to death by now if it weren't for me!"

"GET OUT! GET OUT!" all whispers forgotten, Momma started screaming at Ray.

"For Christ's sake, lower your voice!" he pleaded.

"I will not let you "protect" my daughter the way you supposedly protected Anna. I said GET OUT, DAMNIT!"

Ray was stunned. I had never seen him look so angry. For a moment I thought he might hit her.

"I said get the hell out, Ray."

Ray glanced at me sadly, then turned and left, slamming the door behind him.

Momma collapsed into a chair and began crying. The fire inside me blazed again. "I HATE YOU!" I screamed, right into her face, the way I had wanted to scream at her for years. Then I ran out the door and down the hall as fast as I could, shouting for Ray.

At the end of the hall was a door and I burst through. I ran smack into Ray who lifted me up in a flash and hurried down the stairwell whispering, "sshhh sshhh, everything is okay now."

I held onto him tightly and buried my face in his shoulder as he carried me out into the cold night and away from the only place I had ever known.

That was the last time I ever saw my mother. 'I hate you' were the last words I ever said to her. I carry the weight of that with me every moment of my life. My heart aches with wonder as to why she didn't chase after me. I have to believe that her fear of the outside world was greater than her love for me. There is only one person in this entire godforsaken world that is supposed to love and fight for you unconditionally. Without that love, is it any wonder I am lost.

Ray carried me a long time that night, but eventually he stopped in a park and set me down in front of him.

"Where is everyone?" I had imagined the outside world milling with people.

"They're home," he said kneeling in front of me. "Sleeping," he added quizzically.

"Momma sleeps," I offered. "Do you sleep?"

"Yep. Do you?"

"No."

Ray took my face in his hands, placing one firmly against each cheek the way he always had.

"Reven," he said, "It's very important that you trust me. You can tell me anything. But you need to understand that your Momma was right about some things. One thing in particular is that not everyone can be trusted. Do you understand?"

I nodded yes, cheeks squished against Ray's firm hands.

"You have to understand that you're different. Do you know how you're different?"

Thinking hard I tried to give Ray the right answer.

"Because I don't sleep like Momma?" I guessed, recalling her words.

"Because you are the only living person in the entire world that does not sleep. Ever. And you can never tell anyone, okay?"

"Okay."

He studied me, trying to determine if I understood.

"Okay, then." Ray sighed, forced a smile through pursed lips. But his eyes softened, and he lowered his hands to mine, standing up.

"Hungry?"

"Yes." Hand in hand Ray led me out of the park, and to his apartment.

After he bandaged my hands, Ray told me I would be going to school soon, and I'd make friends. I was excited; I'd never had a friend. "But what will happen to Momma?" I asked, as he tucked me into a bed I would never sleep in.

"She's been afraid for you, Reven," he said. "She lived in fear. Now that you're here with me, she doesn't have to be afraid anymore."

Momma was glad I wasn't there anymore. She had been afraid because of me. That made me sad. I asked Ray why she was afraid and he reminded me that I'm different.

"So?" I choked through the tears rising in my throat.

"So, some people feel threatened by that. People fear what they don't understand, Reven. And when people fear something, they want to observe it, study it . . . control it." That hung in the air for a moment. "I know that you don't understand this right now so you have to trust me. Do you trust me?"

Walking Quinn this early I see a lot of blue collar men heading to work. They remind me of Ray. I miss him and yes, I did trust him; at age nine he was my symbol of freedom. But I didn't understand then. I didn't understand I would carry this secret for the rest of my life; that my choices and things that had happened before I was born would dictate my future. And that I would never see my mother again.

Laying in the darkness of Ray's spare bedroom, my mind raced. Up until now I had only been afraid of Momma's fears. But without her, thinking for myself and preparing for new experiences, the unfamiliar and the unknown scared me more. Ray's voice echoed in my ears: *the only one . . . she's afraid for you . . . never tell anyone.* The pillowcase was hot and damp from my tears. I tossed off the covers, the fire in my chest spreading, making me sweat. *Where is she? How do I get back to her?*

Then I saw Momma leaving her apartment, smiling, relieved that I was gone. The fiery anger that I so often radiated outward turned inward and seared my insides. I wailed like a kit separated from its mother. I grabbed my head and shook it, to put out the flames, to shake out the image of my mother, happy, until stars flashed in the darkness, fists clenched, the cuts on my hands reopening under the cotton bandages, gasping for breath through clenched teeth.

Strong arms hauled me up, and Ray threw me over his shoulder. I screamed and kicked as he carried me into the bathroom, my flailing limbs knocking pictures from the walls.

He dropped me into the tub and turned cold water on, making me gasp for breath. My eyes focused on Ray seated on the rim of the tub with pursed lips, drawn eyebrows and furrowed forehead; elbows on his knees, hands intertwined. Neither of us spoke as I sat there under the cold shower, staring at him defiantly through slit eyes.

After a while, he switched off the water. Wordlessly, he wrapped me in a towel and gave me fresh clothes – girl clothes in my exact size.

When I emerged, mostly dry, he was sitting at the kitchen table, chin resting in his hand. I sat across from him. He stared for a long while.

He didn't seem angry, but I thought for sure I was in trouble. I hoped he realized I was too much trouble, and would be better off home with Momma.

Finally, he asked how I felt. I offered no response, being overwhelmed by the sheer number of possible replies.

"You must feel tired."

I knew the word, but didn't know if I felt it.

Ray continued, "Tired is when someone feels . . . depleted, I guess you can say."

"Depleted?"

"Yeah, like you have no more to give at the moment." He waited while that sunk in.

"Maybe . . . I guess," I began nervously.

His patience and concern put me at ease and I felt safe to continue. "My mind is tired, I think. I don't think it wants to think anymore."

He nodded. "That's called being mentally tired. When people feel tired they go to sleep, but you can't do that so we need to figure out what to do with you when you're tired. You had a very emotional day. Reven, you can't freak out like that. And you are never, NEVER, to hurt yourself again," he said looking down at my bandaged hands. "Do you understand me?"

"Yes," I replied softly, my gaze toward the table.

"Good. You have to understand that you cannot go to Hospital."

"Why not?"

"Well," he hesitated, ". . . it's too expensive."

The next morning, I helped Ray make breakfast, and he explained a little about Branch Columnar, which is where he—we—lived. Branch Columnar was a community that had seceded from Banyan, where I was born and lived with Momma. I was part of the Opposition now, and once I started school I'd be taught how to detect, deceive and destroy Officials.

"If you don't live in Branch Columnar, you are an Official. What does the Opposition do?" Ray quizzed me as he helped me get ready for my first day of school.

"Destroy the Officials, reunite Banyan." I answered, as he had taught.

"If you are not from Branch Columnar, you are not with us. And if you are not with us . . . ?"

"You are against us."

Ray must have been preparing for my arrival for a long while because the spare room wasn't spare at all, but decorated in purples and grays and fully stocked with an entire wardrobe that would take me years to grow into. And he let me wear whatever I wanted, after he helped me find the right size.

My school comprised the lower three floors of a very tall building where Ray worked. I was nervous to meet other people my age, but everyone was nice and welcoming, as if I belonged there and wasn't an outsider at all. It wasn't long before I had a lot of playmates and we invented wild adventures, mostly about us vanquishing Officials. It was more fun than I had ever dreamed in Momma's dreary apartment, with her depressing stories. I loved being with people my age.

With the distractions of friends, books, and schoolwork, it was easy to not think about Momma. I convinced myself that she had moved on without me, so why shouldn't I do the same? But sometimes my certainty wavered, and she was all I could think about.

Sometimes while Ray and the rest of the world slept, I imagined her in our apartment worrying about me, and I wondered if at that very moment she knew I was worrying about her too. I wanted to go to her, but knew that I couldn't. The angry heat sparked again, and I quivered and sobbed, my fists clenching, feet kicking out of my control.

Then the light was on and Ray was there holding my hand, whispering, "Shhh shhh, I'm so sorry, Reven. It wasn't supposed to happen this way."

And I, with my depleted mind, tired of thinking, limbs aching with emotion, never knew how it was supposed to happen.

It was especially impossible not to think of her on the days I saw the creepy janitor. He was an older man with gray hair; easy enough not to notice, except I would catch him watching me. When I did, he'd smile at me, but he was strange so I'd look away and do my best to ignore him.

But sometimes he'd appear out of nowhere and startle me. "Hey, you seem a little jumpy there. Not get enough sleep?" When I ignored him he'd ask, "Did you wake up on the wrong side of the bed this morning or what?" His knowing laugh was familiar. It reminded me of my mother's.

After I caught up with the other kids as far as reading and writing, my lessons changed. I began learning politics, spy tactics: cheating lie detectors, staying calm under pressure, and combat training. I excelled in all of my lessons. After all, I had double the amount of time to study.

As I entered secondary school, I learned to keep my mind occupied all hours of the day to avoid thinking about the things that hurt so much. I read, wrote, studied, worked, cooked. And I excelled at everything, even learning to keep panic at bay.

But it was all a cleverly rehearsed façade. The fact that I alone was incapable of sleep—*different*—stopped being something that was simply a part of me, like a limb. It became a heavy cloak, forever concealing the real me, weighing me down. Over time, I realized this "difference" was the reason for my misery, for my mother's misery. It had separated us, but I couldn't figure out why I couldn't sleep. It gnawed at the edge of my mind constantly, like the low heat of anger that smoldered in my chest.

But there was no one to ask except Ray, and it was clear he preferred to believe I was well adjusted and accepted my new life.

"You seem to be using the extra time to your advantage. Try to think of it as a positive thing; an advantage," he'd say. I began to resent him for his positivity and lack of understanding, and seethed in my solitude.

One night when I was sixteen, I tried explaining this, as well as my more frequent panic attacks to Ray.

"Oh," he said, looking up. "I didn't realize you were still having those."

How would you. You ignore me. "Yes, I still have them," I answered. "I can control them better, but I have one almost every night. While you're *asleep*," I emphasized.

"I'm sorry I didn't notice," he said putting down his fork. "It sounds to me like your panic attacks are like nightmares. Because your mind does not sleep, your brain cannot defragment and process. They most likely can't be helped. All you can do is continue to practice self-soothing."

"Do you ever have nightmares?" I asked.

"I think we both know the answer to that," he said as he pushed out his chair and rose, taking his plate to the sink, ending my questions.

But he was right. I did know, and the answer was yes, he did have nightmares. I had witnessed them myself standing in the doorway to his room, struggling with whether to wake him or to continue to listen to the words he muttered. I knew I was invading his privacy, but I chose to listen.

Anna.

Anna.

I can hear the phone ringing inside my apartment as Quinn and I return from our walk and I rush inside to answer it. To this day, there is still that fleeting moment of hope when my phone rings . . . maybe, just maybe . . . followed by familiar disappointment.

"Hello?" It's still early, so I feign drowsiness.

"Morning, Reven. Did I wake you?" I recognize my superintendent's voice.

"It's okay. What time is it?"

"Nearly six. Listen, a defector wandered into Banyan City Hospital a few hours ago. We're gonna need you to get down here as soon as possible. How long do you need?"

Although I'm fully dressed and ready to go, I tell him I need coffee and a shower and will leave within the hour, a satisfactory response.

That's my job – Defector Assessor. I am the best there is, and it was a condition of my asylum and clemency to do it.

By superior year, I questioned so much and got so little satisfaction in the answers that I spent most of my time alone. Former friends didn't appreciate my disdain for their blind obedience to authority. I said what I was supposed to say and did what I was told, but I withdrew into myself more and more, fearing that I wouldn't be able to maintain the crumbling façade that once was so strong.

I continued to excel in school, but I didn't say much and took interest in very little. This apathy seemed to trouble Ray, but he didn't say much or push me to talk about it. I had remembered my most important lesson: trust no one with your secrets. After all, Ray didn't even trust me with his, so why should I trust him with mine?

At school my teachers kept asking me what my plans were for after graduation. I hadn't really thought about it, but I figured it was time to get a job and move out of Ray's place. The question irritated me and coming up with an adequate answer distracted me.

"Hey, Reven!" I jumped. It was the old janitor. Over the years he and his hair had grown thin. Once gray, it was now white.

"Ya know, I'm gonna miss seeing you around these halls."

"Yeah?" I responded. "Why's that?"

"Because you remind me of my granddaughter, Anna. You look just like her."

I stared at him, stunned. He gave me the familiar smug smile.

"Shut your mouth, old man," was all I could muster.

"Ya know, Reven, it's too bad you never got to meet Anna. You two would have lots to talk about, being that you both have soooo much in common," he said, laughing.

I turned on my heels and marched down the hall.

"I know your secret!" he called after me. And I broke into a run, slamming through the double doors and across the barren lot to home, my mind outrunning my feet.

I opened the door and slammed it behind me. Ray walked into the living room, dish towel in hand. His smile faded when he saw my face. He began to speak, but I blurted, "Are you my Dad?"

He looked at me, shocked.

Furious, impatient and hopeful, I repeated, "Are you my Dad?"

He looked down to his hands and took his time drying them before replying. "No."

"No?" I asked, in disbelief.

"I said no, Reven. I'm not your dad."

For a few moments, it had all made sense; perhaps I was where I was supposed to be. For five minutes I was filled with hope like helium in a balloon, And with one syllable, I was deflated.

I began to cry. I turned to leave but Ray wrapped his arms around me. I let him hold me. I sobbed into his chest, grabbing fistfuls of his shirt. My legs failed under the weight of disappointment and we lowered to the floor in a heap, Ray's arms around me. We sat there like that for a long while until my sobs ceased and my tears ran out and I became so exhausted that I actually closed my eyes.

"I was Anna's Dad," he whispered once I had grown still.

"I know," I returned through parched lips.

"Of course you do," he sighed.

"What happened to her?"

"She died shortly before you were born."

"How?"

Ray exhaled, a long breath. I waited.

"You know the bridge on the outskirts that leads to Banyan? The one over the river?"

"Yes."

"She jumped off of it."

I pulled away, dumbfounded.

"Your mother's father was once the Commander of Branch Columnar. He was a scientist and had very . . ." he paused, "extreme, I guess you could say, ideas as to how we could become superior to the Officials."

"I met your father today."

"My father?"

"Yes, the old janitor at school. He said that Anna was his granddaughter; that we have so much in common and that he knows my secret."

Ray shook his head. "My father died long ago, Reven. You met—" he paused and took an angry breath. "Your mother's father. And my wife's father. The former Commander."

I had to think about that for a moment.

"I married your mother's older sister, Noelle. We had Anna together. Anna is your cousin. I'm your Uncle," he said with a sad smile.

"The Commander? Was—is—my grandfather? My mother once said I can't sleep because of him."

"It's true. Nor could Anna."

"I don't understand."

"Your grandfather developed a vaccination against adenosine, the chemical that makes you sleep. We all knew it was dangerous, but he was so goddamned self-righteous and so damn certain his vaccination would work that he volunteered our unborn daughter as a trial. His own granddaughter."

I felt his anger. "You look pale, Reven. Are you okay?"

"What happened to Noelle?"

"She died in childbirth. People believed that it had something to do with the vaccine, although it couldn't be proven. Your grandfather was impeached, hence his current custodial position. I wanted nothing more than to murder him, Reven. But although he had fallen from grace, he was still a former Commander and therefore, I could not touch him and get away with it." He exhaled. "And I had a daughter. A daughter with no mother. I was all she had."

"The mistake I made," he continued, "the one I swore to your mother I wouldn't make with you, was that I told all of this to Anna. Hate and anger consumed her. Your grandfather wasn't lying when he said you both have a lot in common."

I looked at him quizzically.

"I know, Reven. I know far too well what it's like to be you. I've watched it all before."

My pain and confusion faded as I considered what it must have been like for Ray. Comforting me in Anna's old bed, seeing me wearing Anna's old clothes, watching me grow up into an angry and confused young adult.

But just as soon as compassion kicked in, it faded.

"No, you don't," I said angrily, pushing away. "You have no idea what it's like to be kept in the dark, to wonder why I'm different! What happened to my mother? Tell me who my father is!"

"I don't know."

"Bullshit!"

"It's true, Reven. He was just some guy your mother slept with. I don't think she even knew who he was. She was a little wild before she had you." He smiled a sad, regretful smile.

This was so unlike everything I knew of my mother it left me speechless.

"After Anna died, your mother was devastated. Between the shame of what her father had done, and Noelle and Anna's deaths as a result of it, she fell into a deep depression. She blamed her father for taking everything from her. But that didn't stop him from giving her the vaccine when he found out she was pregnant."

"Why did he do that to her?"

"I guess to show the world that it could be done? To restore his name? Because he likes to play God? I really don't know."

"No one knows about me but us, my mother and him, right?"

"Right."

"How did he do it?"

"Never in her wildest dreams did she think he would do to you what he had done to Anna. Your mother suspected when she was several months pregnant that he had done this to you both. She had the same strange symptoms that Noelle had during her pregnancy. She was afraid the delivery would kill her. And with no father to raise you, she was terrified your grandfather would use you as the face of his insane campaign to take over the world or whatever it was he was planning."

"What did she do?"

"Your mother was far braver than you could ever realize, Reven."

Although I thought I had cried every tear for the rest of my lifetime, my eyes watered.

"She defected. She went to Banyan and met with the Governor there. She told him that she had news of her father and that she would only reveal it if they agreed to offer her clemency and disability so that she could live the remaining days of her life in solitude free from Branch Columnar and her father."

"Oh my God."

We sat for several minutes, understanding dawning. "That's why she hid me. That's why she lived in fear," I said, more to myself.

"After everything your mother had been through, her mind was fragile and she was genuinely paranoid. She had been raised to fear and mistrust her neighbors in Banyan and she was also afraid that her father would find out you were born healthily. She feared someone would discover your secret. You would have been tested and experimented on, Reven. It would be national news, and your grandfather would not hesitate to take the credit. I'm sure he would be happy to sell his vaccine for billions of dollars to all the people who would love to not sleep. And then who knows what he would come up with next. She couldn't take that chance."

"That's why I could never go to Hospital."

"Exactly."

"Why did she tell you?"

"She needed me. Someone had to know in case something happened to her, and you had to eat," he said.

I looked up at him, amazed. "You risked your life for us. The Officials could have killed you."

Ray shook his head slowly. "The bigger threat was here, Reven. I would have been banished if anyone found out I was helping your mother. Or killed."

"Then how did you just show up with me here one day?"

"You were going home with me that day whether your mother liked it or not. It was mere coincidence that it happened the way it did. It had taken me so long to visit you because the leaders here were on to me. So finally, I decided it was time. I swore to your mother that I would protect you, but you needed protection from her. I couldn't let you live that way. You became too reckless and self-destructive. So I told the leaders that your mother was ill, and I was your designated guardian."

"What happened to my mother, Ray?"

Ray looked down at the table, wordlessly.

"Ray? Please," I pleaded, taking his hands tightly in mine.

Just then, at that very moment, there was a loud rap on the door and Ray and I both jumped.

"Open up, goddamnit!"

Ray and I looked at one another, panicked.

"Officials?" I mouthed, and Ray shook his head. We scrambled up, on full alert. Ray put his finger to his lips and I nodded.

"I SAID OPEN UP, GODDAMNIT!" and there were several more loud bangs on the door.

Ray cautiously approached the door. "By whose authority should I open the door?"

"Once a Commander, always a Commander," came my grandfather's voice through the door. "Now open up, Ray."

Ray's eyes darted around the room, calculating. Trained instinct took over, surveying the room for weapons and an escape route.

"What's the problem, old man?" Ray asked through the door.

"Ray, I am going to ask you one more time to open this goddamn door. If you do not, I will break it down and then I will shoot you."

Ray lifted his hand to the doorknob and looked back at me and glanced to my bag.

"Okay, Commander. You win," he said as I silently strapped my bag to my back, always ready for a quick escape, thanks to my education. I stepped into the hall, out of sight.

I heard Ray take a deep breath followed by the click of the lock and the creak of the door.

"What's the problem, old man?" Ray asked as my grandfather stormed into the room.

"Where is she?"

"She's not here."

"Like hell, she's not. She's coming with me."

"And why is that?"

"Because I know!" he screamed.

"You know nothing," Ray responded calmly.

My grandfather laughed a maniacal sort of laugh, this time nothing like my mother's. A deafening shot made me jump. Ray gasped and I heard breaking glass as he must have fallen to the table.

I froze, out of sight in the hall, tears pricking my eyes, terrified that the only person I had left in the world was gone.

"Reven?" came my grandfather's voice. "I know you're here. You need to come with me now. If you don't, I will shoot you too."

I heard approaching footsteps. I was ready. He turned the corner, and the creepy janitor, the man responsible for ruining my life – my grandfather – stood before me.

"Come on now," he said, extending his hand.

"Where are we going?" I asked.

"Thirty-five years I have lived in disgrace. We are going to show the world what I have created."

"And if I don't want to?"

"I will shoot you."

"Kind of difficult to show the world what you created if I'm dead."

"I said I will shoot you, not kill you." He withdrew his hand and offered a clear view down the barrel of his gun.

The years of physical training kicked in and I moved through the door in a flash. I slammed and locked it. There was another shot and a searing heat as a bullet tore through the door and grazed my thigh. I yanked open the window and dropped to the fire escape, scrambling to the ground with my leg on fire.

I ran. I ran as fast as I could, never turning back. It was not unlike the night I ran out of my mother's apartment. Only this time, there was no one waiting to rescue me.

It wasn't until I reached the bridge that led to Banyan, the bridge that Anna threw herself off of, that I dared stop to catch my breath. My blood soaked jeans and searing pain in my leg told me I needed a hospital. Which Ray had told me never to trust.

I was caught between two worlds standing on that bridge. Looking back to where I had come, I knew there was nothing there for me but danger. Looking ahead, there was nothing but my past and the people I was taught to fear. So instead I looked down.

Watching the water rage a hundred feet beneath me, I thought of Anna. How serendipitous that I ended up here now. I had left my mother, not knowing if she was dead or alive. And now I was leaving Ray, equally uncertain about his fate. I was all alone. I had nothing; I was completely and utterly depleted. I knew there was only one way I could ever find rest.

I sat on the edge of that bridge as darkness fell, growing increasingly light-headed with blood loss, fading in and out as the pain seared in waves.

Finally, blackness came.

On the same day every year Ray refused to get out of bed, choosing instead to sleep through it. I know now that it was the anniversary of Anna's death. I prefer nothing more than to sleep through this day, and every day after it until I could catch up for the countless restless nights of my life.

I welcome the distraction of the early morning appointment. I give Quinn a kiss and tell her to be good, and head out. I normally conduct assessments in the government complex near my apartment. The walk to the hospital will take half an hour, but I don't mind. Moving makes my mind slow down.

Ahead of me is the bridge, black and angular against the soft light of sunrise. And on the other side, Branch Columnar.

Seeing the bridge always makes me remember that night, when my life changed again. So many times have I considered going back there, to end the agony of this lonely existence.

I turn the other way, and walk along the river.

I came to punching, kicking and screaming and was restrained by several men and women in gray uniforms.

"Where am I?" I screamed. "Let me go, goddamnit!"

"Calm down, young lady. We need you to calm down. You are in Ark Hospital in Banyan. You were shot and lost a lot of blood. You were found unconscious on the Hudson Bridge last night."

The memories flashed back. Ray, my Grandfather, the bridge. I was still alive, and I was not in Branch Columnar. I screamed as if being tortured. Being alive *was* torture.

I fought strong arms holding me down as a man approached me with a needle. I flailed, but he dodged and jammed it into my arm. It pinched, but I spat at him and kicked the nurse holding my feet.

Bewildered, they looked at one another. I had to be still. So with every ounce of my being, I willed myself to relax and uttered, "I need to speak with your Governor," before feigning sleep.

After a while, I was left alone. I assumed I was being watched, so I planned my next move with eyes closed. These people were my enemies.

Later, I heard a knock at my door. I pretended to be groggy. A man entered, dressed in plainclothes. He approached with a cautious smile.

"Good afternoon, young lady. I'm so glad you're on the mend, and speedily I might add. The doctors expected you would be unconscious for several days," he said.

"Good afternoon," I replied. "Who are you?"

"May I sit?"

I watched as he pulled a chair to my bedside, sitting casually on the edge.

"I'm the Governor of Banyan. Michael Shaw." He extended a hand. I took it cautiously.

"And who might you be?"

"Reven Jason."

He nodded. "Any relation to Nina Jason?"

"She's my mother."

"Yes, she is," he said. He knew who I was. I figured I was already dead. This gave me an overwhelming sense of indifference. I stared.

"I have no intention of harming you, Miss Jason."

I watched as he sat back and rubbed his face.

Several moments passed before he spoke. "I spent the past several hours looking over your mother's files and the conditions of her clemency. Miss Jason, I need to ask you a question."

I braced myself.

"Do you sleep, Miss Jason?"

I intentionally feigned confusion before responding, "Yes, of course."

He looked at me long and hard. "You know, Miss Jason, you're in a hospital. You can't fake something like that."

"You can call me Reven, Governor."

He half smiled. "And you can call me Mike."

He sat there smiling at me for a long moment while I focused all my training on trying to figure out his motive, to no avail.

"Mike," I said, "now I need to ask you a question."

"Yes?"

"Where is my mother?"

He gazed at me intently, eyebrows raised. "Where is your Grandfather?"

Over the next several weeks, Governor Shaw and I became—dare I say it—friends. He visited almost daily, bringing me books and candy. On weekends he sometimes stayed hours, playing cards. He delivered my mother's case files from when she arrived in Banyan seeking clemency. From the rise of my Grandfather to Commander and his experimentations; my Aunt Noelle's death in childbirth; my Grandfather's downfall; and lastly, Anna's death – it was all there.

I felt tremendous gratitude toward Ray for having finally told me the truth; the news clippings proved he was right. I allowed myself to begin to trust, and even to hope. My heart hammered a little faster when I saw Mike's smiling face.

In reading about my . . . family, I learned that Branch Columnar was a tiny, almost insignificant faction. It was embarrassing how much the Officials knew about the Branch, and how little those in Branch Columnar knew about Banyan. And I began to realize what I assume my mother couldn't: that whatever foundation the ideals of

Branch Columnar were founded on were archaic and obsolete and continued based on tradition and sheer ignorance. The Officials had no intention of hurting me, or anyone in Branch Columnar, for that matter.

I had asked Mike again about my mother's whereabouts, and also about Ray.

"In due time," he said, and I respected that. Despite everything I had been through and everything I was taught, he had been honest with me so far so I continued to trust him.

If anyone realized I wasn't sleeping, they didn't let on to it. I felt safe enough, and under their care my leg healed well.

By the time I was released from the hospital, Mike and I had negotiated my clemency, which included my working as an Assessor, and a promise to never go back to Branch Columnar. At first I thought that an easy promise to make. But I still didn't know if Ray had survived. I held back tears as I signed the document, realizing I would never see him again even if he had lived.

"There's something else, Reven," Mike had said.

I rifled through the paperwork, looking for any last minute addendums.

"No, not in the agreement," he said, pulling it away and taking my hand in his. "I have a personal request."

"Yes?" I whispered, longingly. The warmth of his hands was comforting.

"For your own sake, Reven, move forward. You know everything now. Be at peace. Build a life for yourself. And if you need anything, call my office. My staff is here to help." He squeezed gently, then let go of my hands and rose from his chair.

I blinked at the finality of his statement.

"Wait. What?"

His demeanor and tone was all business. Gone was the gentle sympathetic man I had come to care for, and that I thought had cared for me.

"My job was to bring you up to speed and offer you some understanding and clarity. You're a smart, strong young woman. Your clemency is negotiated. You are now a resident of Banyan and you know what is expected of you."

I had been mistaken. I didn't have a friend in the entire world.

I willed the tears away, and choked a response. I couldn't look at him.

"What was that, Reven?"

"You never told me what happened to my mother and Ray," I whispered to the table in front of me.

He didn't even sit. He sighed.

"They died, Reven."

With that, the sound went out of my ears, my sight blurred so I closed my lids, and I gripped the arms of my chair to prevent myself from falling.

"Take care of yourself, Reven."

"Thank you, Governor Shaw," I whispered, eyes closed, as he vanished through the doorway.

I still wish I had thought to ask the Governor how I should best take care of myself. Having no one and trusting no one, my life is a series of motions. I have drank and worked and found temporary solace in the comfort of strangers I never dare form emotional attachments with. I wonder how and when I'll die, and long for the courage to free myself from loneliness and regret. If I hadn't found Quinn, a starved, abused stray, I'd have no reason for breathing. In many ways, she rescued me just as much as I rescued her.

I turn down another tree-lined street, and York City Hospital towers in the distance, forty stories of glass glimmering in the morning sun. I mentally prepare for the meeting with the defector. Many of them I've known personally from my years at Branch Columnar and they're surprised and appear happy to see me. Although I don't care about any of them, their immense relief upon being welcomed by someone they know to a world they were taught to fear brings me a brief happiness.

Upon my arrival, I learn that the patient is classified as mentally unstable, placed in the basement wards. I am cleared for entry and escorted through maximum security, and down to the lowest level. My senses are heightened in these unfamiliar wards, and I am fully alert, reciting in my head the turns we are making in this poorly lit concrete labyrinth. I note the oxidized metal exit doors, in case I need to make a quick getaway.

Walking alongside my escort down the corridor, the sound of my boots on linoleum muffled by the screams seeping through the thick metal cell doors, I catch a name on the one of the cells we pass, and it stops me dead. An icy trail snakes down my back.

"Miss Jason?" my escort asks, far away.

I can't breathe. I'm dizzy. A familiar heat ignites deep within me, fueled by lies and disbelief. But a cold sweat takes over, and I shiver.

"Miss Jason. This is not the patient you are here to assess."

I steady myself against the door with shaking hands. My face is drawn to the wire mesh window, and I feel the cool metal against my damp cheek. I inhale forcefully.

"Miss Jason, are you okay?"

My mouth is dry and I can't speak. Shaking, I lift my face to the window. The tears at the corner of my eyes spill down my face, and my miserable, narrow little world breaks wide open again.

#0708 Jason, Nina.

"Momma . . ."

Reading Glasses

Neal Wooten

Mat swallowed hard as the officer sat beside him. The officer's bulky frame towered above him as their hips compressed into one another. Mat moved his rolled-up burlap sack and empty plastic jug to the other side as the crowded train bumbled along the ragged track. The evening sun bid farewell behind the ruins of ancient cities, the once proud constructs that tickled the sky now a crumbling, contaminated, forbidden zone.

The officer stared at the tin can in Mat's lap, the faded image of a steaming coffee cup and penguin barely visible, perhaps wondering why anyone would carry a container filled with old product labels. It was doubtful he gave it much thought, however, in this age of scavenging. Living quarters were usually decorated with whatever treasures one could drag home from the landfill.

Judging by the dirty clothes, faces, and fingernails of the other passengers on the train, all appeared to be scavengers, people who scoured the massive landfill all day searching for materials to turn in for recycling. It was the only job available to most fringe dwellers, but it earned enough credits to exist. Most stared down at the floor of the train, the pathways worn down to shimmering metal, flakes of old paint adhering to their shoes. Their eyes seemed hollow, lost in the day-to-day grind, made fragile by what the ignoble years had done; lives ground away like the specks of paint.

As the officer peered over at Mat with dull brown eyes that depicted a soul too tired to display a moment of content, Mat smiled and nodded. That was a mistake. The officer removed his small scanner from the pouch on his side and held it face up in front of Mat, his stoic face expressionless with this obtrusive gesture. Mat placed his thumb on the little screen and it displayed a green bar. His paranoia apparently satisfied, the officer slid the device back into its holder without so much as an acknowledgement. Mat made a mental note: don't smile at officers.

Police officers lived in the dome, but a few patrolled the fringe. No one really knew why. There was little crime. The powers-that-be had zero tolerance for crime and people caught committing such were whisked away and never seen again. There was a reward of five credits to turn in offenders as well, so what little crime did exist was usually of the invisible sort, never done in view of others.

The train arrived at Mat's stop and he exited. As it continued with the officer still onboard, he breathed a sigh of relief. Traveling the familiar dirt path between the dismal two-story living quarters, he stopped at the government store in the center of the village to gather enough food for a meager meal. Such was his routine. The rule of thumb was never to keep anything in your quarters that would spoil if not eaten right away.

Two young kids ran around inside as their mother scoured the shelves. It was a blur to Mat, like the blur of every day running together. He ignored the other fringe dwellers in the store and scanned the mundane inventory. Almost everything was wrapped in plain brown paper with symbols to display the contents. No letters were visible anywhere in their world, only numbers and images.

Mat picked out his usual, an imitation meat spread and some stale crackers, and took them to the clerk. Here you could get anything you needed: food, water, clothes, and if you had enough credits, you could even buy a day of electricity. Mat never bothered. He didn't own anything that required electricity. He placed his thumb on the scanner to purchase the items. It totaled two credits. He knew he had over twenty, so he wasn't worried.

Everything worked on credits. One credit a day was deducted for rent. If Mat worked long hours, he could make three, five, and rarely even seven credits a day. Going into the red was a crime, same as any crime, and produced a red bar on the scanners. That you did not want.

He walked outside and stared at the dingy overcast skies. In the far distance he could still see the gloomy outlines of the old cities, an ancient world of an ancient people, dead now forever. Many times over the years, either digging away for treasures at the landfill, or lying in bed at home, he heard the thunderous collapse of another sky-high structure as it succumbed to gravity. Such was life it seemed: decaying cities, decaying landfill, decaying civilization.

Mat often felt the urge to visit the old cities, but they had long been robbed of anything recyclable, so no one ventured into the areas. Plus, it was illegal.

He got to his quarters and entered the cramped room, which consisted of a bed, a tiny table with two chairs, and a sink and toilet in the far corner near a pile of clothes. He was excited to see what treasures he had found this day as he allowed himself the luxury of enthusiasm. Even though paper brought good credits, he had found a more important use for these particular labels.

He decided to wash up and eat first. They were allotted three gallons of river water each day, one of which he lugged to the landfill to prevent dehydration under the relentless sun. After he traded his dirty clothes for less dirty clothes, there was a knock at the door. He knew who it was.

"Hey, Bo. Come on in."

"Hey, Mat."

Bo was the girl who lived across the hall with her grandmother. She was fifteen and very small. Her black hair, which contrasted her deep blue eyes, came down past her shoulders. Mat was not much larger for a guy over twice her age. With the long hot hours spent in the landfills coupled with sparse food supplies, most fringe dwellers were small people.

Bo reached into her pocket, brought out a small object, and handed it to Mat. "Found this for you."

Mat opened his hand as she dumped the short pencil into it. He smiled. "Hey, thanks." Pencils were a rarity indeed.

"Did you do well today?" she asked.

He nodded. "I think so. Did you guys go to work today?"

"Yep," she said as she sifted through the labels. "We worked half a day as usual. Grandma gets tired easily and the sore on her foot is getting worse."

The recycling office was open all day and night so people could work as much as they wanted. Mat usually put in twelve hours a day, seven days a week. But there were some people who actually lived in the landfill. After all, it stretched for hundreds of miles in every direction.

"Can I see the glasses?" Bo asked.

"Sure." He made sure the curtains were pulled tight, went to the sink, and reached up underneath and pulled out the reading glasses. He handed them to her and lit an oil lamp.

"I can't believe you found these in the landfill. We've never found anything so nice. I'm so glad you didn't turn them in."

"Me, too," Mat said. "I was planning to, but it was late and I was on my way home. I set them on the shelf there in front of a coffee can and that's when I noticed the writing."

Bo scanned through the labels as Mat continued with his meal. "Hey," she said, "we have one from Shining Star."

"Great."

Shining Star was one of their favorite writers. They had determined that all of the current writers had fake names. They could tell by how these writers seemed to understand the world as it was today, the dull gray words leaving you longing for a miracle. Some writer's styles of writing was unique and reflected an older world, one as foreign to them as life under the dome. These stories were the best. Their favorite was called *Moby-Dick* by Herman Melville. They had only read a few chapters, but found it very exciting.

"I'm glad your mom taught you how to read," Bo said.

"Me, too."

"Wasn't she worried you'd get caught?"

Mat shook his head. "It wasn't illegal back then. They outlawed it when I was twelve years old, so that's twenty years ago."

After Bo mentioned his mom, Mat thought of how he started going with her to the landfill when he was only ten. She got sick a few years ago and passed away. Most little villages on the fringe have one healer, and if you possessed enough credits, you could get a list of ridiculous home cures for whatever was ailing you. No guarantees; no refunds. His mom went, but it was credits wasted. He knew Bo's grandmother was trying to save enough for a visit. He would offer to pay it if he had any faith at all in the healer.

Mat finished eating, took the glasses, and read the hidden story from Shining Star. It was another great space adventure. The writing on the label was unlike hand writing, it was much neater, and they could only assume it was printed by some type of machine.

"Do you think every single one of the dome dwellers has glasses like these?" Bo asked.

"I don't know."

"I hear they have electricity all the time and even their own personal transports."

Mat had heard the same rumors. "Maybe," he said.

The wealthiest citizens lived under a massive semi-transparent dome that spanned an area even greater than the landfill. The products with the stories printed on them were only available to those people. There were six total companies that printed these invisible stories on their products, as far as Mat and Bo could tell. From the images on the labels, they had assumed the names of the companies were: Penguin Coffee, Lemon & Luster Juice, Hatchet Tools, Harpoon Fish, Mac Beans, and one with just a bunch of random images on the label. The empty canisters, as well as all garbage created by the dome dwellers, were dumped in the landfill.

"Have you ever drunk coffee?" Bo asked.

Mat made a sour face. "Once. Mom would buy a single serving every year or so. It was horrible to me; very bitter."

He read the story written on the coffee can, removing the label to read the second part printed in the invisible letters on the flip side. He was always surprised to find the labels intact, and it made him wonder if the people buying the coffee even knew about the hidden writing.

After he read all the stories, Bo surprised him when she said, "Read me one of yours."

He smiled, went back to the sink, reached underneath and pulled out a few sheets of paper. He read her a story about a boy who discovered a time machine in the landfill and traveled back in time and changed the course of history. Mat concocted stories in his mind all day to pass the tedious hours at the landfill, and wrote them down when he was home. He never turned in pencils for recycling.

"Your stories are better than these others," Bo said. "You should write for these companies."

Mat smiled. After they read all the stories, they said goodnight.

Mat tossed and turned all night. Normally, he slept very soundly, but he couldn't seem to get Bo's words out of his head. Maybe he could be a writer for these companies, like she said. Perhaps the lack of slumber was also in part due to the pang of guilt he felt. Mat had not been honest with Bo about where he found the glasses.

He had found an old pair one day at the landfill, the crusted frame bent and missing one lens. He received two credits for the specialty item. But the glasses he now possessed were in perfect shape when he found them, and it was not amongst the garbage. He was coming home on the train one day when he spotted something by the track, something standing out against the lifeless terrain. He got off at the next stop and walked back to where he saw the object, but only found a clump of damp earth. As he began walking back to the stop to board the next train, upset that he had just cost himself another half-credit, something caught his eye. It was a man running along some old buildings, wearing the glasses.

Then he saw the police transport closing in on him. The last time he had seen a transport was when he reported his mom's death and they came to pick her up. He tried to control his breathing as he hid behind a tree and watched. As the transport closed in on the man, he quickly darted down a short alley. Mat saw the man throw the glasses through a window of one of the old buildings, as if they were the cause of the chase. The two officers in the transport caught up with the man and knocked him to the ground. They proceeded to beat him with their metal sticks until he no longer moved, then dragged his lifeless body back to the transport.

Mat waited until they were out of sight, his heart pounding, before going into the building and retrieving the glasses. He had planned on turning them in the next day, certain they would fetch a great price. But as he had explained to Bo, when he put the glasses on the shelf that evening in front of a Penguin Coffee can, he noticed the red letters though the lens and read the first story. For months he took the glasses to the landfill, making sure to only put them on when no one was around. That's how he discovered the six different company labels with stories printed on them and now knew what to look for.

He thought again about being a writer. All of these companies were located in large buildings in the industrial district next to the dome. The higher-ups lived in the dome, but even the laborers made better credits than scavengers. They lived in villages like his but closer to the dome and much nicer. Once every two months the industrial district opened for interviews. Mat interviewed many years ago to appease his mom, but hadn't been back since. It was an all-day venture to go out there and hard to give up your credits for a long shot like that. But to be a writer was different. That might be worth it.

Mat continued to toss and turn, unable to stop thinking. It was no use. He got up and dressed, then walked to another building in the village and knocked on a door. It was dark in the hall and he saw a light come to life through the crack in the door, not like from an oil lamp, but an instant and even light.

The door opened to reveal a woman clearing sleep from her eyes. "Mat. Should have known. Come on in."

As Mat entered, he noticed the small electric lamp and a fan blowing air toward the bed. Clearly, he was in the wrong business.

The woman walked over to a small bedside table and retrieved her scanner. People who worked from home, like the healers, could purchase their own scanners at the government store. They weren't like the police scanners, however, and were only used to collect credits. She held up the screen for him.

"Two credits?" he asked. "I thought it was one-and-a-half."

"It's been two for a while," she snapped. "If you don't want to pay, go back home."

He placed his thumb on the screen and the scanner beeped. She looked at it to make sure the payment went through then placed the scanner back on the table. She slipped the single piece of clothing she was wearing up over her head and let it fall to the floor. With no emotion at all, she crawled back onto the bed and spread her legs. Mat removed his clothing and joined her.

A few weeks later, Mat skipped work for the first time in years. His short brown hair had been neatly trimmed for the occasion and he dressed in his best clothes, before leaving with much anticipation.

Even though he arrived before sunrise, the line was very long. Every night he dreamt about becoming a writer. He pictured himself in his nice living quarters in the dome working on his next masterpiece for his adoring fans. He had his favorite story hidden in his pants as the line inched forward.

He finally reached the entrance to Penguin Coffee around midday. He was instructed to take a seat in a small office. After a few minutes, a young girl came in.

"Hello. Your name, please."

"Mat."

"What do you do now, Mat?"

"I work the landfill."

She didn't appear happy. "We only have a few openings, so we're looking for people we can trust."

He suddenly realized this was the same questioning he went through many years ago. He decided to let her know why he was there. "I didn't actually come here for these openings."

She looked up with a confused expression.

Mat cleared his throat. "I would like to be a writer for you guys."

Her eyes opened wide and her bottom jaw dropped. She left so fast that Mat began to get nervous and wondered if he should also leave. Minutes passed, which seemed like hours. Finally, a man walked calmly into the room. "My name is Terner. Come with me," he said.

Mat followed him down the hall to another office where he was instructed to sit before what he assumed was Terner's desk. Terner, no longer appearing as calm, looked around nervously before speaking.

"What do you know of our labels?"

"I know about the stories," Mat said. "I read them every day."

"How?" he asked.

"I have reading glasses?"

"Where did you get them?" His tone was demanding, accusing even. "Do you have them with you?"

Mat felt the glasses in his pocket but didn't answer the question. "Look, I just came here to inquire about being a writer for you. I love to write stories and I think mine are a lot better than some of the ones you print."

Terner shook his head. "Our authors are very educated and experienced writers from the dome. I'm sorry, but we can't use your stories."

"How can you turn down something you've never read? Do you make the decisions on what's to be published? Are you the publisher?" Mat demanded, becoming upset.

"No," Terner replied calmly. "But I decide what is presented to the people who do publish. Think of me as a middleman."

"But you haven't even read any of my work. Just read one story." Mat pulled the story from his pants and unfolded it.

Terner pushed backward in his chair as if Mat had pulled out a poisonous snake. "Are you crazy? Don't bring visible writing in here," he said in an urgent whisper. "I think you should leave now."

Mat didn't know what to do. His dreams of being an author and living in the dome had been crushed. He got up and walked toward the door, but his anger stopped him. "I'll keep coming back until you give me a chance."

Terner didn't know what to say. He knew Mat had him over a barrel. All Mat had to do was report what was happening and Penguin Coffee and the world of writing would come crashing down. Mat stood at the door, his hand on the doorknob. "Why do you do it anyway?"

Terner stared at Mat for several seconds as if pondering the question. In a much more polite tone, he answered. "We don't believe in the law against reading and writing. We believe the printed word is far too important not to survive. A lot of people in the dome agree."

Mat nodded. "I agree, also. I respect what you guys are doing. I'd never do anything to jeopardize that. But can I ask you one question before I leave?"

"Sure. What is it?"

Mat took a deep breath. "Can you tell me if Ahab and Ishmael finally kill the white whale?"

Terner smiled. "Ahab harpoons Moby-Dick, but the line gets caught around his neck and he is dragged into the sea and drowns. The ship itself sinks and only Ishmael survives."

"Wow . . . thanks." Mat opened the door to leave.

"Wait," Terner said. He opened his desk drawer, pulled out two ink pens, and walked over and handed them to Mat. "These are special pens," he said with a wink. "Don't walk around with visible writing."

Mat had seen pens in the landfill, but never with any ink. He nodded and left the building.

It was early afternoon and he considered going to work for a while, but he was dying to try out the pens. He went to his quarters, sat at the table, and drew a line on a piece of paper. He put on the glasses and saw the red line as plain as day. He wrote a few simple words.

There was a knock on the door. When Mat answered, Bo was standing there grinning, her hair still wet from when she cleaned up after work.

"Sorry, I couldn't wait any longer. How did it go today?"

They both sat at the table and Mat handed her the glasses. She put them on and noticed the paper on the table that read, "Hey Bo. How was your day?"

"How did you do that?"

He showed her the pens and told her the entire story. "Here, you take one of them."

She took it and smiled. "Thanks. So how did it go at the other companies?"

He shook his head. "I didn't go to any others after what happened at Penguin. I was too afraid."

"But at least you have a contact now and two whole months to get your story ready to take back."

"I'm not going back."

"Why?" she asked.

"They made it clear that they don't want a writer like me. All of their authors live in the dome."

"But he gave you the pens," she said, "so you can redo the story and take it back to him. Right?"

Mat replayed the events in his mind, frame-by-frame, with a genuine desire to understand Terner's actions. "I don't think so."

"I think he expects you to bring it back to him with this ink. You have to try."

Bo had convinced Mat. He spent the next two months working an extra hour a day at the landfill, in an almost mechanical existence. It was inconsequential, however, as he had real direction and purpose now and spent the evenings rewriting his story with the special ink. When the open interview day came around, he was in line before sunrise once again.

"Oh no, you again!" the girl said.

She left and a few minutes later Terner stuck his head in the waiting room. He simply motioned, so Mat followed him to his office. "I really wasn't expecting to see you again, although I can't say that I'm surprised."

Mat didn't hesitate. He took the folded papers from his pocket, laid them on the desk, and sat down.

Terner stared at the blank pages and shook his head. "Mat, I know you heard when I explained that all of our authors live in the dome. I know you understood that."

"Yes, but I don't have a choice. I don't live in the dome and there's nothing I can do about that. I made sure this story is the same length as the short stories you print. I'm only asking that you read this and give me honest feedback." He got up and headed for the door.

"That's it?" he asked.

Mat nodded. "I'll just leave that with you and see you in two months." He smiled and left.

"They haven't read any of them?" Bo asked.

Mat looked up from writing and shook his head.

"How many stories have you taken to them?"

He held up four fingers.

"That's not right. Why won't they read them?"

"Maybe they don't want to encourage me and hope I'll just stop trying."

Bo gritted her teeth in anger. "Or maybe they're just too afraid they'll like them."

Mat laughed. "Yeah, let's go with that."

They both laughed. Tomorrow was the next interview day and Mat was planning to go back for the fifth time. But it was honestly beginning to wear on him as his frustration mounted.

The next morning, he arrived even earlier and the girl led him straight to Terner's office. He smiled and motioned Mat in.

"Here's the next one," Mat said. He handed him the paper and turned to leave.

"Would you like to hear what they said about your last one?" he asked.

Mat rushed back to the chair. "You read it?"

"I didn't, but I had someone read it."

Mat nodded. "Yes, what did they say?"

"They said it was entertaining enough, but lacks a professional writing style. They said your characters seem forced."

"Forced? What does that mean?"

"Not real," Terner said. "It wasn't believable. To write fiction, the key to pulling a reader in is to make sure the story is plausible."

Mat nodded. "That gives me some direction."

Terner laughed. "The thing is; we feel your writing is several years away from being ready. I suggest you work on your writing for a few years, reading as much as you can to see how it's done, and come back then."

"Oh, I see." Mat sat back in the chair. "Did you guys really read it?"

"Honest," he said. "The reader said the premise of an alien invasion attacking the dome was unique and inventive. He also said that the ending where the fringe dwellers repel the invasion and save the world by using ancient weapons discovered in the landfill was very good."

Mat grinned. "Wow. They did read it."

"You have to realize, Mat, that writing is not simply being able to tell a great story. There's a lot more to it than that."

Mat got up and extended his hand, unable to stop thinking about the fact that his story had actually been read. "I'll work hard on it."

Terner shook his hand with a smile. "Hold on," he said. He reached into his desk drawer and pulled out a folded piece of seemingly blank paper. "Study this. These are rules for writing."

Mat smiled back. "Thanks."

"I don't get this at all," Bo said.

"What?"

"These stupid rules," she said as she read the paper given to him by Terner.

Mat sat at the little table across from her. "This is good information to know if you want to be a writer. Like how to break up paragraphs, when to use quotation marks, and a lot of other stuff."

"That's just it," Bo said, "all of these so-called rules and none of the authors they publish follow any of them. Some of them don't even use quotation marks and some of them don't even split up paragraphs when different people talk. And we've read some stories that go back and forth from first person to third person and some that go back and forth from past tense to present tense."

Mat knew Bo had a point. They had pointed out these types of things many times even before Mat first went to Penguin Coffee. "I guess once you're an author, you can bend the rules a little."

Mat shrugged again. He really didn't understand himself.

Over the next two months, Mat studied the rules and worked even harder. Even though he knew Terner was hoping this would deter him, it had the opposite effect. Bo helped him every night as they worked to produce a new story. When the time came around again, Mat returned with another story, but with similar results as they offered up the same reasons as to why his writing was not ready.

This went on for another full year. After six more visits, Mat had heard just about every excuse there was: The story just isn't right for our readers, there is too much narrative, there is too much dialog, it doesn't flow, it's too amateurish, it lacks consistency, etc.

It had taken a toll. Working longer hours left Mat too tired to concentrate some nights. He found himself often getting depressed and began to wonder why he was putting himself through this. Life was hard enough without these sacrifices.

Bo had even started noticing a change in his demeanor.

"Do you want me to leave?" she asked one night.

"No. Why?"

"You just seem upset. I just want good things to happen for you."

Mat smiled. "I know you do. It's just getting to be too hard. I don't care anymore. I'm going to take this one in tomorrow but that's it."

"Are you serious?" she snapped.

He didn't have the energy to argue. "Yes, I'm serious. I don't think I can create a better story than this one. Will you still be my friend if I am only a lowly landfill worker?"

They both laughed. Mat realized it was the first time they had laughed in a while. He hoped she understood. He just wanted to feel normal again. A person can only take rejection for so long.

The next day he walked into Terner's office and dropped the papers onto his desk. He turned to leave without even hearing the latest bad news. He knew he must have looked like a broken animal, but he didn't care; it was how he felt. He appreciated the fact that they had tolerated him for so long, but it was time to admit he would never be an author.

Time passed as time does. Interview days came and went and Mat gave them little thought. He went back to working normal hours, but with one difference—he turned in everything he found. He didn't bring home any new labels to read.

"This looks really bad," Mat said to Bo's grandmother. He lifted her foot and stared at the sore, which was now about two inches across and oozing some sort of green puss.

"She needs to go see the healer," Bo said.

"We can't afford it," her grandmother replied.

It was already late in the evening so Mat made a decision. "Okay, here's what we're going to do. Tomorrow morning, Bo and I will walk you to the healer's quarters and I'll pay the credits. Bo can come with me and work all day at the landfill to make up for it. Are we agreed?"

Bo's big grin was already payment enough. Mat just hoped the healer actually helped.

The next morning the three of them went to the healer. There were four other people waiting as the healer, an older woman with long grey hair, worked with someone in the corner. Her assistant, a middle-aged woman, brought the scanner over and Mat placed his thumb on the screen and paid the three credits. They left Bo's grandmother there and headed to the landfill.

"I don't know why you're smiling," Mat said as they traveled the train. "After working all day, you might not be smiling."

"We'll see," Bo said.

To her credit, she worked hard all day. Mat's bag was almost filled, making it difficult to drag. He drank the remaining drops from his water jug, so he knew they couldn't stay much longer. "Are you ready?" he asked.

She nodded.

Suddenly he noticed something just under her feet. "Don't move," he said in a commanding tone.

She froze. Mat took a steel rod and rammed it under her feet. He motioned for her to back up as he pulled the large snake out from the debris. It measured about eight feet long, its head and tail dragging the ground as Mat held its midsection, the remaining rays of sunlight making the slimy scales glisten.

"Oh my gosh!" Bo gasped.

Mat laughed. "It's okay. They usually won't bite unless you step on them. This is a good thing. We can get you more credits with this."

She looked confused but didn't ask. They headed to the nearest office to turn in their sacks. As they stood in line, Mat took the snake from his bag and held it up. "Anyone?" he asked loudly.

He knew there were people that lived at the landfill and would eat just about anything. A person held up a sack about half filled. Another held up a full sack. Mat walked over and traded the snake for the full sack of recyclable materials. As they reached the front of the line, he gave the sack to Bo to turn in her with her own. They totaled 5.5 credits together. She couldn't stop smiling.

Mat turned in his sack and they gave the empty one back to the person they traded with and walked to the train. The sun was low in the western sky as they boarded. They arrived back home and stopped to buy food for the night. They went to Bo's quarters to check on her grandmother.

"It smells terrible," Bo said.

Mat agreed. Her foot was bandaged and had some kind of leaves sticking out all around it. "How does it feel?" he asked.

"It stings but the healer said it would. She said it would draw out the poison in a few days," she answered, lying on her back.

Mat hoped she was right.

The days passed and Bo continued to work with Mat since her grandmother's foot did not appear to be getting better at all. Mat was very worried.

One night as he lay in bed trying to get to sleep, a feeling of deep depression came over him and he tossed and turned. He finally got to sleep in the wee hours of the morning, but it was not a restful sleep. He had nightmares; one about a young man accused of a crime and fleeing from police. He was not innocent. The man carried a wooden box filled with thumbs he'd collected from the people he had killed. He removed the skin from one and placed it over his own. He used his new thumb to go on a spending spree, using the print for its credits. As the credits ran out, he removed the skin from another and so on until he ran out and went on another killing spree.

Mat woke with a jolt, cold sweat running down his chest. The sun was already halfway up in the sky. He had overslept by many hours. He hurried to get dressed but stopped. He couldn't go to work today; the story was still too strong in his head. He could even see the surprise ending. The man turned out to be a dome dweller masquerading as a landfill worker. He returned safely to his home every few days but his lust for death always brought him back to the fringe for more blood.

Mat sat at his table and began to write. He wrote in pencil first, making corrections, then transferred the story onto clean paper with the invisible ink. He wrote all day as the story poured out of him.

Bo knocked on the door.

"I know," Mat said as he opened the door. "I'm sorry. I couldn't sleep last night."

"I was worried. I kept knocking. I didn't know what to do."

"I'm sorry," Mat repeated. "Come to the store with me."

They walked to the store, and Mat told her the story. She loved it.

"Does this mean what I think it means?" she asked.

"You bet it does," Mat said. "I'm going back next week."

Mat purchased his dinner and they walked back home. As he got to his door, he froze; his mind racing as he felt violated. His door was open about an inch and there were wood splinters on the floor. Someone had broken into his room. He opened the door cautiously and entered. There was no one there, but all of the labels were gone, as were the tin cans holding them. But that's not what worried him. On the table sat the paper with the pencil writing, the visible writing. Thankfully the story with the invisible writing was still beneath that and untouched. The thief had not bothered to steal or even touch something illegal.

"They won't say anything," Bo said. "An outlaw wouldn't want to bring attention to themselves."

Mat could only hope she was right. Still, he was worried. The next morning he went to work, but his stomach churned with fear. He came home and nothing happened. Several days went by before the anxiety completely went away.

Mat found himself at the Penguin Coffee Company again. This time the girl seemed almost happy to see him. He was confused.

"Mat, come in. Come in. Where have you been?" Terner asked.

That confused Mat even more. "I've been busy working," he offered as an excuse.

"Do you have another story for us?" he asked.

Mat nodded and handed it to him. Terner read the title. "*All Thumbs*. Hey, that sounds good. I hope it is as good as your last one."

"My last one?"

"Yeah, we printed it."

Mat couldn't believe it. His breathing escalated and he couldn't find words. "Really?" he finally muttered.

"Yes," Terner said. "It was a huge success. We sold out in record time and had to do another shipment. The reviews have been awesome. Everyone wants to know when we're printing more from *The Junkman*."

"Who's the junkman?"

Terner laughed. "That's you. I had to come up with a name. Hope that's okay."

Mat nodded weakly. He still couldn't believe it.

"We printed two of your older stories as well since we didn't know where you were. We pay five hundred credits per story, so if you'll place your thumb here, we'll get you paid for those three and this new one."

"Two thousand credits?" Mat asked in disbelief as he stared at the scanner. That's more than he would make in a year at the landfill.

Terner nodded. "We want to offer you a standard contract to provide us with one story a week at these rates. Readers seem to love stories told from a fringe perspective, something they've never experienced. What do you say?"

"What do I say?" Mat asked with a chuckle. "I say yes!"

"Now, you'll have to move to the dome," Terner said. "All of our authors live close to me and that's how they get me their stories."

"Well, if I *have* to," Mat said, trying not to burst into hysterical laughter. "I guess I will. How do I do that?"

"There are plenty of rooms in my building," he said. "They run twenty-five credits a day but are fully furnished with three bedrooms and two baths. I can take you when I get off work. There's a direct tunnel from this building to inside the dome."

Mat couldn't believe it. He did it. At first the thought of twenty-five credits per day scared him until he did the math.

"If you need to go home to get anything, go now and come back. But there are plenty of stores that sell clothes, food, and whatever else you need, all within walking distance."

Mat thought about Bo. He had to tell her and say goodbye. But he knew he couldn't do that. Suddenly he had a thought. "Can people live with me there?"

Terner laughed. "Of course. It's your home. You can do whatever you like."

Mat stood and walked toward the door. "Great. We'll be back before you leave."

Mat ran all the way to the train station, his feet as light as his mind, as he floated on air. He could hardly sit still on the train as he imagined telling Bo and her grandmother that they were coming to live with him in the dome. It still seemed surreal. He got off at his exit and walked past the government store.

As he neared his building, he saw Bo walking toward him. He waved high in the air with a big smile on his face, but it disappeared instantly. Bo was crying and walking at an angle as to go around him, as if she hadn't noticed him at all. He looked past her and saw the police transport with an officer standing beside it.

His heart sank; he knew what must have happened. He knew it must be Bo's grandmother. He felt sick to his stomach. If only she could have lasted a little while longer, he could have gotten her a real doctor inside the dome.

When he looked back to Bo, she was staring at him but her head still faced in the direction she was walking. He didn't understand why she was acting this way. She took her fingers and made circles over her eyes. What was she doing? Then it dawned on him as he deciphered the code. He took the glasses from his pocket and put them on. There was red writing all over her face—two words written over and over that made his blood run cold. "Run Mat."

He looked up at the second floor and saw a police officer in his room. He understood. The thief couldn't resist the possibility of credits and had turned him in. Mat turned away and headed back toward the train. If he could just make it back to the landfill he could stay there all night and meet with Terner tomorrow to go to his new home. He could send for Bo and her grandmother later.

Suddenly, the officer called out to Mat, and he bolted, not looking back. He heard the transport closing in behind him and quickly turned down alongside a building, which bordered the forest. He took the glasses and threw them into the trees. He could only hope that the police wouldn't find them.

When Mat emerged from the alley, a second officer was waiting and tackled him hard. Both officers stood over him and wailed away with their metal rods. Mat pleaded and begged, but to no avail. The pain was excruciating at first, but then subsided. Mat thought of Bo and smiled.

I made it, Bo, he thought. *I am an author.* With that thought, the beating ceased to be painful at all.

Finally, everything went black.

The Highborn

K. A. Magrowski

Kwiisa waited in the center of the Temple's main chamber. The worship fire blazed hot on her back. She inhaled the pungent, familiar smell of burning incense heavy across the room. The pillars, a pace across and gilded lightly, lofted into the dark recesses of the ceiling. Although not the Austere Temple in the great city of Bjim B'nar, suppliants still trembled in awe at the sight of the massive statue of Arnusi, seated on Her throne, watching them from above.

They shuffled in like poor vagrants and beggars, although Kwiisa knew two of them to be wealthy residents from town. They had visited her parents' villa on several occasions when she was younger. The three others she didn't know personally, but judging by their well-cut robes and jeweled slippers, she guessed them to be from the upper class also.

"Behold," she said, her voice echoing in the chamber. She held out her arms to each side. The golden bands of twin snakes, coiled around her upper arms, glinted in the dancing firelight. "Behold the Temple of Arnusi, She Who Births, She Who Watches, She Who Judges on the Last Day. Bow before Her and show no false pride."

She stepped to the side of the worship fire on its raised dais to allow the petitioners to walk forward and kneel. They knew what was expected of them. For an instant, she caught a glimmer of light from the wall to her right, in darkness behind pillars. The watcher hole. No doubt the Mother watched the suppliants. Worship was not the only thing expected of them.

Kwiisa had a feeling that the Mother watched her also. She almost missed her cue and flushed with both anger and fear. She, a daughter of one of the highest families, should not be spied upon like one from the common classes.

Kwiisa continued to observe the supplicants. They made the signs, they kissed the ground before the fire, and they chanted in the high tongue the prayers of the most devoted. She watched it all with an impassioned eye. This scene was played out every day by hundreds of worshipers from the city and surrounding towns. Some locals visited several times during every Moon. As priestess, it was her job to guide the believers, but also, and more importantly, to make sure coin filled the coffers.

As the group finished their supplications, she slid the basket off the ledge hidden behind the dais and waited, eyes downcast, as they stood. Each came over to drop coins, jewels, or letters of credit into the basket. She surreptitiously glanced from under her hood to see what was donated, and by whom. The Mother would want a full accounting.

After they left, Kwiisa took the basket into a back chamber while another priestess handled the fire duty for the next group. She sighed when she took count of what had been donated during her watch. She tucked a tendril of her hair that had worked its way from the coils on top of her head behind her ear and recounted.

The Mother swept in as she finished her second count. "How were the takings today?" she asked, looking over Kwiisa's head. Even Highborn priestesses could expect little from the Mother. Although from a well-to-do merchant family and not Highborn herself, the Mother's post commanded respect. At least she demeaned herself enough to speak with Kwiisa. Some priestesses had not yet spoken to the Mother directly; it was only through intermediaries that they communicated with her.

Kwiisa bowed low. "If my calculations are correct, we are down a tithe-full from last Moon, Mother."

Nothing changed in the Mother's demeanor, but Kwiisa could sense that she now walked on dangerous ground. The Mother had been known to have bearers of undesirable news whipped. Although she would not be given a public whipping as Highborn, it would still be no less painful.

"This is the fourth Moon we have lost profit. I assume you and Pimm, as the highest-ranking priestesses, will soon have a plan to reverse this decline. Of course, you may enlist the assistance of some of the others. A few have sharp minds."

Kwiisa bowed her head. "It will be done as you wish, Mother."

The Mother raised one eyebrow. "I expect no less," she said and left the chamber, her embroidered silk gown and cape sweeping along the tiled floor.

Kwiisa stared after her, chewing her lip in thought, when Pimm entered. The other priestess, a head shorter and her skin a deeper shade of brown than Kwiisa's own lighter sun-baked coloring, sighed as she took a seat. Unlike Kwiisa's single coil of hair, Pimm's hair had been half piled on top, with the rest making dark waves down her back. Although Kwiisa was accounted pretty, male supplicants sometimes forgot their duty and obligation when Pimm was near. Her oval face framed sculpted cheeks and lush lips perfectly. Kwiisa often had to quell her own insecurities, despite knowing how rich and powerful her own family was, when Pimm was around.

"You look bothered," Pimm said, twirling a strand of hair around her fingers.

Kwiisa sighed. "The Mother has charged us to find a way to increase revenue. We've suffered another decline. They are not sharp drops, but the decline is steady enough to warrant attention."

Pimm shrugged. "I heard another temple, one for the heathen Serpent God, opened in Jsaur, just two days' ride from here. I am sure once the novelty wears, we will have our proper funding again."

Kwiisa dropped the coins into a leather bag, not looking at Pimm. She didn't have time for willful ignorance. "You don't understand. If this other temple is truly a rival, then how can we be sure the novelty will wear? And what will we do if it doesn't?" She didn't want to continue, but she had to impress upon Pimm how serious this could become. "Do you believe your family will welcome you back with open arms? A Second Daughter?"

She couldn't keep the bitterness from her voice. Despite her pride, she was not a prime daughter, and her family's wealth was tied into the future family of their prime daughter. When firstborn Safira gave birth to twins, her fertility was proven. Kwiisa, no longer needed, was sent to the Temple. Of course, joining the Order of Arnusi was a way to power and riches. One could work up from local, smaller temples to regional centers. One could even go as far as Bjim B'nar. But now, if they continued to lose revenue, there would be no recognition from the Austere Temple.

Pimm's mouth twisted downward in disgust, but she did not reply. She knew it to be true. They would be nothing but caretakers for their sisters' children if they went home. Neither family would invest a dowry for their second or third daughters. It was a way to keep costs down— invest the family money in the prime daughter and use the other daughters, if they were not sent to the temples, as caretakers and nurses for the young. Kwiisa's other sister, born two years after her, was not accepted as a priestess. She was at the family villa with nothing more to look forward to than being a glorified servant.

Just thinking about it all made Kwiisa's stomach turn. She decided that whatever happened, she would not follow that path. Something needed to be done and quickly. Her mind raced as she reviewed the accounting scrolls.

Two days later, the Mother called all the priestesses to the Assembly Hall. The day had wearied them, and by the looks on everyone's faces before the Mother arrived, Kwiisa knew no one wanted to be there. They all had to cut short their ritual bathing and since it was the hottest point of the growing Moons, difficult to leave the cool pools and shaded terrace. Even the high ceilings of the marble-floored chamber and the fanning from the servants did little to alleviate the early evening heat.

Pimm and Kwiisa stood when they heard the Mother approaching from outside the Hall. The five other priestesses lined up behind them. The Mother entered, this time in lightweight linen robes embroidered in thread-of-silver. Pimm and Kwiisa bowed low while the others knelt, including the servants who brought their foreheads to the floor. The Mother stood before them for some time while no one dared move.

"You may address me," she said finally, and they all rose. "An Attendant from the Austere Temple arrived earlier. He will be addressing you shortly. I wanted you to be forewarned."

Everyone appeared surprised and worried at this unexpected news. "I have no reason to fear this visit," the Mother continued. "Although our revenue has been down somewhat, we have not fallen so short that disciplinary action has been taken. Also, I have communicated to the Lord Attendant that my two high priestesses are currently working to improve the donations." She nodded toward Kwiisa and Pimm. "I imagine this is only a perfunctory visit."

So, he did not explain the purpose of his visit, Kwiisa thought. *Interesting.*

While waiting for the Lord Attendant to arrive, everyone busied themselves with the wine and various platters of fruits, breads, olives and cheeses brought in by the servants. They did their best to avoid conversation about the Attendant and maintain a modicum of ease, although some nervously glanced at the entrance. Kwiisa would need to have a talk with them about their manners. As priestesses, they should not let themselves be seen out of countenance.

Finally, three hard raps sounded on the large, wooden double doors to the Hall. The priestesses quickly lined themselves according to status behind the Mother, while the servants stood against the walls. In strode a tall, bald man wearing all black robes trimmed in dark blue, and carrying a staff as tall as he.

"You are now in the presence of Lord Kharmd, Attendant of the Austere Temple and Most Devoted of Arnusi, She Who Births, She Who Watches, She Who Judges on the Last Day," the advisor intoned before stepping off to the side of the doors.

The anticipation was palpable in the moment before the Attendant appeared in the doorway and entered the Hall. Kwiisa tried to peek under her eyelashes while keeping her head bowed as low as possible. An older man, with a halo of white hair and a long white beard, wearing dark-blue robes trimmed in gold, surveyed the room. Other than the richness of his robes, Lord Kharmd seemed like any other noble or well-to-do merchant.

"You may address me," he said and they all stood tall. "Please be seated. I do not wish to stand here to address you." His tone was serious, but his smile belied any ill intent.

After they all sat, the Mother introduced each of the priestesses to the Attendant at his request.

He studied them in turn, a certain weighing look in his eyes.

Once everyone had been properly introduced, he spoke. "As you know, revenues are down. No temple has been unaffected. New temples to some of the old gods and goddesses have appeared ever since Emperor Mandinn ascended to the Blackened Throne and lifted the ban on the heathen religions."

The Mother sighed deeply, shaking her head.

The Attendant nodded. "Yes, the heathen religions. Only through the Goddess Arnusi, the Blessed Mother to All, can we hope to have life after death. But, as we all know, there are deluded souls who will cling to anything new or different or dangerous. The Austere Temple has started to take measures to combat this, but we feel that other changes need to be made as well."

The Attendant paused, surveying the priestesses, before continuing. "The Mother has told me that she has assigned some of you the task of formulating a plan to increase revenues. What you do not know is that the Battle Son, Lord Dvari, the Goddess' human representative on the physical plane, has had a Vision. We believe this Vision was sent to him as a message of the Goddess' wishes."

He paused once more, fingering the silver chalice he held in his hands. Kwiisa thought that perhaps he was reluctant to continue, but that couldn't be. No Lord Attendant would be hesitant to reveal the plans of the Battle Son if he had had a Vision. What was Seen must Be.

The Lord Attendant took a deep breath before continuing. "Your duties here in the Temple will change. It has been Seen that the Goddess wishes a more . . . physical connection to her devotees. With the coming of the next full moon, each temple will have a few Holy Ones available to provide a symbolic sacred marriage to the Goddess."

Shock coursed through Kwiisa. He couldn't mean what she thought he meant. The Battle Son had a Vision of this? That she questioned the Vision at all was a measure of her shock. Glancing at the faces of the other priestesses, she could see they were equally stunned. After all, part of their duty was to remain pure, virgin priestesses to Arnusi.

The Mother slowly nodded. "Yes, yes, I can see this. With the heathen religions flourishing, the Goddess must want to strengthen Her connection to Her devotees. They must be made to feel how strong the Goddess is. She must course through them."

"Yes, exactly," the Attendant agreed with a smile, his assured air having returned. He knew what he said was to be obeyed without question or discussion. He looked to each of them. Kwiisa hoped she had managed to hide her shock. Along with the others, she bowed her head in acquiescence.

Later, after they had been dismissed, Kwiisa and the others quietly readied themselves for bed. Servants brushed hair and washed faces, hands, and feet. There was little chatter or visiting between chambers, unlike other nights. Kwiisa sat on her bed pondering the news for some while after her servant, Maisa left. Finally, she went to see Pimm.

Pimm was finishing up her private nighttime devotions. The muted night sounds of the city strayed through the open doors leading to Pimm's balcony as a warm, fruity breeze rippled the long white sheers.

Kwiisa waited in the doorway until Pimm motioned her in. Kwiisa sat on the edge of Pimm's bed, looking at her friend and her hair that fell in long, thick waves to her waist. Even without the kohl lining her eyes and the lip paint, innocent beauty radiated from Pimm like a fresco painted by a Master.

"What do you think of the Attendant's visit and the Vision?" Kwiisa asked, playing with the edges of her dressing robe.

Pimm stared at her for a long moment then shrugged. "It doesn't matter what I think, or what any of us think. I would have preferred to find another method, but one can't violate the wishes of the Battle Son."

Kwiisa tried to pick her words carefully. "I'm just not comfortable with such a decree. I wonder if the Battle Son and the Attendant realize what they ask."

"They ask nothing of us. It is Arnusi's wish."

Kwiisa wanted to ask if she really believed that, but one look at Pimm's implacable face and Kwiisa smoothed her own and lowered her eyes in apparent submission to the truth.

Kwiisa gave Pimm a quivering smile. "Of course, you are correct. It's just my fear speaking," she said, hoping Pimm hadn't detected her anger and confusion.

Pimm reached out to caress her arm. "All will be well. What we do, we do for Her."

Kwiisa could only nod as she squeezed Pimm's hand.

Two days later, on her day off, Kwiisa walked through the market. Originally, she had decided to eat at the market just to get out of the Temple, but as she walked she became like a twig afloat in a stream, allowing herself to be pulled along by the people, the sights, the smells and the sounds.

Sellers hawked their plates of fruit, or fish, or dough-wrapped spicy meats. One had a wide selection of olives from all the realm and beyond. Another tried to entice potential buyers with samples of roasted meat. Several women offered to spritz her with the latest scents come in to port. But Kwiisa didn't have the heart to shop considering all that was happening around her.

Today, Kwiisa's hair was coiled on top of her head, and wound with gold chains laced throughout. From one golden strand hung a blue stone that rested on her forehead. The day started out warm and only promised more heat, so she had worn her lightest robes; sky blue trimmed in the dark blue typical of Arnusi's priestesses. She did not need protection. It was a high crime to touch any of the temple priestesses without permission, so many moved out of her way just for fear that they might accidentally brush against her.

But that did not prevent the glances. Kwiisa noticed men looking her over when they thought she wasn't looking. It made her skin crawl and reminded her painfully of the Lord Attendant's proclamation.

Approaching midday, she realized she had wandered over toward the harbor side of the sprawling market. Gulls squawked and circled overhead. The tangy smell of the sea filled the air. She continued through the seafood stalls taking in the plentiful shouts of bartering and arguing over the fresh catches, and the sights of the brightly colored fish.

Continuing past the mongers, the noise of all the activity fading, Kwiisa found herself on a surprisingly quiet street. A group of men, talking amongst themselves, headed in her direction. As she passed, she could tell she had caught their attention since they stopped their chatter and paused, gazing at her. Kwiisa maintained her composure, but quickened her pace

"Yes, that's right, temple woman. Hurry now!" one man shouted.

Kwiisa was about to stop and turn when another yelled out, "Temple whore you mean!"

The men laughed. "The Battle Son of Arnusi fears us so much, fears the Serpent God, that he has turned to whores to upkeep the temples and bring in more coin!"

The men continued their raucous laughter as they continued up the street.

Kwiisa, shocked, managed to continue to the end of the street and turn toward the city wall. Through the nearest opening, a promenade overlooked the sea lane. Kwiisa darted through it and gulped in the salty air. Her hands and legs shook, and her eyes brimmed with tears.

So, that's what they think of us. Whores, Kwiisa thought.

Luckily, no one was in sight, so she could cry without shame. After some time, she managed to take a few strong breaths without gasping.

Somewhere deep down stirred thoughts she didn't want to admit existed. Yet considering everything she had witnessed at the Temple—the enticement of the faithful for coin and the Mother's distrust of everyone—she could no longer deny them. She had even overheard not too long ago that the Temple began loaning out coin, but she had dismissed it. After all, they were the Order of Arnusi, not a bank. Yet, now, she wondered . . .

Slowly, she headed back to the Temple, avoiding the way she had come. On the way back, she stopped at the chirographer. She had an idea. She only hoped it was not too late.

Several days later, tired of waiting for a response that might not come in time, Kwiisa knelt on the marble floor of the Temple. The statue of Arnusi, majestic on Her blindingly white throne, towered above her as she splayed her arms in subjection.

"Goddess, oh Goddess, is this truly your will?" Kwiisa cried. "Do you so desire riches for your temples that we, your sacred virgins, must sacrifice what is wholly ours? Please, can you give me a sign? You can see into the deepest depths of my heart and know that I am fearful; that I question not because I doubt my love for you, but because I know you will guide me in what is true."

Arnusi sat silent while Kwiisa continued to kneel, letting her heart flow outward. Finally, with knees stiffened and back aching, she stood and took a deep inhalation, letting the stillness of the Temple instill in her peace. She kissed the feet of Arnusi. Something soft touched her mind just then, as if in confirmation that all would be well.

"I trust you. You know what is in my heart, oh Blessed One," she whispered.

"What are you doing here, Kwiisa?" came a booming voice from behind, making Kwiisa's heart skip as she instinctively clung to the base of the throne.

"Mother. I was praying. I needed guidance," Kwiisa replied, recovering as she turned and bowed.

The Mother tapped her foot, arms folded, studying Kwiisa. The silent Temple, no longer a place of peace and sanctuary, vibrated with disapproval. Was it coming from the Goddess? If so, was it directed at Kwiisa, or the Mother?

"Kwiisa, why were you crying? Do you dare insult the sanctity of this Temple?"

"I . . . I was praying for guidance, Mother. The news of the decree has reached the streets. There was . . . unpleasant reactions from some."

"The decree is the decree. The Battle Son has declared it."

"But why him? Why not Arnusi Herself?"

"Do you dare question the Vision?"

"I ask only for guidance to calm my fears," Kwiisa answered, managing to keep her voice calm.

The Mother narrowed her eyes. "You question. I should have known. And your questioning led you to go so far as to send a message to the Austere Temple. The Austere Temple!" she shouted, then stepped back, visibly trying to calm herself. "Your suggestions for increasing revenue should have come to me first. Instead, you thought to bypass me and take glory for yourself. Well, your ideas will never be implemented."

Kwiisa lowered her eyes to hide her shock. Someone had betrayed her. "I only thought to save us."

The Mother ignored her. "You were never one of us. Not truly. Your rank has given you ideas. Perhaps time spent in contemplation of your heresy would be well spent. Mortification of the Flesh and Spirit might cleanse you."

"That would be most unwelcome, Mother. I obey, as always."

"We shall see." The Mother cast a glance up and down Kwiisa's body as if she were something unclean that needed to be swept from the floor.

Kwiisa stood unmoving for a long time after the Mother departed, her words hanging in the air. Arnusi had not answered her, the Mother found her questioning, and she had no idea what was planned for her as punishment. She swallowed hard, trying desperately to quell the fear growing within.

The next morning, Kwiisa was awakened from her fitful sleep by a rough shaking. Blurred shapes hovered above her as she wiped at her eyes, trying to focus. The barest hint of sunrise gleamed in from the open balcony doors.

"Get up, Kwiisa. No more sleeping for you."

"Pimm? What's going on?"

Pimm shook her again. Maisa, Kwiisa's servant, waited behind Pimm, arms folded.

"The Mother came to me. I am to oversee your mortification. Maisa will take you to get what you need before the Temple opens."

"What? I don't understand."

"Follow Maisa. No more sleeping."

Maisa said nothing as Kwiisa, clothed only in the simple robe Pimm had allowed her to wear, trailed after her. Kwiisa saw a few others peer out from behind their doors, and then duck back in. Maisa led her to the upper floors where the servant chambers were located. Without a word, Kwiisa was given a servant's dress, rags for cleaning, and a wooden bucket.

"There's your stuff. Lady Pimm said you were to wash the Temple floor. Lucky for you it was scrubbed yesterday."

Kwiisa's mouth dropped agape at the realization of what was to be her mortification. The Mother wished for her to be seen as a servant; a Highborn forced to wash floors. Her heart sank, and she realized that this may be only the beginning. She had no idea how mortified she had to become in order to satisfy the Mother's need to punish her supposed betrayal. Bitterness swept through Kwiisa. It was scandalous that she, of all the priestesses, should be accused of treachery.

Kwiisa nodded at Maisa and headed down to the Temple to begin her task.

Of course, the work of washing the Temple floor was only part of Kwiisa's punishment. The other part involved being seen by the servants and other priestesses. Jaslyn and Dinara, both of lesser born families, came to watch her. Kwiisa, forbidden to speak to them, kept her head down as she washed and dried the floor, section by section. Both women whispered behind their hands for a while until Pimm appeared.

"Have you two readied yourselves for the day?" she asked.

"Yes, Pimm," they said in unison. Kwiisa flinched at their sing-song reply. All for her benefit – to underscore their obedience and also Kwiisa's own lowered status.

"Dinara, you will be here in the main Temple, helping me," Pimm said.

Kwiisa scrubbed the floor harder at the realization that Pimm had taken Kwiisa's place and Dinara had been moved up.

"Kwiisa," Pimm called. "After this task, you will go to the kitchens to help prepare the midday meal and assist in serving."

"Yes, of course," Kwiisa said through gritted teeth.

The rest of the day passed much the same with Kwiisa helping the other servants serve the meals, then clean and wash. She fell into bed exhausted, glad she could sleep in her own room. She half-expected to be housed in the servants' chambers for the duration of her mortification.

Sometime after she drifted off to sleep, Kwiisa awoke with a start. Not sure what caused her sudden waking and unease, she went to the balcony. The silent night whispered to her as she watched the darkened streets below. In the distance, the lone eye of the lighthouse swept the shore, its flame burning like a sentinel, leading the ships to safety.

Taking advantage of the quiet, Kwiisa slipped into her silk robes, mortification or not, and left her room. Something touched her mind, very much like the feeling she had the previous night when crying in front of Arnusi.

Slipping through the hallways barefoot, she caught the faint sounds of snoring from her fellow priestesses. Once out in the extensive courtyard that separated the living areas from the Temple, Kwiisa breathed a sigh of relief; she had not awoken anyone. She didn't care to be questioned about her actions when she was so out of favor. Small creatures rustled through the greenery as she walked among the statues and benches, the moon's glow lending a silver sheen to the marble.

Sore from her day of scrubbing and serving, Kwiisa sank down against one of her favorites—the First Priestess Karneia—who helped spread the truth of Arnusi. Kwiisa felt love and admiration for the priestess who had done so much to ensure that Arnusi's legacy would not be destroyed when invading armies swept down from the north almost a thousand years ago, threatening to wipe out all traces of Arnusi. When Karneia, the virgin daughter of a fallen general, heard the news of her father's demise she took up his Battle Cry and rallied the people in Arnusi's name, effectively doubling the volunteers and starting the tradition of virgin priestesses being the only ones who could serve Arnusi intimately.

This statue now had been replicated all over the known world. Kwiisa had a miniature one at the family grotto. As a Second Daughter, Kwiisa's fate had all but been foretold since the day she was born. For the first time, pangs of anger did not stir in her over that fate as she sat bathed in the moon's gentle silver, gazing up at her predecessor. Humility had never been her strong suit, but she realized that this was her calling and she was good at it. No one should deny her that just because she asked for guidance.

Kwiisa made her way to the main Temple. In private, she would once again make her pleas to the Goddess. She had the right.

She opened the side door used by the priestesses and slipped into the Temple, lost among the thick, high columns that spanned her height times four. Whispers floated through the colonnade and Kwiisa froze. Someone was here. *Clink, clink.* Kwiisa moved closer to the sounds. She peered around one of the columns and her breath caught.

The Mother and Lord Kharmd, flanked by two burly guards, counted gold coins.

"This new edict will definitely increase our revenue," the Mother said, dropping coins, one by one, into a bag.

"Once the Austere Temple at Bjim B'nar realizes what we've done, they will see the rightness in it," Lord Kharmd agreed. "The amount of money we've lost over the past year to the new religions will pale in comparison to the amount we will take in."

"Do you think you can convince Lord Dvari to issue the edict of the Vision to all temples? It's risky since he's known to be an adherent."

Lord Kharmd stopped counting. "Lord Dvari may be devout, but even he's feeling the pressure. Something needed to be done and I knew you would understand better than any other Mother. Are you now having second thoughts?"

The Mother shook her head. "No, of course not." She paused. "You did say Dvari was ill? Do you think he will accept what we've done so close to his own meeting with Arnusi?"

"I must ask you something before I answer that. Are you satisfied with being the Mother of this Temple in the outskirts of the empire or would you like something more? Perhaps Bjim B'nar?"

The Mother gasped. "You're offering that to me?"

"I need someone who understands the difficulties of running this religion. Someone who won't flinch at what needs to be done. The false vision was a brilliant idea and I think you deserve to be rewarded."

Kwiisa pulled back into the shadows, mind racing. *False vision? All this talk of money?* Her hands and legs shook, almost unable to support her body. *How can this all be?*

Lord Kharmd continued. "Dvari is ill, yes, but I've been helping his illness along. I stand next to ascend. There is a chance that he might condemn us, but he won't have a chance. I will see to it."

"You never intended to bring our plan before him. You would already be the Battle Son of the Order."

"You're quick, Salima. Do my actions upset you?"

The Mother leaned over and kissed Lord Kharmd full on the mouth. "Nothing you do bothers me."

Kwiisa covered her eyes with her hands, not letting the sting of tears become the falling of tears. If she started crying, she would never stop. Betrayal lay thick on her tongue. A tiny hiccup escaped her.

Lord Kharmd chuckled. "I knew you . . ." He stopped at the sound and motioned to one of his guards.

Kwiisa retreated further and turned to run, but tripped on her robe and went sprawling. Rough hands seized her and dragged her to the statue of Arnusi. The guards threw her down before the Mother and Lord Kharmd, who stared at her.

"So Kwiisa, mortification was not enough to keep you exhausted, you decided to spy on me?" the Mother asked.

No longer held back, Kwiisa's tears streaked her face. "I came down to pray. I have the right," she cried as she rose to a standing position.

The Mother turned to Lord Kharmd. "This is the one I was telling you about. She thought sending a message to Bjim B'nar might save her precious Temple and elevate her. Such a clever one, isn't she?"

"I only wanted to speak to Lord Dvari and give him my ideas as is my right as High Priestess here. Anyone might speak to Lord Dvari. But you . . . you monsters wouldn't want that, would you? There was no Vision, no high decree. You will ruin us for your own ends!"

The Mother opened her mouth but Lord Kharmd raised a hand to silence her. He stepped forward. Kwiisa tried to stand straight, tried to stare him down, but his pale blue eyes, like ice gems, bore into her. "I do not like girls meddling in my affairs. You have no idea what is at stake."

"False visions and the love of money are all that matters to you. What's at stake is the true religion," Kwiisa bravely countered.

Surprisingly, Lord Kharmd laughed. The sound rolled around the high-ceilinged chamber. "True religion? There hasn't been a Vision, real or otherwise, in five hundred years. Other religions are rising around us and Arnusi does nothing. If the false ones can flourish, can masquerade as real ones while our so-called real religion does nothing, maybe then it is all a lie. Either way, I will take control and bring this religion to the top by whatever means necessary."

"So you determine a religion's worth by how much gold it brings in? Truly you are a doomed man if you cannot see what Arnusi means to so many people still."

"Enough, child. I will not debate this with you."

"What should we do with her?" the Mother asked. "She is my High Priestess and Highborn. I cannot dismiss her without scandal."

Lord Kharmd said nothing for a long moment. "She is a virgin priestess, is she not? And now only to give herself in ritual consummation? But isn't it a shame that you discovered her consorting with men of low means for her own pleasure? Even her family couldn't complain at her dismissal then."

Fear snaked through Kwiisa. Lord Kharmd's calculating look and cool tone held no sympathy. She would be ruined. Even her own family would not take her back as a soiled priestess.

Lord Kharmd gestured to the two guards and they leered at her, one unbuckling his breeches. Kwiisa turned to run but the other was quicker and grabbed her. She struggled for her life but he pushed her down and ripped open her silk robes.

"Arnusi, Goddess, please save me! Please! I have been loyal to you. Please!" Kwiisa pleaded. Arnusi stood over it all, watching from her throne as Kwiisa continued to beg.

Lord Kharmd and the Mother laughed. "She doesn't get it and she never will," the Mother sneered.

The guard was on top of her, his heavy, sour breath inescapable.

Kwiisa continued to struggle while Lord Kharmd and the Mother looked on amusingly. Then both guards screamed, as if in terrible pain. The guard on top of Kwiisa rolled off of her. Both men pressed their fists into their eyes as blood ran down their cheeks, like red tears.

Lord Kharmd and the Mother stopped laughing, horror and confusion twisting their features. Kwiisa gathered her robes around her and scrambled to the base of the statue, sobbing and shaking as she prostrated herself before the Goddess.

Lord Kharmd suddenly grabbed at his chest, screaming. He fell to the floor, feet pounding the marble in agony. The Mother gave Kwiisa a terrified look then ran toward the main Temple doors. Before she had taken three steps, she too started screaming. Her elaborate hairstyle transformed from intricate loops of hair to writhing snakes. Her smooth skin crinkled before Kwiisa's eyes and her teeth fell out as fangs sprouted.

"Goddess! Goddess! What have you done to me?" the Mother cried, collapsing to the floor in horror.

A feeling that she was being protected overcame Kwiisa. Despite the horror before her, calm and peace had overtaken her. She looked up to find Arnusi in the flesh looking down upon her from the marble throne. Kwiisa once again prostrated herself.

"Rise, child. Do not be afraid." The voice, like golden liquid sunlight, warm and loving, flowed over her.

Kwiisa stood. "Oh Goddess, Goddess. Thank you for saving me, Goddess!"

"You deserved nothing less."

"I . . . I . . . have questions."

Arnusi smiled. "You always do. Go ahead."

"If you can appear in the flesh, why not go before the people, why let the false religions take over?"

Arnusi's laugh enveloped her in its mirth. "Is that what you think? Child, all paths come back to me. I will be reborn in a thousand incarnations in the future. Have no fear because the name changes."

"And what will become of them?" Kwiisa asked, indicating a now silent Lord Kharmd.

"Word of their treachery will spread. Do not worry. They were not as clever as they thought. Lord Dvari will make things right. As for you, continue to follow your heart." She paused to look over Kwiisa's shoulder, where the Mother lie on the floor moaning. "Her, I will take to a remote island. All who see her will turn to stone at the horror of what hubris and greed can do. Now sleep, child. In the morning, you will know what to do."

Kwiisa awoke at the foot of the throne of Arnusi. No flesh and blood woman sat there now, just the cool statue she had always known. Kwiisa reached up to her throat. A medallion hung from a silver chain around her neck. A snake-headed woman with fangs snarled back at her. Kwiisa smiled and tucked the medallion into her robes. She had work to do.

The Malocchio

Bruce Capoferri

In days long past, in a peaceful village located in the province of Italy once called Abruzzi, there lived a strong, dark and handsome young man named Maurizio. A stonemason's apprentice, he was fair and honest; a hard worker and a generous soul.

But his simplistic life took a complicated turn on the first Monday of October. Because, on that unusually hot and humid autumnal morning, he gazed into the eyes of such beauty that it nearly made him lose his mind.

"Aiee!" old man Paolini cried, swatting the young man on the shoulder. "I'm not paying you to stand around staring at pretty girls all day. Get back to work!"

"Wha'?" the distracted apprentice regained his senses. "Oh! Sorry, padrone." And then he hurried to lift another heavy stone into place. But he still watched the raven-haired beauty in the red dress out of the corner of his eye, drinking in every move as she sashayed enticingly away. When she paused to glance back and smile over her shoulder, he simply could not control himself. He dropped the stone on his foot!

Later, as Maurizio and Paolini shared a simple lunch of ciabatta bread, sharp provolone cheese and homemade sweet, red wine, the wiry, scraggly-haired old man said, "You remember that pretty girl you were gawking at earlier?"

"I wasn't gawking!"

"Well, in any case, you're lucky I'm the only one who noticed. You know why?"

"No. Why?" Maurizio asked, before biting off another mouthful.

"Because she's Don Giovanni's new wife, that's why!" Paolini said, jabbing the young man hard on his chest for emphasis.

133

"Aw, you're kidding," Maurizio said, between chews. "I mean, he's got to be . . . at least sixty-five or seventy years old, right? And she's, what, nineteen . . . maybe twenty? Come on. Stop joking around!"

"As God is my witness," Paolini held up his right hand to swear. "I'm telling you the truth. Her name is Sophia. And Don Giovanni just brought her back from his summer villa in Naples."

"Ah, pitooie!" The young man spat out the suddenly sour bread. "Now you've gone and given me agita! Does ruining my appetite make you happy, old man?"

"Of course not!" Paolini shook his head. "But I can see by the look in your eyes that you're still thinking about her. And, you must stop it! You hear me?"

"Who do you think you are, talking to me like this, Paolini . . . my father?"

"Be happy I'm not! Because if you *were* my son and I found out you were thinking such thoughts about another man's wife, I'd take that wooden mallet over there and knock some sense into that thick skull of yours!"

Maurizio glared at Paolini for a long moment. Then he gulped down the rest of his wine, swiped his mouth with the back of his hand, and returned to his work with a vengeance. And he didn't stop or speak to Paolini for the rest of the day. In fact, he didn't even say goodbye to the old man before leaving when his day's work was done.

That night, the young man tossed and turned. Every time he closed his eyes, he would see the object of his desire swinging her hips and glancing back at him over her shoulder, smiling seductively. And finally, when he did manage to drift off into a fitful slumber, Sophia came to him in his dreams. She slipped into his bed and wrapped her warm and supple body around his like a snake. And then, as they began to make passionate love, he looked into her infinitely deep blue eyes and . . . The sound of the six o'clock church bells startled the young man awake.

Following a light breakfast of biscotti dipped in a hot cup of espresso, the weary young man trudged back to the cobbler's shop in the center of town and began to mix the mortar. By the time the old man arrived, Maurizio was already beginning to lay his second course of stone.

"Nice work," Paolini nodded, absent-mindedly chewing on the stub of his wine-soaked cigar. "Are you still mad at me?"

"Eh! Not so much you as the situation," Maurizio grumbled. "You know, it just isn't fair that an old bastard like Don Giovanni should get such a pretty young thing as Sophia."

"My boy, wealthy old men attract beautiful women like a moth to a flame," Paolini said, fluttering his hand in the air. "It has always been so since the beginning of . . . Uh-oh! Uh, listen, Maurizio . . . I need your help over here. Come on! Hurry up!"

The young man started to turn to see what Paolini wanted, but unfortunately he glanced forward first. And then it was too late! As if in slow motion, Sophia was walking up the street toward him like an erotic dream. And poor Maurizio found it impossible to pry his eyes away from her.

"Don't look at her!" Paolini begged. "Concentrate on your work. The way I do!"

Maurizio gazed upon Sophia's exquisite face and, once again, their eyes met. Suddenly it seemed as if she was gazing into his very soul. The closer she got, the more the young man felt the voracious hunger in those eyes. Even though he sensed they meant to devour him, he willingly opened wide the windows to his soul and . . . suddenly it got dark. And very dusty!

By the time Maurizio had managed to wriggle himself away from Paolini and yank the empty mortar bag off of his head, Sophia was no longer in sight. Coughing and wheezing, doing his best to clear the dust out of his nose, mouth and eyes, he splashed water onto his face and cried, "Have you gone completely *pazzo*, old man?"

"No, but *you* have!" Paolini growled, angrily shaking his finger in the young man's face. "While you were flirting with his wife over there, I saw Don Giovanni and his two henchmen coming up the street over here! They all just met at the corner and went into the café across the street. Now, if I hadn't done what I did, he would've caught you staring at Sophia. And then, instead of laughing when he saw you dancing around with that bag over your head, he would've ordered his men to come over here and slice us both up into prosciutto!"

"Well, then," Maurizio said, wide-eyed, "in that case . . . I forgive you. But, did you see the way she was looking at me? Sophia wants me, I tell you!"

"Sure, she wants you!" Paolini exclaimed, tilting his head and giving his apprentice a cockeyed grin. "She wants you to make her husband's blood pressure go up so high his head will explode. Then, while she's gallivanting around happily spending her inheritance, you'll be hanging upside down like a pig with your throat cut, grinning with your new mouth from one ear to the other!"

Realizing the old man was right, Maurizio fell to his knees, cradled his head in his hands and cried, "But, don't you understand, Paolini? Just the thought of her is driving me mad! Even though I understand what you're saying, I am powerless to resist her. So please, tell me. What should I do?"

"Oh, sonny-boy, I'll tell you *exactly* what you must do," Paolini said, placing his hand gently on Maurizio's shoulder. "Before they come out of that café, you are going to stand up like a man! Then you're going to go jump in the lake and take a long, cold swim. That's what! Then you are going to go home and drink some wine. But not too much! Then you'll take a little nap. *And then* . . . precisely at the moment of sunset, you must head north on the dirt road into the forest. Continue until you reach the old stone bridge. By then the Moon will have risen. And, if you search carefully, its light will reveal a path on the north side of the brook. Follow it all the way up to the top of the hill, and there you will find the house of Signora Volpe. Knock on the door three times. And when she opens it, you will give her this." Paolini dug into his pants pocket and drew out a large silver coin. He pressed it hard into the palm of Maurizio's left hand and continued, "Then tell her Paolini has sent you to seek her help."

"But, isn't she supposed to be a wi—"

"Damn you, Maurizio! I'm not *asking* you to do this," Paolini barked, "I am *begging* you to do this, for *both* of our sakes! Do you understand? So, please . . . raise your right hand and promise you'll do this thing for me?"

"Yes, padrone," the rattled young man said, raising his hand. "I *swear* I will do it!"

With the pledge made, Maurizio got up, collected his things and departed. But, while he was a man of his word, he knew it would take more than a cold bath and a little wine to prepare him to do what Paolini had said. It would require him to muster up every bit of his courage.

North of the village, perched atop a rocky hill in the forest, stood the ancient stone home of a very wise old woman. Those who had reason to fear her peculiar talents called her *La Strega*. But, to the many whose lives she had changed for the better, Signora Volpe was revered! And, so it was that the slightly inebriated young man eventually found his way . . . guided to the threshold of the old woman's sturdy oak door solely by the light of the full moon.

As he hesitantly raised his hand to knock, the door swung inward. Raising a lantern up between them, the rather short and grandmotherly woman took one look at the handsome young man with the wavy, jet-black hair and growled. "Who dares approach my door at such an unholy hour? Only the extremely needy or the supremely foolish would so brazenly risk inciting my wrath! So, tell me, boy . . . which of these are you?"

Scared sober, the shivering young man bowed his head respectfully and stuttered, "My – my name is Maurizio. And I - I am truly sorry to arrive at so – so late an hour, Signora Volpe. But, my employer – uh, Signore Paolini - asked me to personally deliver this silver coin to you. And now that I have done so I – I will beg your pardon and be on my way."

Striking out like a viper, Volpe grabbed the young man's hand, then smiled and said, "No you won't. Because, while Signore Paolini is indeed a generous benefactor, you could have kept this coin for yourself. So now the token no longer comes from the hand of Paolini, but—in fact—*from you*. I sense something is troubling your soul, my son. Tell me . . . what is it?"

Maurizio brought his hands together as if to pray and then, shaking them before his face cried, "Signora Volpe, my heart *yearns* for the most beautiful woman in the world. But I must somehow push her out of my mind because—"

"She already belongs to another," Volpe nodded, matter-of-factly.

Shocked, Maurizio asked, "But, how could you know this?"

The old woman paused to peruse the wooded area beyond Maurizio's back. Then, satisfied that he had not been followed, smiled wryly and said, "The night is brisk, and forlorn spirits dampen the air with their tears. Come inside, my boy . . . warm yourself by my fire and we shall see just how many answers this single coin will buy."

Once inside, Maurizio sat down on a wicker chair next to a magnificent river-rock fireplace. Volpe poured two steaming cups of fragrant tea. After handing one to the young man, she settled down into a quilt-padded oak-wood rocker, gazed into her own cup and said, "The woman for which you yearn is named Sophia. The wife of Don Giovanni. Is she not?"

"Why . . . yes, but—"

"Have you looked into her eyes?" Volpe squinted, studying him.

"Uh, yes, but—"

"And, when you did, *what* did you see?"

"Oh, Signora, she has the most beautiful, deep blue—"

"And how many times have you gazed into those *deep blue eyes?*" Volpe demanded, staring intently at him.

"Only twice, but—"

"Ah!" Volpe nodded with a snaggle-toothed smile. "Then, there is still hope for you, my son."

"What do you mean, *hope?*" Maurizio begged.

"My boy, have you ever heard the saying, 'Three is the charm'?" Volpe asked, holding three age-gnarled fingers in the air.

"Yes, but—"

"If you had looked into her eyes but just *once more*, neither I nor anyone else in this old world could have done anything to save you."

"Save me? From what?"

"The Malocchio," Volpe replied, matter-of-factly. "Surely you have heard of this?"

"Uh, of course I have," Maurizio replied. "It's the evil eye, right? But, the priest in our church said—"

"Priests understand much about the theoretical workings of Heaven and Hell," Volpe said. "But, while they sit in their comfortable chairs studying within the sanctity of their glorious cathedrals, endlessly debating which sins to denounce in the present in order to devise a ritual to counteract evil in the future; Satan and his consorts run rampant every second of the day, joyfully sowing the seeds of sin and wickedness in every corner of the Earth."

"But, Sophia is much too beautiful to be a—"

"Demons wear many disguises, my boy!" Volpe cried. "And, in this case, it really isn't Sophia's outward beauty that tempts you. It is the corruption within!"

"But, how do you know all of this?"

"Simply because you are not the first to be taken in by those eyes," she replied. "At least three other men have succumbed before you. They were brought before me as a last resort. But, by then each was too far gone to save. Driven to madness, one hanged himself from a tree in front of the church. The other two now spend their days bound to their beds, foaming from their mouths like rabid dogs, howling and babbling incoherently."

"Oh, my God," Maurizio said, putting his hand to his forehead. "Is that what is to become of *me?*"

"As this creature is insatiable, and has already acquired a taste for you, we must expect that it will not give up easily," Volpe said. "Now, you could travel far from this place and attempt to begin life anew. But, most likely, you will continue craving this woman until you are compelled to return. But even if you managed to resist her, the evil that possesses her would only exploit her beauty and wreak havoc on others. Something must be done to put an end to this demon's hunger once and for all."

Mortified, Maurizio cried, "Surely you're not saying that Sophia must be killed!"

"Certainly not!" Volpe exclaimed, shaking her head. "Because the death of the host would solve nothing. The evil would survive and simply move on to another. No, my son! What we must do is exorcise *out* the temptress . . . and then confine it in such a way as to render it powerless. But, I warn you, attempting to do so will be extremely dangerous. Because even the purest heart that is the least bit unsure may not survive."

"Signora, asking not for me but for the sake of the innocent, what guarantee can you provide that Sophia will not be harmed?"

"My son, neither of you will ever find peace unless you do this. *That* is the *only guarantee* I can give you! But, if you possess the will – and the courage – I promise to provide you with everything you need to perform this task as safely as possible."

Maurizio paused to consider the old woman's words. Then, finding no alternative, he sighed and, looking her steadily in the eyes said, "Signora Volpe, for the sake of love . . . and all that is right and fair . . . please teach me what I must do."

The following morning, a confident and determined Maurizio strode back into the village. Upon arriving in the courtyard, he found Paolini struggling to place the final stone into the wall and hurried to assist him.

Surprised, Paolini said, "My young friend, as happy as I am to see you, I must admit that I expected you to be far away by now. Why have you returned?"

"It is very difficult to explain, my old friend," Maurizio said. "So, let us just say that I took your advice and, if things go well, we may all find a measure of happiness before this day is over."

"Ah! So, you went and saw her, then?" Paolini stared intently into the young man's face. "And, did Signora Volpe give you something to ward off the curse?"

"Not exactly," Maurizio shook his head. "But, I believe she has provided me with what I need to put an end to it."

Just then, the wind began to blow, and it carried an unnerving sound, like the howling of a ravenous wolf. The baleful cry compelled both men to turn toward the direction from which it had come. And there, at the far end of the cobblestone street stood Sophia.

Paolini crossed his hands to shield his face and cried, "Turn away, my friend! Or, this time she will surely steal your soul!"

But Maurizio stood firm and stared right back at her. And as Sophia began to walk toward them, he reached into his pocket and drew out what appeared to be a ram's horn. Fourteen inches in length, the hollow artifact was encased in pure silver and curved gently as it spiraled outward to a point. He grasped the Corno firmly in his right hand around its two inch thick base, then raised it proudly before him, and smiled defiantly.

When Sophia saw the silver Corno, her face, while still painfully beautiful, grew dark and menacing. Her eyes grew enormous, and glowed like fiery red embers. She let out a beastly roar and— swoosh— in a heartbeat, she was standing directly in front of Maurizio!

Smiling seductively, in a sultry voice she murmured, "This pathetic toy is a poor substitute for what a woman would expect from such a virile man. Throw the disgusting thing away and then I'll teach you ways to wield your true weapon to reach heights of ecstasy far greater than any mortal man's dreams!"

Maurizio paused, as if considering Sophia's offer. And, for a moment, it appeared as if he might accept it. But then, quick as a flash, he swung the curved horn behind Sophia's neck and used it to draw her face toward his. Then, he wrapped his left arm around her waist, pulled Sophia's body tightly against his own and kissed her. Ferociously! As no mortal man has ever kissed a woman before or since! He kissed her with such passion that the Earth trembled beneath their feet! And although Sophia struggled, her efforts only strengthened Maurizio's resolve. Even as the wind began to swirl in a tempest and the rain began to pour! Even as the thunder rolled and the lightning flashed, he kissed her! Love's purifying maelstrom left

Sophia with no other choice but to stare deeply into Maurizio's eyes and surrender her demon soul to the flames of passion!

And then, as quickly as it had started, it was over. In the aftermath, Maurizio held Sophia's limp body in a warm embrace. He gazed upon her creamy complexion, her full red lips and her soft, delicate features, and suddenly realized . . . the uncontrollable yearning was gone!

"My God, Maurizio," Paolini cried while making the sign of the cross. "Are you alright?"

"Uh . . . I think so," Maurizio replied, weakly. "Why?"

"Well, that—that lightning bolt!" Paolini exclaimed. "Don't you remember?"

"I'm afraid I was . . . uh . . . a little busy. Perhaps you could fill me in?"

"Heh-heh! Of course. Well, let's see: Don Giovanni and his henchmen were coming up the street to meet Sophia at the café again. Only, this time, when they came around the corner, he caught you kissing Sophia. By that point, it was too late to warn you. And nowhere to run even if I had. And when I saw his men flash their knives, I knew we were goners. So I started to pray. And that's when it happened! A lightning bolt like none I have ever seen before came down out of the clear blue sky and struck the two of you, making you glow brighter than the sun itself! I was nearly blinded, but somehow I managed to keep watching. And then something miraculous happened! That silver Corno you were holding seemed to soak up all the energy of that lightning as if it was a sponge. Then it flew out of your hand straight at Don Giovanni and . . . *look!*" Paolini pointed at a smoking circle in the center of the cobblestone street and added, "POOF! All three of them disappeared. Just like that!"

"Ohhh," Sophia moaned. "Where am I?"

"In safe hands," Maurizio whispered, as he helped the young woman regain her footing.

"So you say," Sophia said. "But, who do these safe hands belong to?"

"I am Maurizio," the young man bowed slightly. Then, seeing Sophia glance at the old man, he added, "And this is Paolini. My *padrone.*"

"Your . . . boss?"

"Yes. And we are simply two stonemasons who happened to be in the right place and time to aid a pretty lady in distress. So, tell me. How are you feeling?"

"Very tired," Sophia frowned, sweeping her ruffled hair back with her hand. "And confused, as well. You know, the last thing I remember was meeting an old man in a cafe in Naples. Can you imagine? He walked right up to me and said he was rich and was going to marry me. I thought he was joking! So I laughed. But then he got this sinister look on his face. He stared at me with such terrifying eyes. And the next thing I knew . . ." She swatted her forehead a glancing blow and added, "I'm here. Wherever *here* is."

Maurizio turned to the old man and exclaimed, "You see, Paolini? Don Giovanni was in league with the Devil. He used black magic to accumulate all of his wealth and power . . . and then -"

"Hey," Sophia interrupted, "maybe all this jibba-jabba makes sense to you, but where do I fit in?"

"Well, to begin with," Maurizio said, "you should be happy to learn that you are now one of the wealthiest women in all of Abruzzi. However, if you would like to know more than that, allow me to buy you a cup of espresso in that café across the street. Maybe a couple of biscotti, too, eh? Then, while you relax, I'll tell you the whole story. After which—if you wish to return to Naples—I'll make sure you get there safely."

Maurizio nodded slightly, then offered his right hand to her and asked, "Does this meet with your approval?"

Sophia gazed at Maurizio warily for a moment. Then, finding his face, demeanor and offer intriguing, she smiled warmly, nodded her agreement and accepted his hand.

As Paolini watched the young couple crossing the street together, he suddenly heard Volpe's disembodied voice whisper, "They make quite the handsome couple, do they not?"

"That they do, my love," Paolini nodded, while lighting the stub of his cigar. "Sort of reminds me of *us* at that age. No?"

"Funny, but I was thinking the same thing," Volpe said. "With the exception that you were ever more handsome and charming!"

"And *you*, my dear. Ho-ho! *You* were even more beautiful and enchanting. I could not help but fall in love with you . . . despite your hard-headedness."

"Aw, you wicked old man! Must you always spoil the moment?"

"But of course, old woman! It is what keeps my blood flowing," Paolini chuckled. "But, if it will make you happy? I apologize. Okay?"

"Apology accepted . . . you withered old goat!"

Paolini puffed out a smoke ring that formed into the shape of a heart in the air before him, framing his view of Maurizio and Sophia as they paused in the center of the cobblestone street. And when they looked back and beckoned him to join them, the old man smiled and simply waved them on.

"It really is a damn shame about Giovanni, though," the old man lamented after they turned away. "You know, I had such high expectations for that boy. Hoped he would eventually come to his senses. But no. He always had to be the big shot! The Sorcerer of Venice he called himself. Heh! What a joke!"

"Well, perhaps this will finally teach our son a lesson," Volpe said. "Speaking of which, how long do you suppose we should keep the little knucklehead locked up?"

"Oh, I figure about a thousand years should be enough . . . give or take," Paolini said, wobbling his hand in the air. "Any longer than that and I'd miss the little scooch too much."

"But, my dear, you know you can visit him any time you wish. After all, he'll be right there inside of that Corno, sitting on the mantle of the fireplace.

"Sure, sure, I know," Paolini frowned, swatting the idea away like a bothersome fly. Then, watching the happy couple enter the café, he muttered, "And maybe I will . . . in a century or two."

Fox and the Rose

Amy Holiday

Jordan Fox was late, not that this was unusual. He hadn't even planned to go to the Art Museum preview, but his mother had called specifically. "Please. The Peter Fox exhibit is such an honor to our family. And it would mean so much to your father if you were there. He's taking Uncle Clark's death really hard."

That was bullshit, of course. Jordan's presence was requested for PR purposes. His parents donating a famous ancestor's work to the museum; his sister's upcoming high-profile wedding; and most importantly, talking up Fox Run Manor and its renowned gardens, now on the market and actively seeking a buyer.

Jordan dashed across the Parkway against the light and the angry horn of a cab. He took the long stairs of the Philadelphia Museum of Art two at a time, then had to stop to catch his breath.

The exhibit wing was packed with museum members and press. He asked for a vodka and tonic at the bar, and spotted his mother's carefully highlighted red hair on the other side of the room. He threaded his way through the crowd.

"Jordan!" His mother raised her eyebrows. She whispered in his ear as she leaned over to kiss him on the cheek, and Jordan tried not to make a face. "Ted, look who's here."

"Son," his father shook his hand.

"Can you believe these paintings?" Mom gushed. "I never knew that Peter Fox painted all these famous people—Bette Davis is over there! And Vivien Leigh. What a career!"

"I told you, Betsey, he was the black sheep," Dad sounded amused. "Out gallivanting with movie stars while everyone else was working."

She took Jordan's arm. "And look, recognize this one?" She pointed, and Jordan spotted a familiar painting; a woman in a long evening gown from the 1920s, looking back over her shoulder. She stood on a small stone bridge, surrounded by the tall rosebushes of Fox Run, the family's manor home. The Schuylkill River glittered

145

behind her, and a much smaller Philadelphia skyline rose in the distance.

"Is that Uncle Clark's painting?" His great-uncle Clark had spent most of his eighty-four years either in the study at Fox Run talking to this painting, or caring for the gardens and creating exotic breeds of roses.

"That's our Nancie," Mom said. "She looks good all cleaned up, doesn't she?"

The painting was brighter, but the face of the woman in the long black dress was...different. Uncle Clark's Nancie had worn a little smile. This one had a somber, almost sad expression, her eyes wide and melancholy. He spotted the placard next to the painting.

FOX AND ROSES
Oil on canvas. 1928
One of Peter Fox's earliest existing works, FOX AND ROSES depicts the artist's mother, Annette "Nancie" Harbison Fox, in the lush rose gardens of Fox Run, the family home overlooking the Schuylkill River. Nancie, wife of Walter Fox, founder of the Philadelphia financial firm now known as Fox Martin Olivera, died only a few months after posing for this painting. By 1929, Peter Fox had relocated to California and began to make a name for himself as a portrait painter for the nouveau riche in booming Hollywood.
GIFT OF THEODORE AND ELISABETTA OLIVERA FOX

"She looks miserable," Annika said, behind him. She punched him lightly on the arm and said out loud what their mother had whispered. "Christ, you couldn't even shave for a preview at the Art Museum? There are photographers everywhere."

"I had a rehearsal," Jordan said, punching her back.

"Did you get paid for it?" Dad interrupted.

Jordan took a big drink. "No, Dad, not for rehearsal. But we're opening for The Pacers at The Troc tomorrow," he shrugged. "We'll get paid for that. It's a sold out show."

Annika's phone buzzed. "Oh, Mark's here." She looked around.

"Your more boring half," Jordan teased. Annika shook her head.

"Just because he's a good financial analyst doesn't mean he's not interesting," she countered.

"No, I'm pretty sure he's boring. He comes on the eleven o'clock news and that's my cue to fall asleep."

"Jordan, stop it," his mother admonished. "Mark Newton is a sweetheart."

"And when Annika marries him," Dad added, barely concealing a smile, "his father's firm will be that much easier to buy."

Annika gave them a round of dirty looks. "Who says Mark and I won't buy you both out? We're going to look at some other paintings." She put her nose in the air and stalked past them.

"What, and lose your downtown view?" Dad called after her. He chuckled. "Smart girl."

Jordan shook his head. "Greatest con artist ever. I guess it's not that much of a stretch, being a financial advisor."

Dad's eyes narrowed. *Oops.*

"Oh look, there's Jeanie from Philadelphia Magazine," Mom said. "I'll be right back." She slipped away, aiming for a tall brunette with a camera.

Here we go.

"Jordan, you know we've been supportive of your music endeavors. But don't you think it might be time to start earning some of your own income?"

Endeavors. "The band is doing all right. We have a couple of gigs a week, and I'm selling a lot of songs. The band is negotiating a studio deal. We're getting there."

Dad frowned into his empty glass. "You said you had a studio deal last year. What happened?"

Jordan sighed. "I told you about that. They wanted to take away creative control, so we broke the contract."

"How do you know this won't turn out the same way?"

"We don't, Dad, but it's a different studio and we have a better lawyer. Plus, we have a bigger fan base now. We're really getting close," Jordan mustered some confidence. They were not as close as he wished they were, but they were hopeful.

Dad gave him a hard look. "Jordan, it looks like we'll have a chance to get you in soon. There's an opportunity in inside sales. It's a great position to start in, then you can move up to anywhere you want. And it's salaried too, so you don't have to be so dependent on your trust."

Jordan kept his temper. This was a familiar argument. True, he depended on the trust, but royalty checks were getting a bit bigger. "Next month I'm starting some session guitar work in New York," he said. "I'll be there for ten days, maybe more, and I'll probably be invited back."

"Will that cover the rent on your loft?"

Mom came back, and handed them both drinks. "So Jordan, what do you think?" She turned on Human Resource Director mode. *They set me up again*, he thought, more annoyed than amused. He spotted the sad eyes of the woman in the painting.

"It's entry-level, but if you work hard, you'll pick it up and can move up quick." Dad wasn't quite meeting his eyes. "You could start for your securities license immediately, we won't be interviewing for a couple of weeks yet."

She continued, but Jordan wasn't listening. The woman in black glared at him now, and a low roar filled his ears.

"I don't know, okay?" He said, interrupting her spiel. "Geez, can I think about it for a *minute*?" He took another sip, and turned out of her trajectory.

"You can still do the band thing on the weekends," she added. "But this might be the best opportunity we'll have for a while to get you in at the ground level. You should really consider it."

Jordan wasn't listening. The rose garden surrounded him, a fragrant, thorny jungle of green dotted with red. The roar in his head was the little waterfall under the bridge. The woman in the black gown was still posed on the bridge, looking over her shoulder at him. Her face was angry. *Business isn't everything. You have so much life in you. Don't let them kill your spirit.*

Something nudged him sideways, and the roses disappeared, the chatter of the patrons returned. His mother and Annika were standing in front of him, two nearly identical sets of eyebrows knitted together. "What was that all about?" Annika asked. "You totally checked out there for a second."

He shook his head. "I dunno, I think I'm over-tired." *Whoa. Weird.*

His father was next to him now. "I hope you really consider it, Jordan." He hesitated. "We just want you to be successful, that's all."

"Right. I'm sorry you don't want to see me successful as a musician," he said. Annika opened her mouth to speak but he cut her off. "I have a sound check kind of early tomorrow, I think I'm going to head home." The sound check wasn't until two.

"Okay, well, think about it," said Annika. She looked a little worried. "I can help you with the financial stuff. And I promise not to be too bossy to the newbie," she said, punching his arm again.

He grinned half-heartedly. "That's not possible."

Mom pecked his cheek. "Come to dinner Sunday, Jordan. We're eating in the pavilion in the garden."

"The pavilion?" The pavilion was mostly used by the gardeners to store flower stuff.

"We've been cleaning it up since Uncle Clark died last month. It's a lovely space. The Newtons will be joining us, sort of a last hurrah for the Foxes in Fox Run." He realized his mother didn't want to sell the old house, despite all the plans and packing and publicity.

"Uh, sure, Sunday sounds good."

"Wonderful! Cocktails at five-thirty, dinner at six." His eyes were drawn to the woman in black again. Her eyes held an angry, petulant look.

He left the museum thinking about—and trying not to think about—working in an office and a securities license and the mind-numbing boredom that accompanied those things.

And running under his tumbling thoughts and the rumble of traffic, he heard a light, feminine voice in his head. *Business isn't everything, Fox.*

That night he dreamed of the dusty, dark study where the painting had hung his whole life.

The painting filled one wall, candles glowing in sconces on either side. Uncle Clark's chair was directly in front of the painting, and as Jordan sat there the woman spoke from her pose on the bridge, looking back over her shoulder. He leaned forward to catch the words, and in a moment the trickle of water from the pond filled his ears, and birds chirped high in the trees.

"I'm a little tired, Peter." Jordan caught the words, and found himself in the gardens at Fox Run. Surprised, he stepped back, and saw she had spoken to a teenager behind an immense canvas.

"We can stop if you want to, Mother," Peter said, his eyes on the canvas in front of him. She sighed, but kept the smile on her face. Dark red lipstick matched the prized roses framing the bridge, and a few strands of her pale hair flew loose from a tidy chignon.

"I'm sorry," the boy continued. "I know this is tedious. Thank you for letting me paint you. People are more interesting to paint than trees and roses." He looked up and smiled, putting his brush down and removing the palette from his left arm.

"It's nice to see you interested in something that makes you so happy," she said. "The world needs more art." She pulled off the elbow-length black satin gloves, carefully avoiding the sequins on the fancy evening gown.

"That's true," Peter said as he flexed his fingers. "More art, fewer stockbrokers."

Nancie laughed out loud, then covered her mouth and shook her head. "Don't let your father hear you say that."

Peter laughed too, but his face dropped. Jordan turned. A man in an old-fashioned suit and bowtie strode into the pond area, whistling. "What are we doing out here?" he boomed pleasantly. "Nancie dear, why are you all dressed up?" She held her hands out and he pecked her cheek. "And Peter, are you painting something?"

"It's not finished yet," Peter said nervously as the man studied the painting.

"This is a nice hobby, son," he said. "But are you prepared for exams? You'll need to bring up your arithmetic grade so you can apply to Columbia next year. Or maybe Penn, like your sister."

Jordan caught an unhappy look from Peter, but his father had turned away, offering an arm to Nancie. She took it, and smiled at her son.

"Walter, dear, Peter and I were just talking about how business isn't everything. The world needs more art," she said, folding the gloves together.

"Yes, absolutely, which is why I donated thousands to the new museum they're building down the river," Walter answered. "But being an artist is hardly a respectable way to earn a living—if one can be earned at all," he replied.

Jordan saw that Nancie gave Peter a small shrug as he arranged his paints. "Thank you for a lovely afternoon, Peter." Then she looked straight at Jordan with a familiar smile. He felt a rush of anger and a touch of sympathy, and an unspoken wish. He opened his mouth to speak to her, but they were gone.

The concert was even better than they had hoped. Tenth and Catherine's street team had gone all out spreading the word, and the band's small but growing fan base was on their game, singing along and calling for an encore. And the audience response inspired the attention of the CityPaper music reviewer, who caught up with Jordan for an interview at the after party.

After the interview, his drummer DeVaughn found Jordan at the bar. "Hey Jordan, we gotta talk." He ordered a beer and leaned on the bar. "We're losing our rehearsal spot," Dey said. "My uncle is moving to D.C., and turning the building into condos. Our stuff has to be out by the end of the month."

"Well, shit," Jordan said. "That sucks."

"I know another spot," Dey continued, "a startup recording studio. With the rental we can use their mixing board and borrow extra amps and stuff if we need them. But..." he hesitated. "It's another three hundred dollars a month. Is that okay?"

"Hm," said Jordan. "I'll check, but I think I can cover it," he answered, taking a swig from his beer. Three hundred more a month wasn't all that much from his trust.

DeVaughn grinned. "Hey thanks, man, that's awesome. I'll give them a call tomorrow and we'll set it up this week."

"Sure, just send me the address." Dey pulled out his phone. "Awesome. Wait until you see this place!" Kyle the keyboardist joined them, and they laughed about their new status as a band with official studio space.

Hours later, he slept, and found himself back in the garden. He *followed Nancie and Walter up to the house. Nancie still wore the* long black gown. The beige stone of the manor glowed in the sun, looming beyond the last circle of garden called the Sundial.

"I'm worried for that boy," Walter said. "His grades have been awful this year. Brother Stephens says if he doesn't pass all of his exams, he could be expelled from the Prep. And he spends his days out here painting."

Jordan followed to catch Nancie's reply. "He's been working hard. He just gets his letters mixed up, sometimes, and gets the arithmetic formulas backward. Evelyn has been coaching him. Although I think sometimes that might be a bit worse for him. You know how impatient she is with her brother." Jordan felt an angry spike of disdain, and it almost tripped him on the flagstone path.

"Well, maybe we'll hire a tutor. He can't fail, that would be too embarrassing to the Fox name." He pulled a rose off one of the waist-high hedges as they approached the wide patio at the back of the house. "Happy to see you out and about, my dear. I take it you're feeling better?" He handed it to her with a charming smile and a flourish. But Nancie frowned.

"Yes, I am, thank you. But Walter, I've asked you not to pick my roses." She took the flower from him. Jordan recognized it; they had been one of Uncle Clark's favorites. Deep maroon, it could have been made of silk. The petals were uniform, curled back just at the tips. The sepals bent at the perfect angle, and the center stamens were tiny pinpricks of yellow orange.

"Oh, yes, I forgot," he said with a half-laugh. "But you have thousands! Look at these gardens!" He turned and swept out his arm. Jordan turned also, and with some surprise took in the spectacular colors of the gardens; a maze of floral rainbow. The tall buildings of downtown Philadelphia were dark shadows down the river. The gardens he knew now were much smaller, and wilder.

"Of course Fox Run will win the Garden Prize again this year," Walter said proudly. But Jordan turned back to the flower that Nancie held in her hand, and sensed defeat.

Nancie sighed as they climbed up the steps, passing the artful potted flowers that lined the stone rear entryway. "But one makes a difference to the whole."

Walter shook his head as he held the door for her. "My apologies, love. They are still perfect." He kissed her on the cheek as she walked by.

"Mutton for supper," Nancie said, smiling and accepting his kiss. "Will you be joining us?" They passed into the cooler foyer, tan stone with white woodworking, and more roses, these every shade of pink. Strains of piano music echoed from the parlor.

"Afraid not, darling, I have a meeting down in the city. Martin and I have an important merger to arrange," he said, turning to her with a *wink. He crossed the long, open hall to his study. "I'm leaving in about thirty minutes. I'm staying at the Bellevue tonight, but I should be home for supper tomorrow. And," he hesitated a moment, "Evelyn will be joining me." He pushed open the study door quickly.*

Nancie halted in shock, then followed, slapping the heavy oak door wide before it could shut completely. Jordan slipped into the study behind her.

"I beg your pardon?" Walter was at the bar, pouring a brandy. "Our seventeen-year-old daughter is accompanying you on a business trip?"

"Nancie dear, she'll be eighteen in two weeks," Walter said. "Can I pour you a brandy?"

"No, and I would appreciate you answering my questions. What on Earth is Evelyn going to do at your meeting?"

"She's about to be valedictorian at Ravenhill, and you know she's got a great head for business. Plus," he capped the brandy and took a drink, "she's going to meet Martin's son, Stephen."

Nancie's mouth dropped again. Before she could speak, the study door opened, and a young woman stood in the entryway, wearing a trim navy blue suit and a little hat, carrying a small leather suitcase. "Dad, are we going to leave soon? Cocktails are at five. Oh, hello, Mother." She barely gave Nancie a glance. Jordan raised his eyebrows at her rudeness, but a sudden flood of fury made his head spin. A low roar filled his ears.

Nancie leaned on the desk for support. "I can't believe you didn't discuss this with me," she said, with a deep breath.

Walter looked concerned, and walked around to take her elbow. "Nancie, you shouldn't worry so much. You'll make yourself ill again. That was a difficult time for all of us. I don't know how we could manage—"

"I'm all right." Nancie straightened up and placed her hands on her hips. Jordan blinked a few times, and the room slowed its spinning.

"Good." Walter beamed. "Don't you worry, Evelyn will be fine. I'll keep an eye on her. Why don't you change into something more comfortable and rest until dinner." He pulled his gold pocket watch out of his vest, then set the brandy glass down and picked up his briefcase.

Jordan saw Nancie concede defeat. "Fine, enjoy your meeting. Pay my regards to Mrs. Martin." She shook off his arm and walked out of the study behind Evelyn. "And don't you dare marry off our daughter without telling me."

Walter laughed, and Evelyn snorted. "Not likely," said Evelyn. "This is a business meeting." Walter raised his eyebrows.

"Er, yes. All business." He turned the key in the lock to the study. "Have a lovely evening, dear," he said, turning to her for a kiss. But

Nancie turned her back on her husband and daughter, and climbed up the sweeping staircase.

Jordan woke up at noon with a vague headache. *The manor again, what gives? Maybe I don't want them to sell the place after all.* He hadn't given it much thought; they had used it as a summer house for years when he and Annika were younger. And with all his dad's grumbling about upkeep of the place, it had seemed a given they would sell the place as soon as Uncle Clark died. But maybe his summer memories were coming back to haunt him. Amused, he turned off the alarm and got up.

Just after five, he made his way through the maze of roses in full bloom, and found his mother opening a bottle of cabernet at a sleek mahogany bar by the pond. She brightened when she saw him. "Hi, sweetie," she said with a kiss on the cheek. "Don't you look handsome?" He rolled his eyes. Foxes had to dress for dinner, even the non-stockbroker Foxes. "How did your big concert go last night?"

She twisted the corkscrew. "It was a great show, thanks for remembering. We debuted a new song, got lots of compliments. The manager wants us back, and there might be a write-up in the CityPaper. Here, I can do that." She handed him the bottle, and selected a glass from the rack.

"Thanks. Your father is running late, so I thought it would be nice to sit over here and have cocktails first."

Voices approaching on the other side of the clearing made him look up, and in a moment, Annika rounded the corner, followed by her fiancé Mark, the talking head, and Mark's parents. Maureen Newton was looking down her nose, as usual, and Mark Senior was even more boring than Mark Junior. *Oh man. Why didn't I realize what I was getting into?*

"Hey, where've you guys been?" Jordan asked. He reached to shake hands with Mark. *Best behavior for Mom,* he thought. "Lager?" Mark nodded.

"I was showing them around the springhouse. The secret roses." Annika answered.

"Oh yeah, Uncle Clark's lair. Is there still stuff in it?"

"It's a mess. All thorns and vines. What are you going to do with all those plants, Mom?"

She frowned. "I'm really not sure. We are getting a lot of calls from Uncle Clark's flower clubs to donate to this society or that, but we really don't know what they're worth."

He poured a glass of red. "Hm. Since you're pretty much liquidating everything else, does it really matter how much you sell them for?"

"Of course it does," Maureen interjected. "The roses are all part of the estate. Very valuable when planning inheritances." She arched a perfectly penciled eyebrow and sneered. He had to grin as he offered her a glass of wine. She accepted, nose in the air. *God. Rich people.*

"Would you like gin & tonic, Mark? Or maybe a scotch?" Mom asked Mr. Newton, giving Jordan a warning look. He had to turn away so he wouldn't laugh.

"Scotch sounds great. Any word from Ted?" Mr. Newton asked.

Mom frowned. "The meeting out in Warminster went over. We're holding dinner until 6:30. I hope that's all right. I asked the kitchen to send out some hors d'ouevres."

They drifted off to the other side of the pond. Jordan stayed and cleared up the bar slowly, watching them posture and pose, inaudible under the burbling of the pond.

He made his way over to the patio, and settled in a hanging hammock chair. No one noticed him. Mom and Mr. Newton were talking about some kind of international financial crisis; he couldn't even pretend to follow.

Jordan's eyes drifted to the little stone bridge over the stream that fed into the pond. The bridge served as the border to the rose gardens, and the stream beyond was overgrown with trees and ferns.

This had been one of his favorite places as a kid, and it made him a little sad to think he wouldn't have many chances to sit here again. He dangled on the swinging chair, kicking his foot and swirling around. Annika caught his eye across the way and gave him an odd look. Superior. He raised his eyebrows and grinned. He kicked the ground again and closed his eyes. He leaned back in the chair, and the momentum swirled him back to face the bridge.

Uncle Clark's Nancie stood in her familiar spot. *The world needs more art,* she said, pulling off a long black glove. He released his foot, and the chair rocked gently.

Nancie waited in the stone pavilion by the springhouse. It was darker than Jordan remembered, a stone roof arcing over half the space. A fire crackled in the stone fireplace at the far end, occupying half the wall. The pavilion was impressive; carved statuettes accented the arches, and ivy covered the stone columns. White swaths of fabric swept around the eaves, roses punctuating the graceful drape.

But impatience rose up under his observation, and he matched Nancie's paces, from one end of the structure to the other, arms crossed. Jordan saw the table set for two. Hurricane lamps glowed in niches along the wall. A bottle of champagne floated in melted ice on a wrought iron stand. Nancie's heels clicked like the ticking of a clock on the flagstone.

Voices approaching on the other side of the garden wall, and impatience turned to anger. Jordan thought one of the voices was Walter. They grew closer.

"Well that's excellent, Fox," Nancie recognized William Martin's voice. "I'm sure this is going to work out splendidly."

"Provided you can get Duffy's buy-in," Walter answered. "You agreed, so deliver and we'll become partners."

Martin continued. "With Stephen and Evelyn's wedding this fall, of course the firm of Fox and Martin will be that much stronger." Jordan heard a note of self-satisfaction, and Nancie looked shocked. His heart sank.

"And I expect that wedding to be financed by you landing Duffy as a client." A quiet threat sounded in Walter's voice. They rounded the corner.

"Nancie!" Walter broke into a big grin, which Nancie did not return. "What are you doing out here?"

"You're late. We were to have dinner at six, remember?"

Walter looked around at the decorations and the lamps, now dim in the dusk, and recognition passed over his face. "Oh, goodness. Tonight we were celebrating our anniversary..."

"Because you're going to New York City this weekend." Nancie held her head up. Martin looked nervous.

"Oh, my dear, I'm so sorry. Curtis is a difficult bastard. But I think we finally made him happy...over dinner," he finished, shamefaced.

For a moment, the only sound was the fire crackling, and the birds chirping in the late summer heat. Jordan found himself furious, and stepped forward. But Nancie spoke.

"That's the third time this week that you said you'd be home. I canceled dinner with the Junior League and the Lippincotts, thinking you would be home. Peter and Evelyn and I had dinner ready. But your place was left empty. And most of last week, too. Although at least then, I was expecting your place to be empty." A cough interrupted.

"My dear," Walter crossed to Nancie, concern in his face. "I'm sorry. This has been such a busy month. We've done well, though. Evelyn too."

Waves of fury pulsed through Jordan. Nancie's jaw worked.

"I'll make it up to you. We'll go to the nicest restaurant in town. Next week, after I get back from New York."

Nancie grabbed the bottle of champagne out of the ice bucket and hurled it into the stone wall behind them. Walter and Martin jumped out of the way. The deafening crash echoed around the arched stone walls. "Happy anniversary, Fox," she said calmly. A smug sense of triumph made Jordan smirk, and Nancie turned to Martin.

"Congratulations on making partner." *She turned on her heel and stalked out of the pavilion.*

"Well," his mother's heels on the path made Jordan jump. His heart was still racing. *What the hell.* He used his feet to rotate the chair around. "No answer from Ted, and it's six forty-five," she said, annoyed.

"Maybe he's stuck in traffic." Mr. Newton was sympathetic.

"No problem," Jordan said. "It's more fun without him anyway."

Annika laughed. "I am absolutely telling him you said that."

The stone roof of the pavilion had been replaced by a wooden canopy structure with skylights when he was young. The columns, fireplace and low serving wall were still there, although crumbling in places. The space had been cleared out since the last time he'd been there—over ten years, he realized in a bit of shock.

"All right, everyone, let's have a seat, the staff is bringing dinner down." He took a seat next to Annika, across from Mr. Newton. A server poured wine.

"A toast, to Mark and Annika," Mr. Newton held up his glass.

"Oh, of course," his mother said, raising her glass as well, her anger melting away. "To a September wedding!"

Jordan faked a smile. "Cheers." Mark said something he didn't catch, and everyone laughed. So he did too, and the talk turned to wedding plans. *Possibly the only dinner conversation topic more boring than the stock market.*

His dad came in as they were having dessert. "Hi folks, apologies." He greeted the Newtons in turn, then went to the head of the table.

"There's a plate for you in the kitchen," Mom said, with a fake smile.

"Oh, no thank you. Just dessert will be fine."

"Well, none was brought out for you; I suppose you'll have to have some later," she said, brightly, taking the last bite of chocolate mousse and strawberries.

"How was the meeting with Roundtree?" Mr. Newton had to ask about his competition.

His dad sighed. "Didn't close. But we are in the final round."

After the Newtons left, Annika stayed to go through some of her old things. "We have to get a move on clearing out," Mom said. "An appraiser will be here at the end of the month." She shook her head. "Then we have to get the gardens in shape for the wedding." They walked upstairs, still talking about weddings.

Dad invited Jordan into Uncle Clark's study. "I've done a little clearing up in here," he said. "I keep getting stopped by Clark's fantastic collection of aged scotch." Jordan laughed.

The study where his Uncle Clark had spent most of his days was the one room in the house that Mom hadn't redecorated. The dark wood paneling, heavy drapes, and dusty red carpet was decades old. Iron sconces held dim electric lights, and the bookshelves were laden with ancient books. His great-uncle's worn red chair was still in its same spot. In front of it was a large, faded brown rectangle, where "Nancie" had hung for decades.

"Oh memories," Jordan said. "Shame it's such a mess. I used to hide in here and practice guitar when Mom would get after me about summer reading."

His dad went to the sideboard. "And your grades reflected that."

Jordan winced. "I still got into Brown on a music scholarship."

"Hm." Dad took a glass from the set. He held it up to the light. "With respect to his liquor, the old man was fastidious," he chuckled, opening a bottle. "We would have sent you to Harvard, scholarship or no."

"What are you going to do with all this stuff?" Jordan asked, changing the subject.

"An antique book dealer is coming to review the books next week," he said. "Otherwise, we haven't gotten that far yet. Your mother and the housekeeper are handling most of the details while I work on Solarlink." He handed Jordan the glass and got to the point. "Have you thought any more about the position?"

"Uh," Jordan took a sip. *Not really.* "A bit," he said. "I guess I'm not sure what I'd be doing." The liquor burned and he wished it was beer.

"You'd be helping existing customers make trades," his father said, pouring his own glass. "Some in person, mostly over the phone. Offering advice, but mostly making sales."

"You think I'd be good at that?"

"Well, you'd learn," came the reply. "There are plenty of opportunities to learn, and if you just applied yourself..."

"Dad, I have a degree in music. That has nothing to do with securities. I'm applying myself to music."

His dad nodded. *He's as tired of talking about this as I am,* Jordan realized.

"Look, son. You'll be thirty in October. That's five months. Contributions from the family trust to the individual trusts end the month the individual turns thirty, unless the contribution is matched by the individual."

Huh? "And what does that mean exactly?"

Dad sighed. "It means that October first will be the last addition to your trust fund, unless you are also adding to it. So as of next year, if you aren't earning enough to live on, you'll just be draining the funds, and eventually your trust will run out."

Okay. "How long are we talking?"

I don't know, Jordan, you receive a financial statement every quarter, don't you look at them?"

Oh. Those.

"I'm sure you won't be on the street in a year," Dad took a sip of scotch. "But that depends on if you make a bad investment."

"Well, how did Uncle Clark manage it? He was a hell of a lot older than thirty." *I really don't have a right to be angry about this.*

"Believe it or not, he earned quite a bit of income with his heirloom roses." He rubbed his neck. "He wasn't exactly competent, but he knew his gardens."

Jordan finished the scotch with a grimace. "I kind of can't believe you didn't tell me about this until I had five months left."

His father raised an eyebrow. "If you'd read your statement, you'd know. You probably got a letter last year, too. Annika figured it out, and she's still three years from thirty."

The study door opened, and Annika and Mom joined them. Annika waved a hand at the dust.

"Ew, it's gross in here," she put her hands on her hips and turned to Jordan. "So, are you going to take the job?"

Jordan looked at her, nonplussed.

"Come on, you know you want to work for me," she said, with a half-laugh. "I'll be the best boss you ever had."

Jordan laughed. "You've been the only boss I ever had, boss." He took a sip, then her words registered. "Hold on, what? Work for you?"

"He didn't tell you!" His kid sister looked at their father. "I'm going to be the manager of Inside Sales. Someone from the sales team is going to be moving into my old position, and there'll be an opening. And it's totally yours!"

His lip curled. "I'll have to think about it," he stalled.

"I'll get you some of the training manuals, and help you study for the Series 7." Annika took a glass of scotch from Dad and drank without flinching, much to Jordan's annoyance.

"Jordan, honey," his mother interjected sweetly. "I really think you should consider this."

"Okay. I will." He forced a smile. "I think I'll go now. Thanks for dinner."

He went back to his loft, but later that night he found himself in one of the upstairs bedrooms of the old manor.

He perched on a chair, so exhausted he leaned his head in his hands. Nancie slept in a four-poster bed across the room.

A tap on the bedroom door made him lift his head. Peter poked his head around. "Are you awake, Mother? I have something to show you."

She smiled weakly, propped on an arsenal of pillows. "Of course." She drew the bedclothes a little closer in as the door opened, and Peter struggled in, towing a dolly covered by a shroud.

"Remember when I painted you in the rose garden by the pond this summer?" He pulled the white cloth down, and then leaned the painting against the wall.

A flush crept up Nancie's neck as she stared in wonder at the painting. "Oh, goodness, look at that fancy dress. I had forgotten all about this. It's lovely, Peter."

"Well, it took a little longer than I thought. The gardener let me have some space in the west greenhouse, and I made it my studio," he said proudly.

Walter poked his head in. "Aha! I thought I heard voices up here!" He studied the painting. "Well, that is very nice, son. Very nice work on the roses, and the loveliest rose of them all." He came around to the other side of the bed and perched on the edge, close to Nancie, taking her hands. "You're a vision, darling." He kissed her forehead.

"Was," Nancie said, somewhat bitterly. "Was a vision."

To Jordan, the painting breathed sadness. Loneliness, regret, dreams unfulfilled, promises broken. The weight of exhaustion crushed him.

"Thank you, Peter," she said as she pressed his hand lightly. "It's just like being in my favorite place." She took a ragged breath, and held it for a moment. But the cough came anyway, exploding from damaged lungs. Jordan reeled against the wall, and tried to catch his breath.

A day nurse scuttled in, and Walter and Peter shuffled awkwardly to the corner as Nancie's lungs fought against the very act of breathing, throwing her forward in violent spasms. Jordan gasped. The room spun, wavering in and out of focus. Lights popped and flashed. Tears streamed out of Nancie's eyes. Jordan slipped onto his knees, trying to inhale.

Abruptly, Nancie held her breath and exhaled slowly. Jordan's lungs filled with air. Nancie leaned back with her eyes closed, controlling her ragged breath. The nurse fluttered around, fixing Nancie up, holding a handkerchief over her face.

Walter hovered over the bed, taking her hand. "Nancie? Are you all right?"

She took another ragged breath. "I'm dying, Walter, you idiot." She wiped her mouth with a fresh handkerchief. A wall of green filled the room, punctuated with roses dripping blood. A figure in shimmery black blurred, then eased into focus. The roar of the brook filled

Jordan's ears. "I'm dying," Nancie said to the woman in the garden. "And he's leaving again." The woman's face came into focus, a tragic, sorrowful figure.

"Yes, of course he's leaving. He loves his money more than you," the woman replied.

"Dad," Evelyn's sharp voice broke in from the doorway. "We have to go, we're going to be late for the party." What a bitch, Jordan thought, still on the floor gasping for air. The rosebushes disappeared, leaving only the patches in the painting.

"Nancie," Walter said. She opened her eyes. "We'll let you rest now. Evelyn and I have to go to a meeting."

"A party?" She was exhausted but she swore that Evelyn had said 'party'.

He hesitated. "The Kellys are having a party. We've been trying to bring Jack on as a client for months. It's a Christmas party. You could have come, but I didn't want to bother you."

Nancie pressed his hand. "Can you stay? Just sit, and talk to me," she whispered, angling her head back towards him. "Walter? Please."

"I've been trying to meet Kelly for months. But I'll come back straight away. I'll have dinner with you..." His voice trailed off. Nancie slowly shook her head. Evelyn stood in the corner, frowning.

"Goodbye, Mother," she said as she left.

Walter cleared his throat, and kissed her forehead. "You take a rest, and I'll give Martin your love." He patted her hand, then stood up.

She opened her eyes just enough to glare at him. "Tell Martin I hope he rots in hell," she said, louder, the rasp in her throat grating. Walter's back cringed as he walked to the door. "Business isn't everything, Fox," she said as the door closed behind him.

"Mother, I can stay. I don't have to go." Peter sat in the chair at her bedside.

"You're going to a party at Jack Kelly's house too?" she asked deliriously.

"Dad wants me to meet some of his clients." He sounded anxious. "But I can stay if you want some company."

"Son," Nancie reached for his hand. "If I have one dying wish, it's that you don't grow up and work with your father."

"I think Dad's expecting it," he added miserably.

"Your father lies," she said, and anger rebounded in Jordan's head. He stood and paced. "Foxes lie to get what they want. Foxes sneak around, and when you least expect it, they pounce and you're dead." She spoke carefully, controlling her breathing. "They're great at pretending, and they'll lure you with promises. But then they kill your spirit, stomp out your creativity, smother any hint of love. And *they walk away, and you're left in a beautiful, thorny prison with only the dust of your dreams."*

"Mother!" Peter's mouth hung open. "But...I thought you loved the gardens."

"I loved them when your father built them for me, when we spent time there together. I loved taking you children for walks, and I loved our time together this summer." She took in a ragged breath, and gave him a weak smile. "But alone, I hate them."

She spat out those last words and her lungs rebelled again. The room alternated dark, and light, blood red spots exploded, then faded. Jordan sank into the chair, and the room grew black. "Peter," she gasped. "Don't..."

"Nurse Pritchett!" Peter cried, alarmed as the coughs threw her body forward, unable to answer. The nurse handed her a towel, and patted her on the back.

"Peter," she whispered, between gasps, "You don't have to work for your father." Another fury of coughs.

"Mrs. Fox, please, be calm," the nurse was patting her back, and Nancie took a deep breath. Jordan's breathing returned.

The nurse reached to turn Nancie on her side, and she didn't resist. But she tucked her chin so she was still looking at Peter. "You have so much life in you," she whispered. "Don't let them kill you."

She coughed, a dry rasping cough. She inhaled in a faint wheezing breath. Her eyes fixed on the painting. A breath escaped the cage of her infected lungs, and "Lies" floated softly away.

A whoosh of air ruffled the curtains, and in the fury Jordan smashed the ornate mirror over the dresser. Peter jumped, and the nurse shrieked. The room was frigid for a moment, and the glass of water exploded on the nightstand. Then there was a distant roar, and the great painting rattled against the wall.

The vase holding three tall roses on the dresser toppled over. Water ran over the dresser, and the vase rolled. Jordan slammed it to the ground. Then all was still.

Peter and the nurse looked around wildly. Nancie lay still, her eyes open, a trickle of blood coming out of her mouth. The nurse took Nancie's wrist and shook her head. "I'm sorry, child."

The fire inside Jordan slowed, and his chest heaved. His eyes found Nancie's in the painting, and a cool, calculating smile spread across her face.

Jordan woke with a start. His heart raced and he was sweating. *Am I being haunted?* The thought amused him, but the dream was still troubling. *I barely remember that painting from the house. Why am I dreaming about this shit?*

He made coffee, trying to remember who "Nancie" was. His great-great-great grandmother? *Whatever.*

He focused on the pile of unopened mail tucked in a corner. He found the financial statements fairly easily.

He tore open the envelopes, and after a glance rolled his eyes in relief. There seemed to be plenty in the account, although in truth he didn't know how long it would last.

A few hours later, with scratch paper and coffee, he had reviewed the past two statements. He had about three more years on the trust fund. But then he thought of the $500 that was his share of the band's gig last night. He'd have to do that every night just to keep the loft.

Jordan sat a minute. Then he texted Annika. Her enthusiastic response came in about thirty seconds. His mood grew darker as he thought about having to take a test. It wasn't that he was bad at numbers. It was the idea of a suit and a nine-to-five that was bad.

Meet me at the office at four, came another text.

I'll get you the manual and we can schedule your test.

And don't wear jeans.

He fired back.

Right, thanks for the reminder. I'll wear my best swim trunks.

Damn straight, that's how you make an impression. cya then.

He worked through a song he was writing. The melody was off. After a few hours he needed a run to clear his head.

He jogged through the neighborhood and down to Kelly Drive, alongside the Art Museum. Signs advertised the current exhibits, including the one featuring his Uncle Clark's painting. It was a nice day in early summer, and crowds of people jogged and biked in both directions. Carefully landscaped gardens lined the path. He spotted a pack of elderly ladies walking his way, two bikers speeding up behind them with their bells dinging, so he veered off through the Art Museum gardens on the left.

The gardens were pretty; rosebushes and the big purple flowers called ro-do somethings; and lots of other flowers he couldn't name. Even the trees had flowers. He remembered this garden from a decade ago, when he was visiting from college one summer. Uncle Clark had donated some of his roses to the grounds and there was a ceremony of some kind. Something about the pink cherry trees and Japan. Uncle Clark had asked him to play his guitar, and there was a harpist, and there were Japanese musicians and drummers too, and it had actually been pretty cool.

And—the thought bubbled in the back of his mind—he hadn't gotten paid. The realization made him angry; he'd never thought much about money, it was always just...there. He ran under the pink trees, annoyed. If he was going to spend all his time thinking about money, he might as well go be a stockbroker, or securities salesman, whatever securities were.

The pale pink of the trees overhead turned into walls of green dotted with scarlet. Up ahead, the woman in the black evening gown stood on the bridge in the gardens at Fox Run, and over the roar of the water he heard, *Business isn't everything, Fox.*

"What the hell!" he kicked into a sprint and had to leap off the path to avoid a woman with a baby stroller. He bent at the waist, hands on his knees, the low roar in his ears.

"You all right?" The walls of green were gone, and the woman with the stroller was next to him, looking his way but not stopping, in true Philadelphia fashion. He exhaled, nodding, and stood up. He turned around and walked back to the Museum.

The Peter Fox exhibit was mostly empty this time of day. A security guard wandered in a nearby common area. A guy on a ladder adjusted a portrait in the corner.

Jordan stood in front of *Fox and Roses* for a while. *What is your deal, lady?* Nothing happened. He approached the security guard, standing at a booth near the outside of the wing.

"Can speak with the curator?"

The guard was suspicious. "Why?"

"This painting was in my family for a long time; I'd like to talk to the director about it. I'm not sure he knows the whole history," Jordan made it up as he went along.

The guard stared him down, and Jordan stared back. Finally the guard turned and spoke into his radio. Jordan paced around the gallery for twenty minutes, restlessly contemplating old-time movie stars he didn't recognize.

He heard a woman's heels echoing on the marble floor, and turned to see a young black woman in a pale green suit talking to the security guard. The guard motioned to him, and Jordan went back to the booth.

The woman stretched her hand out to Jordan, who took it, suddenly aware that he was a sweaty mess. She couldn't have been older than twenty-four, dressed impeccably with long curls and immaculate makeup.

"Hello, Mr. Fox," he said. "I'm Stephanie Douglas, assistant curator for the museum."

Jordan winced. "Please, call me Jordan. Mr. Fox is my dad."

She gave a little laugh. "All right, Jordan," she said. "What exactly can I do for you?"

"Yes, my family donated this painting, but...I was wondering if...I could have it back?" He felt his face get hot.

Stephanie Douglas cocked her head. "You want it back? I made the arrangements through your father."

"Yes, I'm sorry. That's not right, I can give money to the museum." He blathered on like a moron. "This painting meant a lot to my great-uncle, and it turns out there's not much left to remember him by. At least not once the old house is gone."

She knitted her eyebrows together. "Well, I'm not sure how this works," she said. "I've only been here a year, and I've had deals fall through at the last minute, but no one's ever asked for something back once it's been donated." They were walking through the exhibit, and stopped in front of *Fox and Roses*.

"I'll have to check with the director, but we'd probably have it appraised," she mused, "and estimate a value to see what it would bring at auction...." She trailed off and looked at the painting. "This painting has such depth of expression. From some angles, she seems sad, and from others, she's angry."

After a moment, Jordan answered. "That was what I came here to see. I always remember a smile."

Stephanie turned. "I saw her in the study at Fox Run. I swear she was smiling then."

But Jordan didn't hear the last sentence; the gallery was again wreathed in thorns and roses, the low rush and rumble of the water under the bridge filled his ears.

They all lie, said Nancie. *Foxes lie to get what they want. Foxes sneak around, and when you least expect it, they pounce and you're caught. Peter, don't get caught.* Jordan stared.

"I'm not Peter," he said aloud. "I'm Jordan."

Jordan. The wide, sad eyes relaxed, and the familiar smile returned. *Jordan, don't get caught.*

"Mr. Fox? Jordan?" He shut his eyes and remembered to breathe, and when he opened them, he was back in the Art Museum, and the security guard was standing next to Stephanie.

"Yes." He shook himself clear. "I'm sorry, this was a mistake. My family donated the painting, it belongs here." He tried to smile, but it didn't quite work. "I'll just have to visit."

Stephanie raised her eyebrows. "Sorry to take up your time. Thanks for meeting with me." He turned to leave.

"All right, if you're sure." He nodded and stepped away. She called after him, "Great show at The Troc on Saturday."

He turned back, and she had a small, restrained grin on her face. He waved. "Thanks."

A few hours later, he was back in his apartment with take-out and two enormous study manuals that seemed to have more abbreviations than words. Annika had (fortunately) been too busy to go into much detail, but she had still managed to throw a mess of confusing instructions at him. But along with that, she was being friendly again, offering to help him study in exchange for dinner.

He sat with his food and the first of the big books open in his lap. He had only gotten through about five pages by the time he finished the pad Thai, and it was like reading a foreign language. He tossed the book on the floor.

He cleaned up his dinner and stood over the book a minute. The sun slanting through the skylight was tempting. He picked up his guitar, and went out to the courtyard.

He sat on one of the wooden benches, and recalled the song he had worked on without success earlier. His notes were upstairs. So he played from memory, absently trying new chords, changing some words in his head to see how the combinations worked.

As he played, the bricks of the row homes surrounding the courtyard turned into the green walls of the rose garden, where he had first learned to play the guitar, almost twenty years ago. He picked up the song from the beginning, and the sound of the river rushing into the pond filled his ears.

He strummed absently, seeing the pond in front of him. Then he hit on a chord combination that worked. He tried again, and hummed the words with his eyes closed.

When he was done, Nancie stood on the bridge in front of him, surrounded by her roses. The desperate melancholy in her eyes made him uncomfortable.

You're a great musician, Jordan, she said.

"Thanks." He shook his head. "Wish that meant something in the real world."

Sure it does, said Nancie. *The world needs art as much as it needs business.*

"Tell that to Fox," he snorted.

Maybe you just need to get rid of the outside distractions.

"Like paying bills, and being self-sufficient."

You could be self-sufficient as a musician, too.

"I've been trying. It's a no-go. I'm joining the stiffs."

But you really don't want to.

He paused. "Hell, no."

She smiled. *Well, think about it. I'll help.*

He started. Dusk had collected in the courtyard. The bench was uncomfortable, his guitar was still on his lap. He rubbed his eyes.

What the hell, Jordan thought. *This is getting ridiculous.* The chorus he was working on ran through his head. He tried the tune, and it was perfect. He hit 'record' on his phone, and played and sang it all the way through.

When he was done, the young couple that lived behind him were watching from their doorway. "That was amazing," said the girl with a big smile.

Jordan grinned back. "Thanks. I won't tell you how long it took me to get it right." Back inside, Jordan sent the recording off to DeVaughn and Kyle.

"Dad!" Evelyn rapped on the door to the study. Walter's voice rumbled from inside the room. "Mr. Martin is here, it's time to go!"

She rushed in, pulling a winter coat over a pale blue suit and low heels.

"Dad, come on," she said, buttoning, impatience in her every movement.

Walter was in his favorite chair, a brown leather armchair in the far corner of the room. The desk had a layer of dust on it, but the overstuffed armchair was well worn. Walter sipped from the brandy snifter on the end table, and glanced from his daughter up to the oversized painting of his late wife.

"Sorry, Evelyn, what did you say? I was just having a chat with your mother about the state of the business," he said, shaking his head. "We made it through the worst of it in November, but the market hasn't rebounded." He drained the glass, then set it down with a sigh.

Evelyn almost stamped her foot the way she had when she was a child. "And you are about to lose the last client that can keep us in this house! Mr. Curtis has an opportunity for us and you need to be there."

"Ev, there's a car in the driveway," Peter pushed his head in the open door, rumpled hair and perpetual drowsy look.

"Thank you, Peter, I know," Evelyn snapped. "Tell him we'll be right out." Peter rolled his eyes and disappeared, probably back to the greenhouse. He'd spent most of his waking hours there since the funeral.

"Well?" She walked over to the coat rack and retrieved his pinstriped blazer. "Do you even have a tie on?" she clucked. "Hurry, please." She pulled a tie off the rack as well. It was wrinkled. She sighed. No time to change it. Curtis is expecting us to be at The Bourse at six."

Her father hadn't moved from the chair. "Ah, Ev, dear," he said, not looking at Evelyn, "Ev, your mother is telling me not to go."

Evelyn sighed with impatience. "Dad, she's not here anymore," in a tone intended to be gentle. This had become a familiar argument in the past two months.

"She's not here, she can't tell you what to do. Do you really think she'd want you to ruin your company by ignoring your most important client?"

"So little of that matters in the face of true love," Walter sighed. He poured another snifter of brandy. Evelyn dropped the tie in his lap and snatched away the glass.

"Dad, I don't think you understand how serious this meeting is," she said. "Curtis is our last big client. Please." She was pleading. Walter looked at her with surprise, then glanced back at the painting.

Nancie looked down on them both with the subtle smile. Evelyn shuddered. "I really am not a fan of this painting. But we can talk about that later. Can we go, please? This will be the last time. I know you're ready to retire. But we need you." Evelyn held out his coat.

Walter stood up, his eyes on Nancie. He gave a big sigh and looped the tie around his neck. Evelyn exhaled with relief, then crossed to the heavy door. "Hurry! We only have thirty minutes!"

Walter took the jacket from her and held it over his arm as he blew a little kiss towards the painting. "I'll be back tomorrow, my love," he said, voice dripping with honey. Evelyn rolled her eyes. "Fox and Associates is in good hands with your clever daughter!"

Evelyn tugged on his sleeve and Walter finally tore his eyes away from his late wife, and closed the door of the study behind him. They scurried down the hall, out the front and into the waiting car.

In the study, the brandy bottle hurled itself across the room and smashed behind the desk, soaking Walter's old files. The vase of roses tipped, dumping the water and the flowers on the dark wood table, water seeping into the green carpeting.

Nancie, Walter's rose, glared down at the empty room.

Jordan's phone buzzed, and he looked up.

He was working out the chords to a new melody, an upbeat melody that would go great with Kyle's steel drum. He'd been working for a few hours now, and was almost done. He made a note and kept playing.

A few minutes later, the phone buzzed again. He reached back to the end table, and saw a text from Annika.

I'm at the office. You're bringing me dinner, right?

He was a little hungry, but he almost had this song down. He went back to the tab sheet.

Another buzz. He glanced at the screen. *We're going over the stuff for your test in two weeks so I can get you this job, right?*

Yo, bro. Are you standing me up?

He grabbed the phone and switched it to silent, then tossed it across the room. It slid into the wall and clattered to a stop.

Nancie in the rose garden smiled benevolently, haloed by late afternoon light filling Jordan's loft. He played the song one time through, then met her eyes and grinned back.

Mrs. Rabinski

Richard Voza

10:28 AM. Each compression the EMT delivered to Mrs. Rabinski's chest brought back another memory. Spiteful pride and long-held grudges had knocked her to the kitchen floor, one hand clutching her chest while the other reached up toward the ceiling fan that slowly waved at her from above.

"I'm sorry," said Dr. Landis, "but there's really nothing else we can do. There's nothing you did wrong; nothing we, or anyone, did wrong."

"How long did you say?" asked Mrs. Rabinski.

"A month, maybe two. Anything beyond that is a blessing. A gift." He closed her folder that had been laying open before him on his large oak desk, and clasped his hands, leaning forward slightly. "You should probably start making arrangements as soon as possible."

"What is there to do?"

He looked straight at her without a smile. "Mrs. Rabinski, you were a nurse for almost fifty years. And it wasn't that long ago I told you to do the same for your husband." When Mrs. Rabinski said nothing, he continued. "Contact your lawyer, make sure he has a copy of your will, and make any changes, if necessary. But let your daughter know first."

"She really handled everything for my husband," she said. "Not me."

"Then I'm sure she'll know what to do."

Dr. Landis stood, circled his desk, and offered a hand to help Mrs. Rabinski out of the worn, leather chair that had sat there longer than the twenty-five years he had known her.

"Your daughter is a good woman," he added.

169

Richard Voza

"Usually," Mrs. Rabinski said, ignoring the doctor's extended hand and relying instead on her cane and what strength she had left.

"If there's anything I can do, please–"

"I think you've done enough," she said.

"There truly is nothing else I can do."

She stopped and turned towards him, blankly. After looking him in the eye long enough for him to wish his phone would ring, she said, "I know there's nothing else you can do. That's why I should have gone to someone else."

As Mrs. Rabinski rode the slow, electric chair lift up the staircase to her second floor condo, she sighed in annoyance as the sound of a vacuum grew louder as she neared the top of the steps. Yet again, her neighbor Rosario's vacuum hummed back and forth across the living room on the opposite side of the wall between units B and C in the Coral building of Renaissance Village.

Mrs. Rabinski reached the top, lifted the chairlift arms, and shuffled the few feet to her condo door, which opened to her living room. She tossed her cane on the sofa where her husband had spent most of his life, then settled into her familiar spot across from the television that showed her few things other than CNN, Fox News, and her Philadelphia favorites, the Phillies, Eagles, Flyers, and Sixers. She took a pen and notepad off the glass end table next to her, clicked the pen, and wrote.

Chinese delivery boy

Rosario

Dr. Landis

Alexis

She clicked the pen again and placed it with the notepad back on the table, along with her hearing aids. She glanced at the clock—7:12—and settled in for a short nap.

She had a dream, more of a recollection, about being fourteen years old and sitting in a classroom full of girls in dresses and boys in slacks and polished shoes. She wrote a note, folded it, and tossed it blindly to the student behind her who read it, folded it, and did the same until a soft yet pervasive giggle filled the room.

"Are we all finished?" asked the young, pretty teacher as she stood from her desk. Greeted only by silence, she stepped around the desk and watched. Everyone's head was low and every pencil was moving again. Her new heels clicked, her tapered arms folded, and her

170

admirable legs strode the aisles until she spotted a small piece of paper on the floor near the windows. With ladylike grace, she bent at the knees, eyes and chin up, and then stood with the paper.

Miss Alcott was touching herself in the ladies room when we were at lunch.

Two days and a handful of phone calls later, Miss Alcott began her summer vacation a little earlier than everyone else.

Mrs. Rabinski's ancient air conditioner rattled, hummed, and pulled her from sleep. She realized that Rosario was vacuuming *again.* She reached for her notepad and reviewed the names.

One month. Two is a gift, she thought. She reached for the phone, then squinted at the clock. 9:00. After a brief stint on hold, during which she exhaled impatiently, she cleared her throat.

"Order for delivery," she said. "A quart of beef and broccoli. Quart of pork lo mein. Quart of wonton soup. Six egg rolls. And an extra quart of fried rice." She listened as it was read back to her. "No, *six* egg rolls." She rolled her eyes. "Yes. 448 Thornwood Place." She clicked the pen a few times. "Twenty minutes?" she repeated. "Thanks very much." She squinted again, and saw it was now 9:02. She looked at the cane that lay to her left, but instead gripped the end of the sofa and pulled herself to her feet and headed for the kitchen.

In one of the lower cabinets she found a large bottle of vegetable oil and placed it on the counter top, where it stayed until she returned wearing her black coat. *Too early,* she thought. The cane watched from the sofa as she shuffled to the dining room table to sit for a moment. She gritted her teeth at the sight of the laptop computer that her daughter, Alexis, had given her for her birthday last November. The computer's outer casing showed the crayon scribbles from the two years it belonged to her grandchildren before it was eventually given to their grandmother with a mint green bow, her favorite color.

Mrs. Rabinski had always suspected the main reason Alexis had given her the computer was to avoid the uncomfortable phone calls every night. The awkward silences grew longer and the patience shorter, not just between mother and daughter, but for the grandchildren as well. They were only five years old, so they didn't know any better when they would whine, "But I don't want to talk to

Grandma" when the phone was still too close to their little faces. The kids and their mother could more easily tolerate Grandma by typing messages and sharing pictures. She suspected that it also eased their mother's guilt when they moved across the country and left Grandma alone in her condo. Instead of seeing her grandchildren once a week, she saw Estelle, the home health aide who shopped for her groceries and helped her shower.

Mrs. Rabinski peeked at the clock. 9:18 peeked back. She rose from the computer, took the bottle of vegetable oil, and headed for the door as the cane watched disapprovingly from the sofa. The electric chair carried her down the staircase where she flicked off the outside light and eased open the door to 454 Thornwood Place. In the middle of the day, the squeaky door was no more noticeable than a squirrel rustling a few leaves in a tree. At night, when things you can't see might be watching you, the door was more like a police siren.

It only took about ten steps for her to move from her home, 454 Thornwood, over to 448, the home of Mr. and Mrs. Williams, currently in Florida. A kitchen towel protected her fingers from the heat as she unscrewed the outside bulb just enough to kill the light shining down on the steps. Then she opened the bottle of vegetable oil and poured it over them. The cool temperatures of the late fall evening congealed the oil quickly.

The chair lift was still carrying her upstairs when she heard a small car pull up and stop abruptly out front. She heard no car door close so knew the young man, burdened with heavy bags, hurried towards 448. A smile crawled on Mrs. Rabinski's lips.

At 10:25, once the ambulance stopped annoying her with its flashing lights, Mrs. Rabinski picked up her notepad and clicked her pen.

~~Chinese Delivery Boy~~
She slept more soundly than she had in weeks.

Rosario next door was born in the Philippine Islands and came to America only two years prior when her husband, an Air Force lieutenant, retired from the military and brought his wife to the States. Unfortunately, the adjustment to living in America was more complicated than expected, and they eventually separated.

At first, Rosario had spent an occasional afternoon with Mrs. Rabinski, sniffling over tea and loneliness. Now, however, they did not speak very much simply because Mrs. Rabinski did not like people. Her friends from years back had all moved to an assisted living facility, at which they enjoyed many organized activities and excursions. Mrs. Rabinski sat home alone with not much need for company. Scattered visits with her neighbor were enough since her husband, her only real companion, passed away five years prior.

One recent day, Rosario asked, "Do you still think about your husband?"

"Huh?" muttered the tired, gray-haired woman.

"His name was Stan, right?" she asked. "Do you think about him much? Does it get easier with time? I guess it's been many years, right? Mrs. Rabinski? Are you okay?"

She was not.

Figuring that perhaps enough time had passed since she betrayed the trust of some friends, Mrs. Rabinski—Miss Lefkowitz back then—donned her favorite black dress, and arrived perfectly coiffed and jeweled at their party despite not being invited.

She wasn't inside long enough to even help herself to a cocktail before the hosts marched her into the street.

"You are not welcome here. You proved years ago you weren't the kind of friend we thought you were." The hostess turned on her high heels and rejoined her party, leaving Mrs. Rabinski out on the curb to look through the windows at the elegantly dressed smiling faces as they sipped their cocktails and mingled, enjoying the music and abundant food.

Standing on the sidewalk, she waited for a cab. Instead, a black Cadillac pulled up to the curb. A man in the passenger seat rolled down the window.

"Hey, doll," he said. "Need a ride?"

She estimated that his suit cost at least a month's pay.

"Depends where you're going," she purred.

"Wherever you want," the driver answered.

"You know the supper club at the top of the Madison Hotel?"

"Sure do," said the passenger. He stepped out of the car and opened the rear door for her. She held out a hand and allowed him to guide her into the backseat. He closed the passenger door and slipped into the backseat with her.

They never made it to the supper club. A quick stop at the driver's apartment for more cash turned into two bottles of scotch and an all-night party for three. She woke when the sun forced her eyes open, realizing she had passed out on the floor wrapped in a bed sheet.

She tip-toed around the unfamiliar apartment, gathering her dress and other items, and slipped back into everything without noticing her new collection of bruises.

Tired and hungry, she stopped at the corner bakery, hoping to get there before church let out and the line stretched outside the door. Ten people were ahead of her. Not bad, she thought. When it was almost her turn to order, she caught her reflection in the glass. She considered putting her head down and leaving until a voice came from behind.

"Boy, that was a great sermon today, wasn't it?" a man asked.

"Huh?" She only turned partly around.

"Pastor James, he was great today," the man said. "Well, he's great every week, but today was something special."

"I'm sorry," she mumbled, "I don't mean to be rude but—"

"Oh, gosh," he said, "where's my manners?" He extended a hand. "Stanley Rabinski. Pleasure to meet you. Call me Stan."

He was nearly a foot taller and glanced easily over her head. He tipped his hat, ignored the stare, and smiled again at the woman in front of him.

"Hi," she said, "I don't mean to be rude, but it seems I forgot my wallet and I was just—"

"Oh, here," he cheered. "Please, I insist. Let me get whatever you're ordering." He opened a billfold to reveal more paper than she had spent last Christmas. "What are you going to order?" She decided to stay and make the most of her new friend's offer.

Two months later, she would tell him she was pregnant. Seven months later, when she gave birth to a girl who looked nothing like either of them, Stan asked no questions. As she held his hand on his last living day, he finally asked, and she pretended not to hear him.

It was not unusual for Mrs. Rabinski to silently curse Rosario for having such smooth, olive skin and naturally black hair that made her 55 years seem more like less than 40. So when her ex-husband, Lieutenant Jackson, was thrown out with a little assistance from the police after Rosario called 911, it was no surprise that he was quite distraught. It was also no surprise when he secretly gave Mrs. Rabinski his phone number and asked her to let him know if there was anything that he should know about, such as men visiting his estranged wife.

It wasn't just Mrs. Rabinski who noticed Rosario's beauty. A few months ago, when the humid summer air turned up the volume on her arthritis, she asked Rosario to drive her to Dr. Landis' office. The volume also turned up on the old woman's anger as the doctor could not take his eyes off Rosario, and the attraction seemed mutual. Never in twenty-five years had Mrs. Rabinski seen the man smile so much. She thought his face would break. And never had the man been so eager to schedule her next appointment, requesting she again be escorted by Rosario. It was something Mrs. Rabinski thought about when she reached for the phone.

"Mr. Roth please." She returned the card to its proper place in her box of cards. "Mrs. Rabinski." She checked the clock that revealed it was 10:06 am. "Thank you."

"Hello, David. I want to change my will."

"Again?"

"Have you ever heard of PAWS Farm?"

"The animal place?"

"Yes. They take care of stray and unwanted animals. I want everything I have to be liquidated and given to them."

"Everything?"

"Yes."

"What about Alexis and your grandkids?"

"Everything. PAWS Farm. How soon can you change it?"

"Tomorrow. I'll bring it myself so I can witness you signing it."

"Thank you."

"Mrs. Rabinski, I have to ask, if you don't mind. Why are you doing this?"

She cleared her throat. "I like animals."

He cleared his throat. "I'll call you when I'm on my way."

"Please make it before noon."

"No pro—"

She hung up before giving him a chance to finish, checked her alphabetized index cards, and made another phone call.

"Doctor Landis's office."

"This is Mrs. Rabinski. Can I speak to Doctor Landis, please?"

After a moment, the doctor came on the line. "Mrs. Rabinski. How are you feeling?"

"Do you remember the woman who helped me to your office a few months ago? The Filipino woman, Rosario?"

"Of course. Is something wrong?"

"Well, you might not know this, but she and her husband are divorced, and she's been asking me about you."

"Really?"

"Yes. But she is a bit shy, so she asked me if I would help arrange something."

"Something like what?" She could hear the same smile that she had seen the day he first saw Rosario.

"Something like dinner tonight at seven o'clock." It was Mrs. Rabinski's turn to smile.

"Tonight? That's kind of short notice. I don't know if—"

"Well," she interrupted. "Friday she is taking a trip back to Manila for two weeks, and she just might stay there this time. Maybe you can give her a reason to come back."

"Well," the doctor paused, "I suppose I could make arrangements. What time did you say?"

"Seven o'clock."

"Is that when I'm picking her up?"

"No. She is too shy to go out anywhere and would like to make dinner for the two of you at her place."

"Her place? That sounds cozy. What's the address?"

"Right next door to me, 452 Thornwood Place."

"At seven?"

"Yes."

"How should I dress?" he asked.

"Dress to impress. And I can't stress this enough. Do NOT be late."

She hung up, cutting off his reply. She had two more phone calls to make, and again she plucked an index card from the box.

"Hi, Rosario. It's Mrs. Rabinski." She put her glasses down.

"Oh, hello. How are you today?" she said in her best English.

"I am wonderful, dear, and how are you today?"

"I am good, thank you. Is there something you need from the supermarket?"

"Oh, no, but thank you for asking," she smiled. "Do you remember when you helped me get to my doctor's visit?"

"Yes."

"And do you remember that very handsome doctor you met?"

"Yes."

"Well, I have a great surprise for you."

One hour and another phone call later, Mrs. Rabinski made her way to the kitchen for a tuna salad sandwich with two slices of tomato, the crust removed, cranberry juice with two ice cubes, and a linen napkin. It was 3:17 when she finished. She set her alarm for 6:30 before lying down for a nap.

As most everything in Mrs. Rabinski's life, things happened on time. At 6:30 she was chirped awake by the digital clock next to her sofa where she always napped, and occasionally slept through the night.

Her cane clattered to the floor as she pressed start on the microwave. "Stupid cane," she said, and after an arduous bend picked it up while her food, left unsupervised, scorched in the microwave. She despised the taste of most frozen dinners, but after the fire that almost killed her roughly a year ago her daughter unplugged the electric oven. Regardless of how many times she tried to budge the oven, it held its ground and refused to let her cook anything again.

After the microwave served up bland turkey and dry mashed potatoes, Mrs. Rabinski carried a bag of sour cream and onion potato chips to the dining room from where she could see the parking lot at the front of the building. At 6:55 a polished Mercedes appeared, but the driver stayed put for four minutes before emerging. Armed with a thick collection of white daisies, Dr. Landis strode up the walk and out of view. Mrs. Rabinski heard a knock on the door of 452 Thornwood Place, followed by its opening and closing. Soft murmurs could be heard through the wall between 452 and 454 Thornwood Place.

Mrs. Rabinski quickly returned to the kitchen to refill her cranberry juice and replace the two melted ice cubes. She killed all the lights before shuffling back to the dining room chair where she continued to gaze outside. This close to winter each day grew darker a little earlier. At 7:30, another car entered the parking lot. This one was a dark Jeep with what appeared in the fading light to be splashes of mud and stickers of deer and geese on the back windows. It did not park but only passed slowly before disappearing beyond her view.

Mrs. Rabinski pulled her chair slightly closer to the window and waited. Even in the night she could see a dark figure, silent and quick, move up the path and disappear below her window ledge.

Once again she heard the door to 452 open and close. Immediately, there were raised voices, high-pitched shouts, and guttural barks.

Mrs. Rabinski had placed her phone on the table next to her when she had taken her seat by the window. She thought about calling 911, but decided only if her door was forced open. Voices raised, then lowered, then stopped altogether, followed by the sound of one set of solid footsteps leaving hurriedly. When she saw the bright headlights of the Jeep turning out of the lot, she moved back to the sofa, found the television remote, and joined the Philadelphia Phillies in the second inning where they were trailing the St. Louis Cardinals 3-2. At the first commercial it was 7:59. She picked up her notepad and pen.

~~Rosario~~

~~Dr. Landis~~

Friday morning at 10:02 am, Mrs. Rabinski's telephone rang from the dining room where she had left it the previous night. Ignoring the cane, she rushed to answer it because retrieving voicemail was too complicated.

"Hello?" she huffed.

"Mrs. Rabinski? You okay?"

"I'm fine," she inhaled sharply, "just trying to get to the phone," another breath, "in time. Who is this?"

"David Roth, your attorney," he said. "Did I catch you at a bad time? I have your new will to sign. I'll be there in fifteen minutes."

"No, that's fine," she said, having caught her breath. "Door will be open. Just walk up."

Mrs. Rabinski rode the chair down the steps, unlocked the door, and then rode up again. She had just enough time to change her clothes and adult undergarments. At 10:17, she emerged from her bedroom, opened her condo door, and was greeted by her attorney as he stepped carefully around the chair lift at the top of the steps.

"Good morning, Mrs. Rabinski," Mr. Roth said. "Was there some kind of trouble here?"

"What do you mean?" she said, caning her way into the living room.

"There's yellow police crime scene tape around the entrance down there. Somebody get robbed or something?"

"Oh, no, not that I know of." She avoided eye contact and went to the sofa to find her pen. "You're probably busy, so let me sign the will so you can get on your way," she rushed.

Mr. Roth unfolded several cream-colored sheets of paper from a strong envelope and placed them on the glass coffee table. She quickly scribbled her name in three different places and sat back with a smirk.

"I'll keep one copy on file and return two after they've been notarized. One you keep here and the other goes in your safety deposit box."

"I'm out of checks at the moment," she said, "so could you please send me a bill?"

"As usual, not a problem." Mr. Roth organized his things, folded everything into a leather case, and moved back to the steps. "Have a happy Friday, Mrs. Rabinski."

"I will," she said and quickly shut the door.

She glanced at the clock. 10:27 glanced back at her. She found her notepad next to the sofa and clicked her pen.

~~Alexis~~

She headed for the kitchen but did not make it far before she was again startled by the telephone.

"What do you want?" she griped.

"Mrs. Rabinski?"

"Yes."

"This is Doctor Landis's office." The old woman suddenly stood straighter than she had in a week. "Something horrible has happened."

Mrs. Rabinski tried to conceal a grin, but her solitude made hiding things unnecessary. "Something horrible? Whatever could that be?" The smile spread across her face like butter melting across pancakes on a griddle.

"Your test results from Doctor Landis got mixed up with another patient. A Mrs. Rabinowitz. Yours all came back negative. You have well more than only a month to live. We're very sorry for the mix up, but I'm sure you must be thrilled that there was a mistake. So, please, accept our apologies, Mrs. Rabinski."

Silence.

"Hello? Mrs. Rabinski? Are you there?"

"I. I. Yes, I'm here."

"Are you okay? Did you hear what I said? About the test results?"

"Is Doctor Landis there?" the old woman asked.

"No. And that's odd. He's never late. He should have been here an hour ago. I've been trying to call him but there's no answer. The important thing is that your tests are fine and you're as healthy as can be at your age."

Mrs. Rabinski hung up. Less than a deep breath later there was a knock on the door.

"Hello?" came a voice through the door. "Anyone home?"

"Y-yes?" she stammered as she approached the door. "Who is it?" Peeking through the peephole she saw a man in blue with a silver badge and shaved head.

She opened the door.

"Are you Mrs. Rabinski?" he asked.

"Yes." She wiped at her open mouth as saliva escaped from one corner.

"Ma'am, are you aware that there was trouble next door last night?"

"T-trouble?" She felt behind her for the back of the sofa as tears blurred her vision.

"Are you okay, ma'am?" asked the officer. "You want me to call someone? An ambulance?"

"T-trouble?" she repeated.

"Next door," he said. "There was a homicide there last night and . . . Ma'am, you don't look well."

"T-trouble?" She backed into the kitchen while reaching for the countertop with weak fingers.

"There's an ambulance already here for the woman next door," the officer said. "I can go get one of the EMTs for you."

"Homicide?" she mumbled.

"The woman next door. Her ex-husband beat her up something awful, and she died from the injuries. That's why I'm here, Ma'am. There was a witness, a doctor actually, who said you might know something about it. I have a few questions to ask you, but we can wait until you feel better."

Mrs. Rabinski's vision blurred and it was as if the volume was suddenly turned down on her hearing aids. She wobbled, but the officer reached for her too late, and she landed flat on the floor. The officer was already halfway down the steps before her head rebounded off the linoleum and came to a rest. He quickly returned with an EMT from next door.

Although her vision grew darker she could still make out the glowing red digital 10:28 on the microwave. Each compression the EMT delivered to Mrs. Rabinski's chest brought back another memory. Spiteful pride and long-held grudges had knocked her to the kitchen floor, one hand clutching her chest, while the other reached up toward the ceiling fan that slowly waved at her from above.

Somewhere, far away, she could hear a faint voice with a familiar accent. "Come on, you old bitch. I'm waiting for you."

From the corner of her fading eye she could see the time. 10:29. She did not know which would be better – to live, or not live, to see 10:30.

The Passing of Millie Hudson

J. Keller Ford

Millie cried off and on during the whole car ride back to her old stomping grounds of Dawsonville, Georgia. See, four days ago she got the news her sister, Emma, passed on and well, poor Millie just fell apart. Can't say I blame her. Seeing her sister was gone now, that left Millie the last descendent in a long line of Hudsons, and being a spinster, she ain't never had no kids of her own. Now, Emma on the other hand, been married three times and had a couple of grown-up kids somewhere — last I heard, one had disappeared somewhere in Nevada; the other was living the fancy life in England.

Over the years, Millie'd listen to her sister lament about how she never knew how them kids were getting along and it made Millie so angry sometimes thinking about them rotten youngins. Lawdy, she'd bitch and moan for hours about the way those inconsiderate brats left their mama all alone in that big house out in the middle of nowhere. Now, sitting in the back seat of the Mercedes, she wondered aloud how they'd reacted to the news of their mama's death, if they'd heard the news a'tall.

Millie slapped her gloved hand on the back of the front seat making me and that sweet young driver and caregiver, Jacob, flinch.

"Oh, what am I saying? Of course they've heard. Tell those rotten kids their mama hasn't got much time on this earth and they don't even bother sending her a damn get-well card. But watch. Now they know she's dead, they'll be swarming like vultures wanting a piece of this, a piece of that. Why, they're probably already fighting over who's getting the silverware and china. Trust me. Emma won't be five minutes in her grave before those kids will be putting their names on every damn thing in that house." Millie folded her frail hands in her

183

lap and looked out the window. I saw a slight smile reflect in the tinted glass. "But I've got news for them," she continued. "That house is mine and they'll have to walk on my grave before they take a dust bunny from the premises."

I smiled and shifted in the backseat, unfurling my legs. Now that's my Millie, feisty as ever.

Millie's arthritis started acting up something terrible about an hour outside her hometown and the rain pounding on our car — well it ain't helped a bit. It just made her cough worse and made the ground all soggy and such. I worry about my Millie. She's got a chronic cough, and lately she's taken to having those clear tubes stuck in her nose and a noisy clicky machine that breathes for her. But in spite of all her ailments, she ain't never looked back and felt sorry for herself. She's had a good eighty-one years on this God's green earth and she'd always taken mighty right good care of me over the years. Yep. You won't ever find a better friend than Millie Hudson.

It had taken about three hours to make the drive from Jonesboro to Millie's childhood home in the Blue Ridge Mountains. We stopped at the old general store at Millie's insistence 'cause she just had to have a Coca Cola. Millie loves them Coca Colas. She ain't supposed to have them, being all sickly and such, but she figured the good Lawd gonna take her soon anyways, she might as well be happy. Jacob came back out shielded beneath an umbrella with the owner of the store, Mr. McMurry, at his side. I tell you what. I thought me and Millie was old, but this man — well, he looked like he'd done died and risen again, all skin and bones, but mostly bones. He shuffled over to the car and peeked his powder blue eyes over the top of the window that Millie'd lowered just a little. He offered his condolences then waved us off on our way. Looking at him I must say I suspect he's going to be right behind Millie soon, finding his final resting spot 'neath the azaleas.

We traveled on for a while bouncing and flouncing over the pot-holed roads. Finally, as if God had no more tears to spend, the rain let up and the sun poked its bright head out from behind them old rain clouds. That was right near the time Jacob turned down the old familiar road, the wheels grinding and spitting out the gravel. Millie sat more upright now and slid a little closer to me, though her eyes were focused straight ahead.

Now I gotta tell you, seeing Millie's face light up at her childhood home at the end of the long drive made me happier than a dog in a pool full of raw steaks. The two-story farmhouse, with its gingerbread trim, spindles and round towers, still wore a luxurious coat of bright lemon-yellow. The sky-blue shutters were a little chipped and faded, exposing the wood's natural sensibility and age. Vibrant wild flowers and honeysuckle crept over the prize-winning gardens, and in the front yard, an old horse-drawn carriage tilted up on a tree stump, one metal wheel still deeply rooted in the half-parched lawn. Can't say much was left of the picket fence Millie and I used to play on when we was little; many of its railings have broken or disappeared altogether. As we pulled to a stop, my eyes wandered toward the lone headstone in the side yard. Mama Hudson. To my amazement it still stood strong and upright with the same strength and fortitude of the old woman it honors.

We stepped from the cool comfort of the climate-controlled car into the sweltering Georgia sun. I stretched a bit and lifted my face to the sky, breathing in the scent of the mountains. There's nothing like the smell of earth after a good rain. I glanced over at Millie to make sure she was alright. She pulled her sweater tight about her and re-stuck a bobby pin in the silver bun resting on the nape of her neck. As she waited for Jacob to hook up her breathing equipment, I took a short look around. Lawd, the heat was suffocating, but them robins and blue jays, they don't seem to pay no never mind. They just flitted about, squawking and singing like they be praising the heavens or something.

I stood there buried in my own thoughts watching them birds rustling round the ole oak tree when I heard Millie shuffle up behind me. "My, my," she says. "Look at them. Just as happy as can be. Oh, what I wouldn't do to be one of them for a day, to not worry about anything, especially good for nothing relatives. To not even be privy to my own mortality, but to live each second of every day as nature intended."

I stood still and quiet like I always do when Millie gets into these reflective moods. Sometimes it's just best to listen. Otherwise she gets a little cantankerous, especially if you disagree with her. Why, I remember one time she dumped a bushel of fresh picked green beans on Emma's head just because she said the violets in the field were purple in color, not lavender. I'd never seen two kids argue over something so stupid. Millie'd turned to me at the time and asked me

185

what I thought, but I knew better. Uh uh. I wasn't gonna get in the middle of that one so I got up and went about my business. That's what you had to do with Millie. When she got something set in her head it'd do you good if you just went along, no matter how wrong she might be. It kept the peace, and peace was always a good thing in the Hudson household.

We climbed the five weathered steps to the front porch. A breeze came around the corner unexpected like and caught Millie by surprise. She closed her eyes and tilted her head back. "My, oh my, I can almost smell the biscuits baking. It's been a long time, Jacob." She took his hand. "How about you open these doors and let me inside my home."

Jacob fiddled with the key and inserted it into the old-fashioned lock. The tumblers turned as his hand wrapped around the iron doorknob. The door opened to our past.

I could see nostalgia sweep over Millie's face as we stepped over the threshold into the antechamber. The cherry wood hat stand her Uncle Jake had made still stood in the corner next to the bench her grandfather had built from the same tree. Tears filled her eyes as she stroked a gloved hand along the strong wood.

"I never told you the story about this hat stand did I, Jacob?"

The young man removed his chauffeur hat and shook his head. "No, ma'am, Miss Millie."

Millie withdrew her soft, speckled hands from her gloves and sat down on the bench, her fingertips brushing the haze from the red wood. "I must have been about four, five years of age. There was this horrible storm. I remember flinging myself into the big feather bed with Mama and Daddy, and hiding under the covers. The wind howled something fierce and the rain fell in blinding sheets all night long. Thunder rolled across the sky, shaking the house with each boom, and lightning cracked like a whip. Then something mighty large, like a monstrous beast, crashed to the ground.

"Shivering, I curled my tiny body up next to Daddy, Emma nestled beside Mama, and I remember feeling so safe, as if nothing could ever harm me so long as I lay in Daddy's big, strong arms. He became my hero that night.

"Looking back, I suppose you could say it's because of him I never got married. No matter how hard I looked, no matter how many cotillions I attended, I never could find another man out there with my daddy's saintly soul. He was so kind, such a soft-spoken man, and my, my, was he ever so gentle. You know, I don't remember ever hearing him say a bad word about anyone to anyone, and Lord have mercy, when he sang in the Sunday choir, his deep voice rattled the foundation of the church." A smile rested on her lips for a minute, then it disappeared.

"Anyway, the next morning we woke to sunlight filtering through the windows, dazzling the wallpaper dotted with blue forget-me-nots. The smell of bacon and sausage greeted Emma and me as we made our way to the kitchen. The back porch door was open and I followed Daddy outside. I couldn't believe my eyes when I saw the beautiful cherry tree, fresh with new fragrant springtime blossoms, laying on its side, its roots naked and exposed to the sky. Oh, my, how sad I felt, as if there were something unjust about its demise.

"I remember helping Grams make biscuits that morning. She asked why I looked so downtrodden and I told her. She poured buttermilk over my fingers and helped my small hands knead the soft dough. As she did, she said to me, 'Millie, all things have their time and their seasons. Everything that lives must die. What matters most is not the manner in which life leaves this world; rather it's how others remember the brilliance in the way it lived.' My daddy cut a few sprigs of cherry blossoms. Grams placed them in a special magic vase. 'Together we'll celebrate that magnificent tree's glorious life,' she said." Millie hesitated for a moment and added, "Do you know, Jacob, the buds on those cut sprigs bloomed for nearly two weeks?"

Jacob smiled and opened the interior doors into the hallway leading to the kitchen. I glanced up the stairs to my right, anxious to return to Millie's old room where we used to play for hours, but that would come later. Millie had to say hello to the rest of the home she ain't seen in many years.

We walked down the dark hallway, the floorboards creaking beneath every step. Millie stopped in the threshold of the living room and looked around. She must have been thinking about her mama 'cause the tears started flowing, not so hard like but enough to make her sniffle and wipe her eyes.

"Are you all right, Miss Millie?" Jacob asked. He's such a nice man, that Jacob.

Millie nodded. "I spent many a day in this room, sitting in that couch over there, the one covered in pink rosebuds, listening to Mama tell me her stories of growing up. She taught me how to sew and read in this room. She died in that old chair over there next to the window, a knitting needle in her hand. Oh, how she loved to knit. And she loved that window where she could look out onto the yard and watch Emma and me play." Her voice choked up a little. "Poor Emma. She was the one who found Mama, all crumpled over her latest sewing project, a blanket she was making for Emma's first born. It nearly broke our hearts. It did break Papa's and I guess God knew it because it was no more than six months later he got struck by lightning while out in the field.

We wanted to bury him next to Mama, but his hoity-toity family had such a conniption we finally agreed to let them take him back to Mount Airy, North Carolina. God bless him, he was only fifty-nine years old when he passed. He had no one but us kids, and his two brothers and sister. It's heartbreaking, you know, to have family but never hear nary a word from any of them. Oh well. I guess it doesn't matter where you're buried, does it, as long as you're in the afterlife together?"

We followed Millie from the room, down the hall past the bathroom and formal dining room, which to my knowledge was never used for nothing more than storage, and made our way into the kitchen. Except for the sink stacked with two plates and a couple of glasses, it was just the way I remembered, bright and airy with lots of windows looking out onto the big back yard. Millie brushed her fingertips over the laminated countertop then, appearing somewhat tired, sat down on the long bench seat next to the dining table. Jacob rummaged through the cabinets and brought down a glass, filled it with ice and water, and brought it to Millie who thanked him graciously. We'd sat there no more than five minutes, basking in the peace and quiet, when Lawd have mercy, the front door bangs open and lets in a rambling mess of folks.

I ain't heard so much racket in all my born days. "Bobby Jean, stop running." "Philip, get down off those steps." Why, it sounded like the circus done come to town and the high wire acts were getting their practice in. A herd of footsteps came clomping down the hallway into the kitchen. We all looked up to see Sarah Jane, Emma's first born, stalk into the room all dressed in some garish excuse for clothing. I laughed inside at Millie's face. It got all tight, her jaw set rigid, her eyes got all small and beady like. No, there weren't no love lost between them two.

Sarah Jane kicked off those high heel shoes and hurried over to Millie, falling to her knees and wrapping her arms around Millie. "Oh,

Aunt Millie," she blubbered away. "I'm so glad you came. I don't know what I'm going to do without Mama."

The caterwauling didn't seem like it was ever gonna end. Lawd, that girl's lungs could move some air. Finally, Millie had enough and pushed her away.

"Stop that hawking and crying, young lady. You should have thought more about your mama when she was alive, taking off like that to Nevada, never writing or calling unless you wanted something. You should be ashamed of yourself, child."

Sarah Jane stood up all straight like and fixed herself up a bit, tucking her yellow hair behind her ears. "Well, I got married, Aunt Millie. John's job was in Reno, so it's not like I had much choice."

"We all got choices, Sarah Jane." She peered around her nieces wide hips. "So who are the scallywags you brought with you?"

Sarah Jane stiffened and pursed her lips. She motioned for her children to stand beside her. "Bobby Jean, Phillip, say hello to your great-Aunt Millie."

"I don't want to," whined Philip, a pudgy kid of about nine years of age.

"Me neither, Mommy," curly, red-haired Bobby Jean said. "What's wrong with her anyway? Is she going to die, too? What are all those tubes for?"

Sarah Jane gasped. "Bobby Jean! You shouldn't say things like that. It's not proper."

Millie stood and shuffled forward. She reached up and patted Sarah Jane on the cheek. "Don't try to teach them manners now, dear. It's too late."

I have to say the look on Sarah Jane's face was plumb-right priceless. Millie smiled as she walked past her and down the hall. Almost to the stairs, the front door burst open again, this time letting in a meek little man with round glasses and a banker's look about him. Next to him stood his equally short, plump wife dressed in a more demure manner than Millie's niece.

"Hello, Brock," Millie said with a groan. "I see you made it to the funeral. I'm surprised, seeing you never ventured here for Christmas or any other holiday for that matter."

"I've been in Europe. Surely, Mother told you. I've been teaching economics at Oxford."

"Your mother didn't know where you were, Brock, as you haven't spoken to her in over five years. Funny how you can't even send one letter, but you get a phone call, I'm supposing from your sister, telling you your mother passed away and you're here on the next plane. How convenient for you." She patted him on the cheek. "You're such a fine son." She started up the stairs.

"I take offense to your tone, Aunt Millie," Brock says in that uppity foreign accent he's acquired, all the while tugging on his jacket and tightening the striped noose around his neck. "How long has it been since you returned home? I find your tone and arrogance uncalled for, especially now that Mother has passed away."

Millie turned, her features calm. "Young man, first of all, I am not inclined to answer to you, but if you insist on knowing the difference, it's that I called my sister every day. I never missed a birthday, Halloween, Thanksgiving or Christmas card and more often than not, I sent her 'just because' cards up until the time I couldn't write much anymore. Several times my sweet Jacob brought her to my house so she wouldn't be alone so much. All these years, after everything she's done for both of you, and you good-for-nothing kids never paid any attention to her and never once asked her to come stay with you. She always dreamed of traveling to Europe and she thought after paying for your high-falooting education with the money she and your father saved over the years, you'd invite her to England. How many times had she told you she wanted to see Buckingham Palace and Regent's square? But did you ever ask her to come for a visit? Did you? No, you didn't. Neither of you did," Millie said motioning toward the kitchen. "After all those times she cleaned the vomit from your face and the crap from your pants, neither of you ever called. Hell, she didn't even know you'd gotten married until your sister told her. Now you're both here when it doesn't matter anymore. She needed you when she was alive. She needed to feel a part of something wonderful and you ignored her. You both should be ashamed of yourselves." Millie glanced down the hallway at Sarah Jane standing in the threshold of the kitchen, her mouth open. Millie nodded in her direction. "Yes, you heard me. You should be ashamed of yourself, abandoning your mother when she needed you most." Millie turned and, one step at a time, clung to the banister and made her way to the second floor with me right behind. "Nasty, rotten kids," she muttered as she turned left down the hallway and entered her room.

She sat down on the four-poster bed, and the springs let out a loud squeak. She ran her fingers over the eyelet comforter. The room was exactly the way she'd left it with pictures of her parents and framed photographs of her and me nailed against the blue, yellow and white striped wallpaper. Café curtains dotted with yellow rose buds hung from the sashed window. Seeing she was tired, I helped her lie down on the bed and then curled up next to her and watched her fall asleep.

Afternoon faded into night and more people began to arrive at the house. Millie never ventured back downstairs, choosing to listen to all the mindless chatter from her bedroom. She sat at her dressing table, nibbling with one hand at the food Jacob brought to her while cradling a picture of Emma in the other.

"Oh sis," she said aloud. "If you could see the vultures now, pecking away at your memory. They all have their stories, which I suppose is a good thing, but their stories don't compare to yours and mine, do they? Why, do you remember the time down by the old swimming hole when you slipped on the rocks and fell in and that big old oaf, Samson, came out of nowhere and rescued you from drowning? My, who would have thought he'd turn into the best friend we ever had. We told Mama and Daddy you'd fallen into a puddle in the Spencers' yard. Or what about the time Samson snuck inside in the middle of the night and ate Mama's cherry cobbler she'd left on the counter?"

Millie chuckled. "You and I caught hell for that one didn't we, but what were we supposed to do? Mama would have beat us silly if she'd known we let that boy in her house. Oh, there were lots of times we let Samson in that Mama didn't know about. She almost caught him in bed with me that one time and would've if it hadn't been for you shoving him in the closet. Oh, Emma, those were the days." She ran her hand over the picture in the oval frame. "Soon, my dear sister. I'll join you and we'll talk about all the old times again, but there is one thing I have to do first." She opened up the top drawer of the night stand. "Now where is that notepaper?"

Emma's funeral the next day went as well as could be expected. There were lots of people all dressed in black, sobbing and moaning. Emma was buried next to her mama and beautiful flowers were placed on her grave. Millie left a bouquet of Emma's favorite – daisies. She'd picked them herself from the garden in the rear of the house.

Family and friends mingled about the house for several hours afterward, indulging in the catered affair. Finally, Millie had enough of all the pretense and hypocrisy and excused herself, but not before she took Brock and Sarah Jane into the living room and read Emma's Last Will and Testament. She seemed to find great joy in seeing Brock and Sarah Jane's faces fall with shock as they discovered the house and everything in it belonged to her. I have to say, watching from outside the room, their stunned looks were just downright funny, and if I could have laughed, I would've.

After that, Millie pulled herself upright, held her hunched-over shoulders up straight and walked with pride and dignity from the room. She reached into the pocket of her dress and pulled out a lavender envelope, smiled and kissed it, then laid it on the small table beside the stairs. I followed her up and tucked her in like I'd done for so many years, then curled up on the bed next to her.

The next morning came bringing sunlight once again to the room but something was most definitely different. The room seemed brighter, less noisy. I jumped out of bed, stretched and leaned toward Millie. I just stared at her face. My Millie. She just laid there all peaceful like. That's when I noticed there was no clickity-clackity sound coming out of that blasted machine she always carried about, and them hoses once stuck up her nose was lying on the floor. As the sun moved across the room, I noticed something else too – all them wrinkles and age spots she hated so much – well they was plumb gone. And she smelled like a spring day, you know that kind of sweet honeysuckle sort of smell that hangs in the air after the grass's been cut and it rains. It's the smell all angels get when they've been touched by God.

I nudged my head against her small hand and waited. I knew she'd wake up soon. All angels do. Soon I felt her stir. It wasn't much at first and then I felt her hand pat my head and then, like she'd done when we was kids, she scratched behind my ears. I stood up and nuzzled my cold nose beneath her hand. The eyes of a young girl opened wide. A big smile crossed her face.

"Samson. Is that you?"

I lowered my head onto the bed and wagged my tail.

Millie's eyes teared up as she wrapped her loving arms around me. "Oh, Samson, it is you!"

I jumped up on the bed and licked her all over her face. I couldn't help myself. After almost seventy years of waiting in heaven for my best friend to come home, well it was just a little difficult for me to control myself.

She ruffled my ears and stroked my golden coat that glistened like copper in the sun. She cupped my face in her hands and kissed my nose. "Oh, Samson. You waited for me. You didn't forget me."

I nuzzled her again. How could I forget my Millie? I love my Millie. Always have. I do reckon I understood her surprise though 'cause I wondered about it once, too. See, I was sitting beside a pond in heaven, looking down on my Millie, watching her grow more fragile and ill and the good Lawd, sensing my troubles, sat down beside me one day and he said to me, 'Samson, why you so down in the jowls?' I told him in my own way that I was afraid she'd forgotten about me. After all, I was just a dog and I had died when she was just twelve. God just laughed, rubbed me behind the ears and patted my shoulder. "Samson, dear boy," he said in that booming yet gentle voice of his. "Miss Millie loves you. She always has and she always will. You have nothing to fear 'cause you see, love survives death for all eternity. You'll see."

I should have known then to accept what the good Lawd says but dogs, like folks, well, we don't always want to believe in stuff we're told. But now, I can't believe I ever doubted those words for a minute.

The sound of her laughter lightened my soul. My Millie and I were together again. We laughed and played until we heard footsteps on the stairs. She got all quiet and held her finger to her lips. "The closet," she whispered, a big grin stretched across her face. I remembered the game, jumped down and hid inside even though I knew whoever walked through them doors wouldn't be able to see me. But to make Millie happy, I did as she asked.

A light tapping sound came from the door before it opened revealing Brock all dressed in his travel clothes.

"Aunt Millie?" he asked, approaching the bed. Of course the person he saw was not the one I saw. My Millie was all young, spirited. Alive. The Millie he saw in the bed was old, pale and cold. Lifeless. His hands trembled, his lips quivered. "Oh my God," he said as he turned and flew from the room, running through the angel spirit of a very young Emma as she passed through a wall into the room to greet her sister.

I jumped up on the bed and nuzzled both Emma and Millie's hands. A bright ray of sunlight streamed through the window. I looked at it and barked. Emma hugged Millie and then took her hand and said, "Are you ready?"

Millie smiled. "Just one moment," she said. She looked up toward the ceiling. "Sorry, Grandma. Sometimes it is about the way we leave this world that matters."

Moments later she heard Sarah Jane scream. "Oh my God, Brock! She left it all to the Humane Society. Millie left her entire estate to the dogs!"

Emma smiled. "I take it she found your Last Will and Testament."

Millie laughed. "I should say so."

Millie and Emma linked arms and the three of us stepped into the ray of sunshine. Millie's hand petted the top of my head and said, "Samson, lead us home."

I was happy to oblige.

The Beach House

Christine L. Hardy

Christine L. Hardy

Thunderheads piled in a mushroom formation to the south of Ocean City, New Jersey as if foretelling nuclear destruction. Amber emerged onto the front porch of her duplex in yoga pants and a tank top, clutching her morning coffee, and shook her head in disbelief. Even the sky predicted doom. The headline of the folded paper at her feet screamed *North Korea Proceeds With Test*. She sat down with it and scanned the article as she drank her coffee, already familiar with the scenario that had been playing out for over a year. The North Koreans claimed to have created a "Twilight Bomb" with the power to destroy most of the United States. Although they had been threatening the U.S. for years, their missiles tended to fizzle out like fireworks, either falling into the ocean or failing to launch at all. Still, the President was flying to Paris for yet another NATO security conference.

Amber tossed the paper onto the chair next to hers and drained her cup. Jeeves, her tuxedo cat, sauntered over and batted the corner of the front page with unsheathed claws. A piece tore off with a satisfying rip and he pounced on it.

"Tear it up, Jeeves. Fear-mongering and propaganda."

To the north, early sunshine illuminated the pastel faces of the neighboring houses, all of which had been recently renovated. The porches were emblazoned with school banners, realty signs and flags of the various countries the owners descended from. Amber had bought an Indian flag for her friend Pooja and newlywed husband Dan when they bought this house a year ago, but she took it down after their deaths. They had drowned in a rip current, only four short months after moving in. Their spirits lived on, though, in the sweet scent and glorious profusion of the flowers Pooja had lovingly planted. The climbing pink roses were in their first, unsullied bloom on the trellis beside the porch.

A familiar ache pressed behind Amber's sternum. She wondered if she'd ever get over the pain of losing her best friend. Pooja, a slender girl with dusky skin, big, thickly-lashed brown eyes and an infectious giggle, was the American-born child of Indian immigrants. She grew up to be a dancer and a teacher, and eloped with an American lawyer in defiance of her parents. They had come to like Dan and accepted him with gracious resignation after the initial uproar. Perhaps Mr. and Mrs. Gupta decided they'd rather have her and the man she loved than not have her in their lives at all.

In the end, they'd still lost her. Compared to this intimate pain, the threats of distant dictators seemed laughable.

Gulls cried above in mocking agreement. A couple of surfers carried boards across the street, heading for the beach. A man wearing reflective sunglasses and a flimsy yellow raincoat trudged along the double yellow line toward Amber, surveying each house as if he was looking for something. She recognized the coat as the cheap kind sold on the boardwalk to tourists, which could be folded up into a pouch. As he drew closer, she could see that that his narrow, angular face and limbs were shockingly lean, corded muscles standing out on his legs where his shorts ended, his skin the steamed-crab hue of fresh sunburn. He paused in front of her, tipping his head back to scan the second floor.

"Can I help you?" she asked.

He spoke in a gravelly voice with an accent she couldn't place. "Have you seen a young girl with black, curly hair?"

"No."

She expected him to elaborate or give her a phone number to call if she saw the missing child. Instead, he scanned the property from side to side as if he expected her to pop out of the bushes, and continued down the block. She watched him until he was out of sight and glanced toward the ocean as she pushed to her feet. The thunderheads had spread out, dispelling the mushroom formation. "Come on, Jeeves. Breakfast."

He dashed between her feet just as she opened the sliding door, but she scooped him up before he tripped her. His purr rumbled against her chest. "Gotcha."

Given the looming clouds, Amber opted for a quick run on the beach before heading to work at the realty office. Saturdays were a nightmare of last-minute cancellations and forgotten deposits, which meant she'd do well to burn off her stress ahead of time. The wind from the impending storm kicked up sand that gritted against her legs and face. She turned back after a quarter mile, removing her shoes and socks by the outdoor shower when she reached the house. The little wooden stall was a necessity of oceanside living, sand being responsible for numerous horrible things with the plumbing. Since she was renting this house to help the Guptas out until they could sell it, she did not want to be responsible for horrible things.

She rinsed her legs under the water, shut it off firmly, and reached for the towel on the door hook. Beneath it, freshly etched in the wood, were stick characters in a secret language. Tolkien runes, the kind she and Pooja had used to pass notes in high school. She hadn't seen them in over ten years but knew right away what they said: *Amber, I'm back. Meet me here tonight. Pooja.*

The air left Amber's chest and heat stung her eyes. The runes had been carved in the soft, weathered wood with something blunt, like a stick or the edge of a seashell. She slammed the door shut and ran along the house to the side entrance, head bowed against the glare. Someone was playing a sick joke. Maybe neighborhood kids. How would they have known about the runes, though? Pooja had taught at the local elementary school. She'd probably shown them herself. Horrible brats to use it for a prank.

The sudden coolness of conditioned air hit her when she stepped inside, and the door groaned on salt-corroded hinges. A small sob rose in her throat and she leaned against the kitchen island, covering her face with her hands. Even though Pooja's parents had removed all of the couple's things and had the house repainted for rental, the faint smell of curry still hung in the air. Amber let the memory of helping Dan and Pooja move in on a too-hot April Saturday flood through her. The excitement of carrying boxes into a brand-new space. Petite Pooja delivering instructions with her hair pulled back into a frizzy ponytail. Dan's amused compliance as he wrestled things into place. Amber's own deep happiness at being with them.

She had loved them so much and, would give anything to have them both back.

Amber and the senior realty manager, Jord Maddox, retreated into the tiny kitchen in the back of the office for a quick lunch before the two o'clock check-ins started. Jord was the first friend Amber made when she moved to Ocean City three months ago. He was in his early thirties, had a wrestler's hard body, and devoured things she barely considered edible, like quinoa, chard, edamame and kale.

"You sure you don't want some?" He tipped his bowl of cold beans and what looked like cooked aquarium gravel toward her.

"No, thanks." Removing her cheeseburger from its wrappings, she told him about the sunburned man and finding the message scratched in the shower.

"You should never have moved in there. I know you want to help, but it's crazy to put yourself through this."

"It's just kids." She knew he was referring to more than the shower incident but pretended not to notice, instead admiring the way his dress shirt stretched over his biceps. She wished she felt something more for him than friendship but she didn't, suspecting that maybe grief still numbed her.

"You don't know it's just kids."

"Who else would it be?"

He chewed meditatively and took a sip of bottled water. "Maybe that weird guy with the sunburn. Keep your doors locked and call the police if he shows up again."

"I can't call the police because someone is standing in the street."

"Then call me."

She gave him a small, sideways smile. "Okay."

That night, Amber cooked Indian food for the first time since Pooja's death. Nothing complicated, just red lentil dahl and roti. A heady bouquet of lentils, garlic, cumin and asafetida seeped from the under the lid of the pot on the stove while she fried roti in a skillet. The flat circles of wheat flour puffed as they browned, deflating when flipped with a spatula. She remembered Pooja's mother teaching her in the mustard-yellow tiled kitchen of their house. Pooja's voice echoed in her memory. *You can do it, Amber. It's not hard.*

No, it wasn't, once she got the hang of it, but cooking this food without Pooja was excruciating. She bit her lip, wishing she could step back into those safe, worry-free days. The storm that had been building all day battered the siding in gusts of hard rain.

When the meal was ready, she set three places at the table on her only tablecloth, lit votives in red glass holders and turned off the lights. She felt a little silly, but it was something she needed to do. She'd tried so hard to avoid thinking of Dan and Pooja in order to lessen her pain. It was time to honor them.

She spooned dahl into each of three bowls, added a dollop of yogurt, folded a roti next to it, and poured three glasses of red wine. She had considered cooking Dan a hamburger but thought that would be overkill. Jeeves lapped at a saucer of yogurt on the floor.

Amber lifted her glass. "To Dan and Pooja, wherever you are. Be safe and wait for me."

Her words fell between the pools of light from the candles. No one knew exactly where the couple went the night they disappeared. Their car was still parked in front of the house and they had left their keys, wallets and cell phones behind. Swimsuits and towels had been missing. The police had found no evidence of foul play. The only logical explanation was that they went swimming despite the red flags on the beach warning of rip currents after Hurricane Kelly last August. Part of Amber wanted desperately to believe that Pooja had come back. But if Pooja had, she wouldn't leave messages scratched in the shower. The culprit was certainly not sitting out in the downpour waiting for her, either.

Amber drank most of the bottle of wine before trudging up to bed.

"Amber, wake up." An urgent whisper tore at her wine-sodden cocoon of sleep. "You need to come with me."

Amber dragged her thick eyelids partway open. A small figure stood between her bed and the window. She whispered back to it. "Who are you? What are you doing here?"

The figure came closer and bent over her. In the pale glow cast by the digital clock, Amber could just make out a small face surrounded by a cloud of dark curls. A cold tremor ran down her spine.

"It's me. Pooja." Cool fingers touched Amber's bare arm.

She shuddered and jerked away. "It can't be."

"I wrote you a message in the shower. Didn't you see it?"

"No, you didn't. This isn't happening. I'm dreaming."

"Amber, listen to me. I'm not—"

The distinct creak of the front door opening broke the spell of the dream. Amber sat up and turned toward the hallway, heart pounding.

She listened for footsteps. It was hard to hear with the ceiling fan whirring softly above her. She couldn't recall if she'd locked the doors before going to bed, and reached out for Jeeves' solid warmth. He didn't stir, though a faint purr vibrated against her hand.

She remembered the heavy, long-handled flashlight she kept on the floor and groped for it. It banged against the corner of the nightstand, rattling the lamp. Amber cringed. Whoever or whatever was down there knew she was awake. Maybe they'd be scared off.

She eased to her feet and crept to the doorway, summoning as much bravado as she could.

"Who's there?"

Silence. She switched on the hall light, snuck to the top of the stairs holding the flashlight like a sword and slowly made her way down the steps to the living room. When she reached the bottom, she pressed the switch that illuminated the globe in the ceiling fan.

Everything looked as it should: the secondhand denim sofa, the glass-topped wicker coffee table with its twin stacks of mail and magazines, the flat-screen television and her stereo. The exterior door in the kitchen was ajar a couple of inches. The wind must have blown it open.

Or a ghost.

"There's no one here, right?" A soft rattling sound answered her. She froze as her heart beat so hard she could feel it in her chest. The sound stopped. She let out a breath and it started again. "Holy crap."

She was rattling the batteries in the handle of the flashlight.

She strode to the front door, pushed it shut and locked both the knob and the deadbolt then did the same to the door in the kitchen. She could call the police. But what would she tell them other than she thought she'd seen a ghost and that her doors were open? She wasn't going to call Jord in the middle of the night, though part of her wanted to. She searched both floors for anywhere a person could hide, but no bogeymen jumped out at her. Leaving the lights blazing, she crawled back into bed, clutching the flashlight against her chest.

The cruel brightness of a June morning assaulted Amber when she woke, piercing her throbbing head. The flashlight had rolled to the floor. She shuffled warily downstairs, half expecting Pooja or the sunburned man to jump out at her, grabbed the coffee pot and held it under the kitchen faucet to fill it. There were four bowls in the sink with bits of lentil floating in them. She'd used three the night before.

Had she used a fourth one for something? She couldn't remember. She put the coffee on, head throbbing, slumped into a kitchen chair, and rested her head on her arms while it brewed.

The dream last night had seemed so real. The voice, the face, the figure. The way Pooja got irritated when Amber didn't believe her. *Amber, listen to me. I'm not—.* Not what? Dead? But she *was* dead. The bodies had never been found, but she and Dan were gone forever. Amber muttered into the space between her arms and the table. "Why did you have to go swimming?"

Jord was right. This was crazy. She'd have to find somewhere else to live. She took her coffee to the back deck in order to avoid the sunburned man just in case he came around again. Amber's gaze lifted to the pink roses on the arbor in the corner of the yard, their colors and scent almost obscenely sensual. Pooja had planted them when she moved in. They were called Pink Portal according to the tag with care instructions that Amber found in a drawer. They had been dying from neglect but Amber coaxed them back to life. Now they covered the arbor entirely, sheltering a stone bench. Raindrops sparkled on their ruffled clusters of Barbie-doll pink blooms.

Pooja and her fifth-grade class had submitted some of the rose hips to the town's time capsule project along with stories the children wrote about the future. The project had been accepted after her death, so Amber sent a photo of the couple and a brief letter about their love for each other. The local papers had picked the story up and published her letter. In 2115, the capsule would be opened and with luck the Pink Portal would bloom again in their honor, regardless of what the North Koreans or anyone else did in the meantime.

The capsule was to be buried today in a ceremony. Surely the occasion and last night's tribute had dragged Pooja's image from her subconscious. She wasn't being haunted; she was just grieving. It would be hard on the Guptas to rent the house to someone else, but it was time to move on with her life. Jord had offered to accompany her to the ceremony that afternoon. She'd talk to him afterward about finding a new place. It went without saying that one of the rose bushes would go with her.

Amber crossed the deck and went down the three steps to the shower stall, wondering if anyone had been there last night. It looked the same as ever, no sign of disturbance, except that the runes on the inside of the door had been rubbed out with something like steel wool that left a bare, blonde patch of wood in their place.

Jord picked her up at noon and drove her downtown for the capsule ceremony. On the way, she told him about her night.

"Why didn't you call me?" His voice was almost accusing as he guided his SUV through Sunday traffic.

"In the middle of the night?'

"Yes."

"Jord, I wouldn't wake you up just because my doors blew open."

"I'm not just talking about the doors."

She narrowed her eyes at him. "You think I summoned a ghost by cooking Indian food?"

"No. I think someone might have been in your house and that this is all connected. Did you find any more writing in the shower?"

"No, and the original message was rubbed out."

"So someone did come, at some point. Promise me you'll call me if anything suspicious happens again." He turned his head to fix her with an intense look.

It was a relief to give in. She really had wanted someone last night. "All right."

By the time they found a parking space and walked to the municipal park, a crowd had already gathered. The "capsule" was a fireproof, waterproof safe roughly the size of a Volkswagen Beetle that would be stored in the municipal building for the next one hundred years. The list of items included everything from the rose hips to an iPad. Hers was not the only agricultural contribution, nor the only emotional tribute to a loved one. Thankfully she wasn't asked to read her letter, though one of Pooja's students read his essay.

Jord's solid presence beside her was comforting, and he took her hand as the safe was sealed. She was surprised and touched, squeezing his fingers gently. A sense of finality seeped through her. Time to move on.

He walked her to the car and opened the door for her. "Are you doing anything tonight?"

"No."

"Want to have dinner?"

She slid into her seat and looked up at him. "Okay, but I'm not sure I'll be good company."

"You don't have to be good company. I just don't want you to be alone." He smiled at her. He had a really nice smile.

"All right. Thanks."

He closed the door and went around to the other side. She kept glancing at him, wondering if something significant had just happened.

"I have to stop at the office for a while. I'll come back around six, if that's good."

"Six is fine." She almost said she was okay and didn't need babysitting, but realized it wasn't true. "I appreciate it, Jord. You're a good friend."

"Yeah well, I just don't want you getting spooked and moving away, leaving me short-staffed during peak season." His tone was mild enough to convey the sense that he wasn't serious.

"In that case, you're a good manager."

Jeeves didn't run to greet her when she got home. That was odd. She realized she hadn't seen him that morning, either. He wouldn't have gone out in the storm last night. She picked up a foil bag of cat treats and shook it. When he didn't come running, she went to the slider to see if he was on the deck.

"Jeeves?"

Her heart sank at the sight of bare boards. She ran down the steps and peered under the deck and shrubbery. There weren't many places for a cat to hide. Most of the tiny yard was taken up by the deck and a patch of white pebbles in place of grass. A privet hedge separated her property from the neighbors', with a wooden gate leading to the alley. A few flowerpots, a hydrangea, and the rose arbor with the stone bench underneath it completed the landscaping.

Amber walked down the alley to the side street and back, panic churning her stomach. In all the years she'd had him, he'd never missed breakfast. She walked the neighborhood for over an hour, calling his name and praying he hadn't been hit by a car. Eventually, she found herself in front of a pizza parlor at the south end of the boardwalk, sweat trickling down her back in the heat. She walked in, paid three dollars for a bottle of cold water and slid into a booth to drink it. A television news anchor regurgitated headlines about North Korea and the Twilight Bomb from a screen mounted in the corner of the dining area. The college kid behind the counter kept glancing up at it nervously as he worked. He probably figured New Jersey was sure to be in the danger zone, situated as it was between New York and Washington, D.C.

According to the media, North Korea was planning to test the bomb within the next couple of days. Amber wondered if maybe this really was for real. The anchor and his panel of experts droned on about missile interceptors and potential climate scenarios if the Twilight Bomb exploded somewhere over the Atlantic Ocean. She picked up her bottle of water, slid her sunglasses on and stood up.

That's when she noticed that the sunburned man who had asked her about the missing girl yesterday was sitting in the next booth. He must have come in while her attention was on the television. Was he following her? His skin was lobster red, even his scalp, and yellow blisters crusted his nose. It was the worst sunburn Amber had ever seen. He leaned forward, holding her gaze with hard, pale gray eyes that looked almost silver.

"The quota is full." He spoke in a muted accent she didn't recognize.

"Excuse me?"

"The quota is full. There is no more room. Tell her to come back."

"The girl with the curly hair you were looking for? I told you, I haven't seen anyone like that." But her stomach turned as last night's dream popped into her mind.

She glanced at the kid behind the counter. He wasn't even pretending to work anymore, his attention riveted on the news. A family in the corner laughed at something funny one of the children said. She hurried out of the shop, the sunburned man's flat gaze seeming to bore through her back into her stomach.

She locked the doors when she got back to the house, called Jord at the office, and relayed the encounter in the pizza parlor. "I have no idea what he meant by the quota being full. He said to 'tell her to come back'. I can't help thinking he meant Pooja, like maybe he's a ghost hunter or something."

Jord was quiet for a long moment. She could hear a faint tapping sound, like a pen against a desk.

"Are you still there?" The tone of her voice had risen despite her effort to keep it steady.

"Yeah, I'm here. I don't want you to stay alone tonight, Amber. I'll sleep on the couch."

She didn't want to involve him to that extent, but he was offering and she was scared. "If you're sure you don't mind."

"If I minded I wouldn't offer. I'll be there at six. Keep the doors locked and call the police if he shows up at the house. Don't worry. We'll straighten this all out."

She wondered if he really believed that. "Thanks. I don't want to go out if Jeeves is still missing. I'll make dinner."

"You don't have to; I can pick something up."

"Please, it will give me something to do. I feel like I'm going to jump out of my skin."

"Don't do that!"

She laughed in spite of everything. "I won't."

After hanging up, it occurred to her that Jeeves might be stuck in a closet or under a piece of furniture somewhere. She knelt down to look under the sofa. The distinct sound of human footsteps came down the stairs just when she was most vulnerable, with her back turned and her rump in the air. She froze, listening, then sat up and slowly turned around. Jeeves trilled a feline greeting, bumping his head against Amber's hand. Someone stood on the steps behind him. A small, young Indian girl with curly hair and dark brown eyes. It was Pooja. Amber screamed. Jeeves darted behind the sofa.

"Shhh! Don't be scared. It's me, not a ghost. We have to talk," she said, slowly approaching Amber.

It took a minute for Amber to find her voice. "What do you mean, talk? You're dead. This isn't happening."

"No, I'm not dead." Her gaze darted around the room to each of the windows. "I can't let Gabrel see me."

"Who's Gabrel?"

"Immigration police from the future. He's trying to stop me from bringing you back with me."

"What! This is crazy. I don't know who you are or what kind of drugs you're on, but this is stopping right now."

Pooja's eyes flashed and she spoke in the tone of voice that her adult counterpart had used with difficult children. "No, you're going to listen to me. The Twilight Bomb is real, Amber. It's more powerful than anyone guesses. The test destroyed Asia completely. Tsunamis and earthquakes wiped out South America. The United States was under a radioactive cloud for decades, it blocked crops from sunlight, made people sick." She grabbed Amber's arm. "Electronics failed because of the radiation, and put the world into another dark age. Amber, this bomb *ripped holes in time.*"

"How do you know this?"

"I came from the future. 2215."

Amber buried her head in her hands. "I need a cup of tea."

At Pooja's insistence, Amber closed all of the blinds before putting the kettle on. Jeeves crunched greedily on his kibble while Pooja, perched on a barstool, gazed around the house from which all trace of her and Dan's existence had been erased. Amber thought her eyes looked a little red as she fixed them each a cup of Darjeeling. It was Pooja's favorite.

"Thanks." Pooja poured milk into her tea and added a heaping teaspoon of sugar just as she'd always done.

"It's really you," Amber said.

"I told you it was me."

"Why do you look thirteen?"

Pooja blew on her tea and took a small sip. "I am thirteen. Everyone who comes through reverts to puberty. I don't know why."

"Where have you been?"

"In the future. The arbor is a portal. The roses make connections between times."

"Right. So you went through a portal to the future and got younger."

"Yes. So did Dan. He's watching the other side for us."

"And how did this happen exactly?"

"We were, um, making out on the little bench and fell off."

Novel. Amber lifted her cup and sipped tentatively.

"Why did you come back?"

Pooja leaned forward. "To get you. At first they wouldn't let us out of custody. There are a whole bunch of us who stumbled through by accident, and some that were recruited. They need us. They need our genes. They had to start over completely. New buildings, new technology, new agriculture. But they're dying out from the damage that was passed along from the destruction."

"They?"

"Us. Americans. The rose hips were preserved in the time capsule and found later, along with lots of other things. Corn, soybeans, tomatoes, strawberries. Once the roses were planted, people started appearing wherever a closed arch was covered in flowers. They just stumbled through accidentally, like me and Dan. We were allowed to stay because we're healthy, young, educated and fertile. Others were recruited by immigration to boost the DNA pool. The portals will close tomorrow when the bomb goes off and kills the roses. And all agriculture, for that matter."

Pooja reached across the table and gripped Amber's hand. Her fingers were warm from the teacup. A ghost wouldn't be warm, would it? "You need to come with me. Please, I'm begging you."

It actually was starting to make sense. Jeeves jumped up on her lap, purring and kneading her thighs with his paws. "So I wasn't dreaming. Why did you disappear last night? Where did you go?"

"I ducked down between the bed and the wall. I must have not closed the door tightly enough, or else Gabrel followed me. I thought he was downstairs so I crawled under your bed. I was so exhausted from running in the rain and hiding that I fell asleep and didn't wake up until you were gone. Jeeves stayed with me the whole time. He remembers me."

"But why is he looking for you?"

"Because the quota for refugees is full and he's trying to stop me. But I *had* to come back for you. I couldn't leave you behind."

"What about your parents? My family? Dan's? Are you going to let them all die?"

Pooja's eyes brimmed with tears. "We don't want to, but we can't hide them all. There's no way they'd get past the quota officers and there's no way they'd believe us if we tried to warn them. But we can hide you in our quarters until the portals are destroyed. You're healthy, young, educated. They can't object once it's done. Dan and I talked about it and we agreed we'd have to try, especially when we realized you were right here at the house." Her fingers tightened on Amber's painfully. "Please come."

"This is so much to take in; I have to think about it." She pulled her hand free. "Wait, is Gabrel a weird skinny guy with bad sunburn?"

Pooja winced. "Yes. They're not used to that much ultraviolet and it burns them badly. He's not dangerous, he's just supposed to bring me back."

"Why not just leave you here?"

"I told you, they need me. Plus, I'm kind of a celebrity because my class put the roses in the time capsule. I read the letter you wrote, it was beautiful. I had to come back for you, but I couldn't until the roses had grown all the way over the trellis and completed the portal."

"When does the bomb go off?"

"That's the problem. No one in the future knows the exact time, just that it was July 13th."

Amber stared. "That's tomorrow."

"Then we've got to go as soon as it's dark tonight."

Pooja retreated to the guest room before Jord arrived, accompanied by a burst of rain that spattered on the linoleum. Amber had put a pizza in the oven and was attempting a salad. The television news droned in the living room, a headline banner skating across the bottom of the screen. Her hands shook so badly she could hardly cut the vegetables. She set the knife down. "You're soaked."

"No, just my coat." He set a duffel down on the floor, shrugged the offending jacket off and hung it over a chair. "I can't believe it's raining again. Need any help?"

"Yes, thanks. Here. " She handed him the knife, trying to figure out how to tell him everything. He'd never believe her. She'd already called her family and Pooja's parents, begging them to head for the West Coast, "just in case". Pooja was right. They didn't believe it was that serious. This was only a test, after all. No one was actually firing missiles at anybody. Pooja tried calling her parents herself, but they thought it was a prank and hung up. She'd fled upstairs in tears.

"Thank you so much for coming." Amber poured two glasses of wine and handed him one.

"No problem." Jord flashed her a quick smile and let the wine sit while he sliced cucumbers and tomatoes with quick, precise strokes.

Amber sipped her wine. How could she even begin to explain?

The burst of a musical alert from the television drew both of their attention. "North Korea will launch the test of their Twilight Bomb in just thirty minutes." Amber gripped the counter with tight fingers. Footage of Kim Jong-Sun waving to a group of dignitaries filled the screen.

It was already tomorrow in Korea.

The anchor droned on. "North Korea is warning the United States to withdraw all ships from the North Pacific but the President is standing firm."

They were out of time. She picked up the remote control and switched the television off. "Jord, we have to talk."

He stopped tossing the salad and reached for his wine glass. Faint worry lines creased the corners of his eyes as he met her gaze.

Pooja darted down the stairs, her lithe, young body moving with grace even in haste. Jord's eyes widened and he started, splashing wine on his shirt.

"Amber, we have to leave *now*."

"I was just telling Jord."

"No time for that." She grabbed Amber's hand, tugging her toward the sliding door at the back of the house.

Jord followed. "Telling me what? Who is this, Amber?"

"It's Pooja. She's not a ghost. I can't explain now. We just have to go." She broke free of Pooja. "Jeeves?" she called.

"Amber!" Pooja's voice shrieked with impatience. "Forget the cat."

Jeeves had followed Pooja downstairs and was sniffing some shredded mozzarella that had fallen to the floor from the pizza. Amber scooped him up.

Jord scowled. "Where are we *going*?"

Amber opened her mouth to answer him but saw a figure at the back door. It pressed something to the glass of the slider and it fell like a sheet of water, disintegrating into sand with a *whoosh*. Gabrel lunged through and grabbed Pooja. "Jord, stop him!"

Jord was already moving. He aimed a blow at Gabrel's jaw. Gabrel was forced to use one arm to block it. Pooja twisted free of his other hand and tried to knee him but she was too short. Her elbow slammed into his stomach. He groaned and shoved her aside as Jord came at him.

Amber didn't know what to do. Jord was strong and clearly knew how to fight, but the other guy was wiry and military. Jeeves mewed and struggled. The scene was surreal.

Pooja ducked away from the men and onto the deck. Rain instantly matted her hair. Lightning flashed, briefly illuminating the yard. "Amber, come on!"

Amber obeyed, her sandals skidding on the wet wood.

Pooja stopped at the rose arbor, grabbed Jeeves and tossed him over the bench. He disappeared. She waved her hand, urging Amber. "Go on."

Amber looked back at the struggling men, silhouetted against the light. "I can't leave Jord."

"We won't. Just get through." She raised her voice. "Dan, are you ready?"

A kid's voice answered "yes". Amber couldn't see past the portal through the dark and the rain.

Amber ducked under the rose arbor and jumped over the bench. Her foot caught on the edge and she tripped, falling forward. She cringed, expecting to hit the hedge, but instead she landed on soft, cool sand. A brisk breeze chilled her body, which suddenly felt compact and light. Waves pounded the beach, much rougher than those along Ocean City ever did. The moon was a silvery glow behind the fog.

Thirteen-year-old Dan was a skinny kid with light hair. He held out his hand and helped her up. An obelisk as tall and wide around as a lighthouse loomed over them, encircled by a ring of rose arbors at its base. Amber guessed right away what it commemorated. Through the nearest one she could see Pooja looking through the rain up at her house. Jord and Gabrel were on the deck now. Gabrel had Jord down on the boards. Pooja's voice seeped toward Amber through the storm and the pounding waves. "Let him go, Gabrel. It's time."

"The quota is full." His voice lurched as Jord fought to get up and he twisted to the side.

"If you don't let him go, we'll destroy the portal and trap you here."

Gabrel's head whipped up. "You wouldn't dare."

"Try me," Pooja replied as Dan moved beside Amber and the roses shivered. "Dan's got wires attached to the arbor from the other side. Let the guy through or we'll destroy it."

Amber's mouth fell open. Damn clever. Then it hit her that they had done this for her. Her throat tightened.

There was a moment when everything was still. Thunder cracked on the other side and lightning flashed again. Gabrel shifted and Jord struggled to his feet. Something softened inside of Amber as Jord moved toward the arbor through the rain. "Amber?"

"Here. Just duck through the arbor over the bench. It's okay."

Jord came through, followed by Pooja. Gabrel stood for a moment, his head bowed, then followed. He grabbed the wire from Dan and yanked the roses down and through from the other side, closing the portal. The rain, lightning and thunder ceased, leaving only the pounding of surf. Ahead of them, a pale mass of buildings under a dome glowed on the edge of the ocean.

Jeeves mewed and rubbed against Amber's legs. She felt lithe and young, yet old at the same time. "Is that Atlantic City?"

"The new one." Pooja flung her arms around Amber. Amber hugged her back and breathed in the forgotten scent of Pooja's skin.

A scrawny, adolescent Jord scrambled to his feet, looking around wildly and breathing hard. Dan held out his hand.

"Hi. I'm Dan. Pooja's husband. Welcome to the new Jersey shore."

The Hearing of Memory's Voice

J. J. Steinfeld

Jack Zwick was a great actor. His final performance took place in 1979 on a stage unlike any he had ever acted on before. That stage was a room to which men were sentenced because of the treachery of their minds and bodies, and from which they were removed not fully healed. Its silence was broken by a voice that sounded as if it belonged to a distant world, simply because its origin was from an ambulatory presence. Effortless movement in this large room, located off a hallway branched by a dozen other identical rooms, was always alien and threatening.

"You guys got a new roommate signing on," said the taller of the two orderlies wheeling in a hospital bed.

"Bet you two gonna get along stupendous with our mystery man," the smaller orderly, at the foot of the rolling bed, said with open mockery.

As the two orderlies manoeuvred the unconscious patient onto a bed separated from the other two by cloth partitions, the voice of an excited man burst forth: "Welcome, welcome . . . Welcome to the cerebellum sanctuary. That's a little joke I have with the doctors and nurses, may God protect their *meshuggeneh* souls."

"Save your breath, Old Jack. He's drugged up but good," the taller orderly said after the two had finished situating the new patient. Each movement on the freshly made bed created a crisp sound. "I think this one's got one of them dippacks in him, Old Jack."

"Dybbuk, dybbuk, you scoundrel. When will you get it right?" the old man on the other side of the partition said with annoyance, as if to a child who deliberately refuses to learn an uncomplicated lesson.

"Easy, Old Jack, my man. As long as I can pronounce the drinks I order at the bar, I won't complain."

"You shouldn't mock the transmigration of souls. A restless soul could find your body convenient one day."

"I'm not kosher like you, Old Jack. No dippacks for me."

"Say it right for once: dybbuk . . . dybbuk."

"Dippack is the way I want to say that word."

"The audition is over. You get nothing. You're still a stagehand. You will always be a stagehand."

"So long, Old Jack. My shift is now officially over and I am going to get bombed on dippack juice."

"Dybbuk, dybbuk!" the old man shouted as the two orderlies left, laughing loudly and punching each other playfully on the arms, already lifting the first after-work drink to their lips.

"We have a new friend, Wes," the old man said, suddenly relaxed, as if given a large dose of medication. "You hear me, Wes?" He rotated his neck, seeming to test it for stiffness or defects.

"Shut up shut up . . . up you shut up you shut up you shut . . . shut shut shut . . ." The voice was high-pitched, without menace or cogency.

"Good, Wes, working on your comedy delivery today. *More* gusto, *more* feeling, *more*—"

A low groaning from the room's new occupant silenced the old man. The groaning increased to almost a wail, as if from an injured animal hidden in undergrowth.

"You up, mister?" the old man whispered carefully; he knew well the importance—and danger—of sounds and words in this room.

The new patient answered with a loud growl that broke into uneven groans.

"Welcome, welcome," the old man responded, excited by the assurance of new blood in the room.

The growling and groaning continued. The ruffling of sheets indicated slight movement, discomfort, confinement.

"My name is Jack Zwick. The orderlies neglected to tell me your name. What should I call you, my friend?" The old man was determined to find out the new patient's name, as though a nameless man might possess strange powers over the named.

The pained noises filled the room; the sounds of delirium, of mortality tested and left balanced without sure footing.

"Come on . . . come on, what's your name? What will it hurt you to tell us? Our friend over there, he's Wesley. Call him Wes if he's in a good mood, Wesley when he's surly, which is a lot lately, I'm afraid. Right, Wes?"

"Shut up shut up . . . up you shut up you shut up you shut . . . shut shut shut," Wesley said, gasping for breath and then recovering with a few coughs.

"Wes' delivery leaves much to be desired, but he's rehearsing hard. His wife hit him over the head with a very heavy object. Anyway, that's what I've been told. But don't be fooled, Wes is getting more intelligent by the day. We play Scrabble when he's not in one of his shut-up moods."

"Where am I now?" the new patient asked, the words more a plea than a question.

"That's a good philosophical question. We're in the cerebellum sanctuary. Really, to be truthful, centre stage. Right on centre stage in the best room in the neurological ward."

"Neurological ward neurological ward neurological ward . . ."

"Thank you, Wes. Wes is right on his cue. Humour me, my friend, and tell me your name. An old man asks you most sincerely."

"Don't know," the new patient said, then fell into a long groan that anywhere but in this room would have seemed ludicrous and exaggerated. In this room it was not an unusual sound.

"You really and truly don't know your name?"

"Not yet."

"A name is not to be taken lightly."

"Where's Den-Den-Dennis?" Wesley asked. The old man could hear Wesley's teeth chatter against each other in an uncontrollable echo.

"His daughter took him home this morning, Wes . . . while you were dancing away like a Ziegfeld Girl at physiotherapy. I had to write Dennis out of the play. Meet his replacement, who is now here. We are three again . . . the three *kalikehs*. That means cripples or sick people, my new friend, but I say it only with deepest affection."

"My wife hit me over the head," Wesley said without emotion, seeming to utter a mandatory but unimportant statement.

"I told him, Wes."

"She hit me hit me . . . hit me over the head . . ."

"I don't know who I am," the new patient declared before and after groans barely distinguishable from his words.

"I am an actor," the old man proudly stated. "The greatest actor of the Yiddish theatre. And Wesley used to sell beautiful computers."

"EDP systems . . . EDP EDP EDP . . ."

215

"That's electronic data processing, fancy-shmansy. Until his wife played construction worker and hit him over the head. Bad for the cerebellum, such a heavy object."

"Accident accident accident . . ."

"She had a director without a heart," the old man said to Wesley, then to the new patient, "Rumour has it that maybe Wes deserved it. That maybe he was not too nice of a husband."

"Accident," Wesley said once again.

"That's for the courts to decide, Wes. Have you thought of your name, yoo-hoo, over there, mister?"

"I don't know my name."

"You don't remember your own name?"

"Don't remember anything."

"Aha! Another amnesia person. A little trickery by that *kurveh* Mnemosyne," the old man said, as though he should have known the other patient's affliction all along. One of the doctors who periodically came through this room referred to the Greek goddess of memory as if she were present on the floor, full-bodied and swirling around in capricious dance, her movements dispersing forgetfulness and remembrance with unpredictability. Problems with memory were as common in this room as groans and complaints about the food. "The doctors must know your name. They got files everywhere, even up their big *tochises*."

"I'm trying to remember. I try all the time," the new patient said.

"A human being deserves a name—"

"Name name name," Wesley exclaimed, seeming to make a guess that if correct would be rewarded with freedom or an intact skull.

The old man moved slowly and cautiously onto his side and looked at the cloth partition to his left as he spoke: "But thank God you're not a *meshuggener*."

"What am I not?"

"Another *goy*. All I ever get are *goyisher* co-stars . . . A *meshuggener* is a crazy person, which I know definitely you are not such a person."

"I don't think so," the new patient said without humour, unable even to begin a definition of who he was or what he looked like.

"I tell you, and this is a very old man speaking . . . you are fortunate. Now you can have any name from A to Zed, from Aleph to Tav."

"Aleph Tav?"

"Aleph is the first letter of the Hebrew alphabet and Tav is the last letter."

"Aleph Tav are very good alphabet letters. Aleph Tav."

"You want to be Mr. Aleph Tav until the doctors find your name?"

"I would like a name."

"Settled, you are Mr. Aleph Tav."

"Mr. Aleph Tav."

"*Mazel tov*, Mr. Aleph Tav! Sounds like a good name to me."

"What's your name?"

"*Oy*, another one doesn't recognize my voice. Jack Zwick, I told you, no? That's my stage name. My original name was too long to fit on the marquee. Aleph Tav, you can say, is your stage name."

"Aleph Tav," the new patient said before he fell asleep, and then groaned loudly as he slept.

"Does he play Scrabble?" Wesley asked, dropping to the floor most of the two-dozen Scrabble tiles he had been holding. He usually kept his tiles squeezed in his hands, struggling to regain control over his uncooperative body.

"Shhh, Wes, we'll ask him later. He's dreaming of his new name now," Jack Zwick said.

A large-headed doctor with uncombed hair and accompanied by two nurses and two interns came into the room. The doctor stopped at the side of the first patient's bed, his retinue standing in quiet formation at the foot of the bed. He unfolded a newspaper page and held it like a thin, protective roof over his patient, then said, "Let's hope this gets an answer."

The amnesiac opened his eyes with great effort and looked at the sketch in the newspaper. Only the amnesiac's eyes, nose and mouth were not swathed in bandages, and there was discoloration and swelling in the exposed portion of his face.

"Is that how I look?"

"An artist's conception of you before the beating."

"Hello, doctor," came Jack Zwick's deepest voice, as though he were attempting to reach the last row in a crowded theatre. He vividly remembered himself on stage at the Standard Theatre in Toronto in 1921, fifty-eight years ago. He was one of the first actors to play the Standard. He couldn't remember the name of the play but he could see himself in full costume and surrounded by other costumed actors. All he knew was that the play on his mind now was not *The Dybbuk*. A performance of *The Dybbuk*, in Yiddish or in English, he could place to the second. On the nightstand next to his bed, he kept the first English script he had ever used of *The Dybbuk*, from 1926.

"Hello, Mr. Zwick. I will be with you in a few minutes," the large-headed doctor said, winking to his current patient. When he first met this doctor, after awaking from a coma, Jack thought that the doctor's head was large enough to house an overgrown brain and enough *gefilte fish* for the whole cast of the last play he had been in.

"What's his name, doctor?" Jack asked, still using his theatrical voice.

"We don't know."

"Is that so?"

"Practice listening, Mr. Zwick, until we can get to you. You need to work on your listening."

"I am the greatest actor of the Yiddish theatre ever and that includes Menasha Skulnik and Maurice Schwartz."

"Listen anyway. Let a humble doctor read."

"So read. Who's to stop you?"

"Thank you, Mr. Zwick." The doctor turned the newspaper page around, lifting it close to his face, and began to read: "Hospital officials and the police request the public's assistance in identifying this man, estimated to be between twenty-five and thirty years old, who was severely beaten last week—"

"He was beaten?"

"Yes, Mr. Zwick . . . I will be with you shortly."

"Tell me about this beating."

"I don't think we should discuss it here. It's a police matter."

"Police?"

"No need to alarm yourself, Mr. Zwick . . ." When the doctor was finished reading, he refolded the newspaper page into eighths and slipped it back into the breast pocket of his hospital smock.

"Will it get me my name?" the amnesiac asked.

"We hope so," the large-headed doctor said as he began to examine the patient, the rest of his party leaning forward to watch. "The police are doing everything possible to identify you," the doctor added as he shined a pencil-shaped light into the amnesiac's eyes. He had dealt with battered prizefighters who hadn't looked as bad.

When the doctors and nurses walked around the partition, Jack Zwick was smiling.

"You look very happy, Mr. Zwick," the large-headed doctor said.

"Thinking of the old days. When I was Rabbi Azrael of Miropol and not a sick man . . . not a *farblondjet kalikeh*." Jack began to hum a Jewish melody whose words he couldn't remember. He thought the song might be "My Yiddishe Mama," but he wasn't sure. In frustration, he started to curse himself in Yiddish, then stopped abruptly. Sometimes he would rattle off rapidly fifteen or twenty Yiddish words, the only such use of his old language able to give him any peace. In the early days of Jack Zwick's hospitalization, the large-headed doctor would ask his patient to translate the Yiddish words he used, but the doctor had long since stopped, regarding Jack's Yiddish cursing in the same tolerant way as he did the gibberish some of the other patients used. The Jewish neurologist on the ward knew only too well what Jack was saying but regarded his outpourings as the harmless babbling of an old man.

"The gentleman next to you tells me you keep him entertained," the large-headed doctor said, trying unsuccessfully to sound cheerful and interested.

"I was Rabbi Azrael for him this morning," Jack said. "Hard to believe he never heard of *The Dybbuk* by Ansky, such a great play."

"I'll bet he will never forget it now," said one of the interns who had heard Jack Zwick recite his lines a few too many times.

The large-headed doctor shined the pencil-shaped light into Jack's left eye, holding it there for several seconds, detecting a problem. Then the doctor examined Jack's right eye. After a pensive pull on his nose and a meditative flutter of his eyelids, the large-headed doctor poked and prodded and lifted Jack's body as the other medical people watched. The doctor kept saying "excellent, excellent" no matter what he saw or how his patient reacted.

"I don't want to hear today another cockamamie lecture of yours about me being able to get back on stage in no time."

"You are making progress. We should not dispute that fact, Mr. Zwick."

"*Dreck*, doctor. I can't read, I can't write."

"The problems you are encountering are not unusual for a stroke victim . . . especially an eighty-one-year-old man."

"All I can remember from my sixty years of acting are my lines in *The Dybbuk*, and those in English, not Yiddish," Jack said, pointing with difficulty at the nightstand and the script. "One play. I had forty, forty-five roles, that's a minimum guess, and all I can remember is one—Rabbi Azrael of Miropol. When I was a young man I first played the old rabbi. Such good makeup . . . such acting. Tell me, doctor, you're so brilliant, what kind of actor is that who remembers only one role?"

"You are making excellent progress, believe me. It's just incredible how well you speak and enunciate your words. And you have your identity," the large-headed doctor said, turning his body towards the cloth partition.

"Actors don't need their identities. They need the identities of others," Jack argued.

"You are speaking magnificently. No more stuttering or lapses getting your words out."

"You got a mortician's smile, doctor."

"And you have a sense of humour sharp as anybody's in this hospital."

"Big deal! I still can't read or write. I was such a reader before — what is it again I have?"

"Alexia and agraphia brought on by a cerebral vascular injury, to be technical."

"You make me sound like constipated poultry."

Softly the doctor said, "You can be thankful you're not aphasic also."

"Like Wes?"

"Yes, like poor Wesley," the doctor said in a whisper, shaking his large head.

"What were you showing my new friend?" Jack asked.

The large-headed doctor unfolded the newspaper page once more and held it close to Jack's face. The patient blinked several times attempting to get the page in focus, wheezing slightly at the smell of newsprint.

"This is our amnesia patient without any bandages or bruises, Mr. Zwick."

"Is that how he looks, a little like a famous actor I once worked with? Not as good an actor as me, it needs to be said, but more famous."

The doctor laughed through his nose at Jack's remark, the nurses and interns offering slight smiles. "Your ego is indestructible, Mr. Zwick. Yes, we think that's how he might look. He suffered quite a beating, and remembers virtually nothing."

"I remember all my lines in *The Dybbuk* . . . in English, that is. I was Rabbi Azrael of Miropol, in English and in Yiddish."

"We should be thankful for little things. Mnemosyne is a fickle lady."

"She's a whore, a *kurveh*, and you're a *putz*, doctor. So are your helpers . . . baby *putzes*. Why can't God send me some actors? You medical people don't appreciate Jack Zwick's talent," Jack said, and then began to recite some of his lines from Act III of *The Dybbuk*. When he paused to clear his throat, those gathered around him applauded.

"Good . . . good," came the reaction from the amnesiac.

"Aleph Tav is the only one who appreciates me."

"I don't know if that's fair to say, Mr. Zwick."

"Aleph Tav, Mr. Aleph Tav, that's who I'm being," the amnesiac declared.

"An excellent name. Certainly better than John Doe," the large-headed doctor said as he moved towards Wesley's bed. The doctor stepped on a Scrabble tile and kicked it to the wall as if the tile had bitten him.

Jack was lying flat on his back, depressed. After a testing session—being treated like a slow schoolchild, like a feeble-minded fool, anything but an actor—he always felt depressed for an hour or two, until thinking about acting—the one play, *The Dybbuk*—revived his spirits. No one in the hospital appreciated what went into being a stage actor. Say *actor* and they thought of movies, silly shadows parading ten times larger than life on some fabric screen. Movies, Jack Zwick spit on them; for him there was purity only on the stage.

Jack recalled his latest testing session. He was eighty-one years old and a twenty-nine-year-old baby-faced psychologist had asked him to count in reverse from twenty . . . Now try the letters of the alphabet again, slowly this time, Mr. Zwick . . . *A* . . . *B* . . . *C* . . . That's it, Mr. Zwick, take your time . . . How about *Aleph* . . . *Beth* . . . *Gimel*, young woman? Repeat after me, Mr. Zwick: *dog, order, house, disorder, mouse* . . . Bow-wow, I hope there's no disorderly mouse in your house . . . What month were you born in, Mr. Zwick? The cruelest month . . . Who is the Prime Minister, Mr. Zwick? Do you think I care? What street is this hospital on, Mr. Zwick? Why don't you ask me what streets the Standard Theatre was on? Do you know? I know, young woman. Spadina and Dundas, the location is still in my heart. A picture show, then a burlesque was made out of my Standard, feh!

In the hospital they couldn't comprehend what went into being Rabbi Azrael of Miropol and whoever else he had played in sixty years of acting. Only acting liquidated the foolishness and pain of this *tsedrayt* world, Jack told people, but who listened to an old man? Now Jack lay there and wished he could perform on stage once more.

When Wesley began chanting "My wife's great in bed, my wife's great in bed," Jack snapped back, "She's better at throwing heavy objects . . . a real muscle woman." Wesley didn't break his solemn chant, didn't care about Jack's sarcastic comment, only happy to have escaped his drugged sleep.

By the time the orderlies came in, Jack was halfway through Rabbi Azrael's best speech—"I could make them tremble in Toronto and Montreal and New York with this speech"—and his depression was nearly gone. He was never depressed or not whole on stage.

"Man, did I tie on one helluva drunk last night," the taller orderly said as he gathered and straightened things around Jack's bed. The other orderly was near Wesley's bed and said, "Was it three or four women that came home with us?"

"Why don't you big-mouth troublemakers go to a play instead of drinking like *shikker* fishes?" Jack said, spitting dryly into the air.

"I can't get into plays," the taller orderly said, gently patting Jack on the head.

"If you would have seen *The Dybbuk*—"

"I've heard that play, Old Jack, forwards and backwards and sideways from you. It doesn't make good sense to me."

"And drinking does?" Jack tried to wave a scolding finger but his hand reacted only with tremors. He wanted to trap the shaky hand with his other hand but the task was too difficult. The physiotherapist would say he was doing just fine, Jack thought. Everyone in the hospital believed he was doing just fine if he kept breathing. They knew nothing of acting, nothing of the soul's pain, nothing of trying to please God with your performance.

"Old Jack, you try working at this hospital five days a week, getting here early in the morning. This room is like paradise compared to the others we look after. No real shakers in here." The taller orderly shook his body violently in imitation of an epileptic seizure. He did everything but discharge the contents of his bladder and bowels.

"One woman from last night had the biggest tits I ever saw," the smaller orderly called out, slapping his hands together ecstatically.

"Women should be respected . . . Leah, oy Leah. The torment Leah suffered from her dybbuk," Jack said.

"Ease up, please. We happen to have different views on females . . . Wes, I bet you like big tits," the smaller orderly said, shaping large imaginary breasts in the air over the patient, kissing imaginary nipples.

Wesley responded to the orderly's lecherous movements by saying, "My wife saint my wife saint my wife saint . . ."

"Can I still be Aleph Tav after the doctors find out my name?" the amnesiac said in fright the instant he awoke from a dream that had been filled with murky and rebuking images.

"Of course, my friend. A stage name is handy to have, even in this garbage hole."

"Watch what you call this place, Old Jack. I earn my daily bread here," the taller orderly said, mockingly waving a fist at Jack. "We got to get this place nice and neat for the important visitor."

"A Yiddish-theatre actor from the old days, I can only pray."

"Nope, Old Jack. A newspaper reporter. She got permission to see your mystery roommate."

The newspaper reporter, notebook and pen in hand, rushed into the room, closely followed by the large-headed doctor. As the doctor watched her from a corner, the reporter walked around the room and looked everywhere, seeming to search for buried treasure or hidden microphones, trying to determine what this strange room was all about. She explained to everyone in the room that she was going to do a feature story on the amnesia victim and violence on the streets. The city, she said with a shudder, could be a pretty scary place. The doctor told her she could stay ten minutes, no more than ten minutes.

"Mr. Aleph Tav is my stage name," the amnesiac kept insisting as the reporter gathered material for her story, particularly intrigued by the fact that he had been found beaten and naked on a downtown Toronto street. Jack informed the reporter that Wesley's wife had hit him over the head with an extremely heavy object and suggested that the newspaper do a feature story on him too; Wes was a splendid victim. Send the theatre critic for me, Jack begged, then told the reporter that she would make a beautiful Leah in The Dybbuk. "If you ever need a dybbuk driven from you, just call on

Rabbi Azrael of Miropol, better known as Jack Zwick. I can drive the most ferocious, stubborn dybbuk out of the body," he told the woman as she stood next to the amnesiac's bed.

"You can be sure I'll call you first, Jack Zwick," she said, writing notes as she spoke.

Before the reporter left she gave each of the patients her card and told them to stop by the newspaper's offices when they felt better, speaking to them as if they only had colds. Jack told her he was never going to leave the hospital alive, that she was looking into his *farshtinkener* tomb. The reporter kissed Jack on the cheek and said he was a handsome man who would live many more years. She was escorted out of the room by the large-headed doctor before Rabbi Azrael could attempt to drive the dybbuk from Leah.

Wesley was again proclaiming the saintliness of his wife, the amnesiac repeated his new name Aleph Tav for the hundredth time, and Jack slept as the hospital's head of neurology entered the room and went to the amnesiac's bed.

Jack awoke and said, "That lady reporter was something. I dreamed we were acting together in *The Dybbuk*."

"Yes, Jack," the head of neurology said as he stuck his head around the cloth partition.

"The Jewish doctor," Jack said when he saw the grey-bearded face.

"I trust it isn't just because I'm Jewish that you like me, Jack," he said and moved to Jack's bedside.

"Who said I like you?" Jack told the man, and then added with a burst of excitement that immediately exhausted him, "I'm trying to teach Sender's role to Aleph Tav, my good friend and new co-star, but I'm not having too much luck."

"You're calling our amnesiac Aleph Tav?"

"A good stage name for a young actor."

"I'm sure it is, Jack; however, it might take a long time before your new co-star is able to retain many of his lines."

"I'm determined to teach him Sender's role."

"Keep trying," the head of neurology said with a look of nonchalance that Jack mistook for puzzlement.

"Sender is the father of the bride in *The Dybbuk*. Leah's father, that is. He's a bit of a *shmuck*, I must admit."

"With you as acting coach, Jack, maybe Aleph Tav will be able to learn some of his lines."

"I'd like to put *The Dybbuk* on in the ward before I die. It's my last dream."

"Oh, I have complete confidence that you'll have innumerable more dreams," the head of neurology said. "But, Jack, don't forget that this is a neurological ward and I think a play like *The Dybbuk* is better suited for a real theatre with a receptive Jewish audience."

"*The Dybbuk* speaks to all people, even big-wig neurosurgeons," Jack said, trying to lift himself out of bed, but barely stirring. "Allow me to put *The Dybbuk* on. I'll give you a part. Any part but Rabbi Azrael of Miropol . . . or Sender, which now belongs to Aleph Tav."

"I'll make a deal with you, Jack. The day you leave this ward, I'll get you the best tickets to any play in town. You name the play."

"Put the tickets on my grave, doctor . . ."

"I am happy for you, Aleph Tav," Jack said through the partition when he heard the large-headed doctor tell the amnesiac the encouraging news. The amnesiac was groaning and gasping simultaneously in grueling somersaults of expression, but Jack was certain this must be the happiest day of the man's life. The large-headed doctor had just announced that there was a favourable response to the publicity. Some business associates—the man on the telephone had used that phrase—of the amnesiac's would be at the hospital later in the day to confirm the amnesiac's identity. The doctor had told the amnesiac that he was lucky to be finding out his identity after only three weeks—though it seemed like forever to the patient and less than a day to Jack. There was another patient he was treating who still didn't have any idea who he was after eighteen months. With a few clues, the large-headed doctor said, we can play detective and retrieve some or all of your memory, Mnemosyne willing. After a brief visit with Jack, the doctor left, but the nurse he had entered the room with remained.

"Give this to Aleph Tav, who is going to be who knows who soon," Jack said as he handed the script of *The Dybbuk* to the nurse.

The nurse took the script and walked around the partition to the amnesiac. Then she placed the old script in the patient's hands and curled his fingers one by one around it. He smiled at the nurse but didn't speak to her. When Jack asked the nurse if she would like to read the role of Leah, she told him she had to attend to patients in a non-acting section of the ward, and left the room.

"Over fifty years I've had that script, Aleph Tav. Good luck it's been except when I had the stroke. Now it should bring *mazel* to you. Where I'm going I won't need a script." Jack stopped talking and felt tearful. He uttered several soft moans, and then said with conviction: "I'd love to have only Yiddish-theatre actors as my pallbearers."

"Your script smells so old. I like the smell," the amnesiac said and moved the script to his chest as though attempting to cover a wound with a bandage.

"The script is yours to keep, Aleph Tav. Anyhow, I know all my lines perfectly, so why do I need a script? Jack Zwick never forgets a cue or line on stage . . ."

Jack began to perform from the third act of *The Dybbuk*, during which Rabbi Azrael makes his appearance. The amnesiac grunted his approval and gleefully touched the script. Wesley called out for a game of Scrabble, but Jack kept on with his performance, sure he was on stage performing for God.

He had already gone through his lines in Acts III and IV twice, and was about to start a third performance, when the commotion from the hallway reached the room and its three occupants. Why weren't the ushers doing their jobs? Jack thought. He had once struck a second-row heckler with a cane—Rabbi Azrael's staff—at the conclusion of a performance, as the other actors were taking their bows.

The large-headed doctor backed into the room as if he had been shoved. Three men, all in brown uniforms, followed, the sound of their boots hammering away at the floor and making Jack's bed vibrate.

"Just one visitor at a time," the doctor said, but all three uniformed men entered the room and saw the amnesiac's bed right away.

"Chip! It is Chip!" the first uniformed man to reach the amnesiac yelled, and the other two uniformed men chorused away with the nickname. All three men saluted over the bed, forming a canopy of brown-sleeved arms.

"The way you're all wrapped up, Chip, I almost can't tell it's you," the second uniformed man said, and the third one added, "We knew they couldn't kill you." The amnesiac did not recognize any of the uniformed men.

"Your friends are here," Jack said, trying to push the partition away but his reach was far short of the cloth screen. No one was paying attention to him and he was unable to see what he thought must be a joyous reunion. Suddenly his head stung from pain, furious pain, but he was denied even a scream. Jack, wanting to utter a line from *The Dybbuk*, was unable to move his lips.

"When can Chip come home with us?" one of the uniformed men breathed into the face of the large-headed doctor.

The doctor began to summarize his patient's case to the three uniformed men while he stared at their swastika armbands. If the head of neurology were here, he thought with horror . . .

"What is this?" the man who acted as though he were the leader of the three uniformed men said when he inspected the script of *The Dybbuk* on his friend's chest. He lifted the script and began to skim through the pages. "Chip, what are you doing with *this*?" he said, and handed the script to the uniformed man beside him.

"Aleph Tav is my stage name! Aleph Tav!" the amnesiac screamed at the uniformed men.

Wesley awoke and yelled, "EDP systems . . . EDP EDP EDP," then fell back asleep.

"This is a Jew story, Chip, ain't it?" the man holding the script said.

"Tell them to go away, Rabbi Azrael," the amnesiac pleaded, a frightened boy's voice replacing his own.

"You got a rabbi next to you, Chip?" one of the uniformed men said in disbelief and all three of them looked at the cloth partition as if it were about to explode.

"Everyone must go now, for your friend's sake. He requires rest," the large-headed doctor said, taking a single tentative step forwards.

"Make them leave, Rabbi Azrael . . ."

While the amnesiac was calling Rabbi Azrael's name, an unfamiliar nurse stepped into the room and froze at the sight of the three uniformed men.

"What's wrong, sweetheart, you've never seen uniforms like ours before?" the leader asked. He gave the woman a raised-arm salute and the other two men joined him, one holding the script of *The Dybbuk* over his head.

"Call the police, nurse," the large-headed doctor ordered.

"What do you want the police for? We're not hurting anyone," the leader told the doctor.

The nurse ran from the room before any of the men could stop her. Taking the script away from the man next to him, the leader waved it angrily after the woman.

Without any forewarning, the amnesiac began to deliver lines from *The Dybbuk* in a voice that startled everyone present. Rabbi Azrael's lines, not Sender's.

"Chip, what are you talking about?" the leader asked. The amnesiac did not answer; he was deep in his performance. A moment later, the leader hurled the script across the room.

The three uniformed men attempted to shout the amnesiac's performance to an end, but his delivery grew stronger, reaching every corner of the room and out into the hallway of the neurological ward.

"That Jew rabbi did this to Chip," one of the uniformed men said and kicked over the partition nearest to him, the cloth screen hitting Jack Zwick's bed and collapsing to the floor.

The amnesiac did not interrupt his lines, unaffected by the activity and tension around him. The large-headed doctor, his eyes on the uniformed intruders, took Jack's pulse, and announced sombrely, "He's dead." Wesley, waking from his sleep again, echoed, "Dead dead dead."

With the three uniformed men staring at the body, the amnesiac began the exorcism scene from *The Dybbuk*, in which Rabbi Azrael expels the dybbuk from Leah's body. "Don't spook us!" one of the uniformed men exclaimed, and another said, "Cut out the clowning, Chip." Their words were not heard by the amnesiac, who continued his performance with all the intensity and Yiddish-accented virtuosity of the great Jack Zwick, as Rabbi Azrael of Miropol, on the stage of the old Standard Theatre at the corner of Spadina and Dundas.

The Icarus Option

By *John Farquhar*

With the aid of a cane, Joe Hill shuffled through Rittenhouse Square, the less fashionable part of Philadelphia, and stopped to catch what was left of his breath. Fifty years ago, this area had been very different. There had been a park, for a start. Well, not a park, exactly, but a patch of green with a tree or two. The trees had made it exclusive. Philadelphia's answer to Central Park, New York. Joe shook with what, if he'd been younger, would have been laughter. People had paid five million dollars to live here in apartments the size of his closet. *Fucking idiots!* He thought, his clumsy footsteps echoing off the crumbling buildings. *And they all had fucking poodles.* But when the trees fell to more or less immortal bacteria, so did the property prices. With no more green and a bleak view, people from New Jersey began to move in, so the rich took up their poodles and moved to South Philadelphia, where the poodles still pissed on everything. *Blight, my ass*, Joe thought as he passed a statue of Rocky, forgotten by all except vandals. *It was probably the damn poodles.*

Joe surveyed the next building down. It wasn't quite as shabby as the others. The service it provided was, after all, in demand. He adjusted the grip on his cane and squinted at the bright blue sign.

THANATOS

The sign was not painted, but etched into the building, to suggest permanence, strength and unshakeable resolution. Underneath was their catchy slogan: *There's No Better Way to Leave the Earth.*

There's no cheaper way, at any rate, thought Joe as, head bowed, he passed through the golden door.

A young receptionist was waiting. She flashed him a toothy smile. He was mesmerized for a moment by the carefree promise and exuberance of those teeth. He himself had lost his last tooth ten years ago, to a donut. There is a time to every purpose under heaven: his tooth was wobbly, and, at that precise moment in time had met a donut of just the right consistency. No need for mourning or reflection: everything under the sun has its appointed time to disappear, a law to which teeth are no exception.

The girl confirmed that his appointment was for 10 am, and the doctor would see him at 10:45. Some things never change, no matter how long you live.

He was shown into a waiting room. Twelve people were sitting quietly on comfortable chairs. They didn't bother to look at him. Six were asleep; the other six were looking at the giant screen, where a small animated lizard was cheerfully explaining all the choices that Thanatos could give you, and how much better Thanatos was than its elitist rival Fox in South Philadelphia. Fifty people on the screen yelled: "Thanks, Thanatos!" At the end, a once well-known politician explained how Thanatos was giving the common man the same opportunities the rich had enjoyed for decades.

Joe reflected how he had been a common man all his life. He sat down, and simply stared ahead. He would do what he had done for ninety years: wait his turn.

It came an hour later. The receptionist's brown eyes and gleaming teeth peeped into the room and flashed in his direction. The doctor would see him now. A door slid open opposite him. He went through it into a small room where a young female doctor was sitting behind a desk. The room was painted the calmest shade of blue. Joe took a seat in the vacant chair, which was soft and deep. The doctor looked up and smiled.

"Mr. Hill," she said. "I'm Dr. Deane. How are you?"

"Couldn't be better."

She ignored his sarcastic response. Immaculately professional.

"Have you had a chance to consider all our options?"

"Yes, I have."

"Have you chosen the option that best fits your requirement?"

"Yes, I have."

"And, that is . . . ?"

Joe leaned forward, and quietly spoke the words he'd wanted to say for so long: "The Icarus Option. I'd like the Icarus Option."

The woman's blue eyes betrayed surprise, and her lips closed over her teeth, in a gentle, but firm rebuke.

"The Icarus option. Okay."

There's a special way of saying 'okay' which lets the listener know that it isn't really okay, but if you want to be a bonehead fool, go ahead and do it, and see if I fuckin' care. This 'okay' was the one he heard and fully understood, but didn't mind in the least.

"You are aware that there are gentler options, such as A Minute with Mozart, which are on special offer to seniors at the moment, and which, given your age, might be . . ."

"I've made up my mind. I want the Icarus Option."

"Okay," said Dr. Deane, "bear with me."

Joe nodded, as his hands and mouth began to twitch. He realized that his nose was running. He tried to put his hand in his pocket to get a tissue, no easy task when you have Parkinson's disease. The drip from his nose ebbed and flowed round his top lip, until it dangled uncertainly from the side of his mouth. With no hint of embarrassment, Dr. Deane produced a tissue of her own, leant across the desk, put the tissue around his nose and mouth and wiped both for him in an instant. Joe muttered some inaudible thanks and gazed despondently at the carpet and the young woman's slender legs, while she accessed the computer on her desk.

"I need to take a few particulars," she said.

"Of course."

"First and foremost, you do, I take it, have a verifiably terminal disease?"

"Don't you know?"

"I do, but for legal reasons I need you to confirm it."

"Yes. Yes, I do have a verifiably terminal disease."

"Good. What's the precise nature of your illness?"

"Cancer."

"Cancer." She spoke the word as she typed it. "Of the . . . ?"

"Pancreas."

"Pancreas. Okay. Confirmed. All I need now is a note from a psychologist to show you are in sound mental health, and a death license issued by the state of Pennsylvania no less than twenty days ago."

"It's in the bag."

"Sorry?"

He fumbled as he handed her his shabby green shoulder bag. She sifted through the documents, entering all the details carefully into the computer. He watched her in impotent fascination. He wondered if she enjoyed her job.

"Well, Mr. Hill," she finally said, "I'm glad to say you've been cleared. Your authorization will be through momentarily."

"It's quick, isn't it?"

"We pride ourselves on our professionalism and, once you've made up your mind . . . or are you maybe having second thoughts?"

He looked away from her practiced, professional gaze.

"No."

"Many do."

"Not me."

"And you can, of course, change your mind, up to the last second . . ."

"I won't."

She picked up a small electronic tablet and tapped the screen. "I'm required by law to read this statement aloud to you."

"That's fine."

She read the statement in a slow, solemn, legal voice; he wanted to laugh, but managed to listen.

"This is to certify that Joseph Hill, of 1244 Westbrook Road, Philadelphia, Pennsylvania, is authorized to terminate his life in whatsoever manner he chooses in compliance with Section 4, Paragraph 2 of the Euthanasia Act of 2040. The termination of said life must be made effective no more than thirty days after the date of this authorization. Statutory rights are not affected by this document, which is non-transferable."

When finished, she looked up. "Do you understand all that, Mr. Hill?"

He nodded.

"Then I need you to sign here," she said, sliding the tablet across the desk and pointing to where he should sign.

He leaned forward in his chair and dragged his finger across the tablet, leaving behind a wobbly scrawl, a remnant of his signature, then clasped his hands on the desk. She took the tablet back and tapped again, before moving it off to the side.

Business out of the way, she became less formal. She laid her hand on his; the first time a woman had done that in many a year.

"I must say," she began, "most clients as old as you go for the gentler options: the quiet ebbing away to the strains of your favorite music, and such. Jumping to your death from a plane generally appeals to younger terminals. Icarus was young, after all, when he flew too near the sun. Why, may I ask, did you choose to leave the Earth this particular way?"

"I'm not going to leave the Earth," Joe snapped. "I'm going to die. Disappear without a trace. As we all will. Haven't you seen the painting?"

"The painting?"

"The Fall of Icarus."

"No. No, I haven't. There are so few paintings left."

"I saw it in my youth, when there were still art galleries in Philadelphia. It cracked me up even then. Icarus was supposed to be such a tragic figure; the painting was named after him, but where the fuck was the young Greek hero? There was a landscape, a ship, a few people on the shore, and one or two birds in the sky. I looked for ages, and then there he was, and I got the joke. All you see of Icarus is two little legs sticking out of the water near the boat. He is disappearing, unmourned, unnoticed, without so much as a splash, into the unimpressed sea. Genius!" Joe coughed at the memory; almost a laugh. "Oh, my God, I laughed like a maniac! All the artsy-fartsy types turned around and stared. Icarus fell from the sky, didn't know shit about life, and simply disappeared. That's what I want to feel. Death is the dullest of thrills, and I mean to savor mine."

"I see," said Dr. Deane. She leaned back in her chair, removing her hand from his. Joe realized she hadn't understood a word. She seemed to need a vacation.

"So, you know the procedure, don't you? We fly you eighty miles off the Jersey shore and you jump ten thousand feet into the Atlantic. You don't drown; the impact kills you instantly. And, in your case, just jumping out of the plane might . . ." She paused and cleared her throat. "Anyway, no need to worry about a funeral; as far as red tape is concerned, you'll be classified as 'buried at sea.'"

"Actually," said Joe, "I'd like the Delaware River package."

Dr. Deane looked uneasy.

"The Delaware River package," she said, "has been discontinued. There were teething problems, such as terminals overshooting. You probably read about that one landing in the Franklin Institute and scaring all those school kids. We also had major security problems. People used to sneak through our cordons to watch the terminals fall and cheer them on as they hit the water. People can be such ghouls."

Joe smiled. He himself had been a ghoul. Like so many others, he too had bribed the guard and waited on the bank, watching the bodies fall–*splat!*–into the famous Delaware waters. A novelty at first, but surprising how quickly you get used to it; by four am he had become more excited by the plop of a surfacing fish.

"Okay," said Joe. "The sea was good enough for Icarus, so it's good enough for me."

"When would you like to jump?"

"Tonight."

"Tonight? So soon?" She frowned. Joe could tell he was disrupting her routine. Good.

"No one has ever asked to die the same day," she said, accusingly. "I really don't think . . ."

He waited. She squirmed, but checked the computer anyhow. "Oh . . . hold on . . . ah, you're in luck. There's been a cancellation. Tonight at midnight, we have one place left on the plane taking off from Philadelphia International."

"I'll take it."

"Are you sure?"

"Sure."

"It's very sudden; we like terminals to have time to reflect and–"

"I've had all the time I need to reflect. Everything is in order, didn't you say?"

"Yes. Everything's in order."

"I'm within my rights, yes?"

"Yes, you are."

"Then?"

"Then fine. A car will call for you at 11:00 tonight," she conceded.

"Thank you."

"How would you like to pay?"

"Cash."

"Cash? You have $50,000 dollars in cash with you? Was that wise?"

"I'll hardly be needing it, will I?"

"You should be more careful. You could have gotten mugged."

"There's a thought: maybe you should offer fatal mugging as an alternative form of exit. It could work out well, you know. You could hire sadists to do the deed and offer it to masochists. Kill two birds with one stone, as it were."

"Except that that would be murder. We will never go down that road."

"Fox has."

"We're not Fox."

"No. Did you hear that they're planning Gladiator fights between terminals, broadcast live coast-to-coast from Citizen Stadium? They'll make a fortune. I'd have certainly subscribed. It's one of the few regrets I have that I won't be around to see its launch."

"It's a return to the Dark Ages, if you ask me," said Dr. Deane. "If Euthanasia becomes entertainment for the masses, where, I wonder, will it all end?"

"*Moriturus te saluto,*" said Joe.

"I don't understand."

"*Aequora nomen habent,*" he continued.

She stared, eyebrows knitted.

"Thank you for your help," Joe said, rising from his chair.

"Are you sure you're okay? Is there anything I can—"

"No. It was very professional. I appreciate the service . . . I really do."

They shook hands. He paid the receptionist on the way out.

"Oh," she said, surprised when she looked at his documents.

"Oh?"

"You're off tonight."

"Yes, I am."

"It's very soon."

"I'm in great pain."

"Usually, there's a. . .cooling off period. Sometimes, clients change their minds."

"Are you trying to do your company out of a sale?"

."No. It's just that you seem like a nice man. . ."

"You seem nice as well."

"You remind me of my grandfather."

Joe looked down to the floor.

"I'm nobody's grandfather," he said quietly.

She handed him a tablet with a sympathetic smile. "Would you mind filling out a short survey about our services?" she asked, teeth sparkling. "It will only take a little of your time."

Time is all I have left, Joe thought, and took the tablet.

In response to the question 'What impressed you the most about your terminal service provider?' he wrote: 'She had nice tits'.

He hailed a taxi to take him home and sat in the front, moving the fake steering wheel with all the joy of a child, pretending he were actually driving, as indeed he had done such a long time ago. He missed those days, when cars were driven by people, when middle fingers flashed at you from every direction, when you knew that you were solely responsible for braking, and therefore living or dying. Now, as thousands of cars streamed in front and behind him, all traveling the same speed, all the same distance from each other, and knowing that the last accident in Philadelphia had been thirty two years ago, a feeling of numbing depression overwhelmed him. They had paid a high price for safety.

Arriving home, Joe calculated that he had just enough time to incinerate his life before a last meal and shower. It gave him a quiet satisfaction as he started with the few, old-style photographs of him as a baby and child. He glanced at them, with curiosity, but no nostalgia, placed them in a neat pile on the inciner-tray and pressed the button. The tray slid into the small white oven. He looked through the viewer at the photograph on top, which was of Joe as a newborn baby in his cot, with the date and his weight hand-written on a sign beside him. There was a flash, and nothing remained. He moved on to his clothes and belongings, growing increasingly satisfied: tray, button, flash, gone; tray, button, flash, gone; tray, button, flash, gone. Cancer had removed all traces of sentimentality from him. Of all his possessions, nothing gave him more satisfaction than to place three hundred and fifty pages of the god-damned awful poetry he had written throughout his life on the tray, and consign it to oblivion.

The end of the clean-out was somehow less satisfying. He pressed a button on his computer marked *collect,* and all the electronically stored records of his life were gathered together in one file. He pressed *delete,* and they were gone. Perhaps that was fitting; they had been so insubstantial.

He now had only the clothes he was wearing and a small, foil-wrapped biscuit that tasted like, and had all the nutritional value of, an original Philly cheesesteak.

As soon as Joe got in the shower, the video screen in the living room came on showing a young woman, and a gentle, but annoying ringing set in. Joe cursed, waiting for it to stop. It didn't. He stepped out of the shower and stood naked in front of the screen. A young woman was smiling patiently at him. A choice of options flashed at the bottom: Connect/Reject/Report.

Against his initial judgment, Joe pressed 'Connect'. The woman looked down, looked up very quickly, and proceeded with her eyes focused on his bald head.

"Mr. Hill?"

"Yes."

"Mr. Joe Hill?"

"Yes."

"Joe or Joseph? Which do you prefer?"

"I don't give a shit. Who are you?"

"My name is Mary McCafferty. I represent 'End Well'. I believe you're planning to kill yourself tonight."

Her voice sounded like the woman's at Thanatos. All young voices sounded the same to him.

"Who the hell told you that?" he snapped.

"I'm asking you not to do it."

"It's none of your god-damn business."

"It's God's business, and God's business is my business. God loves you. He doesn't want you to do this."

"He loves me so much he gave me Parkinson's disease and pancreatic cancer to round off an already shitty life."

"I'm talking about your soul."

"You're wasting your time. I don't have one."

"You only think you don't have one because you're in pain. Imagine the shock you'll have when your body dies and you find out that your soul hasn't."

"Imagine the shock you won't have when it's too late to realize that, all your life, you were wrong."

"What does that mean?"

"It means death is just nature's way of taking the garbage out."

"God cares for us all."

"Pull the other one!"

"You have the sin of pride. The best we can do is be humble."

"The best we can do is what I'm doing. Give death the finger."

"The soul never dies, Joe."

"The body dies, the heart dies, the soul dies."

"The soul never dies."

"It does, when the body gets cancer."

There was a pause.

"I can be there with you in twenty minutes," the woman said, trying another approach.

"What for?"

"To comfort you."

"To tie me up more like it. I know you maniacs."

"I'd like to come to see you. Can I come to see you, Joe?"

Joe thought for a moment, before replying: "Sure."

There was a surprised pause before the voice came through, joyful, hopeful and exultant. "Oh, thank you so much. You won't regret it."

"You might. See, I'll be here, waiting, with my Second Amendment gun in my hand. As soon as you knock, I'll blow your god-damn brains out and you'll find out first which of us is right about the soul."

"You wouldn't do that to me, would you Joe?"

"Come around and try me. Hell, what have I got to lose? There are half a dozen people doing well for themselves I wish to God I'd shot when I was younger. You'll be my one and only success story."

"I'm sorry you feel that way, Joe. I believe in God. I trust He will help you. What you are doing is wrong. I will pray for you tonight, and regularly afterwards."

Before Joe could think of a withering reply, the screen went blank. She had gotten the last word. *Don't those religious types always*, he thought.

He finished his shower, ate his biscuit, and waited for the true taste of a Philly cheesesteak to transport him back to happier times. It only gave him indigestion. While he was trying to decide how to spend his last few hours on Earth, his body made up his mind for him, and he fell fast asleep.

He was awoken by the cheerful voice of a limousine on his video screen.

"Hey there, Joe! Are you ready?"

At first he didn't understand, then his rationale self-revived. He gave a short look around his empty apartment, said, "too damn right I am," switched the screen off, and left.

The limousine was cheerfully female in voice, performance and décor. There were luxury snacks and alcoholic drinks. Joe had barely settled in the back when he was asked to confirm his destination.

"We are going to Philadelphia Airport, correct?"

"Too fucking right we are."

"I'm sorry, I did not understand that. Could you say 'yes' if we are going to Philadelphia Airport, or 'no' if we are not?"

"Yes. YES! YES!"

"Thank you. Would you like me to take the fastest route or the scenic route?"

"There isn't a scenic route to Philadelphia Airport, you lying bastard. Never has been, never will be."

"I'm sorry, I did not understand that. Could you say 'fastest' or 'scenic'? If you are speech impaired, non-American, or from a State south of Delaware, could you . . ."

"Fastest. FASTEST!"

"Thank you."

There was a brief pause, after which the limousine resumed their conversation.

"Are you catching a flight?"

"Yes, I am."

"Business or pleasure?"

"Both."

"I'm sorry, I did not understand that."

"Pleasure."

"How exciting. May I ask where to precisely?"

"Hades."

"Hades, Nebraska?"

"No."

"Vacations are so exciting, aren't they? The anticipation, the excitement, the discovery of the new."

"How the fuck would you know, you're a limousine."

"I'm sorry, I did not understand that."

"How the fuck do I get you to shut up?"

"Would you like a little peace and quiet for a while?"

"Yes!"

"Certainly. It was a pleasure talking with you. May I wish you, as the French say, *bon voyage.*"

Joe nodded. He looked at the neighborhood houses flashing past, and thought of all the people inside, none of whom had any idea where he was going. He hadn't spoken to any of them in quite some time. He had thought about telling them about his plans, but decided it was pointless. It would cheapen his death to go out any other way but silently. The death planes, as they were first called, no longer made the news. Not a single reporter would be waiting when he arrived. That was fine by him; he did not want his death to resonate in the world, or even make a splash. Face up to it, that's all. And when that moment came, and if he saw it through, it would balance out so many tedious years.

He didn't eat or drink. He waited for deep thoughts to come to him, but they didn't. He watched all the familiar Philadelphia landmarks drift past, and, to his relief, felt nothing.

*

The limousine arrived at the airport at 11:30, and he was shown to the VIP lounge. He was the last to arrive. Nineteen of his fellow travelers were waiting to board: seventeen men, two women. Six were on stretchers; the rest, though obviously very ill, could stand on their own two feet. All of them—as the doctor had suggested—were much younger than Joe. He felt their concealed hilarity as he shuffled in, but no one addressed him directly. They were all immersed in their final, secret thoughts.

A young man with piercing blue eyes and a shaven head entered the lounge. He was followed by four other sturdy young men. He walked to the front of the room, and raised his hands, as if to quiet them down. Then he bowed his head for a beat.

"Hello, friends," he began, raising his head, revealing brows knitted together in a look of rehearsed sympathy. "My name is Charles, and I'm here to prepare you for the bravest thing you will ever have done."

Charles explained the process. No family or friends were allowed into this room—they had seen them for the last time, unless they changed their minds. There was no disgrace in changing your mind, but there would be a financial penalty—the cost of the flight was non-refundable. Tickets would not be issued, but they needed to have their signed releases and I.D. ready for inspection before being allowed on the plane. The Captain's name was Peter Lister, an experienced and capable pilot. The men behind him—who waved—were their Ultimate Assistants, who would assist them in the final moments if necessary, by undoing the harness for instance, if any terminal became too weak to do so by themselves. They could change their mind at any moment right up to the last. The Ultimate Assistants understood fully how important it was to each and every one of the terminals to die exactly as they had planned and paid for. Everything would be done to ensure absolute satisfaction.

"As you know," Charles continued with a somber, concerned look on his face, "the fall from the plane will not kill you. Death will be instantaneous and painless upon impact. Nobody should be afraid of drowning. If you would prefer drowning, speak up now, and we can transfer you to the Ophelia Project—for a small additional charge." On cue, Charles gave the room a humorless grin and paused, then continued.

No one would survive. No one had ever survived. No boats were in the area. Their bodies—or parts thereof—would not be recovered. They would be classified forever as 'buried at sea'. If there were no more questions—which there weren't—could they line up at the gate, with boarding pass and I.D. clearly displayed.

Finally, Charles wound it up. "I have officiated in many flights of the Icarus Option, and it is, of course, so difficult to know what to say in such circumstances. But I wish you Godspeed, if you believe in God. And if you don't, good luck." He nodded, and bowed his head.

The speech was met with embarrassed uncertainty; a few terminals started to applaud, and then stopped when no one else followed. Charles went around, shaking hands, and stopped to talk to Joe.

"How are you?" Charles asked.

"Old, and about to die. How are you?"

"Even after all this time," said Charles, "I never cease to be amazed by the courage of you people."

"You people?"

"I'm sorry. I didn't mean . . . what I mean is . . . meeting people with such fortitude in the face of death is truly inspirational, truly life-changing."

"And it's meeting people like you that makes people like me choose to do what we do."

"Ah. Well, I'll . . . ehm . . . leave you to your thoughts. Boarding is about to begin."

Charles pointed to the exit. Joe moved slowly towards it. For the first time that day, his heart began to beat noticeably faster.

The plane had been specially converted: there were only forty seats, twenty on either side, so that no one sat next to anyone else. Every seat faced the rear of the plane and there were harnesses for everyone, to help them stand by the door when it opened. There were no flight attendants other than the Ultimate Assistants. Food was not available, but water was given to anyone who asked.

The Captain introduced himself, said the weather was almost ideal, and announced that they had been cleared for takeoff. No one spoke. Joe eyed the other terminals for evidence of second thoughts, but found no such evidence in anyone. They'd all long since had enough of the pointless pain; a feeling of exhilaration and longed for peace was building in them. The screening process was indeed, as the adverts claimed, rigorous in its authorization of terminal status.

The plane took off smoothly and climbed powerfully upwards. Even though it was cloudy, they reached ten thousand feet with effortless ease. In almost no time, the Captain announced that they were approaching their drop altitude. The Ultimate Assistants stood up. People shifted in their seats.

The Assistants moved to the rear of the plane and one of them pressed a red button. A door opened. The wind howled in and the darkness of night mesmerized the terminals. As in a movie theater, everyone had an unrestricted view.

Those in stretchers went first. They were held by harnesses and placed carefully in line. Two Assistants wheeled the first stretcher to the door and positioned it with the man's feet facing the void. They made the final check:

"Ready, Mr. Hanrahan?" asked one of the Assistants, tapping him on the shoulder.

The man on the stretcher lifted up his left arm. His face was calm and passive, with the hint of an ironic smile. He looked back at all the other people in the plane, his hand still raised; they tipped the stretcher gently forward, and he was gone.

After the stretchers, those who could walk moved in line down the plane. They were held steady by the Assistants near the door, until it was their time. One by one, they went to their death in the manner they had chosen and rehearsed so often in their minds: leaps, flops, dives, whoops, or complete silence. Some with defiance, some with awe, some exalting God, others exalting the void. Some faltered momentarily, two asked to be pushed out, but none went back on their decision.

However they went, Joe felt there was something heroic about each and every one, and felt closer to them than any other human beings he'd known in his long life.

He watched them in admiration. His heart began to pound as his turn drew near. The adrenaline kicked in for a moment, and all the pain vanished. Soon, the man before him was being prepared. Joe felt his heart begin to thump even faster. He began to sweat, and in a few seconds his whole body was drenched. It wasn't fear, but how he wished it was.

He had suffered a mild heart attack two years before. He now knew why it had been called 'mild.' This, he knew at once, was the real thing: a primeval, pitiless pain. He doubled up in agony, and began panting for air. He gasped and gurgled and his eyes rolled wildly.

The Assistants were perplexed. They thought he was afraid, and was having second thoughts. The last thing they wanted was blood on their hands. One leaned forward and put his hand on his back, gently, while the wind roared outside.

"You changed your mind, Joe? You had second thoughts? It's okay, you know. You don't have to do this; no-one will think . . ."

Joe shook his head.

"You wanna go on, you mean?"

Joe nodded, and pointed to his heart.

"What are you trying to say, Joe?"

Joe lifted his eyes wearily into the assistant's, who immediately understood.

"Are you dying?"

Joe nodded.

Perhaps they'd seen it before; perhaps it was their training, but they seemed to understand the importance to Joe of having the death he'd planned, and the little time he had left to achieve it. They shifted efficiently into action. They lifted him up. They encouraged him to see it through.

Other passengers were roused from introspection by the activity, and gave him their support. The silence had dissipated. The encouragement was muted, but from the heart.

He'd never felt so loved in all his life.

He tottered like an infant to the door. The harness still held him fast. The noise of the wind should have been thrilling, the feeling of elation should have been all-consuming, but the crippling pain that wracked every nerve in his body overpowered everything else. He felt cheated. All he had wanted were a few moments of mad exhilaration after a lifetime of tedium, compliance and pain. In his mind, he had leapt from that plane a hundred times, and each time the joy and triumph of that moment had been immense. All he wanted was to die as he had chosen, but the pain was making that impossible. He sensed, welling up deep within, the same impotent anger that had defined and shaped his whole life. In a last moment of defiance, Joe pushed everyone away and stood, head bowed and arms outstretched in agony across the frame of the door.

It was then that he realized he wasn't going anywhere. Tears followed the contours of wrinkles in his sallow cheeks and fell at random to the floor. Two Assistants moved forward to ease him gently out of the plane. Even as they released the harness it was too late and he knew it.

He could not speak. There was nothing left of him, but silent, unvoiced words. *God damn it!* he thought. *God damn it! God damn it! God damn it!* echoed impotently in the silent void. So this was what his death would be. He wouldn't even get what he paid for. Pain, and the wish for that pain to end at all costs, and the impersonal granting of that wish would be his fate after all, like all the rest . . . just like all the rest. If he'd had the strength, he would have laughed. If he'd had more time, he might have cursed, but the darkness came as swiftly as sleep. His eyes opened wide, as they do when no light will register in them again.

The living on board the plane followed, for the shortest of time, Joe's spiraling, lifeless body. It tumbled through the dark clouds, spun a while in a self-induced dance, and then magically straightened up at the very last moment in what would have been a perfect dive, before it smashed into the deceptively smooth, impenetrable blue waters.

AUTHOR BIOGRAPHIES

Capoferri, Bruce. "The Malocchio"

Bruce Capoferri sells automobiles, but enjoys writing stories and songs in his spare time and is currently working on a novel. He has four autobiographical stories published in *Primo* Magazine and one in *Buona Salute*. He lives with his wife, Barbara, and cat, Krikat.

Farquhar, John. "The Icarus Option"

John Farquhar was born in England, and educated at Liverpool University and St. John's College, Oxford. He teaches languages and literature at Rutgers University and Temple University.

Feistman, Gregg. "Starstruck"

Gregg Feistman's first political thriller, *The War Merchants*, was published in 2009 by Strategic Book Publishing. He has since completed his second novel in the series, *Unholy Alliance*, currently under consideration. A former freelance journalist and New York City-produced playwright, he is currently an Associate Professor of Public Relations at Temple University in Philadelphia, PA.

Ford, J. Keller. "The Passing of Millie Hudson"

J. Keller Ford is a Young Adult (YA) and New Adult (NA) fantasy author, freelance editor and book reviewer. Her short stories, "The Amulet of Ormisez" (*Make Believe Anthology*) and "Dragon Flight" (*One More Day Anthology)* are published by J. Taylor Publishing. Two of her non-fiction short stories, "Baby" and "Five More Minutes", won reader's choice awards at www.midlifecollage.com. Her first YA fantasy novel, *In the Shadow of the Dragon King*—the first installment in the Chronicles of Fallhollow trilogy—is complete and seeking representation. www.j-keller-ford.com

Hardy, Christine L. "The Beach House"

Christine L. Hardy analyzes data by day and writes fantasy by night. A proud member of the South Jersey Writers' Group, she lives with her son Jeff, her cat Koko, and an escape beagle named Zeke. Their escapades can be found on Facebook as well as at "Write First, Blog Later," aka ChristineLHardy.com. Her stories have appeared in the anthologies *Tall Tales and Short Stories from South Jersey*, *Different Dragons II*, and *A Bard Day's Knight: Tales from Fortannis Vol. III*.

Holiday, Amy. "Fox and the Rose"

Amy Holiday writes stories for children and young adults. She served as the co-editor of the first South Jersey Writers' Group anthology *Tall Tales and Short Stories from South Jersey*. She takes flying trapeze lessons and organizes playtime for grownups in Philadelphia. She is the President of the SJWG until 2015. www.amyhaha.com

Magrowski, K.A. "The Highborn"

K.A. Magrowski has been mangling the English language since 1985. She hopes to secure a book deal before the zombie apocalypse or an alien invasion, whichever happens first. Her work has also appeared in Dreams of Decadence magazine and *We Walk Invisible: A Short Story Anthology* (Chupa Cabra House). She lives in the haunted wilds of South Jersey with her family and feline co-conspirators. She is vice-president of. the South Jersey Writers' Group, and may or may not be addicted to cat videos. www.kamagrowski.com.

Rebmann, Ray. "Sifkin's Fence"

Ray Rebmann raises guide dogs for the sight impaired. His first book of nonfiction, *How Can You Give Up That Adorable Puppy* (Unlimited Publishing) describes a family's years of service as dog trainers. He writes fiction as well. *Chalk Town and the World's Bottle Cap Championship of the Universe* is an e-book published by Wild Child Publishing. *Jersey Devil, The Cursed Unfortunate* was recently published by MuseItUp Publishing. He is also the curator of the Dennis Township Historical Museum. Rebmann lives in the wilds of New Jersey with his wife of 27 years.

Ribay, Randy. "Mason, On His Way Home"

Born in the Philippines and raised in Michigan and Colorado, Randy Ribay holds a B.A. in English Literature from the University of Colorado and a M.Ed. from the Harvard Graduate School of Education. By day he teaches high school English in West Philadelphia, and by night he reviews books for The Horn Book Guide and writes strange stories. He lives in Camden, NJ with his wife and dog-children.

Steinfeld, J.J. "The Hearing of Memory's Voice"

J. J. Steinfeld is a Canadian fiction writer, poet, and playwright who lives on Prince Edward Island, where he is patiently waiting for Godot's arrival and a phone call from Kafka. While waiting, he has published fourteen books, including *Would You Hide Me?* (Stories, Gaspereau Press), *Misshapenness* (Poetry, Ekstasis Editions), and *A Glass Shard and Memory* (Stories, Recliner Books). His short stories and poems have appeared in numerous anthologies and periodicals internationally, and his plays have been performed in Canada and the United States.

Voza, Richard. "Mrs. Rabinski"

Richard Voza is a life-long New Jersey resident. He has written four novels, one of which (*Connecting Flight*) will be released by Start Publishing. Most of his work tends to lean in the paranormal direction, but there's always room for humor in the mix. His film reviews can be found at Cinekatz.com. He sometimes hangs out with the South Jersey Writers Group. His current work-in-progress is a time-travel novel called *Time*.

Walsh, Jessica A. "Unquiet Mind"

Jessica A. Walsh is an avid reader and writer of creative non-fiction. She is a Communications Manager for a non-profit in Philadelphia, PA. She lives in Southern New Jersey and escapes to the beach with her surfboard whenever possible. She has been a member of the South Jersey Writers' Group since 2011. This is her first publication.

Wooten, Neal. "Reading Glasses"

Neal Wooten grew up on a pig farm on Sand Mountain in the northeast corner of Alabama before being dragged kicking and screaming to the snow-infested plains of the American Midwest. He now resides in Milwaukee with his wife and three dogs. He is a contributor to the Huffington Post and a columnist for The Mountain Valley News, cartoonist, artist, and standup comedian. He has a BS in Applied Mathematics and was the director of a math learning center.

ACKNOWLEDGEMENTS

Reading Glasses was funded in part by the contributions of these wonderful people:

Angelica Aguirre; Robert H. Cook; Joanne Costantino; Jordan Fox; Barb Godshalk; Jennifer R. Hubbard; Mike & Rose Jadach; Joseph McGovern; Kathy Notaro; Agnes Peraino; Nanci Rainey; Michael Shaw; Mark Stutzbach; Sharon Trembley; Mohan M. Velpuri; and Anna Katrina Zagala.

Neil Aaronson; Helen T. Cooke; L.D. Davis; Gregg Feistman; Christine L. Hardy; Maryellen Laliberte; Kahuna McCormick; Rob McMann; Nishi Robert; Fiona Kenna Schlachter; Clarice Stasz; Kevin Stephany; Jessica Walsh & Mike Jadach; and Rudy Wolpink.

John Farquhar; Ellen Jaggers; Roman & Danielle Kobryn; Scott McClintock and Heather DeVries McClintock; Sarah Miduski; Tom Minder; Jeff Moore and the Book Asylum in Blackwood, NJ; Loretta Sisco at www.lorettasisco.com; and all our Kickstarter supporters.

Thanks also to our production team: Mike Herold from The O'B View (theobview.wordpress.com); Karen Perkins from LionheART Galleries UK; Shelley Szajner of Shelley Szajner Design.

Book publishing is one thing, book *selling* is another. Huge thanks to our marketing & sales team: Traveling Saleswomen Dawn Byrne and Marie Gilbert; the SJWG social media manager Mieke Zamora-Mackay, and our Patron Saint of Blogging, Glenn Walker.

More gratitude to the members of the South Jersey Writers' Group (SJWG), especially: Steampunk Granny Marie Gilbert for help with the Kickstarter video, author interviews, and endless promotion; Dawn Byrne, Jim Knipp, Mieke Zamora-Mackay, and K.A. Magrowski for countless reading favors; and Janice Wilson for her help with data and admin.

And finally a special thank you to the folks at Kickstarter.com for providing a platform to make this happen, and to Mike Jadach for putting up with recurring meetings in his dining room.

This page intentionally left blank

This page Intentionally left blank